David Butler was born in Sc ... he
was educated at Larkhall A
University. After studying
Dramatic Art, he became
starting with the long-run
During 'Ward 10' he beg
television. Amongst his n
Family, Helen, A Woman of Today,
The Adventures of Black Beauty, Edward VII and
David Butler lives in Hampstead with his wife, Mary.

David Snodin, born in Sweden but now living in London, was educated at Trinity College, Oxford. He began writing at an early age but his first success was with a play, *A Game Called Arthur*, which was staged at the Edinburgh Festival and subsequently at the Royal Court Theatre, London. Several of his plays have been televised including the dramatization of *Wuthering Heights* which was shown on BBC 2 in 1978. He is currently working as Script Editor on a series of Shakespeare plays for the BBC.

Tanya Treacy

Also by David Butler:

EDWARD VII: PRINCE OF HEARTS
EDWARD VII: THE PEACEMAKER
DISRAELI: THE ADVENTURER
DISRAELI: THE GREAT GAME
LILLIE

Also by David Snodin:

A MIGHTY FERMENT: BRITAIN
IN THE AGE OF FERMENT 1750–1850

David Snodin

The Further Adventures of Oliver Twist

Based on the ATV serial by
David Butler

Futura Publications Limited

A Futura Book

First published in Great Britain by
Futura Publications Limited in 1980

ISBN 0 7088 1724 6

Typeset, printed and bound in Great Britain by
Hazell Watson & Viney Ltd
Aylesbury, Bucks

Futura Publications Limited
110 Warner Road
Camberwell, London SE5

CHAPTER ONE

On a summer day especially, with the sound of bees humming industriously, the sight of the white butterflies fluttering amongst humble gravestones, and the scent of flowers everywhere, it is hard to imagine a place more restful, or more conducive to a contented contemplation of life's goodness, than an English country churchyard. Here, for all the world's turmoils, a peace will always prevail. Within the church itself, on this same summer day, there exists a still deeper peace; the thick, plain stone walls keep the sultry heat at bay, the coloured windows soften the sun's brilliance, and there is a stillness unsurpassed.

On one such day, in one such church – a small, homely, low-porched building set amidst smiling fields and waving trees – stood the hero of this history; whose name, as the reader will have guessed if he was not half asleep when his eye first fell on this volume, was Oliver Twist. A handsome, serious, fair-haired youth now in his thirteenth year, he was respectfully contemplating a plain white marble tablet in the wall to the left of the altar. It bore but one word: 'AGNES' – the name of his mother, whom he had never known. Her bones did not lie behind that modest memorial, for they were many miles away, in an unmarked grave, but her shade unquestionably hovered around that tranquil corner at that moment.

Beside Oliver, with a hand on his shoulder and the light from the church's east window enhancing her delicate, kind countenance, stood his late mother's young sister, Rose Maylie – a beautiful being, in the bloom and grace of early womanhood. The wilderness of evil through which both these young people had once travelled, had left not a trace of bitterness on their gentle features. They knew but one thing: that they should be grateful for having suffered as they had done – for it was in that wilderness that they had found each other. It was behind them now, that sorry time.

But the Reverend Harry Maylie, whose church this was, and who also had the incomparable good fortune to be Rose's very happy husband, thought he discerned a small shadow of sorrow pass across Oliver's brow as the boy turned away from the tablet and walked, with his aunt, towards the door. This handsome young clergyman had been fondly watching his radiant wife and her nephew, as they were paying their respects to the memory of Agnes, and he now followed them out of the church and into the churchyard. It was indeed a fine morning. The sun shone brightly in the cloudless sky; rose and honeysuckle perfumed the air. In a corner of the churchyard, the grey-haired sexton, Mr Brittles, was carefully tending the unassuming graves beneath which the old people of the village slept in peace.

Stopping just outside the church's porch, Harry Maylie looked at Oliver. 'Do you know?' he said cheerily, 'I swear you have grown these past months here with us'

Oliver smiled, but could not conceal the suggestion of sadness in his eye.

'Of course he has, Harry,' said Rose, with pride, 'It's the rest and the fresh country air.'

'More likely to be your cooking, my dear,' said Harry. 'Which reminds me – is there time for lunch before the coach leaves?'

'I'm afraid not,' replied Rose, 'I've packed a hamper for Oliver to take with him.'

For Oliver was about to depart from this gladsome place. He was going to London; and here was the reason for that touch of dispiritedness.

'I'll miss you, Aunt Rose,' he said; and it was true, for the months he had spent with her and her husband had been the happiest he could remember.

'We'll miss you, too,' said Rose, laying a comforting hand on the boy's head, 'and think of you, often.'

'Your real home's with Mr Brownlow, Oliver,' said Harry, seriously. 'He is your guardian.'

Oliver understood this, and accepted it. The good Mr Brownlow had spared no effort in pulling him out of the mire of wickedness into which, through no fault of his own, he had once tumbled, and he now owed that kindly old benefactor the affection of a son. He would go to London with all the willingness he could muster. He could derive further comfort from the knowledge that he would still be able to visit his dear Aunt Rose, as often as he liked. She had assured him of that.

'No,' said Rose, as she saw that Oliver was content again, 'we must hurry and finish your packing.'

'May I say goodbye to Mr Brittles?' asked Oliver.

'He would never forgive you if you didn't,' said Harry, with a smile.

Oliver ran towards the sexton and, removing his cap, bowed somewhat formally. 'Goodbye, Mr Brittles,' he said.

Mr Brittles swept off his own wide-brimmed straw hat and returned the bow, with equal civility. Then he chuckled and ruffled Oliver's hair, saying: 'Bless you, boy. A safe journey.' Whereupon the boy and the kind old man shook hands.

Watching this scene at some distance, Rose was not smiling as she quietly remarked, 'I've prayed for him every night.'

'And I,' Harry said. 'It is a miracle he survived, and kept his innocence. But the nightmare is over.'

The serenity of the setting, and the nature of the day, assured them, for the moment at least, that it was.

'So Oliver has come back to you,' declared Mr Grimwig, cocking his head to one side, and regarding his old friend Mr Brownlow out of the corner of an eye. 'He's been away long enough.'

Mr Brownlow smiled. 'I did not wish him to return to

London until his Aunt was sure he had fully recovered.'

Mr Grimwig continued to scrutinize Mr Brownlow with a series of sidelong glances – for such was his manner when suspicious, and he was a very suspicious man – until, apparently satisfied, he straightened his head and grunted, still crustily: 'Quite so.'

The two old gentlemen were in the sitting room of Mr Brownlow's London home – a neat house, in a quiet shady street near Pentonville. The room was full of books, and its window looked onto some pleasant little gardens. Before the window, there was a table laid with three places for tea. A kettle sat on a trivet by the fire.

'And you are going ahead with your plan to adopt the boy?' inquired Mr Grimwig.

'Yes,' replied Mr Brownlow. 'As soon as I discovered that he was the son of my late and unfortunate friend Charles Leeford, my course was clear. I also intend to make him my heir.'

Mr Grimwig's head tipped sideways again and the sceptical look returned. 'Is that wise, Mr Brownlow?'

'Wise, Mr Grimwig?' echoed Mr Brownlow, with playful surprise.

'As a Justice of the Peace,' remarked Mr Grimwig, 'I am forever dealing with quarrels within families, over *wills*. And I'll have to deal with a good many more before I'm finished, or I'll eat my head!' Whereupon he struck his stick upon the ground. Mr Grimwig always carried a stick, for he was rather lame in one leg.

Mr Brownlow smiled again and said: 'I do not doubt it.' Mr Grimwig was in the habit of affirming very often that he would eat his head if such and such did or did not prove to be the case, striking the ground with his stick or tapping his skull, as if to offer further assurance that this was what he most certainly would do if he had to. The difficulties he might encounter, should he ever be called upon to fulfil a pledge of this nature, did not seem to have occurred to him.

'But there should be no dispute,' Mr Brownlow continued, 'for I have no living relatives. And I have become greatly attached to the boy.'

'And he to you, no doubt,' growled Mr Grimwig, 'knowing you will leave him well provided for.'

Mr Grimwig's strong appetite for contradiction might, by now, have seemed more than a little disagreeable to a stranger unacquainted with it. But Mr Brownlow knew the apparently irritable old gentleman very well – and recognized that Mr Grimwig, in the inmost recesses of his heart, was a good man, quite capable of great understanding and kindness. He therefore responded to his friend's latest jibe with a quiet good humour.

'Oliver has no need of money,' he said. 'He has three thousand pounds in his own right, which I have invested for him.'

Mr Grimwig was taken aback by the revelation and exclaimed: 'Three tho ...? How did he come by it?'

'You will recall the villain who was paying that thief-master, Fagin, to turn Oliver into a criminal?'

'Monks,' muttered Mr Grimwig, with distaste.

'Monks,' Mr Brownlow repeated, with equal abhorrence. 'Unmasked, he turned out to be Oliver's half-brother, Edward Leeford.'

'Upon my soul. . . .' interjected Grimwig.

Mr Brownlow continued: 'He was driven by hatred and jealousy. As punishment, I forced him to restore to Oliver what was due to him – a half share in their poor father's estate, which amounts to three thousand pounds. Then I gave him a choice – to leave the country, or be handed over to the police.'

'Fairer treatment than he deserved,' snorted Mr Grimwig. 'Where is Monks now?'

'I understand he has sailed to the Americas.'

'Where, no doubt, he is already up to more villainy,' Mr Grimwig observed, 'or I'll be content to eat my head, sir!' And this time, he rapped himself on the cranium with such vehemence that the powder with which his shaggy wig was dressed flew up in a little cloud all round him.

Mr Brownlow was wondering whether his friend might be right on this point at least, and whether or not he had been too lenient on the malicious creature who had caused poor Oliver Twist to undergo such wretchedness in the past, when there was a knock on the door and Oliver himself walked into the room, in the company of Mr Brownlow's motherly old housekeeper, Mrs Bedwin.

'Bless the boy!' exclaimed this kind old lady immediately, as she set about preparing tea. 'He's been *writing*! To his dear Aunt, sir! *Writing*, sir! His good uncle taught him, and his Aunt Rose and he would read together every day. And he never had a day's schooling before! No wonder they're proud of him. And so am I.' At this she looked briefly at Mr Grimwig, challenging him with her eyes to utter some disparaging remark at her charge's expense. But Mr Grimwig said nothing, and merely cocked his head, glancing sideways at the boy, rather in the manner of a disgruntled parrot.

'Oliver,' said Mr Brownlow, gently, 'I'm sure you remember my old friend, Mr Grimwig.'

Now Mr Grimwig was secretly as pleased to see Oliver as Mr Brownlow and Mrs Bedwin had been when the boy had first arrived, but his natural contrariness prevented him from revealing it even for a second. So when Oliver approached him and said, with a courteous bow, 'How do you do, sir?' Mr Grimwig grunted, and replied, as curtly and as gruffly as ever: 'Uncommon well. And you, boy?'

'Uncommon*ly* well, sir,' said Oliver, with a warm smile which was an instant indication of the fact that there was no malice whatsoever in his thus correcting Mr Grimwig on his use of the language.

More than a touch confused, Mr Grimwig only managed to retort with a mildly petulant 'Hmph!' Quickly recovering, however, he placed a double eyeglass on his nose, and began to examine Oliver with a fierce glare.

After a lengthy perusal, he said: 'You appear to have put on a few inches since I last saw you.'

'Indeed he has,' said Mr Brownlow. 'I shall have to buy him a new suit of clothes.'

'Unending expense,' declared Grimwig, shaking his head and letting his eyeglass drop, 'I, myself, would not consider adopting any boy – at least not until I was assured he had stopped growing.'

Oliver was slightly abashed at this, but Mr Brownlow emitted a low chuckle. Mr Grimwig was very aware of another disapproving glance from Mrs Bedwin.

'And apart from that,' Mr Brownlow asked, 'you have no further objection?'

Mr Grimwig, used as he was to furnishing objections whenever he felt the need – which was most of the time – was not used to being *asked* for them quite so directly; so he could only puff and snort for a while, as he tried to think of one, and finally say: 'Why . . . no . . . no objection . . . whatever.'

Mrs Bedwin beamed, and Mr Grimwig embarked on a loud and long attack of coughing. After clearing his throat for what must have been a good half minute, he tried to change the subject by saying: 'Well then, young . . . uh'; but he could not remember what it was he had wanted to say, if it had been anything at all, so instead he asked Oliver: 'What do you plan to call yourself now? Leeford?'

'No, sir,' said Oliver, 'Mr Bumble, the Beadle at the Workhouse where I was born, gave me the name "Twist". I shall remain Oliver Twist, until I have a real name.'

'And when will that be?' inquired Grimwig.

'When Mr Brownlow has legally adopted me – and I have a real father.'

Even Mr Grimwig found it hard to pretend that he was not touched by this answer, for it was delivered with an absolute sincerity, and he allowed himself to mutter, 'Well said, well said, boy.'

'Tea is ready, Mr Brownlow,' said Mrs Bedwin, as a

maid entered with a plate of toasted muffins.

'Splendid. Splendid!' exclaimed Mr Grimwig making for the table as rapidly as he could, for he very much approved of muffins, and some of his irascibility up to now had perhaps been caused by a fear that they might never arrive.

'One moment, please,' said Mr Brownlow. 'There is . . . another matter.'

Mr Grimwig stopped in his tracks, turned, and stared impatiently at his friend. Mr Brownlow seemed troubled. 'It has to do with the adoption,' he began. 'When I instructed my lawyers, they informed me I would need to furnish some proof of Oliver's identity.'

'Yes,' said Mr Grimwig eyeing the muffins again, 'that would speed the whole business up.' He had taken two more steps in the direction of the table, before it struck him that Mr Brownlow might have mentioned the matter because such proof as was needed did not exist. So he asked if it did.

'Yes,' said Mr Brownlow, 'it exists – in the form of a letter and some papers, given by Oliver's brother for safekeeping to that scoundrel, Fagin.'

At the mention of this name, Oliver froze. Mr Grimwig noted his reaction, and, as if to remind the boy that he was now safe from that wicked old man's influence, he said, nonetheless retaining a tone of fractiousness and impatience: 'But Fagin is in Newgate prison, waiting to be hanged.'

'And refuses to tell us where those papers are hidden,' said Mr Brownlow.

'Even under sentence of death?' declared Mr Grimwig with a shrug. 'Then there is nothing more to be done.'

'There is one last hope,' Mr Brownlow interposed, again halting Mr Grimwig's advance towards the muffins. He hesitated slightly before suggesting: 'If he were appealed to by someone – someone he had grievously wronged – it might, even at this final moment, awaken a spark of conscience in him.'

Mr Grimwig was about to express the opinion that this suggestion was absurd, since no such appelant could possibly be found, when a significant look from Mr Brownlow made him realize that Oliver was the person he had meant. Oliver understood this, and so did Mrs Bedwin, who now said with great anxiety, 'Oh, sir, surely you wouldn't dream of it?'

'Only if Oliver is completely willing,' said the good Mr Brownlow firmly.

Oliver had to force himself not to tremble at the thought of seeing Fagin again. Nonetheless, after considerable internal deliberation, he declared that he would be prepared to accompany his guardian to the condemned cell at Newgate, and to ask the fiend who had once caused him so much misery, where he had concealed the papers relating to his inheritance. The brave determination in Oliver's countenance as he announced this convinced Mr Brownlow that he had succeeded in overcoming his fears.

Yet the dreadful grey stone walls of Newgate, as he and Mr Brownlow stood before them that same evening, sent a shudder of terror through the boy's heart. It could not but occur to him at that moment, that if he had not been saved by the goodness of such as Mr Brownlow and his dear Aunt Rose, his own life might well have been brought to an invidious end in this terrible place. However, when Mr Brownlow asked him if he was still prepared to go on, he replied with quiet firmness, 'Yes, Father,' and the two of them approached the forbidding prison gates; passing, as they did so, a group of workmen who were beginning to build a wooden structure which Oliver recognized at once, even at this early stage of construction, as a scaffold.

Oliver was watching these sombre preparations as the turnkey who had opened the gates examined Mr Brownlow's order of admission. A burly, unshaven, suspicious man, he looked at Oliver for a moment or two before whispering: 'Is the young gentleman to come too, sir? It's not a sight for children.'

Mr Brownlow replied: 'It is not indeed. But my business with this man is intimately connected with him; and as this child has seen him in the full career of his success and villainy, I think it as well – even at the cost of some pain and fear – that he should see him now.'

The turnkey touched his hat, admitted the kind old gentleman and his youthful companion, and led them through innumerable gloomy corridors, to the cell which housed the notorious villain Fagin, who was to be hanged the next morning.

The condemned criminal was seated on his low stone bed, rocking himself from side to side, in the light from the cell's small, high window. His clothes were tattered, his long red hair hung down upon his bloodless face; his beard was torn and twisted into knots. Round his head he wore a blood-stained bandage. Half-crazed, he displayed a countenance more like that of a snared beast than that of a man. He seemed oblivious to his damp, grey surroundings, and was sometimes whispering to himself, sometimes chuckling, sometimes glaring.

'Let him go to bed, Dodger,' he muttered. 'There's things we don't want heard . . . No, no, Bill – never mind the girl. She won't blab. No violence now, no need for violence, Bill . . . Bolter – he's the one who'll split on us. Watch him, Charley, good boy . . . Bolter's throat, Bill . . . Bolter's throat as deep as you can cut. Saw his head off!'

As a kind of satanic accompaniment to the strange words he was giving vent to, and as a reminder of his future, there could be heard through the cell's window, the noise of hammering and sawing, and the throwing down of boards.

'Fagin!' said the turnkey, loudly. Fagin started and glared at his visitors. In his wanderings, he had not heard the key turning and the creak of the cell door as it opened.

'That's me!' he cried. 'An old man, my Lord,' he squeaked as he bowed to the old gentleman who now stood before him, as though to a judge. 'A very old, old man.'

'Fagin?' the turnkey repeated, quietly this time, 'Here's somebody wants to see you, ask you some questions, Fagin! Are you a man?'

'I shan't be one long' Fagin replied, and then screamed, 'Strike them all dead! What right have they to butcher me!' Whereupon he shrank back into the farthest corner of the bed, demanding to know what these people wanted here.

'You mind your manners,' said the turnkey. 'Now, sir, tell him what you want. Quick, if you please, for he grows worse as time goes on.'

'You have some papers,' said Mr Brownlow, 'placed in your hands by a man called Monks.'

'It's all a lie!' Fagin growled, 'I haven't one – not one.'

'For the love of God,' said Mr Brownlow solemnly, 'do not say that now, upon the very verge of death; even now you can make amends if you tell me where they are. You know that Sikes is dead; that Monks has confessed; that there's no hope of any further gain. Those papers can be of no further use to you. Where are they?'

Fagin was silent for a while, gnawing at his cracked lip, apparently only aware of the ceaseless hammering outside the window. Then he suddenly turned and caught sight for the first time of Oliver, who stood by the door, trying to hide the fear within him. 'Oliver?' the villain hissed in wonder, 'Little Oliver?'

'His whole future may depend on those documents,' said Mr Brownlow, but Fagin seemed not to hear this, and beckoned to his former charge.

'Oliver,' he said, almost gently now, 'Here, here! Let me whisper to you.'

Oliver tried his best to overcome his terror, but nonetheless caught hold of his guardian's hand as he approached the villain. 'Will you help me, please, Mr Fagin?' he said softly.

Fagin chuckled, 'I'll whisper it,' he said, and then snarled, 'when we're alone. Only when we're alone.'

'I don't advise it, sir,' said the turnkey to Mr Brownlow anxiously.

'I am not afraid,' said Oliver in a low voice, mastering himself at last and relinquishing his guardian's hand.

'If you harm him. . .' began Mr Brownlow, raising a fist threateningly in Fagin's direction.

'My Oliver?' replied Fagin, with innocent concern. 'My own dear little Oliver? Not a hair of his head.'

After some thought, and with a glance at Oliver, Mr Brownlow murmured, 'Very well' and moved to the open door. The turnkey looked worriedly at the villain and the boy for a few moments, shrugged, and followed the old gentleman out of the cell, closing the door as he went. Oliver was now alone with Fagin. With wide fearful eyes, he stared at his former master, in the manner of a rabbit before a snake, unable to move.

'Nearer, my dear,' Fagin whispered, 'Nearer.'

Oliver began to take a slow step forward but even before he could complete it two gnarled filthy hands had shot out towards him and he found himself so close to the criminal that their faces almost touched.

Fagin held Oliver's arms with an iron grip as he hissed: 'Was it you that gave me away? You that ratted on me, eh? Eh?' He began to shake the boy violently.

'No, Mr Fagin,' said Oliver, terrified, 'I said nothing. I . . . I gave you my word.'

Fagin stared intently at the boy for a few long seconds before loosening his grasp a little.

'So you did,' he muttered. 'Yes. A fine, honourable boy, just like I always said.' And he smiled grimly. Then he looked away and mumbled through clenched teeth 'So it *was* that other one – that snivelling worm, Bolter. . .' and he thought for a while considering perhaps what ghastly revenge he might inflict on the worm in question, if such a revenge was only possible. Such hopes were fruitless, however, for by tomorrow he would be dead, and, suddenly remembering that ghastly truth, he turned to Oliver again, gripping him more tightly still. 'But it was all because of *you* the trouble started. . .' he growled. Then, unaccountably, he slackened his grip and patted the boy's cheek, smiling paternally. 'Still, now you've come to help me . . . I knew my boys wouldn't let me down. So you've come to help old Fagin get away, eh?'

Oliver swallowed hard, glanced at the closed door behind him, and said, as calmly as he could manage: 'I came to ask you about the papers and the letter.'

The old fiend chuckled: 'Oh, you're a hard one . . . But I taught you well. "Always look out for Number One", eh? Yes . . . I always said you'd be the sharpest of the lot . . . next to the Dodger.' Suddenly, he shivered and, releasing the boy, he wrapped his tattered cloak around himself still tighter. 'Listen!' he groaned. 'Do you hear – out there? They're building the gallows, and when it's done, old Fagin's going to swing.'

For a few moments, Oliver tried to listen to the remorseless hammering outside. Fagin listened too. Then Oliver felt the villain's hand clutching his arm again, and heard him whisper: 'You and me, my dear, we'll strike a bargain, eh? The papers.' He pulled the boy still closer: 'The old hideout, remember? The fireplace in the top front room. There's a hole behind two bricks, a little way up the chimney. You'll find them there in a canvas bag.'

'Oh thank you! Thank you, sir!' cried Oliver, unable to conceal his excitement and relief, and began to move towards the door. But Fagin, who was still holding him, tightened his grip and pulled the boy back.

'Not so fast,' he growled, 'You must keep your side of the bargain, my dear.'

'Oh what is it, sir?' said Oliver. 'Do you want me to keep you company till morning? To pray for you? Let me say a prayer. Do! Let me say one prayer.'

Fagin laughed hideously: 'I'm past that! Long past! No, you can get me out of here.' Whereupon he rose slowly, and began to push the boy before him in the direction of the door, looking vacantly over his head. 'Outside, outside,' he muttered, 'Say I've gone to sleep – they'll believe *you.*'

'But they'll see you,' said Oliver, fearful again.

'No, no,' replied Fagin, 'I'm the old gentleman that came in with you. Tell them that, eh? We'll slip past the warders and the turnkey without them even spotting us.'

'Oh! God forgive this wretched man!' cried Oliver, and at that moment the door opened and Mr Brownlow and the turnkey returned, in the company of another warder.

Fagin appeared not to notice their return, but continued, in his distraction: 'Press on. Press on. This door first. We'll slip out past them all, eh? Past the gallows . . . If I shake and tremble, don't you mind, but hurry on. Now, now, now! Faster. Faster!'

The turnkey and the warder laid hands upon him then, and disengaging Oliver from his grasp, held him back. He struggled for an instant, with a desperate power, then sent up cry after cry: 'No, no! I'm with *him*! With Oliver! Tell them, Oliver!'

Mr Browlow put an arm around the petrified boy and led him out of the cell. The door closed behind them, but the condemned man's howls penetrated even those massive walls and pursued them as they hurried through the dank passages of the prison: 'We had a bargain! You cheated me, Oliver! Betrayed me again! I'll see you rot for this!' It was not until they had reached the prison gates that a comparative silence prevailed.

CHAPTER TWO

Whatever dreadful thoughts passed through Fagin's tortured mind that dark night, destined as he was to die in the morning, they cannot have been that much more harrowing than the dreams poor Oliver Twist endured, as he tossed and turned on his bed at Mr Brownlow's – for the afternoon's events had awakened lamentable memories.

As he slept, he seemed to find himself very much awake in a squalid back-room in one of the darker corners of London. With him in this miserable place were three companions – two boys and an old man. The old man was Fagin. His face was close to Oliver's as he smiled and said: 'We'll teach Oliver how to do it. Shall us, Oliver, eh?'

'If you please, sir,' Oliver heard himself reply, meekly.

One of the boys burst into a fit of uncontrollable mirth, spluttering as he laughed: 'He's so jolly green!'

Then a curious game began. Fagin placed a silk handkerchief in one of the pockets of his flannel cloak and turned his back on Oliver, saying: 'See if you can take it out, my dear, without my feeling it.' As he trotted up and down the room, sometimes stopping at the fireplace, sometimes at the door, Oliver followed stealthily; he found himself reaching for the pocket and lightly drawing out the handkerchief. The boys grinned.

'Is it gone?' Fagin inquired at last.

'Here it is, sir,' said Oliver, showing it in his hand.

Fagin put his hand in his pocket, spun round, and gasped in surprise. Oliver felt a flush of pride as the old man patted him on the head approvingly and whispered: 'You're a clever boy, my dear. I never saw a sharper lad.' The two boys guffawed so loudly that their laughter seemed to fill the room with a cacophony of echoes.

Then the room was suddenly silent and dark but for the light of a single low candle. The boys had gone. Oliver thought he must have woken from a sound, long sleep, for he did not feel thoroughly awake, and he was lying on a mattress on the floor. Through half-closed eyes, he saw Fagin seated before a table, with a small box before him. The old man's eyes glistened in the candlelight as he raised the lid, and looked in. With a hideous grin he drew from the box a double string of pearls. 'Clever dogs! Clever dogs!' he chuckled, and scrutinized the necklace for some time before replacing it and extracting a magnificent gold watch, sparkling with jewels, which he surveyed and caressed with diabolic pleasure. Suddenly, he turned and his bright eyes fell on Oliver's face. In no more than a second he had dropped the watch back into the box, closed the lid with a crash, and was standing close to Oliver, a bread-knife trembling in his hand. 'What do you watch me for?' he hissed, threateningly. 'Why are you awake? What have you seen? Speak out, boy! Quick! Quick! For your life!'

'I wasn't able to sleep any longer, sir,' Oliver heard himself reply, 'I am very sorry if I have disturbed you, sir.'

'Were you awake an hour ago?' growled Fagin, fiercely.

'No! No indeed!' replied Oliver.

'Are you sure?' cried Fagin, still more fiercely.

'Upon my word, sir,' replied Oliver, 'I was not, sir; I was not indeed, sir.'

There followed a few long moments during which Oliver thought that his short life was about to come to an end there and then, but Fagin abruptly adopted something resembling a more friendly manner, and he played with the knife a little before putting it down, as if to pretend that he had caught it up in sport. 'Of course I know that, my dear. I only tried to frighten you.

You're a brave boy.' With this he chuckled and rubbed his hands, but could not mask an expression of unease as he glanced at the box.

'Did you see any of these pretty things, my dear?' he said, returning to the table.

'Yes, sir,' replied Oliver.

Fagin turned rather pale at this. 'Ah!' he said. 'They – they're mine, Oliver; my little property. All I have to live on in my old age. People call me a miser, my dear. Only a miser, that's all.' Whereupon he quickly snatched up the box, tucked it under his arm, and snuffed out the candle.

The terrible darkness returned. There are moments in dreaming, when a sleeper begins to wish himself awake, and sometimes he succeeds in waking if the wish is strong enough. But no amount of wishing on Oliver's part could release him from his dark imaginings on this occasion, and he now felt himself climbing a steep narrow staircase. He was surrounded by blackness, and did not know – for he did not dare to contemplate – where the staircase might lead, until he reached a room, smaller, darker and still dirtier than the one he had been in previously. At first the room appeared to be empty, but then Oliver felt a strong hand grasp his collar, and heard a deep, ghastly voice. 'Give me away, 'ave yer?' it snarled. 'Peached on me, 'ave yer?'

'No, Mr Sikes! No, I swear it!' pleaded Oliver, as he recognized his assailant's scowling eyes and huge menacing figure.

'You'd swear to anything, you cunning little devil!' said the horrible shape. 'This time, I'll settle you once and for all.' Still clasping Oliver's collar with one hand, it picked up a thick, ironbound club with the other. Oliver struggled harder than he had ever struggled before, and at last succeeded in freeing himself, by slipping his arms out of his jacket, scuttling from the room and down the stairs as fast as his legs could carry him. 'Come back 'ere!' roared the man with the club, tearing after him.

Now Oliver was scurrying through the backstreets of London – innumerable, interminable streets and alleyways, filthy and confined. He smelt the stench from the gutters, felt the mud splash up into his face. There seemed to be no sign of help anywhere, and whenever he was bold enough to glance over his shoulder, he saw the hefty shadow of his pursuer remorselessly chasing him still brandishing his club. There was worst yet to come, for as Oliver turned a corner, he ran headlong into an equally familiar personage; a very fat man with a red, perspiring face, who wore a cocked hat and a coat embellished with large brass buttons; and who said, as he seized Oliver by the arm and pulled him along: 'Now then, young Twist, you miserable boy. It's back to the Workhouse with you!'

Oliver screamed. His loud anguished cry woke him. For a while he did not know where he was, and stared out into the darkness and silence, still frightened. Within a few moments, however, the door opened and the friendly but concerned figure of Mrs Bedwin bustled into the room, carrying a candle.

'What is it, my lamb? Whatever is it?' asked the kind old housekeeper.

'Bumble!' murmured Oliver. 'Mr Bumble, the Beadle! He caught me!'

'No, no, my child,' said Mrs Bedwin, as she came over to the shivering boy and cradled him in her arms. 'It was only a dream. See – there's no one here.'

At this point, Mr Brownlow hurried into the room in his dressing gown. 'I heard him cry out,' he said anxiously.

'A bad dream, sir,' explained Mrs Bedwin, 'that's all.'

'Sikes!' muttered Oliver, 'Sikes! and Mr Bumble! They were chasing me! They...'

Mr Brownlow came to him and held his hand. 'They are gone, Oliver,' he said fixedly. 'They are gone forever.

You are safe. No one will ever harm you here, I promise.' The quiet assurance in the old gentleman's voice was all the comfort the boy needed. He closed his eyes – for he was still half asleep – and lay back on his pillow. 'Thank you,' he whispered. 'Thank you. . . Thank you, Father. Thank you.'

Within seconds, he had slipped into an untroubled slumber.

Mr Brownlow at once acknowledged to himself that he had been too impetuous in allowing Oliver to encounter Fagin again. He had clearly underestimated the power and terror of the boy's unhappy memories. Moreover, although he had initially thought of asking Oliver to guide him to the place where Fagin claimed to have hidden the documents relating to the inheritance, he now saw that such a course of action was out of the question, for it would only arouse further – perhaps even more painful – reminiscences. Mr Brownlow resolved, therefore, to go to the police and ask them to recommend a reliable agent – someone who knew the wretched underworld through which Fagin and his kind walked, and who would be able to discover without difficulty the hiding-place to which the villain had referred.

The police wasted no time in furnishing him with such a person, and by noon the next day a large-headed, small-eyed, ingratiating and altogether unprepossessing young man who had announced himself as 'Mr Morris Bolter' was in Mr Brownlow's sitting-room. Mr Grimwig was surveying him with a cold distrust, and for once Mr Brownlow thought his friend's suspicions in this case might be more than justified.

'If the property can be found, sir,' Mr Bolter was saying with an air of false gentility, 'I guarantee to find it,' and he added, as he sank deeper into one of Mr Brownlow's very comfortable chairs, 'for a fee.'

'The police spoke highly of you, Mr Bolter,' said Mr Brownlow, in an effort to convince himself of this dubious fellow's worth.

'And that they should, sir,' the young gentleman replied. 'A-considerin 'ow many little services I been and done for 'em.'

'As an informer no doubt,' muttered Mr Grimwig, 'or I'll eat my head.'

Mr Bolter was about to react to this, when Mr Brownlow, who did not wish to waste more minutes than he had to in this unpleasant fellow's company, said quickly: 'These documents are of value only to me, yet I am prepared to pay ten pounds for their safe recovery.'

The creature's eyes lit up at the mention of this sum, and he emitted a low whistle of satisfaction. 'Just tell me where I can come at them,' he asked, eagerly.

'They are hidden in a tenement in Saffron Hill,' said Mr Brownlow.

Mr Bolter's eagerness seemed to desert him as quickly as it had arrived. 'That rookery?' he said hesitantly. 'There's more hidin' places there than fleas on a donkey. I need to know exactly where to look.'

'My ward can tell you,' said Mr Brownlow, and he moved to the door and called for Oliver.

'Do you know the Saffron Hill district, Mr Bolter?' inquired Mr Grimwig with a sidelong glare.

'Only thieves and wagabonds *know* it, yer Honour,' retorted Mr Bolter, thereby hoping to convince the two old gentlemen that he was neither a thief nor a vagabond. Then, realizing that he would not receive his ten pounds if he claimed never to have been there, he added: 'But I – uh – have a slight acquaintance with it, through my perfessional duties.'

As Oliver Twist walked into the room, Morris Bolter was ready to give him the benefit of an unctuous grin. But somehow it never appeared.

'Noah!' cried Oliver, thoroughly startled. 'Noah Claypole!'

'I thought your name was Bolter!' roared Mr Grimwig, with the ferocious glee of one who has discovered his fears to be amply well-founded.

The young gentleman thus identified as Noah Claypole, cowered slightly at this assault before replying: 'Perfessionally, yer Honour. My "perfessional" name.'

'And how do you come to know my ward?' inquired Mr Brownlow, sternly.

Noah Claypole remained silent, and Oliver had to explain: 'We were apprentices together, at Mr Sowerberry's, the undertaker.'

Oliver had told his guardian of the injuries he had had to endure at the hands – or rather the foot – of a certain fellow-apprentice whilst working for Mr Sowerberry, so Mr Brownlow could scarcely restrain his fury as he asked Oliver: 'Is he the one you told me of? The one who ill-treated you so?'

'A long while ago, sir,' interjected Noah Claypole before Oliver had a chance to reply. 'Thoughtless, boyish cruelty, that knew no better. For which I 'umbly asks yer pardon, Master Oliver.' Standing at last, he bowed to his former companion.

After a pause, Oliver said calmly: 'It's all forgiven, and forgotten.'

'Bless yer noble 'eart! At last I can sleep easy!' cried Claypole, grinning with relief.

'This,' declared Mr Grimwig, 'must be the same "Bolter" who turned State's Evidence on Fagin and the man Sikes.'

'Led astray I was, yer Honour,' Claypole explained, hurriedly. 'But at the trial, I saw the error of my ways.'

'And were given a free pardon,' Mr Grimwig snorted, with distaste.

'Well at least you must have been to Fagin's old headquarters,' said Mr Brownlow.

Noah Claypole, alias Morris Bolter, turned pale. He knew the place, certainly, but he was not sure he wanted to return *there*, even for ten pounds.

'A den of wickedness, sir,' he said, unable to conceal the terror in his voice and countenance. 'But it was searched most thorough, sir. There's nothing there.'

'You remember the open fireplace in the top front room?' asked Oliver. 'There are bricks that swing out, a little way up the chimney. The papers are there.'

A thought struck Claypole – a delicious thought; a greedy thought. In his mind's eye, he suddenly saw a way of converting the ten pounds into a considerably larger amount. Like too many young men of his type, Noah Claypole was governed in all his actions by two, and only two, interests: greed and cowardice. The two were often at conflict, but on this particular occasion, greed was the victor. So when Mr Brownlow asked 'You'll fetch them?' he cried 'As good as done, sir!' and made for the door. But then, aware that such a hasty departure might appear somewhat suspect, he turned and said: 'Especially as a means of makin' up to Master Oliver for any little unkindness I may have done 'im in the past.' With another obsequious grin and bow, he was gone. Oliver shuddered.

'I'd have spared you that meeting, Oliver,' said Mr Brownlow, 'if I'd suspected who he really was.'

'No better than a thief himself,' snarled Mr Grimwig, 'or I'll eat my head.'

Once again Mr Brownlow had to concede that Mr Grimwig might be correct in his judgement of the creature who had just left. However, he was able to derive some comfort from the fact that Claypole's obvious knowledge of the hideout would bring the business of retrieving the documents to a speedy end; and Oliver, at least, had been spared the agony of having to retrieve them for himself.

Noah Claypole had every reason to be fearful of being seen, once more, in the vicinity of Saffron Hill, that afternoon. It lies on the fringes of the City near Smithfield market, and there is not a more iniquitous locality in the entire metropolis. It is a labyrinth of narrow streets and filthy courts, which the sun never seems to reach, even on the most cloudless of days. Here, protected to a degree by the darkness, dwell thieves, idlers, vagabonds and ruffians of all sorts. Little wonder, then, that Noah Claypole did his best to keep his bony features well-hidden, as he hurried towards the place in which Fagin had once lived. He was an informer now, and no doubt known as such by some of the district's inhabitants; the possibility of revenge seemed to lurk behind every doorway. But the greed already mentioned drove him on, and at last he reached a house near Field Lane, glanced about him, saw that he was not observed, pushed open the door, and went in. He was met by a sinister blackness. In the light from the door, however, he could identify the beginning of a stairway; groping his way, he climbed it, as stealthily as he could – convinced that the slightest creak would bring the fury of the entire criminal population of London down upon his head. Eventually, and with relief, he reached the room in question. A dim light emanated from a warped, shuttered window. From what he could discern, the place seemed to have been emptied of all its contents, with the exception of a table and a broken chair. In his eagerness to complete his commission as speedily as possible, he moved quickly towards the fireplace – for he remembered where it had been. He ran into something; or someone; crouching on the floor.

With a screech of unmitigated fear, Noah Claypole jumped back, and stood trembling, certain that his throat was about to be cut. The creature on the floor did not move, and appeared to be very small. As his eyes grew more accustomed to the darkness, Claypole saw that it was trembling too, and was clearly as afraid as he was – if not more so. Summoning all the courage he could muster, which was no more than a speck, Claypole shouted: 'Who's that? Who's there?'

A frightened voice answered: 'Ned Fingers – if you please, Mr Bolter.'

Claypole recognized the name at once, and he immediately adopted a tone of vicious superiority, abandoning all his previous fears in an instant. ' 'Ow dare you creep about in the dark!' he cried, 'puttin' the fright up your betters!'

'No offence meant, Mr Bolter. Beggin' your pardon...' the boy began.

'Get up, you sneaky little toad!'

Ned Fingers did as he was bid, and revealed himself to be a skinny, rat-faced, pimply youth – one of the lesser members of Fagin's old gang.

'Now,' said Claypole, 'wot yer doin' 'ere?'

'Nowhere else to go,' replied Fingers, with a shrug. 'After Fagin an' the Dodger was took – an' the gang broke up.'

'So you're livin' 'ere, are yer?'

''Ave to sleep somewhere,' the youth said, with a snivel, and then pleaded: 'Don't turn me over to the Runners... Please, Mr Bolter!'

Claypole pretended to give such a possibility a moment's serious consideration before he said, with a grin: 'Turn yer over? – wot for? Where's the profit? As for the Runners, I only tell 'em as much as is good for them to hear.' He tapped his nose conspiratorially, emitting a low chuckle as he did so.

Fingers stopped snivelling at once and stared at Claypole in surprise and relief. 'So you're still one of us?'

'That's as maybe,' retorted Claypole harshly. Then with a glance round the room, he asked, with affected casualness: 'On yer own, are yer?'

'Never see nobody from one week to the next,' the youth replied.

'You look 'alf starved,' said Claypole, 'I feel a bit peckish meself. Tell you wot, Fingers – hop down the street an' get us two penny worth of saltbeef, and 'alf a loaf.' Whereupon he removed a shining sixpence from his pocket.

'I'll be back afore you've noticed I've gone, Mr Bolter,' said Fingers, snatching the coin.

'No 'urry,' snarled Claypole. 'Take yer time.'

But Fingers was already on his way, scampering down

the stairs. Left alone, Noah Claypole listened for a second or two, then hurried to the empty fireplace. He ran his hands across the back of the wide chimney, until he sensed a slight movement. With a grunt, he pressed at the bricks, and uttered a chuckle of delight as they pivotted and swung out. He reached into the cavity and grinned, hungrily.

Noah Claypole returned to the house in Pentonville that evening, and was shown once again into the sitting-room, where Mr Brownlow and Oliver were waiting. Secretly pleased that there seemed to be no sign of the fractious old gentleman who had been so suspicious of him earlier in the day, he announced, at once and in as rueful a tone as he could contrive, that his search had been unsuccessful; he had found nothing.

'Nothing?' asked Mr Brownlow, sharply.

'Not a sausage,' said Claypole. 'It was the right fireplace. The bricks swung out, the 'ole was behind them, but – empty.'

'Are you *sure*?'

'My oath, sir. The 'ole was only a 'ole. No papers – nothing.'

'Someone must have taken them,' said Oliver.

'Or Fagin lied to us,' said Mr Brownlow.

'More than possible, sir,' opined Claypole. 'He was never persackly the soul, one might say, of weracity.'

'No,' said Mr Brownlow, and walked to the window. 'It is very disappointing,' he murmured, staring into the garden. Oliver turned away towards the fireplace and hung his head.

Thus faced with a pair of very dejected backs, and after a good minute of downcast silence, Noah Claypole sensed that his presence was no longer required – and he, in any case, had things to do – so he said, 'Well, I'll take my leave, sir,' and moved towards the door.

'One moment, Mr Bolter,' said Mr Brownlow, turning.

Noah Claypole froze in fear, but Mr Brownlow appeared to retain a friendly enough countenance as he continued: 'I have not given you your fee.'

For some reason, Claypole had forgotten all about the ten pounds that had been promised him. But now he surprised Oliver, and perhaps Mr Brownlow too, by replying magnanimously: 'Oh I couldn't accept it, sir. Not comin' back empty-handed.'

'You must be compensated for your trouble,' Mr Brownlow insisted, and drew out a purse from which he extracted a number of gold sovereigns.

'Well, sir, if you insist, sir. Thank you kindly,' said Claypole, accepting the coins with apparent reluctance, but pocketing them hurriedly once they were in his hand. Then, with a face full of unctuous remorse, he said to Oliver: 'So sorry . . . Master Oliver,' and left. Only when he was safely out of sight of the house did he allow his countenance to break into a broad smile of self-satisfaction, for several very pleasant thoughts were passing through his mind.

A short while later, however, Mr Grimwig arrived at Mr Brownlow's house, bearing the news that would have killed Noah Claypole's present happiness in an instant, if he had still been there to learn it. Oliver was no longer in the sitting-room when Mr Grimwig was admitted, but downstairs, with the housekeeper. He was reading to her; or rather, doing his best to read, for he was very much lost in his own sorry musings.

'Now then,' said Mrs Bedwin, kindly, as she noticed his sad demeanour. 'Don't be upset, child. It'll only mean waiting a little longer before Mr Brownlow can adopt you.'

'Yes,' replied Oliver, a little despondently.

'Now,' said Mrs Bedwin, 'you go on with that story. I won't sleep tonight, if I don't hear what it was made Robinson Crusoe stop so sudden.'

Oliver smiled and picked up the book again. He read:

'There on the wet sand in front of me was the print of a man's foot.'

'Oh my!' squealed Mrs Bedwin, and dropped her sewing into her lap.

Oliver could not but laugh at this, for all his sadness.

Upstairs at this moment, Mr Brownlow was reading too, but could find no cause for amusement in the words before him. Mr Grimwig had brought a copy of the evening newspaper and, before saying anything, had opened it at a certain page and pointed to an item of particular interest, which read: 'The notorious fence and thief-master Fagin succumbed, in the early hours of today, to a violent heart and brain seizure in Newgate prison. On examination, he was found to be helplessly paralysed and therefore in no condition to undergo execution, set for nine o'clock this morning.'

'I cannot believe it,' muttered Mr Brownlow, lowering the newspaper and looking up at Mr Grimwig.

'Yet there it is, sir,' said Mr Grimwig. 'In black and white. But read on, read on.'

Mr Brownlow did so. 'Being beyond medical aid, and as a gesture of clemency, he has been released to die into the care and custody of his daughter and son-in-law.'

'Clemency!' roared Mr Grimwig. 'To save the prison authorities the cost of a doctor – or I'll eat my head!' Whereupon he struck his stick upon the ground with such violence that the whole house seemed to tremble with the blow.

'Helplessly paralysed' or not, the fact that Fagin was still alive and free again, provoked in Mr Brownlow a considerable amount of understandable unease. The villain's last words rang once more in his ears: 'You cheated me, Oliver! Betrayed me again! I'll see you rot for this!' He determined that Oliver must be sent away from London as soon as possible.

He would miss the boy, naturally, but his prime concern, as it had always been, was for his ward's safety. His first thought was to allow Oliver to return to his uncle and aunt, but when Mr Grimwig declared that the young fellow was now old enough to go to a good school, and certainly in need of a proper education, Mr Brownlow decided to accept his friend's advice and began to make immediate inquiries and arrangements.

Within a fortnight, Oliver Twist was on his way North, in the company of his guardian, dressed in a schoolboy's striped trousers, black swallowtail coat and waistcoat; bound for a new and – so Mr Brownlow hoped with all his heart – troublefree life.

CHAPTER THREE

The school that had been chosen for Oliver's education was not one of the better-known institutions; indeed, it was scarcely known at all – which was precisely why Mr Brownlow had selected it. It had also been recommended to him as a reputable institution by Oliver's uncle, the Reverend Harry Maylie. It was a small, private academy set in the depths of one of the Northern counties, a good hundred and fifty miles from London, and therefore far from the sights and memories of Oliver's wretched past. It bore the impressive name of 'Stalker's Academical Establishment for Young Gentlemen.'

After a long journey, Mr Brownlow and his ward arrived at the gates of this august foundation on a fresh Sunday morning in autumn. They were promptly ushered into the study and presence of its proud owner – Mr Stalker himself; a gaunt and tyrannical gentleman, whose fanatical demeanour made Oliver quake slightly, and forced Mr Brownlow to undergo immediate and severe doubts. He seriously considered putting the boy back into the coach and returning with him to London as quickly as possible. Before he could put this intention into practice, however, Mr Stalker spread his long arms expansively and boomed:

'Welcome to Stalker's Academical Establishment! And, having welcomed, do I now bid farewell, sir? I do.'

'Farewell?' Mr Brownlow inquired.

'Yes, sir,' Mr Stalker reiterated, 'Farewell.'

'Do I understand that you wish me to leave?'

'I do, sir,' replied Mr Stalker.

'But I have only just arrived, sir,' said Mr Brownlow.

'Precisely,' replied Mr Stalker, 'And so has young Twist. The sooner he is left alone, the sooner he will settle in.'

'I see,' said Mr Brownlow, not really seeing at all.

'Thuswise, I must request you to leave, sir,' announced Mr Stalker, 'Perfunctorily. Is that what I mean? No. Precipitately. Yes. *Summa cum celeritate.*' Whereupon he chuckled with the glee of the true pedant, and turned to gaze out of the window.

Mr Brownlow looked at Oliver, and Oliver looked at Mr Brownlow. Tears began to form in the boy's eyes. 'Father...,' he said, weakly.

'I must go now, Oliver,' said Mr Brownlow, with as much firmness as he could manage.

'Can't you stay just a little longer?'

Mr Brownlow heard a warning cough from the direction of the window. 'I'm afraid not, Oliver,' he said, 'It's for the best, I'm sure, so...' and he held out his hand.

In an instant, Oliver had run to him and was in his arms, clinging to him tightly. At the same moment, Mr Brownlow heard a second, more curious sound emanating from where Mr Stalker was standing; it seemed to resemble the noise made by a badly played trumpet. Mr Stalker was blowing his nose, rather loudly. Continued sniffings followed this performance, and Mr Brownlow realized that the awesome old gentleman, far from having a bad cold, of which he had previously betrayed no signs, was simply attempting to conceal the fact that he was weeping; at what precisely Mr Brownlow could not at first imagine, until he concluded that the cause of his tears must be the scene of departure which was at this moment being enacted in his presence. Mr Brownlow warmed to Mr Stalker immediately, for he now understood that underneath his formidable exterior there lay a passably sympathetic heart.

Reassured by this discovery, Mr Brownlow said to Oliver: 'I'll come back to see you again soon, I promise. Now. Obey your masters, attend to your lessons – and I am sure you will be a credit to us all.'

Oliver clung to his guardian for a few moments longer

before releasing himself. 'Will you write to me, Father?' he asked.

'Every week, without fail,' said Mr Brownlow. 'And you will write to me, I trust.'

'Yes, Father,' replied Oliver, attempting a brave smile.

Mr Brownlow patted Oliver on the head, barely able to hold back his own tears. He then turned to Mr Stalker, or rather to Mr Stalker's back, and said: 'Good day, sir. I leave my ward in your hands.'

Mr Stalker nodded, still without turning, and with a last loving glance at his ward, Mr Brownlow left the room.

After a long silence, Mr Stalker blew his nose again, following this action with a little sigh. 'Heigh-ho,' he said, 'most touching,' and when he turned round he had resumed his former authoritative self. 'Now, Twist,' he boomed, 'to business.'

'Yes sir,' said Oliver, softly.

'Your prospective parent, in his wisdom, has placed you in my care.'

'Yes, sir,' said Oliver.

'Shall I tell you what is expected of you?'

'Yes, please, sir.'

'Did I solicit an answer? I did not. That was a rhetorical question, Twist. Hold your tongue.'

'Yes, sir.'

'Will you kindly cease interrupting?' Mr Stalker shouted.

Oliver was about to apologize, but the force of Mr Stalker's glare persuaded him that it might be better to remain silent, which proved to be exactly what Mr Stalker required of him.

Once he had assured himself that the boy was not going to interrupt again, Mr Stalker continued: 'The rules of this academical establishment are simple, and immutable. No lounging, no loafing, nor unnecessary guffawing. No smoking in the Junior School. Spirituous liquors limited to small beer at Sunday luncheon. You will be clean, neat, attentive and, above all, gentlemanly. In short, perfect behaviour. Is that what I expect? It is. If gentlemanly decorum is not inbred, do we beat it in? We do, Twist. We most certainly do. Is that understood?'

Oliver was not sure if he was expected to furnish a reply – he was not very sure of anything anymore – so he did not offer one.

'Well? Is it?' Mr Stalker asked again, with impatience.

'Yes, sir,' Oliver whispered at last.

'I trust so,' muttered Mr Stalker, whereupon he picked up a small handbell from his desk, and rang it very violently for some time.

'I have rung the bell,' he then announced.

Oliver stared at him blankly.

'For future reference, the rule is that the boy nearest the study must answer,' Mr Stalker explained, with exasperation. At that moment, there was a knock and the door flew open before Mr Stalker had the chance to bid anyone enter.

'Ah, Dawkins . . . ,' said Mr Stalker. 'Here is a new boy. Take charge of him. Dawkins will show you round the school and help you to settle in, Twist.'

The boy who had just entered turned to examine Oliver, at exactly the same time as Oliver turned to examine him. Neither of them could believe their eyes, as they gazed at each for several very long moments.

'What is it?' asked Mr Stalker, 'What is the matter?'

'Oh. Nothing, sir,' replied the boy who had just entered, with a smile.

'Very well,' said Mr Stalker. 'Dismissed!'

In Oliver's mind however there was something very much the matter. The boy who had just entered looked thoroughly neat and spruce in his striped trousers and black swallowtail coat, but his snub nose, flat brow, bow-legged stance, sharp eyes and the way he had of keeping his hands firmly in his pockets, even in the presence of Mr Stalker, were immediately recognizable.

'Well I'm blowed,' the boy declared with a grin and

a wink, once they had left Mr Stalker's study and the door was safely shut behind them, 'if it ain't young Oliver!'

For the youth whom Mr Stalker had addressed as Dawkins, was none other than Oliver Twist's former companion in villainy and one of London's most accomplished pickpockets, affectionately known among the criminal fraternity as the Artful Dodger.

At the same time as Mr Brownlow and Oliver were arriving at Mr Stalker's establishment, Ned Fingers was bounding up the broken stairs towards the room which had once housed Fagin and his followers, two steps at a time. The little thief was highly pleased with himself, for he had just robbed a local shopkeeper of a very long cold sausage, and was eagerly looking forward to eating it, in the safety of the room which was still his home. He had kicked the door shut behind him, and was chuckling as he prepared to take his first large bite of the sausage, when he became aware that there was something about the room which had changed since he had left it in his search for nourishment. It was, above all, a good deal less dark. Ned Fingers froze for a moment or two, turned his head slowly in the direction of one of the windows, and saw that the shutter had been opened. He had scarcely had time to register this disquieting fact when a bony hand clasped his shoulder, and he cried out and dropped his sausage, squealing: 'I didn't do it! I didn't do it! Wotever it is – I didn't do it!'

The hand spun him round and poor Ned Fingers found himself staring up at a most sinister-looking creature; a good deal more sinister than any of the many villains he had previously encountered. The stranger was very tall, thin, but strongly-made and well-dressed. He wore a black hat and large black cape, the collar of which was turned up, thereby concealing most of his face; however, the little that Fingers saw of this face was unforgettable. It was pale and haggard, but its most notable feature was a pair of piercing eyes, sunk deep into the head.

'Where are they?' snarled the stranger, clasping Fingers with one hand and brandishing a dangerous looking silver-topped cane with the other.

'I only took one!' shrieked Fingers, 'No, I didn't! I deny it! I never took a sausage! I ain't never seen a sausage!'

'What are you gabbling about?' cried the stranger, tightening his hold. 'Where are the papers? The letters?'

'Eh?' exclaimed Fingers.

'The papers!' the stranger repeated. 'The letter! You stole them!' and he shook the little thief furiously.

'No I never,' he pleaded, 'I don't mess wiv fings like that.'

'If you're lying . . . ,' the stranger hissed, raising his cane menacingly.

'Swelp me!' Fingers cried. 'Papers! I can't even read!'

After a dreadful pause, the stranger released the boy and stood back, considering him. His hand played with the handle of the cane. 'If you *are* lying . . . ,' he muttered, threateningly.

'Me?' said Fingers, with pained innocence. 'Do I look like a liar?'

'Yes,' replied the stranger.

'Well then,' said the boy, sullenly, 'Wot's the game? You're not from the police.'

'No,' replied the stranger.

'So wot you doin' here?'

The stranger seemed suddenly distracted and began to survey the room as he said: 'I was looking for something. Something I left behind.'

'In Fagin's time?' asked the boy, with surprise. 'I don't remember you.'

The stranger fixed the boy once more with his evil gaze, 'No,' he said, 'but I remember you. You're Ned Fingers – a lying, cheating, conscienceless little beggar and a thief.'

Ned Fingers, far from taking this as a condemnation, accepted it as a compliment, and said with a grin, 'Well, I did my best. Fagin allus said I did my best.'

The stranger glared contemptuously at him for a few seconds before looking round the room again. 'Who lives in the rest of the house?' he asked, resuming a distracted air.

'Nobody. It's all shut up,' Fingers replied, bending warily to pick up his sausage. Having retrieved it, however, he almost dropped it again as the stranger caught his arm once more and stared villainously into his face.

'Has anyone been to see you?' he demanded sharply. Then he adopted a soft, silky tone, and whispered: 'Twist, now . . . Did Oliver Twist come to visit you?'

'Oliver? Nah . . . ,' replied Fingers, 'He ran out on Fagin an' went on the straight. He'd get no welcome from me.'

'Has anyone else been here?' inquired the stranger, still with comparative friendliness, 'Anyone at all?'

Fingers thought for a moment, then he shook his head. 'Not a soul,' he said, 'Except . . .'

'Yes?' hissed the stranger, eagerly.

Fingers was growing bolder now, so he said, 'Wot's it worth?'

'You'll save yourself a great deal of pain,' replied the stranger. The threat was presented quietly, but with firmness, leaving Fingers in no doubt as to the certainty of its being fulfilled at once.

'Bolter,' he said, nervously, 'Mr Bolter looked in once.'

'Bolter? The sneakthief who informed against Fagin?'

Fingers nodded, 'Calls 'isself a Magistrate's Agent now,' he said with distaste, 'But it's my belief he's took up Informin' as a trade.'

'It must be him,' muttered the stranger, to himself, 'Where do I find him?' he asked, turning back to the boy. 'You point him out, and I'll pay you well.'

Fingers took a large bite out of the sausage – the first he had managed – and said, craftily, with his mouth full:

'Who do I say's lookin' for 'im, an' wot about?'

The stranger snapped: 'You'll say nothing. You'll keep your mouth shut.' Then, with a brightness in his eye and a slight but terrible grin, he whispered: 'For if you don't, I'll send someone to sew it up.'

Fingers was still chewing as the stranger said this. But now he stopped, and clamped his lips together tightly, his wide eyes betraying true terror.

Noah Claypole, alias Morris Bolter, was out taking the air that morning, as was his custom on Sundays, strolling with a respectable nonchalance through one of the city's more fashionable quarters, arm in arm with his plump companion, Charlotte, whom he had known since the days of his apprenticeship at Mr Sowerberry's the undertaker and who was so devoted to him that she was quite prepared to obey his every wish; to follow him to the end of the earth, if that should be what he most desired her to do.

On this particular autumn morning, Noah Claypole was watching the people of the town as they passed him and his friend. Most of these people were moving in the opposite direction to the young couple, for they – unlike Noah and Charlotte – were on their way to church. A thought suddenly struck Claypole, and he stopped walking.

'What is it, Noah?' asked Charlotte, stopping with him.

'I been thinking, Charlotte,' declared Claypole, 'I been thinking.'

'Thinking what, Noah?' asked Charlotte.

'I been thinking – if you 'ad a list of all the people as went to Church regular of a Sunday mornin', you'd 'ave a list of a lot of empty 'ouses, just waitin' to be turned over.'

'Why, Noah,' gasped Charlotte, 'you'd never go breakin' into people's 'ouses!'

''Course not, my dear,' replied Claypole. 'But I knows

one or two villains I might send to do it for me,' and he tapped his nose with his finger.

Charlotte gazed at her friend in admiration, 'Why, Noah,' she said, giggling, 'Wherever do you get your ideas from?'

Claypole started to walk on. 'Natcheral perspicacity, my dear,' he said, 'Natcheral perspicacity. I am wery perspicacious.' Whereupon he stopped again. 'Speaking of which . . .'

'Yes, Noah?' said Charlotte.

Noah had noticed that ahead of them, only a matter of yards further on, there stood a public house. It was shut, for it was a Sunday. But the publican – a pleasant, rotund individual – could be seen standing inside one of the ground floor windows, smiling as he watched the passers-by.

'Now's yer chance!' hissed Claypole, suddenly.

'For what, Noah dear?' asked Charlotte, with innocence.

'To 'ave a little drink, my dove,' said Claypole.

'But I'm not thirsty,' said Charlotte.

Noah rolled his eyes heavenward for a second or two. He controlled his exasperation, however, and said, with an abrupt expression of apparent concern: 'Charlotte . . . I am grieved to see 'ow sick an' poorly you look, all of a sudden.' Before Charlotte could exclaim that she certainly did not *feel* sick or poorly, Claypole had hurried her forward so that she was standing outside the window through which the amiable publican was gazing. Noticing this personage, and receiving a conspiratorial wink from her companion, Charlotte immediately understood what was required of her, and, without further ado, collapsed in a dead faint into Noah's waiting arms.

'Oh! Oh! Help!' cried Claypole at once, lowering Charlotte to the ground and fanning her face with his hat. 'Oh, my poor dear wife! Oh my beloved! Speak to me! Say but one word to yer distracted spouse!'

As he had hoped, the publican was beside him in an

instant. 'Oh my goodness!' said this genial gentleman anxiously, 'Wot's wrong, sir? Wot's happened?'

'Alas!' replied Claypole, 'We was on our way to Divine Service, when my good lady got took by a spasm.'

'I saw it! I saw it all!' said the publican. 'Whatever can be done for her?'

''Eaven knows,' Claypole moaned. 'If only I 'ad a drop o' something to revive her . . .'

'But of course, sir!' said the publican. 'Why didn't I think of it?' Whereupon he ran quickly back into his hostelry.

'Speak to me, my love!' Claypole continued, looking helplessly at the inert woman. 'Say but one word, I implore!'

'Don't take on so, Noah dear,' replied Charlotte all of a sudden, opening her eyes at the same time.

'Shut up!' hissed Claypole, and Charlotte quickly closed them again as the publican returned with a squat green brandy bottle in one hand, and a glass in the other.

''Ere, sir,' said the publican, filling the glass and handing it to Claypole, ''Ere, try this.'

'A thousand thanks,' said Claypole, as he took it. He tipped Charlotte's head forward and passed the glass to and fro under her nose, but she gave no evidence of reviving. 'Alas,' he said, with a sigh, 'it's too late.'

'Oh don't say that, sir!' pleaded the publican, aghast, 'Don't give up 'ope.'

Claypole put the glass to Charlotte's lips and tilted it. She appeared to swallow a little of the brandy, and coughed weakly.

'A sign of life!' he cried, and put the glass to her lips again. Needing no further encouragement apparently, Charlotte quickly swallowed the entire contents. Her eyes remained firmly shut nonetheless.

'Another!' said Claypole, holding out the glass to the publican. The publican filled it eagerly, and this time, after a small sip, Charlotte allowed her eyes to flutter open.

'Where am I?' she whispered.

'In the arms of yer own dear 'usband,' said Claypole, soothingly.

'Oh, wot a blessing! Wot a relief, sir!' the publican exclaimed, as he helped Claypole raise Charlotte to her feet. Charlotte still did not appear to have recovered completely, however, so her companion continued to support her, and offered her the glass again.

After one languid sip, Charlotte straightened, suddenly very awake, and cried, sharply: 'What's this? Brandy?'

Claypole raised the glass to his nose, and sniffed the contents. 'At a guess,' he said, casually. Then he took a sip himself. 'Five star,' he opined, not without approval.

'Best in the 'ouse,' declared the publican, proudly, and beamed. But his smile soon faded as he saw that Claypole was now eyeing him in a very serious manner.

'Oh dear,' sighed Claypole, 'Oh dearie, dearie, dear.' He looked at the glass, at the publican, at the glass, at Charlotte, at the glass. 'You are doubtless aware,' he said at last to the publican, 'that it is a Sunday morning.'

More than mildly puzzled, the publican replied that he was aware of that fact.

'An' so,' continued Claypole, adopting a judicial manner, 'against the law, to serve hintoxicatin' liquor. Much as it grieves me, I'm afraid I shall 'ave to report this to the Magistrate.'

'But you asked for it yourself!' cried the publican, with understandable indignation.

Claypole remained very calm as he said: 'I asked for somethin' to revive my good lady – expectin' a glass o' water, or a dish of nourishin' tea! No. Sorry. It's my duty to report it.'

'I was only tryin' to help. You know that!'

'Oh *I* know that,' Claypole explained. 'My good lady knows it but the law ...' and he shook his head, as if to indicate that while he was all too aware of the law's harshness in many matters, it was nonetheless the law, and as such it had to be adhered to, whatever the mitigating circumstances.

Sensing at once that his accuser was unmovable on this point, the publican looked very frightened as he said: 'But wot's going to happen?'

'Lose your licence, I should expect. At best – a heavy fine,' replied Claypole, as one who knew the law and all its retributions.

'Ain't there nothing can be done?' said the publican, yet more frightened.

Claypole raised a hand to his chin and scratched it for a few moments before saying: 'Well, you could pay the fine to me. And I'd make it all right with the beak.'

''Ow much?' asked the publican.

Again Claypole appeared to think for a while before declaring: 'Six guineas.'

'Three,' said the publican quickly.

'Four,' retorted Claypole, even more quickly, and to prevent the publican from further haggling he added: 'I do 'ave a witness.' He jerked his head in Charlotte's direction, and Charlotte smiled.

The publican saw that there was nothing to be done and duly handed over four guineas. 'A wery wise decision,' said Claypole, pocketing the money; whereupon he drank off, in one satisfied gulp, the remainder of the brandy and handed the glass back to the publican, saying: 'Wery nice indeed – thanks again for all yer kindness.' He then took Charlotte's arm, and without so much as a backward glance in the direction of the gentleman whom they had thus deprived of four shining guineas, the happy couple continued their morning amble down the sunny street.

The incident related above was a regular Sunday morning occurrence in the lives of Noah Claypole and his faithful and adoring companion, Charlotte; these performances were distinguishable from each other only in very minor respects; the public house and the publican were different on every occasion, naturally, and sometimes, for the sake of variety, it would be Mr Claypole himself who fainted; but the result was always the same – the charitable publican would finish the poorer, and Noah Claypole the richer, by three or four guineas. Such a means of income allowed Noah and Charlotte to maintain a genteel subsistence without too much risk to life or limb, which suited Noah admirably.

On this particular Sunday, however, Noah was in a mood for celebration, for he had decided to embark on a new, and possibly even more rewarding, profession; the nature of which the reader will learn in a very short while. The place he chose to solemnize his decision might provide something of a clue to those familiar with his earlier adventures, as to what this new career was; for Noah Claypole returned to Saffron Hill early that afternoon, in the company of Charlotte; to another public-house indeed, which lay in the darkest and filthiest part of that dark and filthy locality. This gloomy drinking-house, shuttered and curtained from the prying eyes of outsiders, was called the Three Cripples, and with a mute disregard for the law, it stayed open and provided its dubious clientele with as much liquor as they could pay for, on Sundays, and at all hours of every other day and night of the week. The landlord of the Three Cripples knew Noah Claypole to be an informer, and was very well aware that a word from this gentleman in the ear of a magistrate, would immediately deprive him of his licence – if indeed he possessed such a thing – and close his establishment forever. He had no choice therefore, but to admit Noah with all the hospitality he could summon, as the young man strolled into his bar on this Sunday afternoon, with Charlotte in tow, and demanded that he be provided at once with two pots of beer and two portions of cold meat 'in the back room'.

The landlord was more than mildly surprised at Noah's insistence that he and Charlotte should be allowed to sit in the back room, for the backroom was a small room immediately behind the bar reserved for very special customers – in other words, for those who frequented the higher echelons of the criminal community; most notably, for Fagin in his hey-day. Once again, however, the landlord did not consider himself to be in a position to refuse the demand, and Noah and Charlotte were duly ushered into the back-room and furnished with their beer and meat.

Another personage was equally dismayed by the arrival of Noah Claypole, alias Morris Bolter, at the Three Cripples that afternoon; this was little Ned Fingers, who had been sitting in the bar as Claypole entered, but who had gone unnoticed because of the preponderance of dense tobacco smoke in the place, as had the strange customer who was sitting with him. After a hasty word to his gaunt companion, Fingers rose, and followed Claypole and Charlotte into the back-room, carrying his pot of beer. At the sight of Ned Fingers, Noah Claypole could not resist recounting the manner in which he had defrauded a publican that morning.

When he had told his story, Ned Fingers chuckled and said: 'You're a wonder, Mr Bolter, sir. I can't 'elp thinkin' your talents is wasted, workin' for the law.'

At this, Noah Claypole stroked his nose reflectively, and mused: 'As to that, I've been givin' it some thought.' Charlotte and Fingers listened with increasing awe as he went on: 'An' sittin' 'ere in this inn, in this very room as used to be more or less old Fagin's private office, it occurs to me that someone ought to take over where 'e left off.'

'You?' gasped Charlotte.

'As a fence, Mr Bolter?' asked Fingers, with wonder.

'A redistributor of missin' property,' said Noah.

Fingers suddenly seemed frightened, 'Wot about Fagin?' he asked.

''E's dead,' said Claypole, but had to add: 'Well as good as. Anyway, e's finished.' He then continued with his declaration of intent: 'I reckon 'is old gang needs someone to take over an' run the business side; 'specially someone as can steer the law in the opposite direction.'

Fingers' fears disappeared as quickly as they had arrived, and he began to be enthused by the idea of the cunning Mr Bolter as his new master. However, the old gang, or at least those of its members who had escaped hanging, imprisonment, or transportation, would have to be brought together again, and such a task might not be so easy. Fingers remarked on this problem.

'Ah well,' declared Claypole, 'that's where you comes in, Fingers.'

Fingers was thoroughly flattered that the great Morris Bolter should consider him worthy of the sole responsibility of rounding up Fagin's former followers, because it suggested that he would enjoy a position of considerable importance in the gang once it was reconstituted. The thought of becoming Mr Bolter's faithful and respected lieutenant now filled Fingers with such excitement that he quite forgot his original reason for being in the Three Cripples that afternoon. He was sharply reminded of that reason, however, when he caught sight of a pale and evil visage glaring down at him from behind Noah and Charlotte. High in the wall of this room, a single pane of glass was fixed, through which an interested party could observe any guests who happened to be there, with little hazard of being observed himself, except by those who knew of this tiny window's existence. Noah and Charlotte were ignorant of it, and had their backs to the wall in question; little Ned Fingers had also had no knowledge of the window until now, but he was facing the young couple and the window, and the man who was peering through at him clearly had no intention of letting the youth be unaware of his presence at this moment. He glowered at Fingers with a vicious and impatient countenance for a few seconds, before disappearing.

Fingers paled slightly and rose from his seat, saying: 'Uh . . . talkin's thirsty work, Mr Bolter.'

'Quite right,' said Noah, who had seen and suspected nothing. 'So, three more pints to seal the bargain.' He tossed a shilling in Fingers' direction. 'An' when you're my lootenant, I'll cut you in for a share o' the proceeds – or my name's not Morris Bolter.' Fingers nodded, grinned nervously, and left the room, closing the door behind him.

'Which it ain't,' added Claypole, once the youth had gone.

'Oh, Noah, you are a one . . . ,' said Charlotte, with an approving giggle, as her companion leant back in his chair in a most satisfied manner, tucking his thumbs into the armholes of his waistcoat and smiling from ear to ear.

A second later, the door opened again and a stranger stepped into the room, his white face half-hidden by the collar of his black cape and the shadow that fell from his black hat. He was carrying a silver-topped cane. At the sight of him Charlotte gasped. But Noah Claypole, who was in an authoritarian mood, cried at once: 'This 'ere's a private room. Clear off!'

'Morris Bolter?' asked the stranger, in a quiet but dangerous tone.

Claypole sat up and replied warily: 'I might be.'

The stranger closed the door and walked a few steps forward.

' 'Ere!' shouted Claypole, 'What d'yer think you. . . .'

'You have something that belongs to me,' said the stranger.

'To you?'

'Some documents and a letter, wrapped in oil cloth.'

After a pause, Claypole said: 'Don't know what yer talkin' about.'

'Where are they?' demanded the stranger, his voice beginning to quiver with fury.

'Search me,' replied Claypole, with a shrug.

'I intend to,' said the stranger, taking another threatening step forward.

At this, whatever courage Noah Claypole ever possessed deserted him entirely and he leapt out of his seat, scuttling behind the table for protection and squealing 'Do somethin', Charlotte! Keep 'im off me!'

Poor Charlotte, however, was too terrified to do anything but sit and stare at the evil intruder as he walked to the edge of the table, saying, still quite quietly: 'You won't be harmed, if you hand them over.'

'Even if I did 'ave 'em,' retorted Claypole, with a sneer, 'wot makes 'em yours?'

'So you do have them,' replied the stranger, leaning forward and catching hold of Noah's shirt front near the neck. He pulled him halfway across the table with such brute strength that Charlotte had to emit a long and piercing scream of terror.

'You give them to me, you crawling toad,' the stranger snarled, 'before I squeeze them out of you.'

'No!' gasped Claypole, his face now almost as white as his assailant's, and choking with the pressure of the stranger's knuckles against his throat. 'No! Never! I've hid them! Hid them where you can't get them. Not you, not nobody! Only me . . .!'

No person in London could have been more terrified than Noah Claypole at this moment; and yet coward that he was, he had also managed to summon up from somewhere in the depths of his soul, a determination not to reveal the whereabouts of the papers he had stolen from Fagin's old hideout; except, of course, for a very high price. In that battle of greed and cowardice that controlled his every action, greed was winning again. The stranger who held him by the throat must have sensed this victory, for he now, very suddenly, released the quivering Claypole and threw him back into his chair. Charlotte squeaked at this, and Noah set about rubbing his neck.

'You're meddling in things that don't concern you!' said the stranger sharply.

'They concern me all right!' Claypole replied, 'That letter's worth money.'

'Not to you,' muttered the stranger.

'No?' Claypole retorted. 'I know someone as would pay a small fortune for it.'

'Who?'

'Oliver Twist's guardian. It's all about Oliver – an' his half brother – an' how much their father left them.'

'You know Oliver?' asked the stranger, softly.

'Well enough,' said Claypole.

The stranger adopted a deadly gaze, and holding his cane in one hand, began to finger the silver handle with the other. Menacingly, he murmured, 'And you plan to sell the letter to his guardian?'

'Maybe,' replied Claypole, 'maybe not. It's the money 'e's been left that interests me. I wouldn't cross the street to 'elp Oliver.'

The stranger appeared to relax slightly at this, and he let one of his hands leave the cane. Unbeknown to Noah, his life had depended on the nature of his answer, for the cane which the stranger held contained a fine, very sharp blade of steel which could be drawn in an instant.

'Perhaps we can do business after all, Mr Bolter,' said the stranger, calmly. 'You want his money. I want him ruined.'

'Don't listen to him Noah!' Charlotte squealed, emboldened by her companion's apparent show of courage, 'After all, we don't even know who he is.'

But Noah Claypole did know who the stranger was, and now revealed as much, muttering: 'I know all right. 'E's the 'alf-brother – Edward Leef . . .' He was not allowed to complete the name, for the stranger cut him off by crashing his stick onto the table top with such vehemence that it emitted a sound as loud and sharp as a pistol shot. 'Don't ever speak that name, on your life!' he hissed. 'To you – my name is Monks!'

*

Later that evening, Noah Claypole and the man named Monks were standing in an alley-way not fifty yards from Mr Brownlow's house in Pentonville. Claypole was still not sure what Monks wanted him to do with Oliver once he had met the boy again, so now he asked, nervously: 'Yer don't plan to do away with him, do yer? I don't care for Oliver – but I couldn't be mixed up in that.'

'No. Killing him would be too easy,' replied Monks, thoughtfully.

'So wot d'yer want me to do?' asked Claypole.

'Worm your way into his confidence,' said Monks. 'Find out his movements when he goes out and where. And when the time is right, we'll snatch him. Can you do it?'

Sensing no danger in the task that was required of him, Claypole grinned and said, 'None better.' Whereupon he walked boldly up to the front door of the house and rang the bell. The maid opened the door to him and when he asked with great courteousness if young Mr Twist was at home, she told him that the young gentleman had left London, in the company of Mr Brownlow. Noah then asked if he might possibly leave a message for Mr Twist, and the maid hesitated slightly before asking him to step inside and wait while she summoned the housekeeper, Mrs Bedwin.

Fortunately for Noah, the maid was not the brightest of young girls, and did not remember him from his two visits to this house a fortnight previously – or if she did, she did not relay this information to Mrs Bedwin who, also very fortunately for Noah, never answered the front door herself and had therefore never seen him before in her life. Claypole sensed this as the kindly old lady came bustling up towards him.

'Wot a pity,' he said, as Mrs Bedwin showed him into the empty sitting room, 'Oliver and Mr Brownlow not at 'ome. Oh dear, oh dear.'

'Were they expecting you, Mr . . . er?' asked Mrs Bedwin.

'No, I thought 'ow I'd just drop in. A kind of surprise, like. Well, I should've wrote.'

Mrs Bedwin was mildly puzzled by the visitor's appearance and manner of speech, but beyond that she was not in the least bit suspicious of him. 'Are you a friend of Mr Twist's?' she asked.

'Friend's too strong a word,' replied Noah. 'I knew 'im when 'e was a nipper. Bless 'is 'eart.'

'He must have been a pretty child,' mused the gentle old lady, with a smile.

'Oh – pretty. Oh yes,' said Noah. 'Quite a little angel. Shame to miss 'im. When d'yer expect 'im back?'

'Not for months,' replied Mrs Bedwin, with a sigh. 'He's gone to school. Mr Brownlow took him up two days ago.'

'School? Where?' asked Claypole, unable to mask his surprise.

'In the country,' replied Mrs Bedwin.

Claypole's mind was racing now. 'I see,' he said, 'I see ... Some'ow ... I dunno, some'ow I thought, after comin' into all that money ... e'd 'ave been schooled at 'ome.'

'Oh you know about his inheritance?' said Mrs Bedwin, still without a hint of suspicion. 'Yes, it's a wonderful start for him – to have three thousand pounds of his own.'

Claypole had not expected this revelation either – for although he had of course been aware of the inheritance, he had had no idea that it amounted to quite so much. But he succeeded in concealing his utter amazement, and asked, as casually as he could manage: 'Where did yer ... um ... where did yer say this school was?'

'Well,' replied Mrs Bedwin, hesitantly, 'it's supposed to be a secret.' Then she decided that since the stranger had claimed to be such a very old acquaintance of Oliver's, there would be no harm in revealing the school's whereabouts to him, and said: 'It's in Shropshire ...'

'Shropshire?' exclaimed Claypole, 'That's a 'undred miles away!'

'Yes, but Mr Stalker's Academy is said to be a very good school,' replied Mrs Bedwin. 'And there'll be no risk of him getting into bad company.'

'Ow very true . . . ,' retorted Claypole, sanctimoniously, 'That's the last I 'opes for him.'

Unable to conceive of any reason why he should remain in the house, Noah Claypole once again remarked on what a shame it was to have missed his childhood friend, and said he would call another day. When Mrs Bedwin reminded him of his wish to leave a message, he said that there was little purpose in that now, since Oliver was to be absent for so long, and when Mrs Bedwin then asked him if she might at least know his name, so that Mr Brownlow could let Oliver know, when writing to him, who it was who had called, Noah replied that he wanted his next visit to remain a pleasant surprise, and therefore would like to refrain from identifying himself. Mrs Bedwin smiled and showed him to the door. Once safely outside, Noah Claypole hurried down the street to where the mysterious Monks was waiting for him.

CHAPTER FOUR

'And this 'ere's the schoolroom, Oliver,' said the Artful Dodger, 'where we all gets knowledge beat into our little 'eads – through the other end.'

As instructed, he was showing Oliver round the school, and the two boys were now standing in the doorway of a long, high room that was the academy's main place of instruction. At the far end of the room, on a platform, stood a large desk; another desk, still larger and on a higher platform, stood in the centre of one of the side walls. A number of narrow tables and benches faced these respective desks. Beside each desk was a blackboard. A considerable amount of light poured into the room from five tall windows, the window at the end being the greatest of the five.

Oliver walked into the room and surveyed it, slightly puzzled. 'Just one room?' he said, 'I thought there'd be lots.'

'Stalker's Academy is very hexclusive,' said the Dodger. 'In other words, it ain't too big.'

'I've hardly seen anyone except you,' said Oliver.

'Ah,' replied the Dodger, 'that's 'cause they're still on the way back from 'oliday. Even the Masters. You'll see them soon enough.'

'But, Dodger . . .' Oliver began.

The Dodger interrupted sternly: 'The name's Dawkins 'ere. Jack to my friends – of which I ain't sure you're one.' Whereupon he turned in the doorway and walked out of the room.

Oliver was a little hurt by this rejection, and followed the Dodger into the dark corridor. 'But, Dodge . . . ,' he began again hurriedly, then corrected himself 'But . . . er . . . Dawkins?' The Dodger turned back to him. 'It was such a surprise to see you,' Oliver continued, 'I only wanted to ask how you came here.'

'Well, that's another story,' said the Dodger, turning away again and walking on, with Oliver on his heels.

The Artful Dodger was naturally more than a little troubled by Oliver's arrival at Mr Stalker's Academy. He was not at all certain as to what problems it might pose for him; for nobody in this place, with the disquieting exception of Oliver, knew of his questionable past as a highly-regarded member of Fagin's gang; and he could not be entirely sure that Oliver would not now reveal everything. However, he was not displeased to see Oliver again, for he had always been reasonably fond of him. From the very first encounter, all those years ago, he had been constantly touched – reluctant though he was to admit as much, even to himself – by the boy's honest countenance, and by his innocence and naivety. Oliver, for his part, had never disliked the Dodger in the way that he had come to dislike most of Fagin's other followers; for the Dodger, despite being a thief and a vagabond, was blessed with such liveliness and good humour that it was difficult for anyone, however honest, to bear him any resentment whatsoever. Also, Oliver had felt so friendless and desolate after his kind guardian had left him in the presence of the terrifying Mr Stalker, that the sudden appearance of an old acquaintance, even if that acquaintance was a person of dubious character, had filled him with a torrent of relief. He now wished, with all his heart, to gain his old companion's confidence and friendship.

A minute or so later, Oliver and the Dodger were standing in another long room, darker than the one they had just left, with plain white walls, a polished wooden floor, and seven beds, neatly made, set against each wall. There was a small locker beside each bed, and a large cupboard at the far end of the room.

''Ere it is,' said the Dodger, 'the Junior Dormit'ry. That's Latin for where you sleep.'

Oliver looked round the dormitory. He had slept in better places certainly, but he had also in his time slept in worse; in rooms that made this one seem like the bed-chamber of a king. 'Which,' he asked 'which bed do I take?'

'Anyone you like,' said the Dodger, ''cept this one. This one's mine.' He strolled to a bed at the far end of the room, by a window. He opened the window partially and sat on the bed with his back to Oliver.

'You're in the *Junior* Dormitory?' asked Oliver, with surprise; for the Dodger was a good three years older than him, and must have been at least sixteen by now.

'Hacademically speaking, it is where I belong,' replied the Dodger, still without turning. 'By rights, I should be in the Hinfants School.'

The Dodger removed the stub of a small cheroot from a pocket in his waistcoat, and lit it with a match from his locker. Oliver hesitated for a few moments before tentatively moving to the bed beside the one on which the Dodger was seated, and laying his suitcase, which he had been clutching all this while, upon it. The Dodger still kept his back to Oliver, but Oliver could sense a tiny shudder of discomfort nonetheless.

'You're smoking!' he declared, 'But Mr Stalker said ...'

'"No smoking in the Junior School." Right?' said the Dodger, furnishing the correct words. 'Oliver, my lad,' he continued, gazing out of the window, 'the first rule in school, as outside, is all rules are to be obeyed . . . when the Beak's eye is on you. When it ain't . . . ,' and he shrugged, drawing on his cheroot.

There was an awkward silence.

'I still can't get over meeting you!' said Oliver at last. 'I mean, how did you get here?'

There was a still longer silence before the Dodger replied, still not facing him: 'All due to you.'

'To me?' said Oliver. 'The last I heard you'd been sentenced to Transportation.'

'I was quite lookin' forward to Australia,' mused the

Dodger aloud, almost sadly, taking another long puff at his cheroot.

'So how . . .?'

'Did I get 'ere? 'Ow did you?'

'Mr Brownlow, my guardian, was recommended to this school by my uncle.'

The Dodger nodded. 'The Rev'rent Harry Maylie. 'E did the same for me.'

Oliver sat up in surprise. 'How?' he asked.

'When you was stayin' with 'im in the country, didn't you tell your Rev'rent Uncle about me?' asked the Dodger.

'Yes. I think so,' said Oliver.

The Dodger turned to him at last. 'And didn't 'e get it into 'is 'ead that I was another o' Fagin's little wictims?' he said, with a grin. 'Any'ow, 'e asked the Phil-anthropical Institute to look into my case. And didn't I play along? An' didn't they get my sentence reduced to a fine? An' didn't they pay it? An' didn't they send me 'ere, to this school? Taken me under their protection they 'ave. A quiet, cushy life – as long as I go straight.'

Oliver was delighted. 'So you've given up the old life?' he asked, eagerly. 'No more thieving, or picking pockets, or . . .'

'Well,' the Dodger interjected. 'Let's say I've decided to keep me nose clean for a while – an' see wot 'appens.'

Oliver was not unduly disappointed by this last remark, for he understood that it would be difficult for Jack Dawkins to renounce all his former habits at once.

The Dodger turned his back on Oliver again now, and drew once more on his cheroot before saying, carefully: 'One thing – they don't know nothin' about all that 'ere. I wouldn't want . . .'

'Oh you needn't worry!' Oliver retorted, quickly but earnestly. 'I won't say anything. You can trust me, Dodge . . . I mean, Dawkins.'

There was a silence. Then the Dodger turned to Oliver and Oliver was relieved to see a warm smile on his face. 'Call me Jack,' said the Dodger, holding out his hand.

With a happy laugh, Oliver took the Dodger's hand and shook it, firmly. Their friendship was sealed.

'Now then,' said the Artful Dodger, 'one more thing. You said Fagin wasn't 'anged after all.'

This had indeed been one of the first things that Oliver had said to him, soon after they had left Mr Stalker's study. 'Yes,' he now replied, with seriousness. 'They – they couldn't hang him. He had a stroke of some sort and was dying anyway. They released him into the care of his daughter and son-in-law.'

The Dodger's eyes widened in an expression of amazed incredulity. 'But 'e ain't got no daughter or son-in-law,' he said.

Oliver did not have time to register the full significance of this revelation, for at that moment both boys heard someone approaching the room; in an instant the Dodger had thrown his cheroot out of the window and was leaning back against the sill, with a countenance of supreme innocence. He quickly relaxed, however, when he saw who the new arrival was.

'Watcher, Puddin'!' he said, with a grin. 'You're back, then?'

'Hello, Jack,' said the new arrival, panting, 'just off the coach.'

The boy who had entered was of Oliver's age, but smaller and very plump, with a very red face. He slowly dragged a large suitcase down the room towards them, and finally, with a huge gasp of exhaustion and relief, he heaved it onto the bed beside Oliver's.

'Everybody's arrived at once,' he said, in a breathless whisper, and sat on his bed. He extracted a handkerchief from his jacket pocket and wiped the perspiration from his brow.

'Puddin',' said the Dodger, 'This is a friend o' mine, new boy. Oliver Twist. Oliver, meet Tommy Rice – known as Puddin'.'

'Hallo, Pudding,' said Oliver.

'Delighted to meet you,' replied the boy in question, very formally, and proferring a clammy hand which Oliver duly shook. Pudding smiled a friendly smile, and Oliver smiled back. No sooner had they exchanged this greeting than the room was full of chattering boys; all of Oliver's age, and all dressed in the striped trousers and swallowtail coats that were the uniform of this establishment. They threw their cases onto their respective beds and called out: 'Hello, Dawkins!' Hallo, Jack!' Hallo, Puddin'!'

This pandemonium, however, was abruptly brought to an end by the arrival of a tiny boy, far smaller than any of the others, with a bright eager face but a frightened look in his eyes, who now cried: 'He's back! He's back! Craddock's back!'

The silence that followed this announcement was total. Oliver quickly surveyed the faces of his new companions. All of them, without exception, were visibly worried. Oliver then looked up at the Dodger. His visage also betrayed a serious concern. Last of all, Oliver let his eyes fall on the face of Tommy Rice, the boy known as Pudding, and noticed that of all the anxious countenances in the room at that moment, poor Pudding's was the most anxious of all. His plump form was quivering with fear. At last, the stillness was broken by the low funereal tolling of the school bell, and the boys tumbled out of the dormitory, laughing and chattering once more; with the exception of Pudding, who rose slowly from his bed with a downcast look and followed them in his own time.

In a matter of minutes, Mr Stalker's pupils were in the large schoolroom, positioned according to status. Against the far wall surrounding the smaller of the two desks, stood the Senior boys, proud of their standing in the school's hierarchy. In the main body of the room were the boys of the Junior School, larger in number, and obediently standing in line behind the long tables, awaiting the welcoming address of Mr Stalker, who was behind the larger desk. He was murmuring quietly to a peppery scarlet-faced gentleman with large, muttonchop whiskers. A third personage was with them on the platform, a rather lugubrious-looking man in a somewhat threadbare coat, who stood at some distance from the other two, watching them nervously.

As the school's pupils waited for Mr Stalker to give them his attention Oliver, who was beside the Dodger in the centre of the room, surveyed the assembled company 'Which one's Craddock?' he whispered.

'Over there,' replied the Dodger, out of the corner of his mouth. 'The one with the fancy tie.' He jerked his head towards where the Senior boys were gathered. Oliver saw Craddock at once. He was immediately distinguishable from the others, not only because of his necktie which was made of the finest lavender silk, and was attached to his shirt front with a jewelled stickpin; but because of his highly coloured silk waistcoat. Moreover he was the tallest boy in the room, and possessed a handsome mean face.

' 'E's the school bully,' whispered the Dodger. 'An' the one on 'is left, that's Gurney, 'is friend. You keep out o' their way.'

Oliver looked at Gurney. He was by no means as immaculately dressed as his companion – not one of the other boys was – and he wore the pinched countenance of a coward and a sycophant. As Oliver's eyes turned to Craddock again, there was a sharp pealing sound. Mr Stalker had rung his bell. Setting it down he said in booming tones: 'Have I just rung the bell? I have.' He then asked, still more loudly, 'Does it signal the start of a new term?'

'It does,' whispered the Dodger, in anticipation.

'It does!' Mr Stalker echoed. Oliver just succeeded in preventing himself from laughing out loud.

'A term in which,' continued Mr Stalker, 'I am determined we shall achieve the same standards of scholastic achievement, and, most importantly, of gentlemanly conduct, as in those past. I myself, as usual, shall tutor the Senior School. While the Juniors shall be in the more than capable hands of my Deputy, Mr Meikle.' At this, the scarlet-faced gentleman with the mutton-chop whiskers coughed and nodded fiercely, thus identifying himself as the Deputy referred to. 'Ably assisted,' Mr Stalker went on, 'by Mr . . . um . . . ah . . . Mr . . . um . . . ah . . .'

'Trent,' muttered Mr Meikle, helpfully.

'Mr . . . er . . . Trent,' said Mr Stalker, and glanced in the direction of the other gentleman on the platform, who returned his glance dolefully before looking away with a most mournful expression. Then Mr Stalker announced:

'Subsequent upon the retirement of the School Porter and the difficulty of finding a replacement for such an onerous position, charged with maintaining discipline and delivering punishment upon wrongdoers, does this mean that good order is at an end? It does not. And do I now place each boy upon his personal honour to behave in an exemplary fashion? I most solemnly do!' Whereupon he proclaimed, striking his fist upon the desk in emphasis:

'Laxity, levity and loafing shall be dealt with summarily!'

There ensued a silence, during which Mr Stalker surveyed the entire company with his steely glare. 'Now,' he said at last, 'welcome again to your tuitionary Home from Home.' He once more rang his bell very violently, crying 'Dismissed!'

A short while later, and after a brief but not insubstantial supper, the Junior boys were in their dormitory preparing for bed. Like all boys of their age, they did not seem capable of doing this without making a great deal of noise, and throwing themselves about in a mad abandon. In the midst of the turmoil, however, Oliver Twist was calmly and neatly setting out a number of books on the top of his locker.

'You goin' to read all those then?' asked the Dodger, who was standing at the foot of Tommy Rice's bed, watching Oliver with interest.

'I want to do well at school, so that my father will be proud of me,' Oliver replied.

'I thought 'e was dead,' said the Dodger.

'I meant Mr Brownlow, my guardian,' Oliver explained, a little abashed. 'He's going to adopt me.'

'Well, well . . . , the Dodger murmured, thoughtfully, returning to his own bed.

Just then, the door flew open and all the boys in the room froze into an awed silence, as the school bully and his faithful assistant stalked in. 'Have you all gone deaf?' screamed Craddock, 'I've been shouting "Fag!" for the last half-hour.'

Nobody dared reply. 'Perhaps they were arguing over who would have the honour of answering,' suggested Gurney, with a snigger.

'I believe you're right, Gurney,' said Craddock, smiling maliciously. 'Well, let's settle it for them, and choose our own servants.'

The bully then swaggered slowly down the aisle between the two rows of beds, enjoying the terror he had invoked, and examining the boys individually. Not one of them had the courage to return his evil gaze, with the exception of Oliver, who stared intently at him out of fascination, if for no other reason. Craddock reached the end of Tommy Rice's bed before he noticed this, and said quietly: 'Well, now, what have we here? A new innocent to the slaughter. What's your name, Innocent?'

'Oliver Twist,' replied the innocent, without looking away.

'Say "sir" when you speak to me!' Craddock snapped.

Oliver wondered whether or not to defy Craddock immediately by saying nothing, for he already disliked this creature intensely. But his hatred was not yet powerful enough to provide him with the required degree of courage, and he had to glance at the Dodger for guidance. The Dodger, far from urging him to do his worst, merely shrugged and muttered: 'It's a kind of unofficial rule, Oliver.'

'Is he a friend of yours, Dawkins?' said Craddock. The Dodger did not answer, but simply stared back at him, with an expression that betrayed nothing. Oliver thought he detected a hint of uncertainty in Craddock's face at that moment, but it was gone in an instant. 'You mind your manners, Twist,' said the bully, turning his attention to Oliver once more, 'and you *may* survive.' A low gurgling noise emanated from the direction of the door. It was Gurney, laughing.

While this was going on, poor Tommy Rice, who was sitting on his bed, was doing his best to make his plump frame as small as possible, in the hope that Craddock would not notice him. It was a vain hope indeed, for now the bully turned on him savagely and, grabbing the boy by both ears, pulled him to his feet, causing him to emit a sharp shriek of pain. 'On your feet, Rice Pudding!' bawled the bully. 'There's my bed to make and my boots to clean!'

'But I fagged for you last term, Craddock!' squeaked Tommy Rice.

'And did so well, you can carry on,' Craddock snarled. 'Now! Cut along!' and he pushed the sobbing boy towards the door. Tommy Rice fell to the floor at the force of his thrust, but picking himself up as quickly as his fat form would allow, he scurried out of the room, holding his ear and howling.

Gurney watched him go, then turned back to the boys, all of whom, except Oliver, knew what was going to happen next. 'Now,' said the school bully's loyal follower, 'which lucky fag shall *I* choose?' Whereupon he pretended to look round the room in search of a possible candidate, allowing his eyes to light at last, as he had initially intended, upon the tiniest boy present; this was the little creature who had come scuttling into the dormitory earlier that day, bearing the terrible news that Craddock was back; his name was Shrimpton, but because of his diminutive stature, it had been shortened by his fellows to "Shrimp". Well aware that he would be the boy whom Gurney chose, for this was invariably the case, the Shrimp without looking up, began to shake his head in terror and whisper: 'No . . . no, Gurney . . . please.'

'My room needs to be tidied, Shrimp,' said Gurney, softly, as he approached his miserable victim, 'and my clothes pressed.' The Shrimp continued to whimper and shake his head. 'So get there!' boomed Gurney. The Shrimp jumped off his bed and scuttled out.

'The rest of you innocents will all have your turn,' declared Craddock, who had been watching this performance with much amusement, and with a final threatening glance at Oliver, he ambled back down between the beds and out of the room, followed by his cruel friend. A gloomy despondency prevailed in the dormitory for some minutes after the two Senior boys had left.

'How can they get away with it?' murmured Oliver, turning to the Dodger. 'What right do they have to behave like that?'

The Dodger shrugged and said in a resigned manner: 'They're the Seniors. You can't change it. Keep your nose clean. You'll be all right.'

Oliver did not consider such an explanation to be very satisfactory.

The next morning he and the Dodger were in the schoolroom with the rest of the Junior boys, attempting to fathom the finer points of the art of multiplication. They had to do this in silence, for at the start of the lesson the scarlet-faced Mr Meikle, far from offering them any instruction in the art, had merely scribbled a number of sums on his blackboard, and told them sternly to get on with it. He had then sat down at his desk, perched a pair of spectacles on the end of his long nose, and settled down to read a book. He was now absorbed in the volume, only looking up occasionally with an air of sharp suspicion, searching for mischief.

Oliver was doing his best to follow Mr Meikle's instructions when he became aware that the Artful Dodger, who was sitting beside him, was concentrating, not on the sums on the blackboard, but on something below the level of the table top. Glancing down, and with considerable surprise, Oliver saw that his neighbour had an exercise book on his lap, upon which he was busily and quietly rolling a pair of dice. Noticing that Oliver was watching him, the Dodger looked up with a grin, and winked at his companion. He then returned to the business in hand, and threw the dice again. Unfortunately, his thrust was a mite too forceful this time, and one of the dice spun over the edge of the book and landed on the floor beneath the table. Even more unfortunately, it decided not to end its journey there, but to roll on and out from under the table, far from the reach of either of the two boys. They were sitting at the front of the class, and they now watched the tiny cube come to a halt in the middle of the wide open space between their table and Mr Meikle's desk. The Dodger quickly laid his exercise book aside, concealed the other die in his pocket, and sat frozen in suspense. After a few agonizing moments, however, it became apparent that Mr Meikle had seen and heard nothing. Oliver decided to retrieve the recalcitrant die. He was seated at the end of the table and therefore concluded that he might manage to carry out the task without attracting attention; if he did it as quickly and as softly as he could. The Dodger now watched in wide-eyed amazement as his friend rose from his seat, tiptoed round to the front of the table, picked up the die, and began to return to his seat with relief.

'What are you doing, boy?!' boomed Mr Meikle.

A busy silence had prevailed in the schoolroom until that moment, so now, at the sound of Mr Meikle's voice, everybody looked up and round – including all the Senior boys, who were working at the far end of the room; and Mr Trent, who was seated at the other desk; and Mr Stalker, who was in the process of scribbling a Latin quotation on the far blackboard. All the eyes in the school fell on Oliver, who was the only boy standing.

'Nothing, sir,' said Oliver, softly.

'You're out of your seat!' said Mr Meikle. 'Must be doing something.'

'I was . . . I was just picking something up, sir,' replied Oliver.

'What! Show me! Here!'

Mr Meikle sharply pointed to a spot directly in front of his high desk, and Oliver had no choice but to walk there, raise his hand, and slowly open his fist to reveal the die lying in his palm.

Mr Meikle's scarlet facc turned purple. 'Dice in the classroom!' He barked. 'Gaming, when you should be working! This is unforgiveable!'

'What's this? What's all this?' cried Mr Stalker, marching over from the far end of the room. As he approached, Oliver had time to glance at the Dodger. He was the only boy in the school who was not looking up at this moment, but was leaning over his book, apparently absorbed in his work.

'Show Mr Stalker, you reprehensible boy!' snapped Mr Meikle. Oliver did as he was bid.

'Can I believe my eyes?' declared Mr Stalker, glaring in horror at the object in Oliver's hand. 'Is it your intention to corrupt the entire school? Twist? Well? Have you nothing to say?'

In the silence which ensued the Dodger hunched his shoulders and closed his eyes tightly, convinced that Oliver would plead innocence and denounce him. But Oliver, to the Dodger's considerable surprise, said nothing.

'Very well,' said Mr Stalker, when it became clear that the boy was not going to defend himself, 'Very well, I promised that wrong-doers would be summarily dealt with, and do I keep my word? I do! Mr Meikle!'

Mr Meikle, without answering, reached behind his desk and withdrew a long, thin birch cane, which he handed to the headmaster.

'Twist! Bend over! Grasp your ankles!' barked Mr Stalker.

Oliver Twist did as he was instructed, and received his punishment as philosophically as he could manage, in the circumstances. The Artful Dodger must also have felt some of that pain, as he sat with his book in front of him, not daring to look up into the face of his friend.

That night in the quiet dormitory, with the lamps out, and the room lit only by moonlight, the Dodger could not sleep for he was troubled, as he had been all day, by unaccustomed pangs of conscience. Finally he could bear it no longer. Restlessly, he turned to the bed next to him and whispered: 'Oliver! Are you awake?'

'Yes,' replied Oliver softly. He was lying on his back, staring up into the near-darkness.

'Listen,' the Dodger said, 'I didn't ask you to take a beatin' for me, did I?'

'No.'

'So why didn't you give me away?'

Oliver said: 'You don't let down your friends. You wouldn't tell on me.'

'Oh, wouldn't I?' the Dodger retorted. 'That's just stupid. It goes right against what old Fagin said. "Always look out for Number One," he said.'

There was a silence, after which Oliver said firmly: 'Then Fagin was wrong.' And he turned away.

No sooner had he turned than he thought he noticed the door at the far end of the room opening, and three shapes creeping in silently. One of the shapes carried an oil-lamp, and remained by the door, as the other two tip-toed to the centre of the room.

Suddenly, and very loudly, the tallest shape shouted: 'It's bouncing time! Come on, you lucky innocents! Bouncing time! Who'll be first?' It was Craddock. The other shape sniggered in a low, gurgling fashion, thereby identifying himself as Gurney. The shape by the door must have been another Senior boy: perhaps he was some variety of apprentice bully.

'Now!' cried Gurney, 'Who's first? You? You? Where's Shrimp!'

'No! Please, Gurney!' squeaked Shrimp, burying himself under the covers, as squeals of fright began to emanate from all the other beds.

'Come on, you little cowards!' bawled Craddock, laughing. 'Who's first? I know. Pudding! We'll get Pudding!' Whereupon he hurried to the bed next to Oliver's and stripped it of its covers, revealing the plump, quaking, pleading figure of Tommy Rice underneath. 'Here!' Craddock snarled, holding up one of the blankets, 'We'll bounce him in this! Come here, you!'

With surprising alacrity, Tommy Rice had already scrambled off the bed and was now doing his best to conceal himself beneath it, begging for mercy at the same time: 'Don't hurt me again!' the poor boy screamed. 'Don't touch me! Leave me alone! Ple-e-ease!'

'Come out of there, you little brute!' growled Craddock, running into the space between Tommy's bed and Oliver's, and reaching down for his victim.

Before he could stop himself, Oliver cried out: 'Leave him alone!'

Craddock turned to him briefly and hissed: 'Keep out of this!' but Oliver, far from obeying this command, scrambled out from under his blankets in an instant, and pushed Craddock so forcefully that the bully fell forward and sprawled across Tommy's bed, rolling onto his back. Gasps of shock from all the boys greeted this extraordinary act of temerity on Oliver's part.

'Gurney!' Craddock roared, rising and glaring murderously at his brave assailant. Oliver picked up a pillow and swung it in the direction of Craddock's chest, causing him to fall back onto the bed again.

Gurney would have dearly loved to come to his leader's aid, but he was busy trying to shake off Shrimp who, himself emboldened by Oliver's act of courage, had leapt onto his back and was now clinging on to it with all the might in his tiny body. The Senior boy by the door was too staggered to do anything.

'Gurney!' Craddock shrieked again, and rose once more to wreak his vengeance on Oliver. However, Tommy Rice, who was still under his bed and had also been encouraged by Oliver's bold example, now seized hold of the bully's legs, allowing Oliver to jump onto his own bed and begin to flail at Craddock with his pillow. Seeing that the two Senior boys were now defenceless, the other boys in the dormitory leapt out of their beds with one accord and, shrieking with joy, joined in the pandemonium; surrounding Craddock and Gurney and hitting them delightedly with their own pillows. The triumphant uproar continued for a good half minute before two more figures stalked into the room and a strong adult voice bellowed 'What is the meaning of all this?!'

Silence and stillness fell upon the scene in an instant. Mr Stalker and Mr Meikle were standing in the middle of the room. Mr Meikle was carrying a lamp. The anonymous Senior boy had disappeared. Staring round at the confusion, Mr Stalker continued: 'Can this be Stalker's Academical Establishment for Young Gentlemen? Or is it Bedlam?'

Nobody answered: but some of the boys began to creep stealthily back to their beds.

'Will someone tell me what is going on?' roared the furious old gentleman.

'Please, sir, it was . . .' Shrimp began, meekly.

'Was I addressing you, boy?' cried Stalker, 'I was not! The Senior boys. Craddock!'

The bully rose from Tommy Rice's bed, brushing a number of feathers from his jacket. 'We . . . we heard a disturbance, sir, and came to investigate.'

At this, Tommy Rice piped up: 'Please, sir, they were . . .'

'Silence!' Stalker snapped. 'Continue!' he barked, staring at Gurney, who was lying on the floor.

Gurney stood up. 'We found them rioting, sir,' he said, 'and we tried to stop it.'

'Very commendable,' said Stalker.

'Get into bed, all of you!' growled Mr Meikle. The boys who were still out of their beds, including Oliver, did as they were commanded. The Artful Dodger had not moved from his bed throughout the battle, but had simply sat, with his arms folded, watching the events.

Once everyone was in bed, and a semblance of order had returned to the occasion, Mr Stalker declared: 'Has horseplay here got out of hand? I fear so. Craddock – Gurney – until the arrival of the new Porter, I make you entirely responsible for discipline in the Junior School.'

An audible gasp of dismay from all the boys greeted this announcement. Craddock and Gurney did their best to conceal their delight.

'Now,' said Mr Stalker, striding towards the door, 'Let us have no more of these disturbances!' He left the room.

'Get to sleep!' cried Mr Meikle, and followed his superior.

A terrible pause ensued, during which the boys wondered whether or not Craddock and Gurney would embark on some dreadful revenge there and then. But the bully and his assistant merely ambled towards the door, as Craddock said, 'We'll see you in the morning, innocents. Pleasant dreams.' And they were gone, closing the door behind them.

Oliver thought he heard a boy weeping in the darkness at the far end of the room; then he heard the Dodger whisper: 'You can't win, y'see. Now you've stuck your neck out, Oliver. An' they're goin' to chop your 'ead off.'

CHAPTER FIVE

The new authority now invested in Craddock and Gurney strengthened their tyrannical hold over the Junior members of Mr Stalker's Academical Establishment. Oliver soon became aware that they, and not Mr Stalker, or Mr Meikle, or Mr Trent, were the school's true rulers; indeed at times Mr Stalker appeared to be as much in awe of the two bullies as the boys were themselves. As the Artful Dodger explained: 'He won't see what 'e don't want to see. Gurney's father's on the Board o' Guvnors, and Craddock's uncle's a Dook. As far as old Stalker's concerned, that makes them perfect.'

'So even if we all complained, he wouldn't believe us?' Oliver asked.

'Couldn't afford to.'

'Then there's nothing we can do,' said Oliver, ruefully.

' 'Course there is,' replied the Dodger, with a hint of sarcasm. 'You can kick up a fuss an' get chucked out as a trouble-maker. Or grin an' bear it, till the new Porter gets 'ere.'

Tommy Rice was with them on the occasion of this conversation, and he now said, by way of encouragement: 'The Porter keeps an eye on everyone, even the Seniors. They won't dare to bully us so much, with him watching.'

'Let's hope we get one soon then,' said Oliver, for they were now some weeks into the term and there was no sign as yet of any Porter; and therefore of an end to Craddock and Gurney's merciless reign.

What distressed the boys most particularly was that in previous terms they had at least managed to escape from the evil attentions of the bullies in the schoolroom, during the day; but now even that comfort had been removed, for Mr Stalker had allowed Craddock and

Gurney to supervise lessons; or at least those lessons in which the boys required no direct instruction, but merely had to sit in silence, working problems out for themselves in their exercise books.

On these occasions no master would be present, and Craddock would pace up and down between the tables, wielding a tapered, wooden pointer and glaring at his terrified charges, as they did their best to ignore his malignant gaze and concentrate on their work. As soon as a boy had finished the exercises that had been set, Craddock, instead of giving him the liberty to enjoy his achievement, would send him immediately up to his study to clean it or to make his bed, or to lay out the tea, or to polish his boots. Such labours were usually the prelude to greater cruelties. Shrimp, who was the cleverest as well as the smallest of the boys, was invariably the first to finish, and therefore the first to be sent off on one or other of these chores. Oliver, too, would complete his work quite early but, on the Artful Dodger's advice, would pretend to continue it long after he had finished; and thus managed to avoid the onerous tasks which Craddock and Gurney seemed to derive such pleasure from inventing. The Dodger himself, who always sat beside Oliver in the schoolroom, reaped a certain benefit from this practice, for it allowed him the time to examine his friend's answers and copy them into his own book.

It became increasingly evident, however, as the weeks passed that, together with the Dodger, Oliver was being exempted for some reason from having to perform the duties imposed on his fellows, even in the early morning and evenings. Oliver had not once been ordered to go either to Craddock's or to Gurney's respective studies. Moreover, that terrible revenge which the Dodger had sworn would be visited upon him, had somehow not materialized. He was being left in peace, or comparatively so, and the real sufferers at the hands of the Junior Dormitory's tormentors were still Shrimp and poor Pudding. Oliver was not to know that it was because of the Dodger that he was enjoying such a privileged position.

He had established himself as the Dodger's closest companion, and Craddock and Gurney, dearly though they would have loved to subject him to the most dire tortures, were both very wary of the Dodger (or of Dawkins, as he was known to them). Dawkins was as old as they were, and although he had as yet given no indication of being moved to anger by any of the cruelties which they inflicted on the other boys, they were not so sure that the same passivity would prevail if they were to be excessively vindictive towards his friend Twist.

Late one afternoon, however, towards the middle of Oliver's first term at Mr Stalker's Academical Establishment, Craddock resolved to put his fears regarding Dawkins and Twist to the test. The day's lessons were over. He was on his way to the Junior Dormitory with the intention of ordering Tommy Rice to come and clean his study; but as he reached the door of the dormitory, he decided that he would tell Twist to come as well. He would then note Dawkins' reaction. Pausing only to let a wicked grin pass briefly across his face and then to adopt the sternest of countenances, he kicked the door open and barked: 'What's this? Loafing? No work to do? Can't have that, can we? Rice! Twist! Get up to my study!'

Dawkins was stretched out on his bed with his arms folded. Twist and Rice were seated on theirs. Rice rose at once, but Twist did not move. There was a tense silence, which lasted for some seconds before Craddock said dangerously: 'Did you hear me? I gave you an order.' Rice hesitated at the end of his bed, glancing at Twist, who still refused to move. Dawkins, to Craddock's considerable relief, appeared to be ignoring the proceedings entirely. Craddock was about to take courage from this apparent lack of concern on Dawkins' part, and began to walk down the dormitory threateningly, when

Shrimp raced into the room and, before he could stop himself, ran directly into the bully's back.

'Ooh, sorry, Crad . . . er . . . sorry, Mr Craddock, sir!' squeaked Shrimp.

Craddock turned on him with a snarl: 'I sent you to fetch more bread from the kitchen. What are you doing here?'

'Please, Mr Craddock, sir,' Shrimp explained, 'the Headmaster stopped me. He wants to see Twist straight away.'

'Twist?' said Craddock, turning to Oliver once more. 'Been telling tales, have you, Twist?'

'No,' said Oliver calmly.

'You'd better not. What does he want you for?'

'I don't know,' Oliver replied.

The Dodger then whispered to Oliver: 'Only one way to find out then. 'Op it!'

Oliver looked at the Dodger, rose, and strode from the room without giving the bully even the briefest of glances. Craddock glared at the Dodger, but only received in return a familiar, expressionless gaze. A slight hope had begun to rise in Tommy Rice and, as unobtrusively as he could, he sat on his bed again.

'You needn't think I've forgotten *you*, Pudding!' Craddock bawled. 'Get up to my study!'

Whereupon poor Tommy Rice, with the resigned look of a true martyr, rose from his bed and dejectedly trudged towards the door.

Upon entering Mr Stalker's study, Oliver was surprised and delighted to see his guardian standing by the desk. He was dressed in a travelling cape.

'Hello there, Oliver!' said Mr Brownlow, smiling warmly.

'Father!' cried Oliver. So pleased was he to see Mr Brownlow's friendly, welcoming countenance, that his immediate impulse was to run to him and throw his arms around the kind old gentleman's neck. But a loud cough from Mr Stalker, who was seated at the desk, prevented him from moving so much as a yard.

'As I was saying, Mr Brownlow,' said Mr Stalker, sternly, 'it is not our practice to encourage unscheduled visits during term. However, since you are only, as it were, passing through. . .'

'Very good of you, sir,' said Mr Brownlow.

'Most kind,' said a shrill sharp female voice from behind Oliver. The boy turned and saw a lady in a black cape and bonnet, sitting rather primly upon a small chair in the corner of the room. She was of middle years, dark, and clearly took considerable care over her appearance. Though not unattractive, her eyes seemed somewhat cold, in Oliver's opinion. She certainly did not smile at him as he turned to her.

'Not at all, madam,' said Mr Stalker, most politely, rising from his desk. 'Does the Headmaster not stand, so to speak, in loco parentis? He does. Here at Stalker's Academy, do we not comprehend the affections of a father's heart? We most certainly do.' Whereupon, much to Oliver's surprise, he moved round the desk and, with a smile that Oliver had never seen cross his face before, patted the boy, almost affectionately, on the head. 'You will wish to spend some time alone,' Mr Stalker continued. 'Accordingly, I accord you – oh, what a vile phrase! Accordingly, I *allow* you . . . five minutes.' He smiled once more, this time most particularly at the lady, and left closing the door behind him. Oliver watched him go, wide-eyed.

Mr Brownlow chuckled and approached his ward, laying a hand on each of the boy's shoulders and looking fondly into his face. 'It's good to see you, my boy' he said.

'And you, Father,' said Oliver, 'I can't believe you're here.'

'Well,' said Mr Brownlow, 'I had some business to attend to in the Midlands. But I'm forgetting my manners.' He turned to the lady. 'Mrs Carraway, this is my ward Oliver. Soon to be my adopted son.'

'How do you do, ma'am,' said Oliver, bowing. The lady did not reply, but merely inclined her head, still without smiling.

'Mrs Carraway is to be my new Housekeeper,' Mr Brownlow announced.

Oliver could conceal neither his surprise nor his concern. 'But . . . what's happened to Mrs Bedwin?' he asked. 'She'd never leave you.'

'Alas,' Mr Brownlow replied with a sigh, 'she has had to. You remember her widowed sister? She has now become a permanent invalid and Mrs Bedwin has had to leave to look after her.'

'I wish I could have said goodbye to her,' said Oliver, ruefully. 'The house won't seem the same without her.' He sensed Mrs Carraway shift very slightly in her seat.

'Yes, she had been with me a long time,' mused Mr Brownlow, but he then smiled and said: 'Still, I have been fortunate in securing the services of Mrs Carraway.'

'Yes,' said Oliver, smiling at Mrs Carraway. She now permitted herself the merest hint of a smile in return.

'Perhaps I should wait outside, Mr Brownlow,' she said, making as if to rise.

'Oh no,' said Mr Brownlow. 'I wish you two to become acquainted.' Mrs Carraway relaxed into her seat again. 'Mrs Carraway is from Birmingham, where I had business affairs to settle,' Mr Brownlow explained to Oliver. 'It seemed only sensible to travel back to London together. And I could not resist the temptation to call in here. I've missed you, my boy.'

'And I you, Father,' replied Oliver. 'I wrote to you just last night.'

'I look forward to receiving the letter,' said Mr Brownlow. 'I have read all your letters to Mrs Bedwin. And to Grimwig.'

'Mr Grimwig?' said Oliver, with surprise.

'Oh, he takes a considerable interest in your progress,' Mr Brownlow explained, and continued, in a more serious tone, 'I must say, he detects from your letters – although I did not – that the school may be somewhat strict. Not too strict, I hope?'

'No,' said Oliver, but added, after some hesitation, 'Mr Stalker is a great believer in discipline.'

'He would need to be, to control so many boys,' Mrs Carraway interjected, sharply.

'Quite so,' murmured Mr Brownlow, with a brief, mildly irritable glance in her direction. He then coughed and returned to the desk, from which he picked up his hat and gloves. 'Well,' he said, 'perhaps we should not overstrain his patience. And we must catch the London coach. Will you walk with us to the gates, Oliver?'

'Please!' Oliver replied, eagerly.

'Good.'

Mrs. Carraway rose, and slipped on her gloves in a most meticulous manner. Oliver held the door open for her as she left the room. Mr Brownlow did not follow her out immediately, but paused for a moment or two and looked seriously into his ward's eyes.

'I am sorry it is such a fleeting visit,' he said quietly, 'but I had to assure myself you were well. You have settled in?'

'Yes,' Oliver replied, for it was true.

'And are making friends?'

'I have made some very good friends,' replied Oliver, for this was also true.

'Splendid,' said Mr Brownlow. 'I want you to be happy. If you are not happy here, I would not wish you to remain.' And he added, laying an affectionate hand on the boy's shoulder, 'For your schooldays should be the happiest days of your life.'

If Tommy Rice's schooldays were the happiest days of *his* life, the poor creature did not dare to imagine what life would be like once they were over. As Oliver was walking his guardian and Mrs Carraway to the school gates, Tommy was in Craddock's study, polishing the bully's boots, trying hard not to be noticed as Craddock and Gurney lounged before the fire, discussing the subject of higher education.

'University, my uncle says. Insists on it,' drawled Craddock.

'So does my father,' Gurney droned.

'Hanged if I see the point,' said Craddock. 'If a gentleman's educated enough to sign his bills, what more does he need?' Gurney sniggered.

'Haven't you finished those blasted boots yet, Pudding?' Craddock snarled, without so much as a glance at the boy.

'Just finished, sir,' replied Tommy Rice, meekly.

'Well, put them on!' the bully barked, swivelling his stockinged feet lazily in Tommy's direction. On his knees, Tommy Rice moved towards Craddock and set about this task, as the bully continued: 'It's not as if one planned to *do* anything. There's only the law and the army, and they're both so absurdly boring that . . . *You infernal brute! Look what you've done!'*

Tommy had manoeuvred the boot onto Craddock's foot with a trifle too much force, causing Craddock to jerk his hand, which was holding a sherry glass at the time: as a result one or two drops of sherry had spilled onto the bully's embroidered waistcoat; as a further result, the arguments for and against attending university were forgotten in an instant.

'I'm sorry – sorry, Craddock,' Tommy Rice muttered.

'You clumsy . . .! You did that deliberately!' Craddock bawled.

'No. No, I . . . I swear it . . . ,' Tommy pleaded.

'Don't start lying to me!' cried Craddock, sitting up and dabbing his waistcoat with a handkerchief. 'It's ruined! It's ruined!' But he did not seem especially distressed, for a malicious gleam entered his eye as he continued: 'I think this brute needs to be taught a lesson, don't you, Gurney?'

'Oh, most definitely,' replied Gurney, calmly. Whereupon he rose and turned towards the study door, which was slightly ajar.

'No, no . . . please,' Tommy Rice whimpered.

Gurney leant his back against the door and it shut softly behind him. He grinned, as Craddock picked up a long thin stick from beside his chair.

I shall respect the reader's sensibilities and spare him from learning the precise details of the tortures poor Pudding had to bear as a result of his minor act of clumsiness. It will be quite sufficient merely to state that the degree of pain which Tommy had to undergo, far outweighed the nature of the deed that was its justification. That night, the boys of the Junior Dormitory were kept anxiously awake by the sound of muffled sobbing from the direction of Pudding's bed. Most wakeful of all was Oliver Twist. Although he himself had not as yet suffered unduly at the hands of Craddock and Gurney, he was beginning to experience a burning sense of injustice on behalf of those who had. However, in his weeks at Mr Stalker's Academy, he had also learnt something of that spirit of manly independence which is the English schoolboy's cardinal rule of behaviour, whatever dire agonies he might have to endure. It is a code of practice which almost without exception prevents a boy – however inwardly frail or secretly concerned he might be – from expressing his feelings too openly. Oliver therefore, even though Tommy Rice's every whimper sent a shudder of distress through his own heart, and dearly though he wished to comfort the poor boy in some small way, merely by patting him on the shoulder and offering a few soft words of comfort, could not bring himself to do so. He glanced at the Dodger to see if *he* might be demonstrating the slightest show of sympathy, but the Dodger was lying with his back to Oliver, and appeared to be the only boy in the dormitory who was sound sound asleep. Unbeknown to his friend, however, the

Dodger was also very much awake, and his eyes were wide open. He too was wincing inwardly at the sound of Tommy Rice's sobs.

On that same dark night, in the silence of his study, Craddock was considering how best to make life thoroughly miserable for Oliver Twist. Most of his waking hours, indeed, were spent conceiving of ways in which he and Gurney might torment one or other of the smaller boys, and now, encouraged at last by Dawkins' apparent unwillingness to give Twist any support that afternoon, he was busily thinking of an array of suitable hardships for the one boy, apart from Dawkins, whom he had not as yet had the pleasure of persecuting. He would commence the campaign, he decided, immediately after the next day's lessons. He would force Twist to participate in a game he had just invented, and which he felt sure that the other Senior boys would enjoy playing. The rules of the game were simple enough: the older boys would stand in a circle, and would push, or sometimes kick, as hard as they could, two Junior boys, one of whom would be blindfolded, from one side of the circle to the other. The boy who was not blindfolded would try to avoid being hit by the boy who was, and the Senior boys would try to prevent him from doing this by propelling him towards the blindfolded boy as hard as they could.

The following day therefore, when the lessons were over, and the masters had left the schoolroom, Craddock ordered the desks and tables to be cleared from the centre of the room, and his eager colleagues formed their circle. Craddock had explained the rules to them that afternoon.

'Twist! Shrimp!' barked Craddock, 'You're first! Twist to wear the blindfold!'

Before Oliver could make any show of defiance, Gurney had pinned his arms behind his back and another Senior boy had quickly tied a rolled handkerchief tightly round his head and over his eyes. He was hurriedly marched into the circle, and the game began. He felt himself being caught by a pair of rough hands which sent him hurtling across an empty space until he reached a second pair of hands which then thrust him in the opposite direction, stumbling as he went.

'Missed!' he heard Craddock bawl, and he was again thrown towards the centre of the circle. He brushed past someone whom he presumed to be Shrimp. 'Good shoot!' cried Craddock.

'Nearly got him that time?' cried Gurney, and flung him back. Again he thought he sensed Shrimp leap aside desperately, avoiding him by a hair's breadth.

'Missed!' Oliver heard Craddock cry once more.

This delightful pastime continued for several minutes, and the speed and force with which Oliver was hurled across the circle, seized, swivelled round and hurled back again, increased with each thrust. He heard the cries of glee and the laughter grow ever louder and more enthusiastic, and he became dizzier and more exhausted with the effort of trying to retain his balance. At last, the game came to a halt as Shrimp, with a squeal of pain, cannoned into him directly and sent him reeling and winded onto his knees. 'A hit! A hit!' bawled Craddock, and the Senior boys cheered.

Oliver remained for some seconds on his knees, too weak to rise. He felt a pair of small hands trying to help him up, and supposed that they belonged to Shrimp. But soon a stronger and less merciful hand had grasped him by the collar, and he heard Craddock snarl: 'On your feet! Come on!' He was hauled into a standing position which lasted only for a short while, for no sooner had the hand left his collar, than he fell to the floor again.

'These little oafs have no sense of sportsmanship!' Craddock remarked disgustedly, as Gurney tore the handkerchief from Oliver, almost dislocating his neck in the process, and at once set about binding Shrimp's eyes. Oliver now had to do what the Shrimp had to do, attempting to leap out of the way of the blindfolded Shrimp, as the two boys were once more thrown with ever greater force back and forth across the circle, and towards each other. Oliver was too dazed and feeble by this time to avoid Shrimp for long, and collided with him almost immediately, once again collapsing onto his hands and knees as a result, and soliciting a groan of displeasure at his incompetence. 'Next two!' bawled Craddock, and Oliver and Shrimp were allowed to crawl from the circle at last, fighting for breath. As Oliver emerged from between the legs of his tormentors, one of whom – he was certain it was Gurney – kicked him to help him on his way, he could think of only one thing: that he would never allow himself to be brutalized in such a fashion again. Through swimming eyes, he looked up at the Junior boys, who were gathered at the end of the room, cowed and apprehensive, awaiting their turn to be summoned by Craddock. Two of them, Tommy Rice and another, had already been dragged submissively into the circle and the game had recommenced. As his sight began to clear, Oliver scanned the faces of his friends in search of the Dodger, but the Dodger was not amongst them, or indeed anywhere in the room.

Unbeknown to Oliver, he was at that moment sitting in the fork of a tree in a wooded corner of the school grounds, secure in the knowledge that this secluded area was rarely visited and he therefore stood little chance of being disturbed. He had been present in the schoolroom at the commencement of the game, and had seen Oliver being thrust into the ring, but had soon tired of having to watch a sport from which he could derive no pleasure. He was now trying to glean what satisfaction he could from smoking a clay pipe in reposeful surroundings; this was not an easy task, for he was deeply troubled. Until now, he had always managed to retain a cheerfully acquiescent attitude to all life's hardships, accepting injustice and cruelty as inevitable facts of existence. Seeing his honest and innocent colleague being unjustly persecuted by the school bully, however, had now made him angry; anger was a feeling to which he was unaccustomed, and it made him uncomfortable. What caused him the greatest distress though, was the conviction that, however incensed he might be at the cruel hold Craddock had over the school, there was nonetheless nothing that could be done to overthrow it; especially now that it was very evident from the behaviour of the Senior boys during the game, that they were on Craddock's side. His was an impotent fury, which is the most comfortless fury of all.

When he had mused over these novel emotions for some time, and had concluded that his pipe was incapable of providing the necessary solace, he slipped from the tree and walked back to the school with a hung head and doleful countenance, his hands thrust deep into his pockets.

So dejectedly pensive was the Artful Dodger that he did not at first notice, as he entered the Junior Dormitory, a cord of thin rope that had been stretched directly in front of the door and across the aisle between the beds at shin level; he now almost tripped over it. Fortunately for those responsible, however, he caught sight of it in time. His morose cogitations were forgotten in an instant. ''Ere,' he cried indignantly. 'Wot silly Charlie did that? I could've broke me neck!'

'That's the whole idea,' said Tommy Rice, with a grin. He was standing at the far end of the room with the rest of the Junior boys; Oliver was amongst them, smiling at the Dodger.

'It's Oliver's battle plan,' Shrimp explained excitedly.

'Wot you talkin' about?' asked the Dodger, carefully stepping over the cord and approaching them.

'We're going to war,' said Shrimp, eagerly.

'Against Craddock and the Upper School,' said Oliver.

'They'll murder you!' cried the Dodger.

'Not if we all stick together!' Oliver replied firmly, and the other boys nodded and murmured their agreement. 'We have to do something,' he continued. 'It was bad enough when Craddock and Gurney were the only ones bullying us.'

'And now,' Tommy Rice said, 'without even a School Porter to keep order, all the other Seniors are joining in.'

'So,' the Dodger interrupted impatiently, 'Craddock and Gurney are two rotten apples, spoilin' the rest of the barrel. And what do you think you can do about it?'

The boys looked to Oliver to explain. 'The next night they raid the dormitory,' he said, 'we'll be ready for them.'

'*That's* not going to stop them,' said the Dodger, pointing to the cord.

'That's just to give us warning,' said Oliver. 'With luck, the first one who comes in will trip over it – maybe two or three. That'll give us time.'

'For wot?' asked the Dodger.

'To build a barricade.'

'You'll still need somethin' to fight with.'

'We'll have the fire buckets filled with water!' suggested one of the boys.

'And peashooters,' said Tommy.

'And ink bombs!' said Shrimp.

'Ink bombs?' asked the Dodger, who had never heard of them.

'Pellets of blotting paper soaked in ink,' Shrimp explained.

'Splosh!' cried Tommy, with enthusiasm, 'Right in the middle of Craddock's fancy waistcoat!'

Despite his misgivings, the Dodger could not pretend to disapprove of such a pleasurable image. Nonetheless, he shook his head and said: 'Sounds good, but it'll only make 'em mad. Then you'll 'ave a real battle. One yer can't win!'

'We're not going to let them just walk all over us,' said Oliver, with increased firmness. 'At least we'll go down fighting.'

'Hear, hear!' Shrimp squealed, with all the fierceness

he could muster. The Dodger could not resist a grin at the contrast between Shrimp's diminutive size and the strength of his apparent determination. But the smile soon left his face as he looked up at the other boys, all of whose countenances revealed a fixity of purpose that demonstrated the seriousness of their intentions. The Dodger was more than mildly alarmed by what he saw, but he was nonetheless about to express his support for their cause, when the school bell suddenly tolled three times.

'Wot's that?' said the Dodger.

'Three rings,' said a boy.

'The bell for assembly,' said Oliver, with bewilderment.

'At this time?' said the Dodger. 'Wot's up?'

No-one ever questioned the authority of the school bell, however, and duly summoned, the boys began to run for the door. Tommy Rice was at their head, and therefore suffered the misfortune of tumbling headlong as he tripped over the forgotten cord.

'I was just goin' to say,' the Dodger remarked cheerily, 'better untie that before someone comes a cropper.' The boys laughed as they helped Pudding to his feet, and even Pudding smiled broadly. The sight of his cheerfulness filled Oliver Twist with hope as to the success of the coming revolution.

CHAPTER SIX

'Silence!' bellowed Mr Meikle. 'This is a schoolroom! Not a bear-garden! Seniors! Set an example! Come along now! Settle down!'

The babble in the schoolroom, prompted by the knowledge that a call to assembly at such an unusual hour must betoken an announcement of very special import, began to die away.

'I have an announcement to make,' Mr Meikle declared, once an acceptable silence had prevailed, 'and have no intention of bellowing it like a towncrier.'

'Oyez, oyez,' murmured the Dodger, loudly enough to cause a ripple of amusement along the ranks of the Junior boys. Mr Meikle glared down at them from his desk.

'This is not a moment for levity!' he barked. 'Desist!' The boys did their best to desist, and Mr Meikle continued, in a tone of great authority: 'The Headmaster has asked me to announce the arrival of a new and most welcome member of the staff, who will combine the functions of School Porter and Proctor, in charge of moral conduct and all matter of discipline.'

A second ripple passed through the ranks; this time influenced not by amusement, but by a mixture of excited anticipation and relief. Oliver glanced towards the far end of the schoolroom and was pleased to note a scowl of annoyance pass across the countenance of the school bully and his loyal lieutenant.

'A watchdog, guide and guard shall he be unto you,' Mr Meikle now intoned gravely, 'and verily shall ye rejoice thereat.' Whereupon the doors of the schoolroom opened and Mr Stalker entered, accompanied by the new School Porter. He was a large man; indeed he was so enormously large and so exceptionally rotund, that he appeared to dwarf even the tall Mr Stalker. His bulk was encased in a long-skirted brown coat with deep pockets, a buff waistcoat, breeches and gaiters. His face was very red, far redder even than that of the scarlet-visaged Mr Meikle, and also very fat, and heavy-jowelled. A pair of small, close-set eyes peered from somewhere within this excess of flesh. It was a wonder, many of the boys now remarked to themselves, that such a colossally corpulent creature could walk at all: but walk he did now, or rather he waddled, at Mr Stalker's side, towards the room's main desk.

'Boys of the Upper and Lower Schools,' Mr Stalker announced magisterially once they had reached the desk. 'I present to you our new Porter. Having held for many years a responsible parochial position, does he not come to us with the highest qualifications? He most certainly does! Boys, you will welcome as your Proctor . . . Mr Bumble . . .'

Oliver's worst fears were confirmed at the sound of this name. At the first sight of Mr Bumble, as he had come through the door, he had not permitted himself to believe that this gross personage was the same individual as the one who had once been almost entirely responsible for the wretchedness of his earliest years, and who had inhabited his nightmares ever since. But it *was* Mr Bumble; it could be no-one else. Oliver stared up at his former tormentor, who was surveying the boys now placed in his charge with a small, complacent grin.

A cry from Craddock broke the train of Oliver's thoughts. 'Sir!' the bully now pleaded indignantly, stepping forward. 'You made Gurney and myself responsible for discipline in the Junior School!'

Mr Stalker turned to the bully and replied smilingly: 'And have you not acquitted your task admirably? Now, however, you may lay down the burden. The responsibility devolves upon Mr Bumble.'

Before he could prevent himself from doing so, and because he was so thoroughly delighted at the downfall of Craddock and Gurney, Tommy Rice now cried: 'Three cheers for Mr Bumble!' Equally overjoyed, the other boys cheered loudly and happily. Mr Bumble beamed, accepting their adulation. Oliver Twist tried very hard to join in the cheering, but there was no enthusiasm in the ragged 'hurrah' which he succeeded in emitting, after considerable effort.

He wasted no time, however, once the boys had been dismissed, in informing the Dodger as to who exactly the person now responsible for the school's discipline was. 'He was the Beadle in the Parish where I was born, the one who gave me my name,' he explained.

'Well, I'll go to Putney on a pig,' remarked the Dodger, aghast. 'The one you was so scared of?'

Oliver nodded. 'He bullied the whole Workhouse,' he said. 'And after he married, he became Master of it himself.' The Dodger gave vent to a long low whistle of amazement. 'But what I don't understand,' Oliver went on, 'is this. They were both dismissed for stealing from the inmates.'

The Dodger grinned knowingly and said: 'You can bet 'e didn't tell old Stalker that.' The grin disappeared as he added: ''E won't like finding you 'ere – with you knowin' . . .'

'I was just thinking that,' Oliver said anxiously.

'Is it possible, I asked myself?' a familiar, unctuous voice interposed at this point. The two boys were alone in the dormitory, and they now turned to see the subject of their conversation waddling towards them. 'Is it possible?' Mr Bumble repeated with a joyous smile. 'Do my heyes deceive me, or is that young Oliver?'

'Yes, Mr Bumble,' replied Oliver, with extreme wariness.

'Little Oliver what I reared and nurtured as if 'e was my very own! What a coincidings! What a joyous reunion!' Oliver instantly received the surprised impression that this former tyrant was exerting himself to be as affable as he could be. 'An' now,' Mr Bumble continued, turning his gaze in the direction of the Dodger, 'who might this be?'

'Dawkins,' said Oliver.

'Jack Dawkins,' said the Dodger.

Mr Bumble beamed and bowed as deeply as his bulk would permit, which was no more than an inch or so. 'Delighted to make your acquaintance, Master Dawkins.'

'Likewise, Mr Bumble,' the Dodger replied.

Mr Bumble gave Oliver the benefit of a mildly anxious glance before saying hesitantly to the Dodger: 'No doubt Oliver has told you of the interruption to my – uh – parochial career?'

'No,' the Dodger replied innocently, 'Wot was that, Mr Bumble?'

Pleased to hear that the precise reasons for his dismissal had not apparently been imparted, Mr Bumble beamed once more and declared: 'A hunfortunate misunderstanding, now 'appily cleared up.' Again he turned to Oliver: 'I was completely hexonerated,' he said.

'I am very glad to hear it,' said Oliver, truthfully.

'Yes-s-s,' said Mr Bumble, surveying Oliver with an almost affectionate expression. 'You're a credit to the upbringin' I gave you, Oliver. 'Ard I might have been, in the commission of my parochial duties. I did not spoil the rod.'

'I'll bet you didn't,' the Dodger remarked quietly, soliciting a sharp stare from Mr Bumble which nonetheless quickly vanished.

'Firmness and fairity is my motto,' said the former Beadle, with a smile, 'as you shall see.' Whereupon he looked at Oliver once more and added: 'But now that our paths 'ave so mysteriously recrossed, bygones, shall we say, is bygones?'

An anxious silence ensued during which Oliver reached the conclusion that Mr Bumble was sincere in his desire to have done with the past, and to continue his relationship with him on a fairer and friendlier footing. 'If you wish it, Mr Bumble,' he said at last.

'Most decidedly,' declared Mr Bumble, smiling hugely. 'Depend on it. I shall keep a most particular heye on your welfare.' Whereupon, with a brief but distrustful final glance at the Dodger, he turned upon his heel and began to move towards the door.

A polite enquiry from Oliver stopped him abruptly in his tracks. 'And how is Mrs Bumble?' the boy asked.

There was a pause before Mr Bumble remarked in a most doleful manner: 'Mrs Bumble? Her that was such a forceful woman? Best not to ask.'

'Not dead, I hope?' asked Oliver.

A second pause followed before Mr Bumble replied, with a slow shake of his head: 'A shadow of her former self, Oliver. In the work'ouse infirmary, poor soul. Let us hope she'll remain there a long, long time.' By this last remark, Mr Bumble meant to express the wish that Mrs Bumble would be allowed to live for several more years, but the prospect of an existence free from the attentions of his beloved wife was too pleasant for him to conceal his delight in it; despite his efforts to retain a dolourous countenance, as he left the room.

'He's changed!' declared Oliver, when Mr Bumble had gone. 'He's trying to be nice!'

The Dodger, however, remained thoroughly sceptical. 'Nice?' he said, 'He's a snake inside a tub of butter. I wouldn't trust 'im as far as I could throw 'im. An' that wouldn't be 'alf an inch!'

We must now leave Oliver Twist to his cogitations regarding developments that might occur as a consequence of Mr Bumble's sudden re-appearance in his life; and return, if only briefly, to the streets of London. In one of these streets, on that same evening, stood Noah Claypole, otherwise known as Morris Bolter, with a smile on his lips that betokened satisfaction, and a change of clothing that betokened some success in the new profession he had recently chosen for himself. Most notably, he was now sporting a silk waistcoat of an intricate weave, spanned by a fine gold watch-chain. There appeared to be no reason for his being in that particular street at that particular moment; except the simple but pleasant one of watching the ladies and gentlemen of the metropolis stroll by.

'Psst! Psst!' said a small voice, very suddenly, at his side.

'I can see you! I can see you!' replied Noah Claypole, with some irritation, but continuing to gaze smilingly at the passers-by. He had no need to look down at the person who had approached him, for he knew it to be little Ned Fingers.

'Never take *you* by surprise, Mr Bolter,' whispered Fingers, admiringly.

'Remember that, Fingers,' retorted Noah, still without so much as a glance at the boy, 'I got eyes every which where.'

'Then cast yer glims on this!' said Fingers, eagerly. Noah Claypole allowed himself a brief glimpse in the direction of what the little thief was now holding up for his perusal: to his considerable horror, he saw that it was a bulging wallet, made of the best morocco leather; and that Fingers, in his pride at having stolen it, seemed to have forgotten that bulging morocco wallets were not the sort of item that small boys were in the habit of displaying quite so openly in the streets of London for anyone to see. 'A fat wallet,' Fingers continued, with relish, 'stuffed wiv . . .'

In an instant, Claypole had slapped the boy's hand away and was holding out the side of his jacket in an effort to conceal the offending object from the world's gaze. 'Ow many times I got to tell yer?' he hissed urgently, 'Keep the money – throw away the wallet!'

'But it's worth a guinea or two!' Fingers protested.

'It's worth a laggin' if yer caught with it,' retorted Claypole. 'Get quit of it!'

'If you say so, Mr Bolter,' said Fingers, somewhat morosely, for he had hoped that his achievement might have provoked just a glimmer of approval from his master.

'Now, vanish!' Claypole snapped. 'I'll see yer at the Cripples in 'alf an hour.'

Fingers sidled quickly away. Noah Claypole glanced anxiously about him, wondering if he and the boy had been observed. Satisfied by the oblivious countenances of the people who were passing that all had gone unnoticed, he smiled again, straightened his jacket and waistcoat and began to saunter down the street in the opposite direction to that which Ned Fingers had taken. He had walked only fifty yards or so, and was passing the darkened entrance to an alleyway, when he was abruptly halted by the sudden appearance of a black cane, menacing in its slimness, which caught him across the chest and barred his way. He had barely had time to emit a gasp of fright, before a long thin hand had caught him by the arm of his coat and hauled him into the alley. In an instant he found himself pinned against a wall and staring into the pale half-hidden face of Monks.

'You've been avoiding me, Bolter,' the villain snarled softly.

'No, no, Mr Monks!' squealed Noah.

'I think you have,' said Monks, 'and I think that means my plan is going well and that Mr Brownlow is proving co-operative.'

'A wery affable gen'ellman – like you said,' Claypole replied nervously, 'I calls on 'im every second day.'

'And?'

'Seen the error of me ways, I tell 'im. Eager to turn over a new leaf.' Noah's courage, such as it was, was beginning to return, and he now said, with a grin: 'He's willin' to 'elp.'

'And you,' murmured Monks, still menacingly, 'are trying to turn that to your own advantage.'

'No!' Claypole pleaded hurriedly, 'It's all part of the plan, so 'e'll trust me.'

'I could almost pity him,' Monks muttered with disgust.

'With one of us on the inside,' said Claypole, 'we've a better chance of gettin' our 'ands on Oliver's money.'

'That's your interest, not mine,' Monks retorted.

Noah shrugged: 'I don't see that either of us can do much, not with 'im at school so far away.'

'I've taken care of that,' Monks now revealed, lowering his voice still further.

' 'Ow?' asked Claypole, interestedly.

Monks gazed around for some while, desperate not to be overheard. He then stared at Claypole, and whispered: 'I've planted someone at the school. Someone with as much reason as myself to wish to see my dear brother's reputation and future destroyed.' He announced this in a tone of such malicious glee that Noah Claypole involuntarily but visibly shivered.

That revelation was the reason for our short visit to London. Having absorbed it, and having given grave consideration to all that it implies, we must return at once to Mr Stalker's Academical Establishment, where events consequent upon Mr Bumble's arrival had already begun to take an interesting turn.

A week or so after Mr Bumble assumed office as school porter, the Junior boys were due to sit their midterm examination. However, two days prior to this test of their ability, the list of proposed questions mysteriously disappeared from Mr Meikle's desk. Mr Meikle's disquiet at this occurrence was occasioned not merely by a moral indignation at the list having been stolen, but by the realization that he would now have to think of an entirely new list. Understandably, therefore, he was furious. As soon as he discovered that the questions were missing, he relayed the sorry fact to Mr Bumble, who accompanied him at once to Mr Stalker's study. If anyone was more capable of fury at the idea of theft than Mr Meikle, it was Mr Stalker. He did not at first understand why any of his pupils should want to steal the list, and Mr Meikle had to explain that the guilty pupil, whoever he might be, presumably intended to copy the questions down and return them, undetected.

Once he had fully comprehended the terrible reason for the theft, Mr Stalker bellowed: 'Monstrous! When the culprit is found, he will be expelled at once. Who could commit such a crime?'

'I cannot imagine,' Mr Meikle replied.

Mr Stalker then turned to the School Porter, who had said nothing as yet, and asked: 'Mr Bumble. Have you any suspicions?'

Mr Bumble appeared to think hard for several seconds before saying: 'Well, sir. . . I 'ave been aware of one or two boys a-'angin' around of Mr Meikle's desk. But I regret to say, who they were I can't recollect. . . Except . . .'

'Who?' barked Mr Stalker.

After further consideration, and with apparent reluctance, Mr Bumble enunciated a single short name: 'Twist'.

'Oliver Twist?' said Mr Stalker. 'I shall summon him instanter.'

He was about to give the bell on his desk a characteristically violent ring when Mr Bumble stepped forward, raising a large hand and saying: 'Er, Mr Stalker, sir. If I might make so bold?'

'Yes?'

'Proof,' declared Mr Bumble, 'is what we need.'

'Exactly,' said Mr Meikle.

'In which case,' Bumble continued, 'might I suggest we make a search of all the boys' possessions in the Junior Dormitory? That would be more fair.'

'And more incriminating,' Mr Meikle rejoined, 'if the list were found.'

'Exactly,' remarked Mr Bumble with a smile.

'Very well,' announced Mr Stalker, after considering the plan. 'And when shall we carry out this search?'

'When least expected, sir,' Mr Bumble suggested. And then he asked, 'P'raps we could call on some o' the Senior boys to assist?'

'An excellent idea!' said Mr Stalker. 'Shall we root out the malefactor, gentlemen?'

Mr Bumble, who was not as yet fully cognizant of Mr Stalker's habit of answering his own questions, was about to declare that they most certainly would, when a restraining gesture from Mr Meikle prevented him.

'We most certainly shall!' boomed Mr Stalker.

Not a quarter of an hour after this conference in Mr Stalker's study, the Artful Dodger, who was once again seated in the fork of his favourite tree, and enjoying a pipe of tobacco, became the unseen witness of a most remarkable conversation. Lost in his thoughts, and gazing at the smoke rings he was forming, he suddenly heard the sound of bushes being parted, of twigs being snapped and of the dry autumn leaves being crushed under a pair of very heavy feet. He at once concealed his pipe in his coat pocket, fearful of being discovered in his illicit activity, and also a trifle annoyed at the tranquillity of his surroundings being thus disturbed. He looked down from his vantage point high up in the tree, and saw, directly below him, the immense figure of the School Porter, quite exhausted by the effort expended in fighting his way through the foliage, and mopping the perspiration from his fleshy brow. Fortunately for the Dodger, Mr Bumble appeared to be far too preoccupied to look upwards. He was clearly waiting for something, or for someone. Soon enough, that someone appeared; it was Craddock, who was in turn followed by Gurney.

'You said,' said Craddock, quite loudly, 'to settle our score with Twist.'

Mr Bumble began to flap his huge hands violently and uttered a long low spluttering sound, which Craddock interpreted correctly as a request to lower his voice. 'You said,' he now whispered, 'to settle our score with Twist.'

Mr Bumble glanced worriedly about him, but not upwards, before replying: 'Which, I 'ave reason to believe, you'd welcome?'

'He's caused nothing but trouble since he came here,' snarled Gurney.

'Stirring up the Juniors!' hissed Craddock. 'He's a bad influence.'

'Just so,' said the Porter. 'Which is why I 'ave deputized you to assist in the search of the Junior Dormitory.'

'If the exam papers are there, we'll find them,' declared Gurney eagerly.

'You could make certain,' said Mr Bumble, emphasizing each word.

'How?' asked Craddock.

The Dodger watched intently as Mr Bumble, after another quick look round, now withdrew from the inside pocket of his coat three folded sheets of paper covered in handwriting, and passed them to Craddock.

Craddock unfolded them and saw what they were in an instant. He stared aghast at Mr Bumble. 'The list of questions!' he gasped. '*You* took them!'

Mr Bumble could not resist a small grin of satisfaction at his own cleverness. In a second, however, it had vanished and he now said seriously: 'Slip 'em amongst his things, when you're a-searchin' of 'is locker. That's all you have to do.'

Keen though they were to revenge themselves on Oliver Twist, Craddock and Gurney now glanced nervously at each other, and then at Mr Bumble. 'Why are you doing this?' asked Craddock.

'To oblige someone,' Mr Bumble replied, mysteriously, 'an' to please myself. Which is all you need to know.'

'It's a bit risky, isn't it?' said Gurney.

'Easy as pie, young sir,' retorted Mr Bumble confidently. 'An' leave Twist to be searched last. To make it more positive.' Whereupon he turned and began to make his heavy way back through the bushes, panting vigorously as he went. Craddock and Gurney watched him go and glanced at each other again. The Dodger then saw Craddock determinedly place the three sheets of paper in the inside pocket of his tailcoat. Gurney grinned, and the two Senior boys followed the school porter.

The Artful Dodger knew at once what he had to do. When he was confident that the three conspirators were far enough away not to see him, he shinned quickly down the tree and ran as fast as he could towards the school.

''Ere! Oliver!' the Dodger cried as he burst into the Junior Dormitory. All the boys were in the room, and Oliver was in the process of helping Tommy Rice to bind the broken handle of a cricket bat. 'Oliver!' the Dodger repeated, breathlessly.

'Just a minute,' said Oliver, who was concentrating deeply on tying a knot.

'No, listen! It's important!' cried the Dodger, with a tone of such urgency that he caused Oliver to look up at him in amazement.

'Right!' bellowed an authoritarian voice at that moment. 'Attention everyone! Stand by your beds!' It was Mr Bumble. His massive frame filled the dormitory door. As he stepped forward, Mr Stalker, Mr Meikle, Craddock and Gurney followed him gravely into the room.

'Oliver,' whispered the Dodger in desperation, 'you mustn't let . . .'

'Sharp about it!' barked Mr Bumble, with a glare at the Dodger. 'No talking!'

The Dodger had no choice but to obey. Morosely, he moved to his bed, and stood beside it, while the other boys stood by theirs. They watched puzzled as Mr Stalker now commenced a slow progress along the aisle between the beds, saying, as he did so: 'You wonder why I am here? Why do I quiver with indignation, you say? Does one of you already know the answer? Who is afraid to meet my eyes!'

At this, he stopped walking and stared suddenly and for several seconds at Oliver. The boy was a trifle alarmed by the Headmaster's penetrating gaze, but his expression, as he returned it, did not reveal a hint of guilt. Mr Stalker soon began to be embarrassed by the open innocence in the prime suspect's countenance and, with a cough, he looked quickly away. 'The list of questions for the Junior Midterm Examination having been purloined from Mr Meikle's desk . . . ,' he now began, but was silenced by the loud gasp of astonishment which met this revelation. Once more Mr Stalker glanced sharply at Oliver, who, to the old gentleman's further consternation, appeared to be as surprised by the news as the others. Again he had to look hurriedly away. 'Will the perpetrator own up?' he thundered threateningly. 'Will he come forward?' Not one of the boys made the slightest movement. 'So be it,' Mr Stalker then announced. 'Each and every one of you will be searched. Immediately. Proceed!' With a wave of his hand, he indicated that the proposed search should now commence, and stood watching the proceedings from his commanding position in the centre of the room.

Starting at the door, Mr Meikle and Gurney began to search the boys on one side of the dormitory, while Mr Bumble and Craddock searched those on the other; amongst whose number, as it happened, were Oliver and the Dodger. The two Seniors concentrated on rummaging through the bedside lockers, while Mr Meikle and Mr Bumble examined the contents of the boys' pockets. The Dodger noticed that, as far as Mr Bumble and Craddock were concerned at least, each search lasted only a matter of seconds. They both seemed over-eager to reach Oliver's bed, which was the last bed but one, the last bed being the Dodger's own. In a suspiciously short time, it was Oliver's turn to be searched, and, as Craddock moved round to search Oliver's locker, the Dodger detected a swift conspiratorial glance being exchanged between the bully and Mr Bumble. In an instant, the Dodger had stepped forward. 'What about me?' he said.

'Wait your turn,' said Craddock, sharply.

'I'm fed up waitin'' said the Dodger. 'If someone's accusin' me, I want it cleared up.'

'No one's accusin' you,' retorted Bumble, with impatience.

'I demand to be searched!' protested the Dodger, loudly; whereupon Mr Stalker, with a familiar cry of 'What's this? What's this?' began to approach.

'A honest impulse, 'Eadmaster,' Mr Bumble explained unctuously. He then turned to the Dodger and said, with a malicious gleam in his eye, 'I am sure we can accommodate him.'

The Dodger was duly accommodated. Craddock, ignoring Oliver for the moment, moved round the Dodger's bed towards his locker, which he now opened, as Mr Bumble hurriedly examined the Dodger's pockets.

'Nothing,' announced Craddock, after a most cursory search.

'Satisfied?' said Mr Bumble to the Dodger. 'You are off the 'ook'; and he once again turned his attention to Oliver. Craddock began to move back towards Oliver's bed, passing behind the Dodger as he did so. The Dodger suddenly turned and collided with the bully.

'Mind where you're going!' snarled Craddock.

'Sorry,' said the Dodger, with a smile. 'Wasn't thinking.'

He quickly dusted down the lapels of Craddock's tailcoat and gave him an affectionate pat on the chest. Craddock glared briefly at him and shrugged him away impatiently.

'Well now, young Twist!' declared Mr Bumble, 'You appear to be last.' This was true, for Mr Meikle and Gurney had long since completed their fruitless examination of the boys on the other side of the dormitory. 'Raise your arms!' Mr Bumble snapped.

Oliver did so, and there was a breathless tension in the room. The fact that Twist was the only boy who had not yet been searched was virtual proof of his guilt. The boys began to crowd round Oliver's bed, as Mr Bumble commenced his exploration of the suspect's pockets. The Dodger moved forward to join the throng, but collided with Mr Meikle, who was approaching Oliver's bed at the same time.

'Out of my way, boy!' cried Mr Meikle. Once again, the Dodger made a gesture of profuse apology. Mr Meikle brushed him aside impatiently, eager to enjoy a good view of this moment of truth. To his initial disappointment, however, Mr Bumble now concluded his search with the declaration that he had failed to find anything. All eyes then turned to Craddock, who was busily rummaging through Oliver's bedside locker. Only the Dodger, who had been watching Craddock while everyone else in the room was concentrating on Mr Bumble, had noticed the bully slipping his hand surreptitiously into the inside pocket of his tailcoat. Only the Dodger had noticed the look of startled astonishment on the bully's face as he discovered the pocket to be empty. He had then hurriedly put his hand into his other pocket, in the confused hope of finding something there. Aware now that he was being watched by everyone in the room, including Mr Bumble, he made a final desperate pretence at searching the locker, before turning at last and staring disappointedly up at the Porter.

'Nothing,' he said, almost voicelessly, 'Nothing there.'

The boys were immediately and audibly relieved; so, to be fair, was Mr Stalker. Mr Meikle was mildly annoyed, but no expression in the room could match the astonished distress on Mr Bumble's face at that instant.

'Look again! Look again, boy!' he snapped, frantically.

Craddock made a further brief show of examining the locker's contents, but could only repeat at last, with a shamefaced expression: 'Nothing.'

'Has this entire search been a fiasco?' thundered Mr Stalker. 'Have these papers vanished into thin air?' He glanced sharply at each boy in turn; allowing his eye to fall finally on the boy Dawkins, who appeared to be looking up at the ceiling in a most abstracted manner, his hands thrust deep into his pockets; a very study in supreme innocence.

'The culprit must have secreted them elsewhere, Headmaster,' Mr Meikle suggested.

'I am well aware of that, Mr Meikle!' barked Mr Stalker, and continued furiously, 'We shall search and search again! Not a stone shall be left unturned! Each boy will write a detailed report of his movements from the last time the list was seen in Mr Meikle's desk! Every statement must be verified by witnesses! I shall . . .'

'Headmaster,' Mr Meikle now interjected, in a softly apologetic tone.

'What?' snapped Mr Stalker, 'What is it now?'

'The list,' said Mr Meikle, weakly.

'List?'

'Of examination questions. I have . . . found it.'

'Found it? What are you . . .?'

And indeed there they were, in Mr Meikle's hand; the three leaves of paper containing the questions for the Junior Midterm Examination.

'I am at a loss for an explanation,' Mr Meikle now continued. 'It was . . . in my pocket.'

Mr Meikle, who was at the time suffering from a mild head cold, had reached into his jacket pocket with the purpose of withdrawing a handkerchief, and had, to his understandable amazement, withdrawn the papers instead.

A slight titter began to make itself heard through the ranks of boys as they understood what had occurred, but it was immediately silenced by a glare from Mr Stalker. 'Is hilarity called for? It is to be borne? It is not!' he boomed, and turned again to his abashed colleague. 'Mr

Meikle! Do you have the temerity to tell me? . . . Words fail me, Mr Meikle, I . . .'

Mr Meikle now said: 'I can . . . I can only apologize . . . most sincerely . . . to everyone concerned.'

Mr Stalker glowered ominously at him for a few seconds and then marched from the room, saying no more. Mr Meikle followed him apprehensively. Craddock and Gurney were both far too confused by this strange turn of events to do anything but move sheepishly towards the door, and leave as quickly as they could, not daring to look into the faces of any of the boys; but Mr Bumble allowed himself a final venomous glance in Oliver's direction before departing, magisterially, slamming the door behind him as he went. As soon as they were left alone, the boys, with one accord, began to laugh in puzzlement and relief.

'What did you make of that, Dodger?' Oliver asked.

The Dodger replied mysteriously: 'What do I make of it? This is what I make of it. That some o' the things old Fagin taught us still come in handy!'

'What do you mean?'

'Tell you when I get my breath back . . . ,' the Artful Dodger retorted, collapsing onto his bed, unable to restrain for a second longer his need to break into uncontrollable mirth.

A hurried conference was instantly convened in Craddock's study. Present at this meeting were the School Porter, the bully and his assistant.

'So? What happened?' demanded Mr Bumble.

'How should I know?' replied Craddock, still thoroughly confused. 'The list was in my pocket one minute. And the next . . .'

'In Meikle's!' said Gurney. 'It was like magic!'

'There's no such hanimal,' snapped Bumble. 'Anyone who believes in witchcraft is a imbecile. That list wasn't magicked – it was snitched. Someone was on to us.'

'Twist?' suggested Gurney, eagerly.

'Or someone a-'elping of him,' Bumble mused. 'It'll be ten times as difficult to get 'im now.'

'But it still won't save him,' Craddock now remarked, firmly.

'Meaning?' inquired Bumble, in a silky tone.

'Now that we know you're on our side and won't interfere,' Craddock replied, smiling.

'Depend on it!' said Bumble.

'Then Gurney and I,' snarled Craddock, 'will make his life a hell on earth. He'll wish he was back in your workhouse.'

'Spoken like a fine young gentleman,' Mr Bumble declared, spreading his huge arms and placing a fleshy hand on each of the bully's shoulders. He sealed the conspiracy with a most malicious grin.

CHAPTER SEVEN

One of Mr Bumble's many duties as School Porter was to issue the boys' mail every afternoon, as soon as the day's teaching was over. He would stand self-importantly beside the larger of the two desks in the schoolroom, and call out the names of those who had received letters or packages; each boy, as his name was called, would come forward excitedly to collect whatever Mr Bumble was holding out for him.

Oliver Twist was a most exemplary letter-writer. He would loyally and willingly write to Mr Brownlow, and to his Aunt Rose, every week without fail, and occasionally with even greater frequency; his guardian and his Aunt invariably replied by return. Oliver looked forward to their letters as much as they did to his. Naturally, therefore, he began to grow somewhat concerned when a week and a half had passed without a word from either of them. Each afternoon, he would anxiously wait for his name to be uttered by Mr Bumble, but was disappointed every time. Eventually, he approached the Porter as this gentleman was waddling majestically towards the door after having completed the ceremony of issuing the day's post, and asked: 'No letter for me, Mr Bumble?'

'Hif I 'ad called out your name, Twist,' Mr Bumble retorted sharply, 'there would of been a letter for you. Since I don't reckerlect a-doin'-so there was not.' He continued on his journey.

'I can't understand it,' said Oliver morosely, as he and the Dodger were leaving the schoolroom. 'I haven't had a letter from Mr Brownlow for over two weeks. Nor from Aunt Rose.'

'Too busy to write, I 'spect,' the Dodger suggested.

'Not *both* of them,' said Oliver. 'And I've written to them every week, as I promised.'

'You'll 'ear soon enough,' said the Dodger, 'No point

worryin'.' He ran off, eager to enjoy his daily pipe in the seclusion of his favourite hiding place.

Oliver was too despondent to join in the delight occasioned in the Junior Dormitory that afternoon by the arrival of a large parcel for Tommy Rice. As he now entered that room, Tommy was busily unwrapping this parcel, surrounded by several ardently curious companions.

'Look!' cried Tommy Rice, holding up a bottle of round, multicoloured objects, 'My favourites. The sweets my grandmother makes!'

'Are they any good?' asked one of the boys, doubtfully.

'Of course they are!' declared Tommy indignantly, 'Here. Try one!' He opened the bottle. The boy snatched a sweet from Tommy's grasp delightedly. Realizing that he had been tricked, Tommy began to protest, but then he grinned and said: 'Oh all right! Help yourself, everybody. I was going to share them out anyway.'

'Good old Pudding!' squeaked Shrimp, and the sweets were handed out to the assembled company. Oliver accepted one, too.

'Oh look!' Tommy then squealed. He had extracted a larger object wrapped carefully in a cloth. There were now further reactions of approval from his friends as he removed the cloth to reveal a large, golden, currant-filled manorhouse cake. The boys eyed it hungrily, but Tommy laid it aside, saying 'And there's something else'. A third object was then extracted, flat and rectangular. 'Ooh . . . what's this?' said Tommy excitedly as he unwrapped it.

'It looks uncommonly like a slab of marzipan,' replied a vicious voice, and the boys spun round to see Craddock approaching Tommy's bed. Predictably enough, Gurney was at his side.

'Well?' said Craddock, 'Is it?' He stood menacingly before Tommy, and held out his hand. Reluctantly but powerlessly, Tommy handed over the marzipan. Craddock broke a piece from the slab and tasted it. 'By Jove!' he declared, with false friendliness, 'that's just what it is! And not at all bad. Don't you agree, Gurney?' He broke off another piece and gave it to his friend.

'Not bad. Not bad at all,' opined Gurney, as he put it into his mouth.

'Oh, and what have we here?' Craddock now remarked. 'A splendid cake, I do declare.'

As he was bending to pick up the cake, Oliver stepped forward and cried: 'That's Tommy's cake, Craddock!'

Craddock turned sharply to Oliver and snarled: 'In case you've forgotten, Twist, you address me as "sir"! And speak when you're spoken to!' Oliver fumed silently, as Craddock lifted the cake from Tommy's bed.

'I was . . . I was going to share it all out, Mr Craddock, sir,' said Tommy, nervously.

'But of course you were,' said Craddock, with an evil smile. 'And I'm extremely grateful. Aren't you, Gurney?'

'Extremely,' Gurney echoed as Craddock handed him the cake.

'Oh, and what's *this*?' Craddock now inquired, eyeing the bottle of sweets. 'Who sent you these?'

'My – my grandmother, Mr Craddock, sir,' Tommy replied.

'How thoughtless of her,' said Craddock, with a shake of his head. 'Doesn't she know they're very bad for your teeth?'

'Very bad,' said Gurney, also shaking his head.

'I'll see they're disposed of,' said Craddock, picking up the bottle.

'But, sir . . .' protested Tommy, softly.

'No, no, don't thank me, Pudding,' Craddock interposed, 'It's I who should thank you. Such a generous little fellow.' He patted the wretched boy on the head, and left the room with the bottle of sweets and the slab of marzipan. Gurney followed with the delicious-looking cake.

*

'What's going on?' asked the Dodger, as he entered the dormitory a while later and saw nothing but an array of dejected countenances, the most dejected of all being poor Tommy's.

'Craddock and Gurney have taken all the things Tommy was sent from home,' Oliver explained.

'His cake!' squeaked Shrimp.

'And his sweets!' declared another boy.

'I never even had one myself,' muttered Tommy, miserably.

'Well,' said the Dodger, making for his bed and throwing himself headlong onto it, 'I told you it was goin' to get worse.'

'We should complain to the Porter!' cried Shrimp, stamping a tiny foot.

'Bumble?' the Dodger retorted. ''E's a bully 'isself. 'E's on their side. Make no mistake – they'll be back.'

'And there's nothing we can do,' muttered Tommy, even more miserably.

There was a long unhappy silence. At last Oliver said quietly: 'You certainly can't beat bullies by giving in to them.'

'What do you mean, Oliver?' asked Shrimp.

'Remember the plans we made?' said Oliver.

The boys began to murmur to each other. 'The battle plans?' asked one of them.

'It's time we went over them again,' said Oliver, more firmly. 'Jack's right. We can't take it lying down!'

'Wait a minute,' the Dodger interposed, 'I didn't mean . . .'

But Oliver was now determined; his indignation had reached the point of no return. 'We said, the next night they raid the dormitory, we'd be ready for them. It's up to us! Are you with me?'

'I am!' piped Shrimp.

'Me, too!' cried another boy.

'I told you before,' the Dodger protested, sitting up,

'You'll bring the lot, the Masters an' Bumble, the 'ole Upper School, down on you!'

'But at least,' Oliver retorted fixedly, 'we'd have stood up for ourselves! Just for once!'

'Hear, hear!' squeaked Shrimp, at once prompting a chorus of assent and support from all the boys. 'Oliver's right! I'm with you! What do we do?' they cried ardently. The Dodger watched, sceptical and concerned, as his dormitory mates now crowded round Oliver, asking a host of eager questions, and as Oliver began to remind them of the proposed procedure, with a quiet urgency in his voice.

All the boys were watchfully awake that night, but they lay quite still, and some of them even pretended to snore, as Craddock, Gurney and another Senior boy – the apprentice bully again, Oliver presumed – crept stealthily into the Junior Dormitory in the small hours of the morning. Craddock was carrying a lantern. Gurney held a length of thin rope, stretched taut between his hands.

'Get Twist first,' Craddock was heard to whisper, sharply. Gurney nodded and proceeded to tiptoe down the room between the beds, followed by the other boy. Craddock set down the lantern on the small table by the door. No sooner had he done this than he was startled by a loud crashing sound followed immediately by a howl of pain from Gurney. Only a moment later, there was a second crashing sound followed by a second howl. Craddock spun round and saw Gurney and the apprentice bully sprawled headlong on the dormitory floor, one on top of the other. He hurried forward but stopped abruptly, for his eye now fell on the reason for what had happened; a cord was stretched across the room at shin level between two of the beds. Craddock scowled and glanced round the room; he saw that all the Junior boys were wide awake, and sitting up in their beds.

'You little devils!' he roared. Knowing full well who

the chief culprit was, he quickly stepped over the cord and advanced rapidly towards Oliver Twist's bed. Once again, however, he had to stop, for he now nearly fell over a second cord tied at thigh level between two beds still further down the room.

Taking advantage of the brief pause in the proceedings, Oliver was out of his bed in an instant, and now cried: 'Get them!' With a cacophony of yells and delighted squeals, the Junior boys leapt from their beds; some had pea-shooters, and began to use them enthusiastically; others concentrated on pummelling Gurney and the apprentice bully, who were both still prostrate, with their pillows. In the confusion, Craddock was still determined to lay his hands on Oliver, and lunged at him. But Oliver had darted behind his bed, which he now pushed towards Craddock, knocking the bully backwards and over the end of the bed on the other side of the dormitory. The owner of this bed, overjoyed that the privilege should be his, at once proceeded to assault Craddock with his pillow, forcing him to cover his face with his hands. At this point, the apprentice bully, recovering from his fall, began to rise slowly from the floor; but was instantly persuaded to descend again by a powerful barrage of very painful projectiles from an array of pea-shooters aimed in his direction. Gurney appeared to remain too dazed and winded to do anything but lie flat, groaning at the blows he continued to receive from several pillows. Craddock now caught hold of the pillow with which *he* was being struck, wrenched it from the hand of his assailant, and proceeded to fight back, knocking the boy sideways off the bed. The bully flailed with the pillow in the direction of another boy and sent him flying too. Unfortunately for Craddock, however, the force of the blow now rendered the pillow useless as a weapon, for it burst and its contents began to flutter around the room. An accurately timed hit on the back of his head, from yet another pillow, sent him tumbling into the space between the bed upon which he had been standing and its immediate neighbour. Oliver now speedily pushed his own bed against the ends of the two beds on either side of the bully, and Craddock found himself imprisoned. The boys with the pea-shooters, seeing him thus caged, now concentrated their attack on him, allowing the apprentice bully to rise again and run for the door. He was halted, however, by a cascade of very cold water from a red fire bucket held by Shrimp, which drenched him from head to toe. Another boy, stationed on his bed by the door, was holding a second bucket filled with sand, and immediately upended it, depositing its contents all over him. Spluttering, coughing, and howling, the apprentice bully reeled from the room, escaping at last and vowing never to enter the Junior Dormitory again.

Gurney then made his first attempt to raise himself from his prone position, for Craddock had become the main object of the attackers' attentions; however, one boy caught sight of him in time and subjected him to an immaculately aimed blow on the head with his pillow. Gurney collapsed; the pillow burst open and more feathers began to fill the room.

'Stop it! Now stop it! Do you hear me!' screamed Craddock, but he was not yet repentant, for he added: 'You'll pay for this! Gurney! Help me!' The bully was in severe need of help, for several of the boys were now trying to push the two beds on either side of him towards each other with the intention, it seemed, of crushing him between them. This rendered Craddock incapable of protecting himself from the battery of painful missiles from the pea-shooters, for his hands were fully occupied in trying to keep the beds apart.

Gurney heard his master's cry for help, however, and once more began to rise by grasping the end rail of the nearest bed and pulling himself up. Apparently unnoticed, he succeeded in standing, and proceeded to move to Craddock's aid; his progress was immediately curtailed by the fact that his ankles had been tied together with the very rope that he had brought with him; once more he fell helplessly to the floor with a crash and a yell; once more he was assaulted by innumerable blows from innumerable pillows. He acknowledged defeat. 'Pax!' he screeched. 'All right! Pax! I give in! I give in!'

Gurney's cry caused a momentary halt in the squealing and shouting and battering and shoving, as everyone in the room turned to look at him; whimpering, he sat up and morosely began to unwind the rope from around his ankles. Craddock, however, was infuriated by his friend's cowardly declaration of surrender, and he now glared at Oliver and screamed: 'Don't think you've won, Twist!' A perfectly prepared and expertly directed ink-soaked pellet struck his tie at this point, and the ink spilled onto his splendid, cream-coloured waistcoat. As far as Craddock was concerned, no crime in the world was worse than the ruination of his tie and waistcoat, and with a gasp of horror, he glared round the room in search of the offender. Almost at once he saw that it was Tommy Rice, who was at that moment bending a ruler with another pellet on its end. Tommy now let this second pellet fly; it hit Craddock on the forehead.

'Good shot, Tommy!' cried Oliver. With a monstrous roar, Craddock then wreaked his revenge; his anger rendered him unstoppable. He rose in an instant, kicked Oliver's bed from his path, leapt towards Tommy and grasped the boy by the collar of his night-shirt. Aghast at the power of his fury, the other boys immediately fell back; with the exception of Oliver, who succeeded in catching hold the arm with which the bully was about to strike his hapless captive. Craddock let go of Tommy and turned on Oliver; the two boys fell onto Tommy's bed in a desperate struggle. Encouraged by Oliver's refusal to succumb, the boys advanced again, and pandemonium was resumed as they climbed on top of Craddock and began once more to strike him with their pillows.

The events so far described lasted a considerably shorter time than it has taken to describe them; a minute or so perhaps, and certainly no more than two; long enough at any rate for the School Porter to be woken from a deep slumber by the chaotic noises emanating from the direction of the Junior Dormitory, and to set about investigating their cause. Rising from his bed, and pausing only to slip his coat over his nightshirt and pick up a large heavy stick and a lantern, he waddled towards the dormitory with all the speed he could summon. The distance from his own room to the room in which the younger boys slept was only a short one; a sprightlier person could have covered it in twenty seconds at the most; it took Mr Bumble well over a minute.

As he strode into the room and raised his lantern, he discerned what appeared to be a very noisy mountain of flailing limbs and pillows on one of the far beds. Feathers floated about him as he peered into the semi-darkness. 'Desist!' he bellowed, 'Leave off! D'you hear me?' Desist! At once!'

The mountain quietened and fell apart in an instant. Mr Bumble began to approach its components, brandishing his stick and roaring: 'Wot d'you think you're a doin' of?! I'll brain the first one of you that – oh – ah – ... ow!! H-e-e-elp!!'

The floor, it must be understood, was very slippery by now, covered as it had become with a treacherous mess of feathers, sand, and water. Mr Bumble had advanced no more than a yard or two before his feet proceeded to slither about uncontrollably beneath him, and he lost his balance. With the above cry, he teetered dangerously and reached frantically for the nearest object of support; this happened to be Gurney, who was rising from the floor at that moment. Gurney immediately sagged and swayed under Mr Bumble's immense weight. It was a sight that caused the Junior boys a great deal of amusement, and they began to laugh. Their laughter was cut short, however, by the entrance of Mr Stalker, in his nightgown and cap, followed closely by Mr Meikle, clad in similar attire. Both gentlemen stopped at the door, appalled by the shambolic scene before them.

Mr Stalker, indeed, was so very appalled that he could not speak for several seconds, but could only cast a pair of disbelieving eyes around the room. When he did speak at last, he could barely manage, to begin with at least, a hoarse whisper. 'Do my eyes deceive me?' he muttered, 'Am I living in a nightmare? Shall I awake to . . . to find myself in Stalker's Academical Establishment for *Young Gentlemen*? Or in some *barracks*, some . . . some . . . *cattleshed* . . . some infidel den of *iniquity*!!!' By the end of this declaration his voice had found its familiar force, and had risen to an almost incoherent bellow. It was answered only by a long silence, during which Craddock rose slowly from the bed to which he had been pinned, and advanced towards the Headmaster. His hair was dishevelled, his fine clothes were torn in several places, and his face was streaked with ink.

'Craddock?' inquired Mr Stalker, uncertainly, 'It is Craddock, isn't it?' At this, some of the braver boys proceeded to laugh nervously.

'Silence!' barked Mr Meikle.

'Do you have a rational explanation for your appearance and your presence here, Craddock?' asked Mr Stalker.

'Yes, sir,' said Craddock, fighting for his breath. 'Mr Bumble asked the Seniors and myself to look out for disturbances in the Junior School. We came to investigate the noise and were attacked.'

'That's a lie!' Oliver cried, stepping forward.

Mr Stalker stared at Oliver. 'Indeed?' he said.

'Indeed, sir,' Mr Bumble now remarked, after a glance in Craddock's direction, 'Indeed, it is not a lie. 'Eadmaster, I collaborate Master Craddock's weracity.' A loud groan of protest emanated from some of the boys, provoking a second bark of 'Silence!' from Mr Meikle.

'Furthermore,' Mr Bumble now continued, glaring at

Oliver, 'I suspicion Twist of bein' the ringleader of the disturbance.'

'Is that so, Twist?' said Stalker, approaching him, 'Is that so? Speak up! Did you begin this – this uproar?'

'Yes, sir,' replied Oliver, truthfully.

'He wasn't the only one!' cried a courageous voice; it was Tommy Rice's.

'Silence!' snapped Mr Meikle, a third time.

Mr Stalker sternly surveyed Oliver for a few more moments before saying: 'Very well, Twist, you have confessed. And shall you suffer the utmost punishments? You most certainly shall! You shall be flogged in front of the entire school. You shall be...'

He was about to embark on a list of all the torments he could think of, when Mr Bumble interposed in an unctuous manner. 'Hif I might be so bold, Mr Stalker...'

'Yes? Yes? What?'

'You gave me responsibility for discipline, sir. So if I might suggest...'

'Well?'

'Twist should be treated like a common criminal, since that's 'is obvious destiny. 'E should be locked up on bread and water, as a Awful Example. Solitary Confinement, that's the answer.'

The boys were too horrified by this suggestion to protest audibly; they merely watched in wide-eyed silence as Mr Stalker gave it due consideration. 'Very well, Mr Bumble,' he declared at last. 'I leave it in your capable hands. And the rest of you, shall any of you go to bed before this disgusting mess is cleared up? You most certainly shall not! As for you, Twist, you miserable boy, shall you go forthwith with Mr Bumble?'

'I most certainly shall,' replied Oliver, flatly, as the Porter clasped him tightly by the arm and marched him from the room.

The Artful Dodger, who had sat on his bed with his arms folded and had watched the entire proceedings with an amused and distant air, now became doubly convinced of the fruitlessness of any form of rebellion against the state of things at Mr Stalker's Academy.

The pleasant place chosen by Mr Bumble for Oliver's imprisonment was a broom cupboard, no more than four feet wide and three feet deep, behind the largest of the two desks in the schoolroom. The wretched boy was brought there immediately, escorted by Mr Bumble and Mr Meikle. The porter unlocked the cupboard door, opened it, and removed two buckets and a mop which were the cupboard's only contents. 'Inside with you, Twist,' he said. Oliver had no choice but to enter the dark and cramped cupboard.

To his surprise, he then heard Mr Meikle protest in an unfamiliar and apparently concerned manner: 'There's nothing to lie on! Not even a chair or a stool!'

'You do not provide the comforts o' Buckingham Palace in Solitary, Mr Meikle,' Bumble retorted.

'Nevertheless,' said Mr Meikle firmly, 'he shall at least have a chair.' Whereupon he took one from beside the desk and placed it in the cupboard, to the porter's obvious disapproval.

'Thank you, sir,' said Oliver, very quietly, and sat down, looking up into Mr Meikle's face, which did at that moment betray more than a touch of genuine sympathy.

'You 'ave three days to contemplate your wiciousness, Twist,' said Bumble, and Mr Meikle caught a glimpse of the boy's eyes widening in shock as Mr Bumble slammed the heavy door shut, and turned the key.

In the darkness of his tiny prison, Oliver heard Mr Meikle protest again: 'Three days? Is that not excessive, Mr Bumble?'

As one well-versed in the effects of various forms of punishment, Mr Bumble replied authoritatively: 'The minimum needed to bring a 'eart full o' wickedness to repentance, Mr Meikle.'

There was a pause, and Oliver heard Mr Meikle's footsteps as he left the schoolroom.

'Can you 'ear me, Twist?' a soft, gloating voice now snarled from the other side of the door, 'I'm sure you can. While you're in there, just think of 'ow your guardian, your Mr Brownlow; just think 'ow 'e's goin' to feel, when 'e 'ears o' this. Shame, that's what 'e's goin' to feel: the shame that you've brought on 'im.' Then Oliver heard Mr Bumble's slow, heavy tread as he too left the schoolroom.

The poor boy's thoughts now turned once more to his guardian and his Aunt Rose, and to how neither of them had written to him for well over two weeks. He felt friendless and unloved, and therefore thoroughly despondent. Soon, however, exhausted by the night's events, he fell asleep, still sitting on his chair; it was the deep, resigned repose of one who cannot hope for comfort from any quarter.

When the cantankerous Mr Grimwig called on his old friend Mr Brownlow at his house in Pentonville the following afternoon, the latter gentleman was in his study, having just completed the task of composing yet another letter to his ward. He was sealing the envelope as Mr Grimwig entered the room. Mr Brownlow looked up and smiled at Mr Grimwig, but Mr Grimwig could not avoid noticing his friend's tired and care-worn countenance. He did not express his concern vocally, however, but merely inquired if the letter was to Oliver.

'Yes, yes . . . to Oliver,' replied Mr Brownlow. 'Would you oblige me by ringing the bell?'

'With pleasure,' said Mr Grimwig, pulling the bell-pull by the fire. 'I trust that you did not fail to send him my . . . my remembrances?'

Mr Brownlow replied, smiling softly: 'I'll tell him that my friend, Mr Grimwig, misses him as much as we all do.'

'Ah, quite,' Mr Grimwig retorted, and adopted a fierce expression, thereby concealing the gratified affection he felt in his heart. 'And he has settled in at the school?' he asked.

'Very well, I have every reason to believe,' replied Mr Brownlow, with some hesitation in his voice. 'The Masters are strict, but fair. And he has made some congenial companions.'

'Having the time of his life,' declared Mr Grimwig, 'or I'll eat my head!' He was prevented from accompanying this remark with a blow on the floor from his stick, which was his usual practice, by the entrance at that moment of Mrs Carraway, Mr Brownlow's new housekeeper.

'You rang, Mr Brownlow?' this lady now inquired, somewhat crisply.

'Thank you, yes, Mrs Carraway,' replied Mr Brownlow. 'Would you ask the maid to take this to the post for me?'

'Certainly, sir,' said Mrs Carraway, and took the letter. Mrs Carraway was of a curious mind when it came to letters, and she could not avoid a glance at the name of the person to whom this one was addressed. As she turned to the door, she remarked: 'It is a pity, when you write so often, that there's never a reply. He must be a very ungrateful boy.'

Mr Brownlow stiffened, 'I have no reason to believe so,' he retorted, a trifle sharply. He noticed at the same instant that Mr Grimwig had summarily adopted a very suspicious expression upon hearing the lady's last utterance.

'I hope I did not speak out of turn, sir,' said Mrs Carraway, in response to her employer's apparent displeasure. 'Your kindness is well known, and I am concerned not to see it abused.'

'Yes,' Mr Brownlow replied softly, 'I appreciate that, Mrs Carraway. Thank you.'

'Am I to understand that you have not heard from

Oliver?' Mr Grimwig snapped, as soon as the housekeeper had left the room.

'Not for some time,' Mr Brownlow now admitted, a little sadly 'Although I write to him at least twice a week.'

Mr Grimwig could not hide his alarm, 'Surely you don't think there's something wrong?' he asked.

'No. No,' replied Mr Brownlow, without much conviction. 'New surroundings, new companions, his studies – he'll have many distractions.'

Mr Grimwig snorted disapprovingly. 'In short,' he declared. 'he's enjoying himself too much to consider the feelings of others.'

'Well,' mused Mr Brownlow, morosely, 'it's in the nature of boys to be thoughtless. Though, I confess I am disappointed.' He sighed and stared gloomily out of the window.

After a pause, Mr Grimwig said, with serious concern: 'I'm troubled about you, old friend. Are you quite well?'

'Tired, that's all' said Mr Brownlow.

'Perhaps you should see a doctor.'

'I have already. Mrs Carraway insisted.'

'And what did he say?'

'Plenty of rest – a tonic. I'll be fine again, when the weather changes.'

'Or when you finally receive a reply from Oliver,' declared Grimwig, 'or I'll eat my head!' and he struck his stick upon the floor.

'Yes,' said Mr Brownlow, nodding with a mournful smile. 'That would be the best tonic of all.'

CHAPTER EIGHT

'The time 'as come for Twist, what has been made A Awful Example of, to be released from confinement,' announced Mr Bumble majestically. 'Normally, when a person 'as accepted 'is punishment, we say, 'let bygones be bygones, the slate is wiped clean.' But in Twist's case, to avoid contamination, I recommend 'is bein' sent to Coventry. I advise each an' every one of you to ignore 'im – or risk sufferin' the same fate. Do I make myself clear?'

A cowed silence was the sole response to this inquiry. Three days had passed since that mutinous night in the Junior Dormitory, and Oliver was about to be freed from his place of imprisonment. The entire school had been assembled to witness the ceremony. Mr Bumble was standing beside the broom cupboard, and, once he had satisfied himself that the Junior boys were by now too terrified of him to do anything but obey his instructions, upon pain of having to endure a period of confinement themselves, he turned the key with a great flourish and opened the cupboard door. 'Out of there, Twist!' he barked. 'Let's be seein' you – let's see the woebegone face of a subjugated sinner!'

Oliver emerged, hesitantly. He was still in his nightshirt. In Mr Bumble's opinion at least, he seemed suitably repentant. He was pale and thin, for he had been fed very little during his detention. He now blinked in the bright light that met his eyes, having to raise his hand to shade them. None but the hardest of hearts could have felt sympathy for the released prisoner at that moment. Mr Meikle, who was seated at the larger desk, and who had spent the past three days inwardly questioning the irregularity and severity of Oliver's punishment, was perhaps more horrified than anyone.

After several silent seconds, Oliver lowered his hand and gazed at his assembled companions, surveying their anxious faces. He did not, even briefly, look up at Mr Bumble.

Suddenly, the awed hush was broken by a loud cry from Tommy Rice. 'Hurray for Oliver!' he shouted.

'Hip, hip!' squeaked Shrimp. In an instant, the room was filled with the clamour of cheering and applauding boys. Thunderstruck, Mr Bumble glared about him, but his infuriated, threatening stare could not silence the acclamation, which only increased in enthusiasm and volume as the seconds passed. Some of the boys now climbed onto their benches, clapping their hands above their heads. Many of the Senior boys, too, began to join in the general uproar; naturally, Craddock and Gurney merely scowled, surprised and incensed at the same time.

Mr Meikle could not resist a smile of satisfaction as he saw Oliver straighten with pride at the sight and sound of such unanimous approval from his fellows.

'To be thwarted like that,' snarled Bumble. 'Flouted an' 'umiliated by a pack of *boys*!' He had left the schoolroom hurriedly and was now sulking in the porter's lodge. Mr Meikle had followed him there, and was deriving considerable pleasure from watching his consternation.

'Well, you could hardly lock up the entire school, could you?' declared Mr Meikle, with ill-concealed amusement. However, he quickly adopted a more serious tone and countenance and added: 'I must warn you, Mr Bumble, against being unnecessarily hard on young Twist.'

''E's a bad influence!' Bumble growled.

'Maybe so,' retorted Mr Meikle, 'but you are fast turning him into the hero of the Lower School.' Mr Bumble stared at him as he continued: 'Now, I find little harm in the boy. Perhaps he has reacted too strongly against the school's system of fagging and other traditions.'

''E's a trouble maker,' snapped Bumble.

'Maybe so,' Mr Meikle repeated. 'But he is also an idealist, a champion of the underdog. So I look to you, Mr Bumble, to be not too narrow nor prejudiced in carrying out your duties.'

Mr Bumble was beginning to understand that Mr Meikle, whom he had initially assumed to be an inflexible authoritarian who would support him in all matters of discipline, would now have to be dealt with more subtly, for he was demonstrating a dangerous preference for fairness and even leniency. The Porter was a trifle baffled by this newly discovered quality in Meikle, and, since this gentleman had given, until recently, not the slightest indication of possessing an almost fatherly concern for the manner in which his pupils were treated, Mr Bumble could only conclude that he had undergone a change of heart, occasioned by the severity of the punishment inflicted on Oliver Twist; so he now smiled unctuously, and said, almost gently: 'Justice an' fairity; that's my motto, Mr Meikle.'

'Well,' said Mr Meikle, 'that's all I ask.' He left the lodge, apparently satisfied.

In the secrecy of his own heart, of course, Mr Bumble was still determined to see Oliver broken, if it was the last thing he did.

Oliver had been released from his cell in the morning, before the commencement of the day's teaching. In the late afternoon, when lessons were over, Mr Bumble embarked on the daily duty of issuing the post. Oliver was still hopeful, naturally, of receiving some communication from Mr Brownlow or his Aunt Rose, for it was now three weeks since he had heard a word from either of them. Yet again, however, he was to be disappointed.

'Swinnerton . . . Linley . . . Dukes. That's all, 'declared Mr Bumble, and waddled from the room.

'I just can't understand it,' said Oliver to the Dodger,

as the assembled boys began to drift off. 'I still haven't had a letter.'

'I've *never* 'ad one; never in me 'ole life,' the Dodger retorted, with a grin.

'But Mr Brownlow promised. And Aunt Rose. They'd never break a promise.'

'Looks like they just 'ave. I told you – you can't depend on nobody. Come on. Let's walk down to the river before tea.' Whereupon the Dodger joined the stream of boys heading for the door. Oliver was about to follow when he chanced to glance back over his shoulder, and saw poor Tommy Rice standing between Craddock and Gurney. Gurney was behind the boy, clasping him tightly by the arms, as Craddock addressed him softly, punctuating his every sentence with a painful prod in the ribs.

'You owe me for that waistcoat, don't you, Rice Pudding?' Craddock hissed, 'Don't you? Did you think I'd forgotten? Think you'd get away with it? Well, you can report to my study after supper and we'll see what . . .'

'Leave him alone!' said Oliver, approaching the bully.

Craddock turned his head. 'What did you say?' he snapped.

'Leave him alone,' Oliver repeated, 'Haven't you bullied him enough?'

Craddock stared at Oliver menacingly, clenching his fist.

Oliver heard Gurney whisper urgently: 'Bumble said we were to let him be for a while.'

'Bumble,' Craddock snarled, 'doesn't have to endure his insolence!' Whereupon, incapable of controlling his fury any longer, he swung his arm and struck Oliver brutally on the side of the face, knocking him to the ground. The noise of the blow and the accompanying squeal of concern from Tommy caused those boys who had not yet left the room to stop in their tracks and turn round. Oliver shook his head to clear it, for Craddock's swipe had almost rendered him insensible; he began to rise, only to be felled again immediately by a second assault from the bully's fist.

'Get up!' Craddock bellowed. 'Get up, you little brute!'

'All right!' That's enough!' cried a voice. Craddock looked up sharply. Dawkins was pushing his way through the crowd of boys towards him. 'That's enough!'

'Stay out of this, Dawkins!' Craddock barked. He realized in an instant, however, that Dawkins had no intention of obeying his order, and was quite prepared, if necessary, to return a punch on his friend's behalf.

'What happened? What's up?' said a Senior boy, coming forward.

'Twist started it,' Gurney explained, surlily

'He challenged me,' said Craddock, eyeing Dawkins a trifle hesitantly, 'I'm only protecting myself.'

'Get off,' said Dawkins, 'You're more than twice 'is size.'

By now, Oliver had risen, and said, with quiet firmness: 'I'm not afraid of him.'

Craddock was about to resume the attack when Dawkins caught his arm, holding him back. ''Old it!' he cried. 'If there's goin' to be a fight, it's gotta to be done proper.'

'That's right,' concurred the Senior boy who had come forward, and whose name was Farningham. He now looked at Oliver. 'Are you determined?' he asked.

'Yes,' said Oliver.

'All right, Craddock?' said Farningham. 'Do you accept?'

Craddock glanced at Gurney, who grinned. The bully then looked at Oliver. Presuming that the boy's size would be certain to preclude him from victory, even in the fairest of fights, he now grinned too, and said: 'I accept.'

'All right then,' declared Dawkins, not without a hint of trepidation in his voice, 'Sportin' rules. Gloves, seconds, an' proper rounds, in the gym, tomorrow. Right?'

'Right,' muttered Craddock.

'Right,' said Oliver, courageously.

The Dodger now decided to devote all the time available to him to preparing Oliver for the fight. Oliver's experience in the art of combat amounted to no experience at all; as the Dodger was to discover all too soon.

'Ain't you never learnt 'ow to fight?' he inquired, after he and Oliver had practised a few thrusts and parries in the schoolroom that evening.

'No,' Oliver replied.

'Well, 'ow 'ard can you 'it?'

'I don't know. I've never hit anyone.'

'Well, I'll be a monkey's uncle,' declared the Dodger, who had hit several people in his time. He thought for a while before saying: 'Look, Oliver – I only fixed up this fight to give us time to think. We can find a way out of it.'

'No,' retorted Oliver, firmly. 'Somebody has to stand up to Craddock; to show him we're not afraid of him.'

'All right,' said the Dodger, after further thought. '*I'll* fight him *for* you.'

'No, Jack,' said Oliver. 'Thanks, but it has to be me. Maybe you could beat him . . .'

'Course I could beat him!' the Dodger interposed.

'Yes,' said Oliver, 'but it wouldn't prove anything.'

''E'll *murder* you!' cried the Dodger.

'Oh don't you see?' said Oliver, with impatience, 'That's not important.'

'Ain't it?'

'No. It doesn't matter if I win.'

'Maybe not,' mused the Dodger, 'but it'd 'elp.'

Oliver's lack of expertise did not detract from his enthusiasm. His willingness to learn, under the Dodger's patient instruction, proved boundless. The Dodger, however, could barely conceal his concern as to the depressing certainty of the battle's outcome.

Most of the other Junior boys were equally despondent at the prospect of Oliver's defeat. Tommy Rice seemed the most downcast of all; but Shrimp did his best to cheer everyone:

'Good for Oliver! That's what I say!' he squeaked, brightly.

'*You* don't have to fight Craddock,' observed a boy, morosely.

'D'you think he'll be all right?' asked another, with anxiety.

'He *has* to be,' cried Shrimp. 'He's fighting for us all.'

'Well,' said a third boy, in a querulous tone, '*I'll* cheer for him anyway.'

The time appointed for the conflict was the next afternoon, when the day's lessons were concluded, and the Masters were at tea, thereby guaranteeing that there would be no interference from any figure of authority higher than Mr Bumble, who, for his part, had assured Craddock and Gurney that he would not intervene. Indeed, he had declared that he was very much looking forward to the fight, and would be an eager spectator. He had instructed Craddock, however, to ensure that it lasted for five or six rounds, so that it would have the appearance, at least, of being fair; 'Then *smash* 'im!' Bumble had added, with malicious glee.

Every single pupil in the academy had arrived at the school's gymnasium well before the chosen hour, so as to be certain of a good view of the battle. If some enterprising boy had decided to sell tickets for the fight, not one would have remained unsold, however high the price, and the seller would have emerged a rich and happy gentleman. A constant murmur of barely controlled excitement accompanied the preparations for the contest. A large space was cleared in the centre of the room, the opponents were stripped down to shirtsleeves and trousers, and gloves were donned as the seconds –

Gurney in Craddock's case, the Dodger in Oliver's – murmured words of encouragement.

'Make it last. Teach him a lesson!' Gurney whispered.

'I intend to,' declared Craddock.

Tommy Rice was standing close to Oliver in his corner, and now said softly, but anxiously: 'It's all my fault! You'll be hurt and it's all my fault!'

'Don't blame yourself, Pudding,' replied Oliver. 'It was bound to happen anyway. And don't worry – I'm not beaten yet.'

'That's the spirit, Killer,' muttered the Dodger, 'Now, remember, keep your 'ands up. And try to stay out of his reach. Wear 'im down.'

Farningham had been appointed referee and when he saw that the contestants were ready he called them both into the centre of the circle.

'Craddock says if you apologize in public and accept a whipping,' he announced, 'he'll be satisfied.'

'Never!' said Oliver, firmly.

'You're still determined?' said Farningham. 'Very well. Back to your corners; and come out fighting.'

The bully and his challenger returned to their corners briefly and Farningham rang a small handbell to signal the commencement of the battle. The two boys advanced towards each other, their fists raised. The Dodger raised his eyes to heaven in a moment's silent prayer.

'Come on, Oliver!' shouted Shrimp, only to be met by an anxious chorus of hushing sounds and a whisper of rebuke from Farningham: 'Keep the noise down, or you'll fetch the Porter!'

Unbeknown to all but Craddock and Gurney, of course, the Porter was already present, watching the proceedings from a dark balcony set high up in one of the walls of the gymnasium. He had a perfect view of the contest, for he did not need to conceal himself unduly, as all the eyes in the room were directed, like his, towards Craddock and Oliver.

The two boys circled each other for a good while before either of them struck a blow. It was immediately apparent, simply by the manner in which they moved, that Craddock was the more experienced fighter. Oliver, however, being the smaller and the lighter of the two managed to leap out of the way with considerable agility when Craddock swung his fist towards him at last; he then continued to dodge a series of attempted punches on the part of the bully.

'Stand and fight!' Craddock snarled.

'What's the matter, Twist?' hissed Gurney, 'Afraid, are you?' This remark was greeted by laughter from some of the Senior boys, which in its turn inspired Shrimp to call out again, as softly as his anxiety would permit: 'Come on, Oliver! Come on!' Craddock began to enjoy his opponent's evasive tactics, and embarked on a succession of quick jabs in Oliver's direction, making each jab fiercer than the last, and forcing his challenger back towards the edge of the ring of spectators.

'Get out there!' said a Senior boy.

'Coward!' Gurney whispered into Oliver's ear, and pushed him back towards the centre of the circle. Craddock grinned as Oliver continued to avoid his darting fist. Over a minute had passed, and Oliver had not yet made a single attempt to strike out at the bully. He became aware of growing and derisive laughter from the Senior boys, and of an accompanying anxious silence from the Juniors. He caught sight of his friend the Dodger, who was covering his face with his hands; a sight which was incitement enough for him to throw caution to the winds and commence an attack. He threw a wild punch at Craddock. With his long reach, Craddock succeeded in blocking it with great ease and took immediate advantage of Oliver's unguarded state by landing him a violent blow in the ribs. Oliver staggered back winded, and a gasp went up at the first hit of the match. In his concealed position, Mr Bumble delightedly struck the air with his fist. To everyone's considerable surprise, however, Oliver quickly recovered and resumed his attack with a flurry of desperate blows, but every lunge was easily parried by Craddock, who finally planted a perfect punch on the side of his opponent's head. Oliver sank to his knees, prompting a loud cry of mingled disappointment and pleasure from the spectators. In the growing excitement, the boys were forgetting to keep their voices down. As Oliver proceeded to rise, Craddock raised his fist, but Farningham prevented him from striking out by pushing him away and calling, 'Stand back! Stand back!'

Craddock backed off, reluctantly; only when Oliver was on his feet again, did Farningham allow the fight to continue. Craddock advanced once more. 'Keep your 'ands up!' the Dodger cried: this was a timely instruction, for Oliver was so dazed that he had forgotten to put up his fists for protection; in the nick of time he lifted his arms in front of his face and succeeded in blocking a deadly uppercut from Craddock. All the boys were shouting by now. 'Stay out of 'is reach!' bellowed the Dodger, and Oliver resumed his tactic of leaping out of the bully's way; but he was too exhausted to avoid being hit by a succession of short, sharp, vicious strokes. He tried to fight back as best he could in his battered state. A loud ring of Farningham's bell at this point did not quite save him from being knocked into unconsciousness, for Craddock appeared to want to ignore the sound and to continue his assault; he was stopped at last by the Dodger who ran into the ring shouting: 'End o' the round! End o' the round!', and pulled him away from Oliver. Craddock swaggered back to his corner, smiling at the acclamation of his supporters.

'Try to keep him on his feet a *little* longer,' said Gurney, with a grin.

Farningham approached the bully. 'I think I should stop it,' he suggested quietly.

'No you shan't!' snapped Craddock. 'He has this coming to him.'

Oliver was immediately surrounded by a number of

Junior boys, all of them openly concerned, with the exception of Shrimp, who squealed excitedly: 'You hit him! I never thought you could do it! You hit him – twice!' This was not of course true.

'Are you all right?' asked Tommy, anxiously.

'Not too bad,' Oliver panted, 'he didn't really hurt me.'

'No,' said the Dodger, 'he was only playing with you.' Oliver at first understood this remark to be in jest, but when he looked up and noted his friend's worried countenance, he saw that it had been meant as a serious statement of the truth; that was exactly what Craddock *had* been doing – merely playing. 'Look,' the Dodger now whispered desperately, 'you're goin' to get *mangled,* Oliver! The only thing to do is 'ave a real go at 'im. Make 'im finish it off quick!'

As the bell rang for the second round, and the spectators scattered back to their places, he continued: 'Get in there! Go for 'im.'

Oliver nodded determinedly and advanced towards Craddock. Mr Bumble was hugging himself in gleeful anticipation of the imminent slaughter. No effort was made to restrain the loud cries of encouragement from all sides, as the fighters began to circle each other once more. Craddock was supremely confident of victory; he allowed his opponent to weave and dodge for a few moments before striking out sharply and hitting Oliver in the stomach, knocking him back. A second still harder blow to the chest sent Oliver reeling towards the edge of the circle.

'That's the way!' cried Gurney exultantly. 'Show him Craddock!'

Craddock could not resist a slow turn and a grin in Gurney's direction. For no more than two seconds the bully allowed himself to drop his guard, but this was time enough for the Dodger to see that it was Oliver's only chance, and he barked: 'Oliver!' Needing no further encouragement, Oliver at once took advantage of

Craddock's momentary lapse of concentration. To the bully's understandable surprise, he now found himself the object of a wild, desperate assault. He had to raise his arms for protection, for his opponent had lost all concern for his own safety, and was swinging at him with a series of flailing punches. Some of the blows found their mark, but poor Oliver's reach was simply not long enough to do any damage. Craddock confidently brought the pummelling to an end by bringing up both his fists and knocking the boy's glove aside. As his arms circled back, however, his chin was left unprotected; only for the smallest fraction of a second admittedly, but that was, as it happened, all the time his challenger required to swing out his right fist and land a clean punch on the bully's jaw. Craddock took two steps backward and stared at Oliver in utter amazement; then, to Oliver's even greater amazement, and to the amazement of all who were gathered in the gymnasium at that moment, not least of all Mr Bumble, the bully's eyes took on a distant gaze and he crumpled to the floor, wholly unconscious.

There was a long moment of total and stupefied silence. Mr Bumble gaped from his balcony. Gurney opened and shut his mouth over and over again, noiselessly, failing to express his disbelief in words. Farningham hurried to kneel beside the prostrate Craddock, examined him for a second, then stared up incredulously at the assembled company. 'The fight's over,' he announced quietly. 'The winner is Twist . . . by a knock-out.'

An absolute pandemonium broke out at once. All the Junior boys rushed forward to surround the flabbergasted victor, cheering and shouting themselves hoarse with excitement. Some of the Senior boys came to offer their congratulations too.

'Well done, Killer,' said the Dodger with a wink and a grin as he removed Oliver's gloves. 'Knew you could do it.' Oliver, in his astonishment at what had occurred, could not reply. Very fortunately, everybody was too jubilant or dismayed to notice what the Artful Dodger did next. Carrying Oliver's gloves, he slipped unobserved to the outer edge of the crowd, and glanced about him briefly before putting his hand into one of the gloves, and extracting from its lining a small iron horseshoe, which had been concealed within it all this while. He quickly stuffed the incriminating object into his pocket; opportunely, as it happened, for no sooner had he hidden it than he heard Gurney shouting furiously: 'Let me see those gloves! Let me see them!'

The company fell silent. 'Show me the gloves you were wearing!' Gurney demanded.

''Ere they are,' said the Dodger, calmly, returning to the centre of the crowd and handing over the gloves for inspection. Gurney examined them eagerly, but naturally found nothing to imply that his friend had been knocked unconscious by any but the fairest of means.

'What's wrong, Gurney?' inquired Farningham.

'I just didn't . . . ,' Gurney muttered, staring at Oliver. 'I just didn't . . . didn't think it was possible.'

Oliver had by now recovered from the shock of winning and was flushed with success. He stepped towards Gurney hotly and said: 'If you're accusing me of something, perhaps *you* want a fight too.'

''Ere wait a mo', Oliver,' whispered the Dodger, suddenly worried. ''Old on, Oliver!' But he had no need to fear a resumption of hostilities, for Gurney was backing away with a terrified look in his eye.

'Keep him off me!' he squealed, 'I'm not a fist-fighter! I don't want to fight *him*!' With that single sorry plea, he brought his bullying days at Stalker's Academy to an end, for with his protector lying unconscious, and threatened with an assault from the boy who was now the school's hero, he had revealed himself to be what he really was and had always been: a consummate coward. The Junior boys wasted no time in subjecting him to a loud and lengthy outburst of jeers.

Nemesis, however, was at hand. Mr Bumble saw it first, and hurriedly backed into the shadows of his vantage point. Mr Stalker had entered the gymnasium. With his gown flying, he thrust his way through the crowd of boys, crying: 'What is this?' Is there to be no day without pandemonium?'

A hush descended instantly. Mr Stalker glared about him and at last saw Craddock at his feet. The bully was dazedly regaining consciousness and Farningham was helping him to sit up. 'Craddock?' inquired Mr Stalker. 'What has taken place? Is he all right?'

'He's coming round, sir,' Farningham explained. 'It was a fair fight.'

At the word 'fight,' Mr Stalker appeared to become positively apoplectic. 'Fight?' he bellowed, 'Is there such a thing as a fair fight? There is not! Fighting is an abomination! Ah, Mr Bumble! Why were you not here to prevent this fracas?'

The School Porter had apparently just arrived on the scene, and he explained between puffs, as he pushed his huge bulk through the boys: 'Just 'eard the commotion, 'Eadmaster – an' came at once.' He then stared about him in seeming astonishment and declared: 'What's this, what's this? Fisticuffs? What was it about? You!'

He directed this enquiry at Farningham, who replied: 'Twist challenged Craddock, sir.'

'Twist?' barked Mr Stalker. 'That abominable boy again? Twist, where are you?' Oliver stepped forward obediently, flushed and unhappy. 'You – you – you perpetual malefactor!' Stalker thundered.

'It *was* a fair fight, sir' the Dodger pleaded, in the hope of soliciting a degree, at least, of leniency.

'Is Pugilism not strictly forbidden? It is! Mr Bumble! Lock him up!'

Mr Bumble promptly grasped Oliver by the back of his neck; marching him at once from the gymnasium and towards the schoolroom.

'Do the rest of you think this is the end of it?' Mr

Stalker continued. 'It is not! One hundred lines from every boy in the school! And you, Craddock? Have you recovered?'

'Nearly, sir,' responded Craddock, who was now on his feet and nursing his jaw. 'I'll be fine in a minute.'

'Very good,' snapped Stalker, 'then take one thousand lines, since you are older and should know better.' The Headmaster swept from the gymnasium, leaving the bully speechless with indignation.

But let us reserve our sympathies for Oliver Twist who, within less than two days of being released from a wretched confinement in the schoolroom's broom cupboard, was about to have to endure a further period of imprisonment in the same dark place. This time, however, the length of his stay was not defined.

'An' you'll stay there,' growled Bumble, as he locked the door, 'till the 'Eadmaster decides otherwise!'

CHAPTER NINE

'Rose, my dear,' asked Harry Maylie, in a concerned tone, 'Is something wrong?' It was a Sunday evening in November. Cold winds were prevalent, but in the vicarage parlour all was sweet comfort and warmth. The good clergyman and his lovely wife were seated before a large log fire; he was reading, she was sewing. Glancing up briefly from his book, Harry Maylie had noticed that Rose was apparently unable to concentrate on the task before her and was staring into the flames that leapt happily beside her; her soft brow betrayed a touch of anxiety, thereby prompting the above inquiry.

'I was thinking about Oliver,' she now replied. 'I cannot understand why I have not heard from him.'

'It's only three weeks, surely?' said her husband.

'Nearly a month! And I know that Mr Brownlow has not heard from him either; even though I have written to tell Oliver that he is unwell, perhaps seriously.'

Harry Maylie leant forward and laid his hand gently on hers. 'You must remember the circumstances in which Oliver was brought up, my dear,' he explained. 'I am sure that neither in the Workhouse, nor in the clutches of that villain Fagin would he learn the social niceties of regular correspondence.'

'You cannot humour me out of it, Harry,' Rose responded, seeing him smile. 'I cannot believe that Oliver would ever be indifferent to his guardian's illness; nor to my letters, when I have begged for a reply.'

'And if you have begged,' said Harry, 'what more can you try?'

'I don't know. But I must do *something*!'

What Rose did that evening will be revealed in a very short while; for the moment, however, we must return to Stalker's Academy, for it would not be fair to leave

Oliver Twist for longer than necessary in his sorry predicament as a prisoner in the schoolroom's broom cupboard. He was kept there for four days, catching a brief glimpse of the world outside the cupboard only when his food was brought to him twice a day by Mr Bumble; this consisted merely of what was considered sufficient to keep a boy of his age alive and reasonably healthy; in other words, its sole components were bread and water. When Oliver was at last released, he was surprised to see the schoolroom empty apart from Mr Bumble, Mr Stalker, a concerned Mr Meikle and a lugubrious Mr Trent. Mr Stalker addressed him at once in the sternest of tones: 'You were expecting to find the entire Academy assembled to admire and applaud you, were you not, Twist? Would I give you such encouragement in your revolutionary crusade against Authority? I most certainly would not! Mr Meikle has spoken for you, and so has Mr Trent. Why, I cannot imagine. Or perhaps I can – could? No matter. Otherwise, you would not still be here. So, do I now say to you, watch your step? I do. One more breach of discipline and shall you be expelled? Sent home in disgrace? You most certainly shall. Do I make myself clear? Do I make myself clear, Twist?'

'Yes, sir,' replied Oliver, meekly.

'Good. Dismissed!'

Oliver was allowed to leave the schoolroom and almost immediately ran into his friend the Dodger, who appeared to be unusually excited; only that day he had, he announced, received a letter; something he had never received before in his life.

'Who from?' inquired Oliver.

'You'll never guess,' said the Dodger, 'Your Aunt Rose!'

'What does she say?' asked Oliver, puzzled.

The Dodger seemed momentarily embarrassed and glanced about him to check that he would not be overheard before declaring: 'Well . . . that's just it . . . I'm still not too clever at readin'. So I could only make out a word or two. There's somethin' about you, though, an' your guardian, 'im that's goin' to adopt you.' The Dodger then explained that the letter was upstairs in his bedside locker, and asked Oliver if he would accompany him there now, in order to read it to him.

When Oliver entered the Junior Dormitory, Tommy Rice and Shrimp were there, together with two other boys. They leapt from their beds to greet him, delighted that he had been freed.

'They let you out!' cried one of the boys.

'How are you? How was it?' asked Shrimp.

'Not too bad this time,' said Oliver, smiling bravely, 'I'm all right. A little bit hungry.'

'I saved you a piece of cake!' announced Tommy, hurrying to his locker.

'It was funny sitting in there, hearing you all have lessons,' said Oliver.

'I bet it was!' squeaked Shrimp.

'I'd have changed places with 'im gladly durin' Algebra,' exclaimed the Dodger, with a grin. The boys laughed as Tommy returned with a large wedge of sponge cake.

'Thanks, Pudding,' said Oliver, accepting the slice. 'So Craddock didn't take it from you this time?'

'That's just it!' said Pudding, 'We hardly see him anymore.'

'Ever since the fight,' said Shrimp, 'he's stopped bullying us!'

'And Gurney nearly faints if you just look at him,' rejoined Tommy. Once again the boys laughed, exuberantly.

'So it was worth it after all,' Oliver observed.

'Worth it?' squeaked Shrimp, 'The whole school's a different place!'

'All right,' the Dodger now interposed with impatience, 'save it for later. I want to talk to 'im.'

'But Jack...,' protested Tommy.

'Later,' said the Dodger, 'This is important.' He led Oliver to his bedside and opened his locker, extracting the letter. ''Ere!' he whispered, holding it to Oliver, 'read it.'

Oliver did so, to himself at first, and appeared immediately shaken by what he read.

'Well go on!' demanded the Dodger, 'What's it say?'

'Dear Master Dawkins,' Oliver read.

'That's me,' said the Dodger, grinning proudly.

'I take the liberty of writing to you, knowing that you are a school-fellow of my nephew Oliver.'

'That's you,' said the Dodger.

Oliver continued: 'Forgive me, if I ask you a favour. Would you entreat my nephew, most earnestly, to write to me – or, if not to me, at least to his guardian, Mr Brownlow.'

'Wot's the point o' that?'

'...'as neither of us have heard a word from him for some considerable time. Even though his guardian has written to him frequently, as so have I, to tell him of the worsening state of Mr Brownlow's illness. I would not ask you this, except that ...,' Oliver broke off and stared up at the Dodger, deeply upset. 'But I *have* written!' he protested, 'over and over! You know that!'

'That's the truth,' said the Dodger, 'An' you've waited an' waited for a letter from either o' *them*.'

The two boys sat thinking silently for several seconds. At last, with a snap of his fingers, the Dodger cried: 'That's it! Bumble! Bumble's the answer! Piggy in the middle. 'E collects all the letters from the school postbox to post them in the village – an' all the ones comin' in go to 'im first. 'E must've snitched both the ones you sent out, an' any that was sent to you.'

'But why?' asked Oliver, in bewilderment.

''E's got it in for you, that's plain enough,' said the Dodger. 'The kind o' thing 'is sort enjoy. Give 'em a little power an' they use it to cause upset an' misery.'

Oliver was wretched with helplessness. 'What can I do? She says Mr Brownlow's ill; very ill.' He returned to the letter and read: '"Even now a word from Oliver could cheer him – if it is not too late..."'

'Listen,' suggested the Dodger, 'you write to your Aunt an' *I'll* post it. Better still, we could post it in the village. You could send one to your guardian too.'

'"If it is not too late."' Oliver repeated. 'What's wrong with him? How can I find out?'

'Ask them to write back to me,' said the Dodger. 'It'll take a week maybe, but at least you'll 'ear from them.'

Oliver nodded, but was growing more visibly worried and miserable. 'You'll just 'ave to wait,' the Dodger announced, as comfortingly as he could; he saw, however, even then, that Oliver's deep concern at the news of his uncle's illness made waiting an impossible prospect.

Winter was approaching, and the night of Oliver's departure from Mr Stalker's Academical Establishment was a frosty, bitter one. The mist hung heavily on the fields that surrounded that isolated institution, and a thick blanket of low cloud prevented any moonlight from illuminating the dreary scene. But no degree of climatic inclemency could hinder Oliver in his avowed intention; which was to escape from the place under cover of darkness, while everyone was still asleep, and to embark on a journey to London.

The Artful Dodger awoke at first light. In his slumbers, he had lain facing Oliver's bed, and upon opening his eyes he saw at once that it was empty. He immediately considered rising and setting off in pursuit of his friend, but soon reached the conclusion that Oliver was almost certainly a good many miles away already, and that even if he did catch up with him, no amount of hard persuasion would succeed in making him retrace his steps; so the Dodger merely turned over onto his back, and lay staring at the dormitory ceiling, wakeful and troubled.

Oliver was indeed several miles away by then, tired and hungry, but walking determinedly on across the damp fields, as the cold air sharpened with the approach of morning.

CHAPTER TEN

Three days later, on a more charitable morning, Oliver was fast asleep in the back of a cart that was travelling down a country road towards London. The driver of the cart, a genial pleasant-faced gentleman, had seen him lying exhausted and hungry by the roadside on the previous night. He had fed the boy with what nourishment he was able to provide, and, having heard the reasons for his eagerness to get to London, had taken pity on him and told him to snatch what rest he could amidst the cart's cargo of bundles, barrels and boxes, as it continued on its journey. Thoroughly grateful, Oliver had quickly fallen into a deep slumber.

He was now awoken, after a good eight hours' sleep, by the carter's kind voice and the realization that the cart had come to a halt. 'This is where I have to set ye down, young master,' said the carter.

'Are we at London?' Oliver inquired, sitting up and looking about him; he saw only the open countryside, fresh under a bright winter sun.

'Not quite, no,' replied the carter, with a chuckle. 'The closest I come, though.' He pointed to a fork in the road ahead of them. 'I turn this way,' he said, 'an' that's the Barnet road. You put a stout foot forward, an ye'll be home before night.'

'Thank you, sir, thank you very much,' said Oliver, relieved and heartened, and he climbed from the assortment of objects that had been his place of rest and jumped down onto the road.

'Bless you, but no need for thanks,' the carter responded. 'I 'ope your father's better when ye find him.' He clicked his teeth, flicked the reins of his horse, and set off down the left-hand fork.

'Thank you, sir!' Oliver called after him again. The

carter did not turn, but merely waved a hand in farewell, as he travelled on. Oliver watched him go for a few seconds, then commenced his own determined journey down the Barnet road, refreshed from his rest. He must have seemed a curious spectacle, for he was still dressed in his school clothes, which were now torn and dusty.

As he walked, memories were revived; for it was down this road that he had tramped on his very first journey to London, some five or so years previously. As he reached the town of Barnet, he remembered how he had once gazed in wonder at the number of taverns in this place, and at the innumerable busy coaches passing through; he also recollected that it was here, whilst wondering, that he had first encountered the Artful Dodger; and now he began to consider how that same personage would be reacting to his disappearance from Mr Stalker's Academy. But Oliver's cogitations did not prevent him, even for a second, from hastening onwards towards his intended destination. He had reached Barnet by the early afternoon, and the evening was rapidly advancing by the time he reached the turnpike at Islington and turned right into Pentonville.

He was again tired, and again very hungry, when he at last arrived at the street in which Mr Brownlow resided. He was thoroughly happy, nonetheless, that his travels were over, and he pulled eagerly at his guardian's door-bell, smiling with relief. After a moment, the door was opened by a creature who drove all joy from his heart in an instant.

'Noah!' Oliver gasped.

'Well, well, now,' exclaimed Noah Claypole, with equal surprise; he then smiled unctuously and declared: 'Wot a sight for sore eyes!'

Before Oliver could say anything further, he felt himself being pulled roughly into the house and marched into Mr Brownlow's sitting room.

'Mrs Carraway,' announced Claypole to the lady who

was seated there, 'we 'ave an unexpected visitor.'

Oliver glanced hurriedly about the room for some sign of his guardian; but there was none. Mrs Carraway rose quickly and approached him. 'Oliver?' she said. 'What are you doing here?'

'I came to see my father,' replied Oliver.

'Came? You were not sent for?' Mrs Carraway seemed mildly alarmed.

'I heard from my aunt that he was unwell,' said Oliver. 'Where is he?'

'He is resting,' Mrs Carraway replied, quickly.

'I must see him,' declared Oliver, turning to the door.

'Out of the question,' snapped the lady. Oliver felt Noah's grasp tighten round his arm. 'I can only presume,' Mrs Carraway continued, more quietly, 'that your aunt did not inform you that Mr Brownlow's illness was partly caused by reports of your appalling conduct at school. In the circumstances . . .'

'Who could have told him about that?' Oliver interposed, in a shocked tone. 'It's all untrue.'

'I am relieved to hear it,' remarked Mrs Carraway.

'I didn't even get any of his letters,' Oliver protested. 'I must go to him and explain!' Once again he turned to the door and once again Claypole's grip grew tighter.

'He is far too ill to be disturbed,' said Mrs Carraway, with sharp authority, 'I shall take you up to him later; but first he must be prepared for the shock of seeing you. I am surprised your Headmaster did not write to warn us of your arrival.'

'I didn't tell him I was coming,' said Oliver.

'So you left without his permission?'

'Yes.'

'Indeed,' said Mrs Carraway, severely, 'it does not inspire me with much confidence in anything else you have said. Take Master Oliver to the kitchen, Bolter. He may have something to eat – once he has washed. Then report back to me.'

'Wery good, ma'am; as you wish, ma'am,' said Claypole, with an ironic bow. 'Come along then, Master Oliver.' He smiled evilly at the boy and pushed him out of the room.

Oliver was to encounter yet another familiar figure from the past as he and Noah entered the kitchen; for at the kitchen table, her head resting on one hand, with a dark green round-bellied bottle of spirits and an empty glass before her, sat Noah Claypole's faithful companion Charlotte. She was, Oliver noticed at once, a little the worse for an excess of drink, and barely stirred at their arrival.

'Charlotte, my dear . . . ,' said Noah.

'Gerraway,' mumbled Charlotte, without turning. 'Why'nt yer lerra body sleep?'

'We 'ave company, my love!' declared Noah, sharply. Charlotte deigned to turn then, and her eyes took some time to find or to focus upon any new arrival in the room. When they did, however, they opened wide with surprise.

'No, yer ain't mistook,' said Noah. 'It's our werry own little Oliver, come back to us.'

'Well I never!' exclaimed Charlotte.

'I'm sure yer reckerlect my dear Charlotte, don't yer . . . "Master Oliver",' said Noah.

'*Master* Oliver!' Charlotte echoed, with a giggle.

'Yes,' said Oliver, unable to conceal his distaste at the sight of the slatternly creature before him, 'I remember.'

'I'll never forget the day,' Charlotte now announced, 'I'll never forget the day Mr Bumble brought yer from the Work'ouse to Mr Sowerberry's the undertaker.'

'Pale an' shiverin' like a little, frost-nipped radish, 'e was,' said Noah.

Charlotte continued her recollection: '"Wot d'yer need another 'prentice for?" Mrs Sowerberry asked. "He'll make a perfect mute," old Sowerberry said, "most melancholic at children's funerals." "At least 'e won't eat much," she said.'

Both Noah and Charlotte found the memory exceptionally amusing, and embarked on a lengthy session of highly raucous laughter.

'An' now look at 'im,' Charlotte continued, when she had managed to control her mirth to an extent, 'all dressed up like a proper gentleman.'

'A gentleman of eddication, Charlotte,' declared Noah, ''Cept 'e's done a bunk an' run away from school.'

'Whyever did 'e do that?' inquired Charlotte.

'I want to see my father,' said Oliver.

'Yer father?' retorted Charlotte, blankly.

''E means Mr Brownlow,' Claypole explained. This occasioned a further outburst of wild amusement.

'Where are the maid, Dinah, and William, and Mrs Noakes, the cook?' Oliver asked, with rising impatience.

'Gone. Packed off,' replied Claypole.

'But they've been with Mr Brownlow for years!' protested Oliver. 'He'd never dismiss them.'

'Ah, but Mrs Carraway's 'ousekeeper now,' announced Claypole, 'an' she didn't see no point in keepin' them – not with Charlotte an' me willin' to take over.' He then turned to Charlotte and said: 'Now, my love, you get "Master" Oliver some pickles an' a nice slice o' that cold brisket we 'ad for luncheon while I pops up for a word wiv Mrs C.'

'When can I see Mr Brownlow?' Oliver demanded, crossly.

'Not up to me, is it?' retorted Claypole. 'Now, mind yer stay 'ere, nice an' quiet.' There was a threatening look in his eye as he said this; and then he left the room. Oliver was too tired and hungry to be anything but thoroughly confused by the changes that appeared to have taken place in his guardian's home, and he sank exhaustedly into a chair.

Charlotte set about preparing a platter of cold meat for the boy, giggling as she did so. 'We wus jus' wonderin' 'ow you was gettin' on,' she murmured. 'Not a word of a lie. Noah was jus' talkin' about you. An' you run away from school to come back to us . . . Well, I never.'

Twist's disappearance from school naturally aroused a particularly fine frenzy in the extremely irascible Mr Stalker. As soon as the boy's absence was discovered, stern inquiries were made amongst those of his friends who might know of his whereabouts. Receiving no enlightenment from that quarter, Mr Stalker then sent out a number of parties to comb the surrounding countryside for any sign of the absconding pupil. Every boy in the academy was involved in this search, which was organized by Mr Bumble, and which lasted for three whole days. Lessons were suspended for the purpose. At last, on the morning of the fourth day, Mr Stalker decided to accept that the quest was fruitless, and to resume the education of his young gentlemen. He did not allow the day's teaching to begin, however, until he had given full vent to his fury in front of the entire school.

'Twist!' he bellowed, gazing at the assembled ranks before him. 'Can I ever again speak that name without emotion – without a shiver of revulsion? Never in the history of this Academical Establishment has there been such a wolf in sheep's apparel. A wolf? Nay, a tiger in lamb's wool! Was I not warned repeatedly against him by Mr Bumble?'–Mr Bumble nodded most complacently – 'I was! Has he not proved his evil nature by slipping away like a thief in the night? He has! In the entire history of Stalker's Academy has such a thing ever happened before? Most emphatically not! Have we not searched for him for three days without avail? And shall I tell you why I was so eager to retrieve him?' This was an interesting question, and everyone in the room breathlessly awaited the answer, which duly arrived: 'So that I might have the pleasure of expelling him, myself! And do I do so now, in absentia, as a warning to others? I most certainly do!'

This speech was followed by a slow, burning glare which included every boy in the schoolroom; then Mr Stalker left, his gown flying, followed by the lugubrious Mr Trent, whose countenance revealed nothing but a blank indifference to everything, as always. Mr Bumble was about to begin the task of issuing the school's mail, prior to the commencement of lessons, when Tommy Rice and Shrimp approached him tentatively.

'Mr Bumble, sir,' said Tommy, nervously.

'Yes? What is it?' snapped Bumble, with irritation.

'Does it mean that Oliver can't come back?' asked Tommy.

'Yes,' replied Bumble, sharply.

'Not ever?' asked Shrimp.

'You 'eard the 'eadmaster,' said Bumble. 'He 'as pronounced 'is hirrevocable judgement. Twist 'as been expelled – as a hevil hinfluence.'

'But Oliver isn't evil!' Tommy protested.

'Hevil is as hevil does, Master Rice,' announced Bumble, authoritatively. 'Particularly if the 'eadmaster an' myself say so. Twist's name is never to be mentioned again inside the Academy. An' since you seem so determined to defend 'im, Master Rice, *and* Master Shrimpton, I shall be keepin' my custodial eye afixed on both o' you from now on. So beware . . .' whereupon he waddled majestically to the main desk to proceed with the handing out of the post.

'Did you hear, Dawkins?' whispered Tommy to the Dodger, as Bumble began to call out the names on the letters and packages he was holding. The Dodger nodded.

'Isn't there anything we can do?' asked Shrimp, softly.

'Oliver made up 'is own mind,' said the Dodger, after a pause. 'He'll 'ave to take care of 'imself.'

'But shouldn't we try to follow him?' asked Tommy.

'An' get expelled, too?' retorted the Dodger. 'Wot good would that do? We'll 'ave enough trouble keepin' Bumble from stampin' on us. Oliver'll be all right.' He was not at all certain, however, that he meant what he said, for he had great fears for Oliver's safety in London, if indeed he had reached London at all.

These sad musings were passing through the Dodger's mind on the morning when his friend reached the outskirts of the metropolis. We must now rejoin Oliver on the evening of that same day; several hours had passed since his arrival at his guardian's house, but he was still sitting in the kitchen under the watchful eye of Charlotte, for Noah Claypole had expressly forbidden her to allow the boy out of her sight. Few words had passed between either of them during the time that they had both been there. Oliver had eaten the food that had been provided for him, and now sat morosely watching the cooking range; he felt exceptionally tired. Occasionally he would turn to look at his keeper, who was pouring herself glass after glass of a very evil-smelling liquid from the dark green bottle that stood before her on the table.

'I'm really very tired, Charlotte,' said Oliver at last. 'Can't I go up to my room?'

'Which one's . . . which . . . which one's that?' mumbled Charlotte, pronouncing her words with some difficulty.

'On the second floor,' replied Oliver, 'the little one at the back.'

Charlotte emitted a low gurgle of mirth. 'Oh, no,' she said, 'oh no, yer can't . . . yer can't go up there, 'cos . . . 'cos that where 'e is.'

'Who?'

'The old geezer . . . whassisname . . . Brownlow. 'Im yer call yer farver.'

'But why . . . why isn't he in his old room?' asked Oliver, in sudden astonishment.

Charlotte poured another glass and tittered quietly before saying: 'Don't make much difference to 'im where 'e is. Not no more.'

Oliver was so shocked by this announcement that he

forgot his exhaustion in an instant. 'How ill is he really?' he now demanded. 'Why won't anyone tell me?'

Charlotte drained her glass in one gulp, and yawned, leaning her head on her hand. 'Don't . . . don't take on so, love,' she mumbled.

'Why can't I see him?' said Oliver, 'Does he even know I'm here?'

'Won't do no good gettin' worked up,' retorted Charlotte, almost inaudibly. 'You'll see 'im when it's time. Now, be a good boy an' sit quiet – like Noah said.' Whereupon she lowered her head towards the table and laid it on her folded arms.

Some minutes elapsed before Oliver realized that the drunken woman was sound asleep; or certainly seemed so. After a long moment of watching her for the smallest indication of wakefulness, he rose slowly from his chair and moved softly to the dresser, eyeing her still form all the while. He took up a candle that was providing the room's only light and crept carefully towards the door. Raising the latch, he gave her one final glance, and, concluding that she was truly dead to the world, he slipped from the kitchen.

The house was ominously silent as Oliver stealthily ascended the two flights of stairs that led to his old bedroom, holding the candle in one hand and shielding its light with the other. He stopped occasionally, listening for the slightest sound, expecting to be apprehended at any moment. At last he reached the room in which he had once spent so many happy days. He paused for some while before entering, for he had no idea of what to expect inside. Eventually he slowly turned the handle of the door and went in.

The homely little chamber was lit only by a single lamp beside the bed, turned to its lowest level of illumination. In the bed lay Mr Brownlow; or someone at least, who bore a faint resemblance to that kind old gentleman, for he appeared to be so frail and thin and white that the boy could barely recognize him at first, as he lay there, so frighteningly still, with his eyes closed. Oliver set down his candle on a table by the door and approached his guardian. He had seen many dead people in his time, during his days at the Workhouse, and more particularly while he was an apprentice to Mr Sowerberry the undertaker; he now reached the conclusion that Mr Brownlow might well be dead, or if not absolutely so, as near to death as made very little difference. Gently, the boy knelt beside his guardian and tremblingly touched one of his hands, which lay outside the covers of the bed. 'Father . . .' he whispered, lovingly.

He did not begin to hope for a reply; but to his understandable joy Mr Brownlow now opened his eyes, weakly, and muttered with a soft smile: 'My boy . . . My boy . . . you've come back to me.'

'Oh, Father . . . ,' Oliver repeated, and could say nothing more for a long while. At last, however, he continued: 'I'd have come sooner, Father. At once, only your letters were stolen. And mine . . .'

'No matter, no matter,' murmured Mr Brownlow. 'No matter. You're here.' Oliver felt his hand being gripped tightly; or with all the strength that his guardian could summon in his frailty. 'Grimwig . . . ' Mr Brownlow began, with great effort, 'Grimwig . . . Mr Grimwig . . .'

'What, Father?' said Oliver, with concern. 'What?' Is there something you want to tell me?'

A sharp shrill female voice broke the stillness of the scene. 'What is the meaning of this?' it demanded.

Oliver turned to see Mrs Carraway standing in the door, sharply outlined against the light from a lamp held by Noah Claypole, who was lurking behind her.

'Is this how you obey my orders?' snapped Mrs Carraway, in open fury.

'I just wanted to talk to my father,' Oliver explained, releasing his guardian's hand and rising from beside the bed.

'Even if it meant endangering his life? See! You have exhausted him!'

Oliver glanced at Mr Brownlow who, with flickering eyes, did indeed appear to be considerably more restless than he had been previously; he was struggling for breath.

'He was trying to tell me something,' said Oliver.

'How disappointed he is in you, no doubt,' retorted Mrs Carraway. 'I told you he was not to be agitated, under any circumstances. Take this boy back to the kitchen, Bolter.' She stepped aside and Claypole came forward obediently.

'But he was pleased to see me!' Oliver protested.

'Come long, Master Oliver,' said Claypole, with a certain pretence at deference, presumably for the benefit of the old gentleman on the bed.

'I won't disturb him, I'll just sit quietly and . . .'

'I said come on, young 'un,' snarled Claypole, dropping all signs of servility in an instant and grabbing hold of the boy's arm. He dragged him, struggling, into the passage. Before Oliver could cast one final glance in Mr Brownlow's direction, the door had been shut firmly behind him. As he was pushed roughly down the stairs, he gave serious consideration to the possibility of never seeing his kind old protector again.

Charlotte was very much awake when Oliver re-entered the kitchen with Noah, and, upon seeing him, she launched into an immediate diatribe of offended abuse. 'Of all the ingrates!' the woman cried, pacing up and down the room. 'Of all the . . . After I fed yer and treated yer nice. Sneakin' out when a body's back is turned!'

'Yer can stow that!' interposed Claypole, hotly. 'I'll be speakin' to yer later, my dear. An' so, no doubt, will Mrs C.'

The prospect of the harsh vengeance that Mrs Carraway would wreak upon her for her negligence quickly silenced Charlotte and she subsided into her chair, sulkily resentful.

'You can't stop me seeing my father!' exclaimed Oliver.

'Yer wot?' snorted Claypole. ''E ain't yer father; not yet, not by a long chalk, *Work'ouse.*'

At this last word, Oliver stared in horror at his tormentor; he recollected at once that this was the name with which Claypole had invariably addressed him when they had both worked at Mr Sowerberry's. 'Yeah,' continued Noah, with a vicious sneer. 'Remember that. Work'ouse born an' work'ouse bred, an' that's where you'll end up.' Oliver turned and tried to make for the door, but was pulled back sharply: 'Jus' where d'yer think yer goin', Work'ouse?' Claypole barked. 'I'll tell yer where – nowhere! Since yer can't be trusted, yer'll stay 'ere – locked in!' whereupon he dragged the struggling boy towards another door, which he opened. 'An' sleep in the cellar with the cockroaches!' he yelled, thrusting Oliver through the door and down a short flight of damp steps into utter darkness. As the boy landed on the cold stone floor of the cellar, he heard the door slam quickly shut. He saw nothing but blackness, and heard nothing but silence. He was too exhausted even to weep.

That same night, there were considerable festivities in the private room of the Three Cripples tavern, Saffron Hill. The assorted petty vagabonds now under Noah Claypole's charge were celebrating a day of highly successful thieving. Most of the members of this tattered, villainous collection had previously worked for Fagin; they now often reflected upon how much more luxurious life was under their new master, Morris Bolter. Ned Fingers had by this time firmly established himself as Mr Bolter's deputy; and whenever the great man himself was absent, as he was on this occasion, the little thief would exercise a swaggering authority over all proceedings, as if he himself was the leader of the finest gang of criminals in the world.

'Another drop o' gin, gen'lemen,' he now exclaimed, 'on Mr Bolter's slate!' The villains surrounding him chuckled. 'More than we'd ever 'ave got of old Fagin!' Fingers added, as he rose to summon the landlord. There were murmurs of cheerful agreement.

At this point, the famous Morris Bolter himself appeared in the doorway. 'Wot's goin' on?' he demanded savagely, surveying the revelry before him. The effect of this inquiry was to quell all signs of jubilation at a stroke. Morris Bolter's followers may have preferred him to Fagin, but they were nonetheless frightened of him, especially when his mood was not at its best, as it unquestionably was not at that moment.

Ned Fingers also underwent a sudden change of character. 'A little celebration, Mr Bolter,' he now said nervously, 'seein' as 'ow it's been such a good day for pickin's.'

Noah Claypole, alias Morris Bolter, affected to ignore the large canvas bag on the table, filled to the brim though it clearly was with stolen objects of various kinds, and continued to glare angrily at the company. Under the force of his gaze, the villains set down their glasses and rose; one by one, they proceeded to slink out of the room past their commander and his lieutenant. Fingers was about to follow them, but Claypole snapped: 'Not you, yer slimy little toad!' Poor Ned Fingers had no alternative but to remain where he was. Claypole shut the door behind the last of the thieves.

Fingers looked up at his master anxiously; then, in an effort to rid him of his black look, ran to the bag on the table, and declared eagerly: 'Oh my life, Mr Bolter! Look! One o' the best days yet! Fobs an' tickers an' . . . wallets an' . . .'

'I'll look them over later,' Claypole interrupted sternly. 'Where is 'e?'

Fingers knew at once who it was who was being referred to: 'I couldn't find 'im, Mr Bolter,' he replied. Morris Bolter took a threatening step towards him; Fingers darted behind the table for protection and pleaded: 'Straight! 'E's 'opped it – gone out o' town!'

'Where to?' asked Claypole.

'Oo knows?' responded Fingers. ''E never tells nobody nothin' – not Monks. Gone off to the country, they say.'

'Well ain't that rich,' observed Claypole, after a troubled pause. 'Jus' when there's a problem. Jus' when 'e's needed for once.'

'A problem, Mr Bolter?' inquired Fingers interestedly.

'None of yer business!' snapped Claypole, before attempting to assume a less agitated manner. 'Nothing much,' he said, as calmly as he could.

'I'll wait tell 'e gets back,' suggested Fingers, craftily, 'tell 'im somethin's come up.'

'Yer'll do nothing o' the kind!' retorted Claypole. His mind was racing as he mused: 'Wot 'e don't know won't 'urt 'im. Maybe *I'll* 'ave took care of it – by the time 'e gets back.' Then, to Fingers' bewildered surprise, and relief, all traces of anxiety left his countenance in an instant. He grinned: 'Right, Fingers,' he said. 'Let's 'ave a look at the stuff.'

Fingers proceeded to lay the day's treasures out on the table; it was a fine haul indeed, but if the crown jewels themselves had been displayed before Claypole at that moment, he would barely have registered the fact; for he was concentrating on other matters; most particularly, on what benefits he might accrue from the apparent disappearance of Monks.

CHAPTER ELEVEN

The next morning Mr Brownlow's doctor, a gaunt but amiable personage named Hyssop, who was highly regarded in the town, called upon his patient. He had not examined Mr Brownlow for some days, and was now immediately troubled by an obvious further deterioration in the old gentleman's health. Ushering the doctor downstairs and into the sitting room, Mrs Carraway explained that this decline was almost certainly the result of a very great shock Mr Brownlow had received on the previous night; he had been disturbed by the sudden arrival at his bedside of his ward Oliver, who had thoughtlessly disobeyed her firm instructions not to agitate him in the slightest way; but then Oliver was an uncaring and mutinous boy, she said.

'And where is the boy now?' inquired Dr Hyssop.

'I have had him confined to the kitchen,' replied Mrs Carraway.

'Will he continue to try to contact his guardian?' the doctor asked.

'He won't succeed,' said Claypole, who was present. 'Not with the doors locked.'

There was a degree of savagery in Noah's voice as he announced this, and the physician stared at him with some distaste and concern. The doctor's musings were suddenly interrupted by the sound of the front doorbell being rung in a very violent fashion.

'Was you expectin' anyone?' said Claypole to Mrs Carraway.

'No,' replied the lady, who seemed suddenly anxious. After some thought, she said: 'Very well. Answer the door. I am not at home.'

Claypole appeared to resent the curtness of this command, and left the room sulkily as the doorbell rang impatiently once more. Not many seconds had passed before raised voices began to emanate from the direction of the hall; one of these voices sounded especially choleric. 'Out of my way, sir, d'ye hear?' it barked, 'I will not be put off! Stand aside at once!' Moments later, the owner of the voice had marched into the room; a stout, cantankerous old gentleman in a blue coat, nankeen breeches, and gaiters. He was brandishing a thick stick, and immediately demanded: 'Where is he? Where is Mr Brownlow?'

'I couldn't keep 'im out,' explained Claypole, following him in nervously.

'Ah, Mrs Carraway!' exclaimed the newcomer. 'This impertinent jackanapes told me no-one was at home!'

'On my instructions, sir,' responded Mrs Carraway, coolly.

'And why so, madam?' growled the gentleman. 'When before have I been denied entrance to my old friend's house? Not once – or I'll eat my head!' Whereupon he rapped his wig with sufficient vehemence to make Claypole rear back from the explosion of powder. 'I have come to see Mr Brownlow!' the furious old man announced.

'I regret that it is not possible, Mr Grimwig,' said Mrs Carraway, retaining her calm exterior with some difficulty. 'He is too ill.'

'And that,' remarked Mr Grimwig, 'is the only information I have been given for weeks! This time, I refuse to budge until I have been told more of the details!' And he sat himself determinedly down upon a chair before the fireplace.

A silence ensued. 'Then,' said Mrs Carraway at last, 'it is perhaps fortunate you arrived now, Mr Grimwig. This is Mr Brownlow's physician, Dr Hyssop.'

Mr Grimwig cocked his large head to one side and surveyed the physician out of the corner of his eye, suspiciously. 'Hyssop?' he said. 'Hyssop? I believe I have heard of you.'

'I am gratified, sir,' responded the doctor, with a bow. 'I have been treating Mr Brownlow for some time, for general tiredness and loss of energy.'

'Yes,' remarked Grimwig. 'I'd noticed the tiredness.'

'Quite so,' said the doctor. 'Unfortunately, it turned out to be the symptom of a very serious kidney condition, affecting the circulation of the blood and the brain with resulting impurities.'

Mr Grimwig's expression of scepticism changed rapidly into one of genuine worry and compassion. He stared into the fireplace. 'My poor old friend . . . ,' he murmured.

'Above all,' continued Hyssop, 'he needs complete rest and constant attention, positively no agitation.'

'Yes, yes, I see,' muttered Grimwig, and appeared thoughtful for a while. 'Now,' he said, 'tell me frankly. What are his chances of recovery?'

'I shall do my best, sir,' replied Hyssop. 'But we must brace ourselves. They are very slim.' Again there was a despondent pause.

'And now,' said the doctor, 'if you will excuse me. I should return to my patient.'

'Yes, yes, of course,' said Grimwig softly. 'If you find a convenient moment, do give him my – regards.'

'Certainly, sir,' replied the doctor, and bowed again.

'Bolter will take you up,' said Mrs Carraway.

When Dr Hyssop and Noah Claypole had left the room, Mr Grimwig gazed wretchedly at the fireplace for some time before muttering: 'My apologies, ma'am. I had no idea it was so serious. I suppose I am the one who should write to inform young Oliver?'

'To inform him?' said Mrs Carraway.

'He must be told,' said Grimwig.

'He has been, sir. And sadly, he has shown complete indifference.'

'Indifference?'

'Worse than that,' replied Mrs Carraway. 'Hearing of his guardian's collapse, he reverted to his true colours and disappeared from school, to return to a life of crime.'

'You . . . you don't say so, ma'am,' declared Grimwig, in utter astonishment.

'Most regrettably it is true,' said Mrs Carraway, calmly.

A further silence followed, yet more morose than the last. 'Upon my soul,' sighed the old gentleman, 'I never heard anything that caused me such a heavy heart - or I'll eat my head.' He tapped the ground with his stick in a most melancholy manner.

A minute or so later, Oliver Twist, sitting dejectedly in the kitchen that was his prison, heard the front door slam upstairs. He glanced up. Charlotte was stirring a large pot of soup at the range, with her back to him. He rose cautiously and moved to the barred kitchen window, which looked out upon a grey area below the level of the street. By leaning forward over a broad sink that stood before the window, and craning his neck to look upwards, Oliver could just discern whoever might be coming in or out of the house by the main entrance. His eyes widened as he saw that the person in question, on this particular occasion, was Mr Brownlow's old friend Grimwig, who appeared to be in a state of mournful contemplation, as he paused beside the railings above the window. Oliver immediately forgot all concern for his own safety and proceeded to wave frantically in an effort to catch the old man's attention. Failing to attract any notice by this means, he then began to call out: 'Mr Grimwig! Mr Grimwig, sir! It's Oliver. I'm down here! Here, Mr Grimwig! Help! Mr Grim . . .'

He was silenced by a hand clapped firmly over his mouth. 'Shut yer gob, yer sneaky little devil,' hissed Claypole, who had just entered the kitchen and now dragged the flailing boy away from the window. Charlotte had come running forward too, and helped Noah push Oliver sharply back into his chair.

'Yer 'ave to 'ave eyes in the back o' yer 'ead for this one!' declared Charlotte.

'Don't try that again, Work'ouse,' snapped Claypole,

'or ye'll spend all day in the cellar! Hear me, Work'ouse? There ain't nobody goin' to 'elp you! Not nobody! Never!'

Oliver gazed up at his tormentors for a few seconds, then lowered his eyes, robbed of hope. For his part, Mr Grimwig was too deeply lost in his own sorry cogitations to have seen or heard anything. He sighed lugubriously, and set off down the street.

The schoolroom of Mr Stalker's Academy was at the end of a long straight corridor, at the other end of which was the main entrance to the school. Beside this entrance, appropriately enough, was the Porter's lodge. Between these two extremities, at various intervals along the corridor, were a number of doors of different shapes and sizes; the most obviously important of these because the largest and the most ornate, was the door to Mr Stalker's study. One afternoon, about a fortnight before the end of the term, the Artful Dodger was walking pensively down the corridor, having just emerged from the schoolroom. He had been sitting alone in that room for some time after the conclusion of the day's lessons, wondering in his solitude about the fate of his friend Oliver Twist. He was still sunk in thought as he ambled along the corridor towards the Porter's lodge, and as a result he almost collided with someone who was walking in the opposite direction.

'Oh, sorry,' said the Dodger, looking up. He found himself gazing briefly into the half-hidden face of someone he thought he recognized; a narrow-faced, fashionably dressed gentleman in a tall hat and cape, the collar of which was turned up to conceal the lower half of his visage. He was carrying a silver-topped cane.

'Look where you're going, young man,' said the stranger, flatly, as he strode on without a backward glance.

The Dodger was instantly alert. He turned to look at

the man who was walking away from him. The gait was unmistakable; that cane could have belonged to no-one else; the voice had been the final confirmation. The Dodger began to follow the man, but stopped when he saw Mr Stalker emerge from his study. The visitor raised his hat politely to the Headmaster. Mr Stalker appeared to hesitate for a moment before nodding and ushering him in, closing the door behind him. The Dodger hurried forward and, reaching the door, he put his ear to it in the hope that he might be able to listen to whatever strange conversation the two men were about to have; but the door, as well as being large and ornate, was very thick, and he could hear nothing. He was deeply troubled. As was his custom when anxious, and when alone, he took a small flask from his hip pocket and uncorked it. He was about to take a ruminative sip when a heavy hand fell on his shoulder, startling him. It belonged to the School Porter.

'Wot's this, wot's this?' said Bumble. 'You knows the rules, I presume, Dawkins?'

'I was just . . . er . . . ,' began the Dodger.

'Breakin' them,' declared Bumble, snatching the flask from his hand. 'Spiritous liquors not allowed to members of the Junior School. I shall confiscate this 'ere flask – an' think yerself lucky I don't report you to the 'eadmaster.' Whereupon he gave the offending flask an openly appreciative sniff, recorked it, and waddled pompously down the corridor towards his lodge. The Dodger gave his retreating back the benefit of a dismissive sneer, and turned again to the door. He tried to listen once more to whatever might be being said behind it, but he could still hear nothing.

If the door had not been quite so infuriatingly impenetrable to the ear, this is what the Dodger would have heard.

'You wish to enrol perhaps a youthful relative here?

A son perhaps?' inquired Mr Stalker, uncertainly.

'No, Mr Stalker,' replied the stranger softly. 'I come to enquire about my younger brother.'

'A brother? Did you mention your name, sir?'

'I did, sir. It is Monks.'

'Monks? Should it strike a reverberating chord? It does not. We once had a Bishop.'

Monks did his best to remain patient. 'I should explain,' he said, 'that I am making enquiries about my *half* brother, Oliver Twist.'

If the name Monks had not produced an especially powerful reaction in the Headmaster, and there was no reason why it should have done, the name Twist most assuredly now did. 'Twist?' he exclaimed, stiffening. 'Twist! If you have come to beg me to take him back, sir, do I refuse? I most certainly do!'

'Take him back?' echoed Monks, in bewilderment.

'Do you affect not to know that he has run away, after causing more disruption than any single boy has ever done before?'

There was a pause. 'You'll excuse me,' said Monks, 'did you say, "run away"?'

'Gone!' retorted Stalker. 'Vanished! Run off! Much as it grieves me to tell you. *Does* it grieve me? Not a whit!'

The mysterious gentleman's already white visage, or that part of it which Mr Stalker could discern behind the collar of his black cloak, appeared to turn still whiter. 'Then . . . forgive me, sir,' he muttered 'my journey has been unnecessary.'

'If you came to beseech me to pardon him . . . ,' Mr Stalker began.

'On the contrary,' interposed Monks, 'I came to warn you,' Mr Stalker stared at him as he continued, in a tone of apparent reluctance, shaking his head sadly. 'My poor brother Oliver is the black sheep of the family. My intention was to warn you, privately, against the criminal tendencies he has shown since early childhood.'

Mr Stalker was horrified. 'A noble gesture, sir,' he declared, 'what further wrongdoings have we not been spared? Oh worthy Mr Bumble! How right you were!' Then, assuming that the gentleman did not know the personage to whom he had referred, he explained: 'Mr Bumble, sir. The School Porter and Proctor. A man of sterling character.'

'I have no doubt,' replied Monks, with a slight movement of the mouth which Mr Stalker presumed to be a smile. The strange gentleman then turned to the door and said: 'Well, sir, I shall not trespass any longer. Pray do not trouble to see me out. I may pause for a word with your sterling Mr Bumble on the way.'

'Do, sir!' exclaimed Stalker. 'And once again – my gratitude – and commiseration.'

As soon as he was in the corridor and had shut the door of Mr Stalker's study behind him, Monks dropped his expression of unctuous civility in an instant and adopted a furious scowl in its stead; he strode rapidly and determinedly towards the Porter's lodge, not noticing, as he did so that the pupil with whom he had almost collided a few minutes previously was still in the corridor, seated on a bench against one of the walls, his head studiously lowered over a book.

Mr Bumble was now dozing pleasantly in his lodge, seated on his chair beside the hatch which looked out into the corridor. The hatch was open, but Monks did not use it to communicate with the Porter; rather, he entered the lodge directly by means of the door, which he slammed noisily behind him once he was inside, promptly rousing the Porter from his slumberous state.

'Why, Mr Monks!' declared Bumble, with a beam of surprised pleasure. 'Wot a joy it is to see you!'

'Is it?' retorted Monks, coldly.

'A joy unfeigned!' exclaimed Bumble. 'Thuswise, I can report a job well done.'

'Can you?' replied Monks, yet more coldly.

'Your orders was carried out, sir, just as you wished,'

announced Bumble, in a complacent tone. 'All Twist's letters was diverted – straight into the fire. While 'is life 'ere was made a misery. The upshot, three days ago, 'e ups an' offs.' He chuckled. 'Now ain't that music to yer ears,' he said, 'worth maybe a little bonus?'

'No, you fat oaf, it is not!' thundered Monks. 'You great, stinking windbladder! Can't you *ever* get anything right?'

Mr Bumble gaped at him in indignant amazement. He had not been quite so harshly or loudly abused for a very long time; for fear that the offensive tirade might continue and, worse still, be heard by anyone who happened to be passing down the corridor, he quickly shut the hatch. ''Ow dare you!' he cried. 'What are you 'inting?'

'Hinting?' hissed Monks. 'I'm reminding you, you incompetent idiot, that I sent you here to get Oliver expelled for bad conduct – not to drive him into running away!'

''E'd of been expelled if 'e'd stayed!' Bumble protested.

'That,' said Monks icily, 'is something we shall never know.'

'You're just tryin' to get out of payin' me,' said Bumble.

'I hoped,' snarled Monks, 'to recover three thousand pounds I was forced to give him. You'd have been paid out of that. Now you can whistle for it.'

'You – you – you're goin' back on your word!' squealed Bumble, rising from his chair.

'If you thought I'd keep it, you're an even bigger fool than I imagined,' said Monks, and turned to the door.

'Well, see if I care, Mr 'Igh an' Mighty!' Bumble suddenly announced, with some pride. 'I 'ave no need to work for such as you anymore. I 'ave a splendid position 'ere, authority an' security for the rest o' my life! I shall stay 'ere forever!'

'Tormenting schoolboys. It's all you're fit for,' Monks

muttered dismissively, and left the lodge.

Alone in his indignation, and exhausted by his last cry of defiance, the Porter puffed, blew and waddled up and down the small room for some while, before collapsing back into his chair and pulling open his neckband. 'Gratitude?' he muttered to himself in a self-pitying tone. 'Gratitude is a illusion . . .'

The hatch of the Porter's lodge was considerably less thick than the door to Mr Stalker's study, and the Artful Dodger, in placing an eager ear to it, had heard every word that had passed between Monks and Bumble. However, when Monks emerged from the lodge, the astonished boy was once again seated on his bench, busily occupied in reading a book. Monks had barely noticed him before, and did not notice him now, but moved quickly towards the main entrance of the school and out into the open air, without a single glance to the right or to the left.

When this evil man had gone, the Dodger laid down his book, which he had extracted from a convenient pile on the bench and which, to his amusement, he now discovered he had been reading upside down. He rose, thoughtfully, and thrust his hands into his pockets. 'Three thousand pounds,' he murmured to himself, and whistled softly through his teeth.

'Dawkins!' thundered a tyrannical voice from the far end of the corridor. The Dodger glanced round and saw Mr Stalker standing beside the door of his study. 'Did you not hear the bell, Dawkins? Did I not just then ring the bell? I did. Fetch Mr Bumble this instant!'

'Right-oh, Mr Stalker, sir!' said the Dodger, and Mr Stalker retreated, shutting the door behind him. The Dodger hesitated for a few seconds, eyeing the closed hatch, behind which, he presumed, Bumble was still seated. He then reached a sudden, very firm decision, and, far from obeying the Headmaster's instruction, he left the corridor through another door and ran up a flight of stairs towards the Junior Dormitory.

''Ere,' he inquired as he entered this room, 'got any money?'

'My grandmother put some in the bank for me,' squeaked Shrimp, who was involved in a game of chess with Tommy Rice.

'No,' said the Dodger, 'I mean brass – tin – ready money.'

'I've got tuppence,' declared Tommy.

'Tuppence,' muttered the Dodger, with distaste, 'Shrimp? Wot about you?'

Shrimp extracted a coin from his pocket. 'Only a penny till Saturday,' he announced dejectedly, 'Why?'

'I need it, that's why?' said the Dodger. 'Come on – I'll give it back.'

Shrimp handed over his penny. Reluctantly, Tommy dug into his pocket and gave the Dodger his two pennies.

'Ta!' said the Dodger, and ran from the room. He returned hurriedly to the corridor and advanced towards the Porter's lodge. The hatch was now open again, and Mr Bumble was seated behind it, fast asleep, his plump hands tucked round his huge belly. Silently, the Dodger opened the door of the lodge and stepped inside. He saw his recently confiscated flask on a table. Quickly and quietly, he uncorked it and proceeded to sprinkle some of its contents, very carefully, onto Bumble's lapels, then onto the table, and then onto the floor. He also gave the portly gentleman's hat, which lay in front of him, the benefit of a few droplets. He then set the open flask down beside the Porter and slipped from the lodge. No sooner had he emerged into the corridor once more than he saw Mr Stalker bearing down towards him, irritably.

'Have I not been waiting?' barked the Headmaster. 'I have. Did I not send you for Mr Bumble?'

'You did, sir,' replied the Dodger, with great innocence. 'I'm sorry, sir, I couldn't wake him.'

'Wake him? Wake him?' inquired Stalker, pushing the boy aside and marching into the lodge. The Dodger grinned as he heard the following explosive conversation:

'What's this? Brandy! Bumble! Arise from your drunken stupor.'

'Drunk?' protested Bumble's drowsy voice. 'I never touched a drop!'

'Do you not reek of brandywine? Can you deny the evidence?'

'O' course I deny it!'

'Adding falsehood to inebriation? Imbibing spiritous liquors in the hours of work, have you not betrayed your position of sacred trust?'

'Oh lemme be,' grumbled Bumble, 'I've 'ad enough o' being' accused of things this afternoon.'

'Have you indeed?' retorted the Headmaster dangerously, 'Then you will not be distressed if you are dismissed summarily, on the spot? Which you most certainly are!'

Thus it was that Mr Bumble's second career as Porter and Proctor of Mr Stalker's Academical Establishment came to a sudden and ignominious end.

Another personage left the school that afternoon, but of his own volition; this was the Artful Dodger, who did not wait for nightfall to make his departure. No sooner had he overheard the above conversation than he walked through the academy's main entrance, and briskly set off across the fields on the long journey to London, whistling blithely as he went, jangling his three coins in his pocket, and murmuring occasionally, with a grin: 'Three thousand pounds . . . three thousand pounds. . . .'

CHAPTER TWELVE

On the third morning of Oliver's imprisonment in the kitchen of Mr Brownlow's house, Noah Clapole was surprised, upon unlocking the door of that room and entering, to see the boy facing him with a determined glare in his eye, and a poker, which he had taken from the range, in his hand. He was alone, for Charlotte had been sent shopping. Noah was somewhat frightened, but he nonetheless decided to adopt a manner of affected servility.

'Well, well, *Master* Oliver,' he said. 'So 'appy you could stay, *Master* Oliver.' His voice then hardened into a snarl: 'But then it's yer 'ome, ain't it? Yer wery own 'ome, ain't it, Work'ouse? An' when the old boy croaks...'

'I have a right to see Mr Brownlow,' said Oliver with a quiet firmness, tightening his grip on the poker.

' 'Ave you then, Work'ouse,' sneered Claypole.

'I do. And you have no right to keep me from him, Noah.'

'Morris Bolter!' snapped Claypole, '*Mister* Bolter to you, Twist.'

'I mean to see my guardian,' said Oliver, 'and you're not going to stop me.'

'Oh, ain't I, Work'ouse?' hissed Claypole, with a wicked smile, which abruptly vanished when Oliver raised the poker threateningly.

'Because if you do,' announced Oliver, 'I'll put this poker through the window and shout and shout and shout until someone comes to find out why.'

Noah was inwardly relieved at this statement of purpose, for he had initially presumed that *he* was to be the victim of an assault from the poker. He now decided to bring the boy into Mrs Carraway's presence at once.

'Right,' he said, appearing to give in, 'if yer insist,

Master Oliver, I'd better take you up.' He swung the door wide open and moved aside deferentially, motioning to Oliver to pass through.

'After you,' said Oliver, suspiciously. Claypole's small eyes narrowed for a moment before he shrugged and stepped from the room. Oliver followed with caution.

'Oh really!' declared Mrs Carraway as Noah and Oliver stood before her in the sitting room. 'I cannot understand! When you know how agitated I am! How we all must be!'

Her irritation appeared to be directed more at Noah than at the boy. This may have been because the boy was still carrying the poker and looked somewhat dangerous; nonetheless, Claypole felt the need to defend himself: 'I'm sorry, Ma'am,' he explained unctuously, ''E – 'e made me. 'E threatened me.'

'I did not!' Oliver protested.

'Oh really, this is quite too much!' said Mrs Carraway, staring at the boy. 'When half the cause of your kind benefactor's illness is yourself.' Claypole, relieved for the moment from the lady's steely glare, stepped back smirking.

'But how could that be?' demanded Oliver.

'At school!' exclaimed Mrs Carraway. 'Your conduct! Your appalling behaviour!'

'But everything that happened at school . . . ,' Oliver began. He was interrupted by the sound of the front doorbell.

'I'll answer it, ma'am,' said Claypole, slipping from the room.

Oliver did not have a chance to continue the defence of his conduct at Mr Stalker's Academy, for now the lady glowered at him coldly and said slowly and in an icy voice: 'Mr Brownlow has been unwell for some time. The attentions of Mrs Bedwin – well-meaning as she may have been – did not help. And when we heard from the school that, if you had not yourself decamped like a thief in the night, you would most certainly have been expelled, it prostrated your guardian.'

Oliver believed this, and was stricken, but he did not comprehend how it should in any way alter his need to see his benefactor. If anything, the need was increased. He began to plead: 'I still have to see him. I have to see him even more. I have to explain.'

'Dr Hyssop to see you, Mrs Carraway,' said Claypole, ushering the gentleman in question into the room.

'Ah, Doctor,' said the lady.

'Mrs Carraway,' said the gaunt physician, with a bow.

'And someone I believe you have not met, Doctor,' said Mrs Carraway, 'Mr Brownlow's ward.'

'Young Oliver,' said Hyssop, turning to the boy with a friendly smile, 'Well, well! Your guardian speaks of you often.'

Oliver was greatly relieved to see what appeared to be a sympathetic countenance for the first time in many days, and he now replied at once, and with urgency, 'Dr Hyssop, I have to see him, to talk to him.'

The doctor was abruptly grave. 'Ah now that,' he declared glancing at Mrs Carraway and receiving an expressionless stare in return, 'now that raises difficulties.'

'I'm sure if I could just explain,' said the boy quietly.

'Your guardian's condition, my boy,' interposed the doctor, with a shake of his head. 'Recovery – even if it is possible – must be many long months away. You do realize that?'

Oliver looked at Mrs Carraway briefly, then, at the doctor, before replying, with some reluctance: 'Yes.'

'Then I suggest,' said Dr Hyssop, 'that like all of us you must just possess yourself in patience, and hope.' Oliver opened his mouth to protest again but the gentleman raised his hand authoritatively, and continued: 'As to your not being allowed to visit the sickroom, it is, I am afraid, myself you must blame. I advised most strongly against any excitement, any disturbance, to that poor man upstairs; which you, I feel, albeit with the best intentions, might cause.'

'Even hearing his voice,' rejoined Mrs Carraway, sharply.

'Indeed,' said the doctor, 'I fear so.'

Oliver realized that any further attempts to demand admission to his guardian's bedroom would be fruitless. He respected Dr Hyssop's advice, not merely because he was a medical man, but because Mr Brownlow had often spoken of him as a person of great judgement. When Noah now approached the boy, therefore, and said, almost gently: 'All right, Master Oliver? Yer 'eard it now. An' it's back down we goes,' the boy went, obediently, with his head bowed.

'Doctor?' said Mrs Carraway, hesitantly, once Oliver and Claypole had gone, 'Keeping Mr Brownlow isolated, with the boy in the house and friends calling, friends like Mr Grimwig, is becoming increasingly difficult.'

'Mmm. Yes,' muttered the doctor. 'Difficult. Perhaps.' He thought gravely for a few moments before offering the very suggestion that Mrs Carraway had been hoping for. 'I own a small nursing home, a private sanatorium, in the country,' he said, 'And with money being no problem, as I'm sure it is not . . .'

'No indeed,' retorted Mrs Carraway, hastily. 'It was all arranged by Mr Brownlow himself. I may draw on his account for all expenses of the house and servants, and professional fees.'

'Yes, yes of course,' remarked the doctor. 'A most thoughtful and farsighted man.'

Arrangements were immediately made to remove Mr Brownlow to the comparative quiet of the sanatorium; indeed, so prompt were these arrangements that the frail old gentleman was carried from the house and into a waiting carriage that very afternoon.

'Well, that's 'im gone,' announced Claypole as he returned to the kitchen after having seen the carriage drive off. Oliver had also watched the departure from the kitchen window. 'Gone, Work'ouse,' Claypole repeated. 'You 'ear? An' maybe never comin' back. Yer a orphan,

Work'ouse an' yer going' to stay a orphan.' The boy turned from the window and stared at him with a blank, shocked expression. Claypole grinned. 'Orphan,' he snarled, 'Orphan. *Master* Oliver. Master *Nobody*! Old Mr B. ain't never goin' to adopt you, nowise. An' there ain't nobody in the whole, wide world to care one little bit wot 'appens to yer, nor 'elp yer.'

If further desolation was possible, Oliver felt it now.

Early the next morning, however, someone who cared very deeply about what might happen to Oliver Twist was sleepily approaching London.

'We'm there, lad!' announced the carter, pulling sharply at the reins of his horse and bringing him to a halt. He turned to look at the boy who was lying behind him.

The boy opened his eyes, raised his head slowly, blinked and looked about him. 'London?' he asked, with a yawn.

'No, I wouldn't say that,' replied the cater, with a chuckle, 'Far as we go together though, I'm turning east now. But down there's Barnet. An' keepin' straight on, London.'

'Well,' said the boy, staring at the fork in the road ahead, 'well thank ye kindly.' He shook the carter's hand and leapt to the ground. 'All the best,' he said.

'An' to you,' replied the carter. 'An' let's 'ope you'm the last.'

The boy stared up at him. 'The last?' he said.

'From your school,' replied the carter, with a grin. 'Looks like all the roads to London are full o' boys runnin' away from your school.'

'You met another one?'

'Well, 'e was dressed the same. An' on 'is way from Shropshire like you. Must be a 'ard place that school.'

The boy paused thoughtfully for a moment asking: 'Did you catch 'is name?'

' 'E wouldn't give it,' said the carter, chuckling, 'made one up, though. Funny sort o' name. Wot was it?'

'I'll bet you a penny 'e called 'isself Twist!'

'Well, well, I'll be . . .'

'Did 'e say where 'e was 'eaded?'

'Lemme think,' said the carter, 'Pentonville was it? That's right – to see 'is father.'

'Ta,' said the boy, 'Ta again,' and set off immediately down the road, whistling cheerfully, his hands thrust firmly into his pockets.

Noah Claypole had prepared a document which declared, in a straightforward manner, that he would from that day be entitled to withdraw, at any time, and in whatever quantity he wished, the money that had been invested by Mr Brownlow in Oliver's name. Naturally, such a document would not be valid until it had been signed by the boy; late that afternoon, therefore, Noah entered the kitchen with the piece of paper in one hand and a freshly-inked pen in the other, and placed both on the table in front of Oliver, saying, 'Sign it, or make yer mark.'

'Not till I've read it,' replied Oliver.

'Wot?'

'Not till I've read it,' Oliver repeated.

'*You*, Work'ouse?' sneered Claypole, '*Read*?' Come on, make yer mark an' 'ave done with it.'

Oliver's eyes rapidly scanned the document and he said: I can tell you already I won't. Nor sign it.'

'Do what Mr Bolter says, Oliver dear,' said Charlotte softly. 'I'm sure 'e knows best.'

'I'm sure he does,' rejoined Oliver, knowingly.

'For the likes o' you an' me,' said Charlotte.

'For himself,' rejoined Oliver. 'This gives him the right to draw out money invested in my name – to steal it, in other words.'

Charlotte gave a gasp of affected shock. 'Oliver, dear!' she cried.

''Old yer gab, Charlotte!' snapped Claypole, catching hold of the boy's arm and squeezing it. 'You'll sign,' he snarled, 'or I'll break this off.' Oliver winced with the pain.

'Noah!' protested Charlotte.

'I said shut up!'

'Noah! You promised! No 'urtin 'im!'

Claypole glared at her for some moments, before releasing Oliver's arm. 'Eddication, eddication,' he muttered, 'wot a meddlesome thing.' He was inwardly annoyed with himself, for he had unthinkingly supposed that the boy was illiterate, and would not be able to read the document. He was not sure what to do next, until he decided that the only course of action would be to force Oliver into submission by a more lengthy, but equally cruel means. 'All right, Work'ouse!' he now barked. 'Off with yer coat! An' yer weskit!' Oliver stared at him in puzzlement. 'You 'eard me!' thundered Claypole. 'Off with 'em!'

Oliver rose, bewildered, and removed his coat and waistcoat, laying them on the table. Claypole scooped them up. 'Yer won't be needin' these,' he announced, and proceeded to push the boy towards the cellar door, saying: 'It's the cellar for you, Work'ouse. An' bread and water, once a day. That'll soon change yer tune. A powerful eddicator, 'unger.'

'Couldn't I keep my coat at least?' pleaded Oliver.

'Inside!' barged Claypole, holding the cellar door open. Oliver was powerless to do anything but obey, and, with a shrug, he entered the cellar. 'No, Master Eddicated,' said Noah, slamming the door shut and turning the key, 'yer won't be wantin' them. But there's them as will. They'll fetch a shillin' or two.' Whereupon he cast a wicked grin in Charlotte's direction and strode from the kitchen.

He went at once to the Three Cripples Tavern in

Saffron Hill for his daily inspection of the articles stolen by those under his charge during the previous twenty-four hours. Morris Bolter's reputation as a fence, or, as he continued to call himself, 'a re-distributor of missin' property', was growing rapidly; almost every day yet another young vagabond would arrive at the private room of the Cripples, eager for the privilege of becoming a member of his gang. One such youth, pimpled, and sharp-faced, was waiting for Mr Bolter now; he had deprived an inattentive old gentleman of a silver hunter watch on a fine silver watch-chain that morning. Once the youth had been introduced to the great Morris Bolter by Ned Fingers, Bolter examined the watch carefully, peering at it closely, holding it to his ear, checking the key in the winding hole. Apparently satisfied with its condition, he withdrew several coins from his pocket and handed them to the young thief, who beamed, touched his forelock, and scurried from the room.

'You give 'im too much,' announced Fingers, when the boy had left.

'Did I then Fingers?' said Claypole.

' 'E'd 'ave settled for 'alf.'

'Would 'e now,' said Claypole, with a knowing smile. 'But who'll 'e come to with 'is next pickin's? An' who'll 'e make sure the others come to? An' who'll 'ave a top team in next to no time, workin' direct for 'im? A team better'n Fagin's ever 'ad?'

'You're a wonder, Mr Bolter, you truly are,' exclaimed Fingers, with a low whistle of admiration, as he emptied a large black leather bag of its contents onto the table.

'A good 'aul for one day,' declared Claypole, proceeding to pick his way through the pile of watches, rings, snuffboxes, coins, notes and silk handkerchiefs that lay before him.

Fingers watched him proudly for some moments before he was struck by an unpleasant thought. 'Only one fing,' he said.

'Wot?' said Claypole, not looking up.

'Supposin' 'e 'ears.'

'Who? Supposin' who 'ears?'

'Fagin.'

Claypole chuckled. 'Ol' Flat'at's gone,' he retorted. 'Finished. We got nothin' to worry about. Nothin' wotsoever.'

There was a low gutteral laugh from just outside the room. Claypole and his young assistant suddenly stared at the door in terror. Noah threw his arms over the pile of stolen goods on the table. 'I wouldn't be too sure about that,' said a cold, quiet voice. A second later, Monks was standing in the doorway. 'I wouldn't be too sure about that,' he repeated, dangerously, and took a step forward.

'Mr Bolter!' squealed Fingers, rising.

'Take this,' said Claypole hastily sweeping the pile off the table and back into the leather bag. 'Put it – you know where.'

Thoroughly relieved at being thus excused, the little thief snatched the bag and hurried from the room. Monks shut the door.

'No, I wouldn't be too sure about that,' he said a third time, advancing to the table and sitting opposite Claypole, 'I dislike wild goose chases. Intensely.'

'Wild goose?' murmured Noah.

'To deepest Shropshire,' said Monks, 'To find Twist gone. And back, to find you've had him a week without saying a word to me.' Whereupon he slowly lifted his cane and held it parallel to the table top.

'Don't yer try nothin'!' exclaimed Claypole, unable to mask his fright. 'While I've got them papers, we're still partners!'

'I wouldn't presume on it,' Monks replied quietly, toying with the cane. 'All you're after is his money. I want him ruined, branded, *destroyed.*' On this last word, he subjected the table top to a long, vicious scratch with the point of his cane.

'A week,' Noah whined. 'A couple at most. We'll both

'ave wot we want.' Monks stared at him expressionlessly, ''Unger and thirst,' whispered Noah, leaning forward. 'You'll see. No more'n three weeks an' 'e'll be beggin' to oblige. Then we does with 'im whatever you say. I got connections. Another week an' we'll 'ave 'im transported. Or sent to the 'ulks.'

To his relief, he saw the villain's cold eyes light up dimly: 'The prison ships?' muttered Monks, 'To rot? I'd enjoy that.' He laughed. 'Oh yes. Oh yes. Yes, I'd enjoy *that*!'

Charlotte was sitting at the kitchen table, staring at the locked cellar door, and feeling wretched. She was seeing increasingly less of Noah as the days passed. He seemed to be spending more and more of his time upstairs, with Mrs Carraway, or else in the private room of the Three Cripples, with his friends, and she was rarely permitted to accompany him there. Their pleasant Sunday morning strolls, too, had come to an end a long time ago. In short, poor Charlotte was lonely. Suddenly, she called: 'Oliver? Oliver dear? You there?'

'No,' replied a sarcastic voice from behind the cellar door. 'I escaped through the coal-hole.'

'But there ain't no . . .' Charlotte began to exclaim: 'Oh, Oliver!' she cried with a little laugh, realizing her stupidity. She rose from the table and crossed to the cellar door. 'Oliver?' she said softly, 'Listen. Noah's left us both alone, 'asn't e? If I let you out, will you give your word? To be good? Will you, Oliver?' The boy did not reply. 'Oliver?' she repeated.

'Yes,' said Oliver at last. 'Yes, I will.'

'An' not try to open any doors?'

'I promise,' replied Oliver, with a sigh.

Charlotte unlocked the door and opened it. Oliver stepped out from the cellar's darkness momentarily blinded by the daylight.

'Least,' said Charlotte, beaming, 'this way we'll both

'ave a bit o' company, won't we?'

Just then, the front door bell rang. Charlotte froze, staring nervously at the kitchen door.

'Shouldn't you answer it?' suggested Oliver, when it became clear that she was not going to move.

'I can't,' whispered Charlotte, anxiously, 'I can't leave you alone.'

'I gave you my word, didn't I?' said Oliver.

Charlotte glanced at the boy, and thought for several moments. As she was thus occupied, the bell rang again. 'No,' she said at last. 'No. I can't.'

Upstairs, Mrs Carraway was not in the slightest bit pleased at having to open the front door for herself, but she nevertheless did so, when she had allowed the bell to be rung at least four times. Standing on the doorstep was a snub-nosed, flat-browed youth, dressed in a swallowtail coat and striped trousers, who raised his cap and bowed politely the minute the door was opened; he smiled broadly: his name, he said, was Jack Dawkins.

CHAPTER THIRTEEN

'I really cannot imagine what can have happened to that stupid girl!' declared Mrs Carraway as she ushered the smiling youth into the sitting-room. 'Do sit, Master Dawkins,' she said, seating herself on a straight-backed chair.

Dawkins sat in a chair beside the fireplace. 'Thank you, ma'am,' he said, with great politeness. 'It's most kind o' – *of* you to see me.'

'Oh I recognized the uniform at once, of course,' said the lady. 'But I must confess to profound shock at what you tell me. Poor Mr Brownlow in a nursing home grievously ill, and now Oliver, run away from school.'

'You'd no idea?' inquired Dawkins.

'None,' replied the lady, in an apparently distressed tone.

'An' you've seen neither 'ide nor – I mean, no sign of him at all.'

'None,' replied Mrs Carraway, shaking her head sadly, 'As I have said, a profound shock. But most kind of Mr Stalker to let me know, through you.'

'Well 'e – *he's* that kind o' man, ain't – *isn't* he?' said the youth. 'And sendin' me rather than a peel – a *porter*. The uniform, sort of 'elping recognition. Distinctive.'

'Yes, I'm sure,' observed Mrs Carraway eyeing him curiously. 'Can I offer you some refreshment, Master Dawkins?'

'No thank ye, ma'am,' replied Dawkins, rising from his chair. ''Avin delivered my message, I'd best catch the jolly old coach back to Shropshire.'

Mrs Carraway rose too. 'Well, if you're sure,' she said. 'It seems such a long way to have come, only to go back.'

'I miss it,' said the youth, 'the old school, ma'am. I'll tell Mr Stalker we'll just 'ave – *have* to look for that misbeguided boy elsewhere, prob'ly not even in London.'

'This,' said Mrs Carraway, crossing to the door, 'is the last place he would come, I imagine.'

'Quite so, ma'am,' said Dawkins, with a smile and a bow. Mrs Carraway allowed herself a half smile in return.

The Artful Dodger stood outside the front door of Mr Brownlow's house for some while after it had been closed behind him, with an expression that was at once both confused and mildly sceptical, and when at last he descended the steps and began to set off along the street, he paused again, still thoughtful. He peered down over the railings into the house's basement yard. Suddenly purposeful, he opened a gate in the railings and hurried down the steps; he knocked gently on what he presumed to be the kitchen door.

'Who's that, I wonder,' said Charlotte, tensing. She was sitting opposite Oliver at the kitchen table. The knock was repeated. Finally, she rose reluctantly and went to the door that led out into the basement yard. She unlocked it and opened it only slightly. 'Well, what d'you want?' she demanded.

Oliver heard a cheerful voice reply: 'I was wonderin', ma'am, if I might trouble you for a glass o' water. Thirsty day for walkin', if it is Thursday. Could be Tuesday, o' course.'

Charlotte was instantly and utterly charmed; she giggled and said: 'A glass o' water?'

'An' a bite to eat to go with it,' retorted the cheerful voice. 'Something to chew, if it's Tuesday.'

Charlotte laughed again. For his part, Oliver had risen from the table in surprise and delight, for he had recognized the voice at once. 'I think you'd best come in,' said Charlotte, opening the door wide.

'Not only young an' pretty, but kind with it,' remarked the Dodger with a grin as he entered the kitchen. His eye fell immediately on Oliver. 'Oops, sorry!' he said. 'You got company.'

Charlotte glanced at Oliver, thereby allowing the Dodger to put his finger hastily to his lips for his friend's benefit. Oliver instantly understood that he should on no account reveal recognition. ''Im?' said Charlotte. 'Oh, don't mind 'im! That's Oliver. 'E's . . . 'e's the 'ouseboy.'

'Well,' said the Dodger, his grin widening. ''Ow d'you do, Oliver.'

Oliver answered the greeting with a nod and a countenance that betrayed nothing.

'You don't look like a beggar,' observed Charlotte, surveying the newcomer.

'Beggar? Me?' said the Dodger. 'I'm a lawyer's clerk.'

Charlotte smiled. 'You've cheek enough for it,' she said.

'Tell the truth,' the Dodger announced. 'I really don't like to go back to the office looking like this.' He did indeed look more than mildly dirty and dishevelled; he had also removed his tie and coat, which he carried over his arm. 'Wot I'd really like,' he continued, 'is a bit of a wash. You wouldn't 'appen to 'ave a towel 'andy?'

'I think we could manage that,' said Charlotte, laughing, and began to move towards the door that led to the rest of the house. She halted abruptly, however, and glanced at Oliver. She then crossed once more to the basement door and closed it, putting her hand tentatively on the key.

'Don't worry,' exclaimed the Dodger. 'Oliver 'ere'll stop me runnin' off with the 'ouse'old silver.'

The woman hesitated for some seconds, eyeing both boys with a hint of suspicion; then she giggled again and locked the door to the yard. 'You can keep an eye on each other,' she said. Leaving the key in the lock, she crossed to the main door of the kitchen, and with a final sweet smile at the charming stranger, she left the room, closing the door behind her.

'Come on then!' the Dodger whispered sharply, ''Ow long d'you think we've got? No more'n a minute.'.

'I can't,' said Oliver, in a subdued tone. 'I gave my word.'

'Wot?' said the Dodger, unable to believe that he had heard correctly.

'I gave my word.'

'Who to,' said the Dodger, 'to 'er?'

Oliver nodded. 'I promised I wouldn't open any doors.'

'You *promised*!' exclaimed the Dodger, in exasperation, 'Well, *I'll* unlock the blasted door, won't I? All *you* got to do is walk through it! Come on!' He crossed to the basement door, turned the key, and held it open. Oliver remained uncertain. 'Come *on*, Oliver!' the Dodger whispered urgently. 'Walk! One foot front o' the other!'

At last, Oliver proceeded to move in the direction of the door, but he had only taken one step towards his freedom when the Dodger whispered 'Too late!' and both boys heard the sound of someone hurriedly descending the steps outside. The Dodger stepped quickly backwards, as Noah Claypole and Charlotte entered the kitchen simultaneously through their respective doors.

'Ello,' declared Claypole, stopping abruptly and glancing distrustfully from one boy to the other, 'Wot's going on? Wot's 'e doin' out? An' who's this?'

''E's a clerk, Noah, dear,' explained Charlotte nervously, 'Just dropped in for a wash an' a glass o' water.'

'A wash?' Claypole exclaimed incredulously.

'That's it, Guvnor,' said the Dodger. 'Bit of a wash an' brushup like.' He smiled uncertainly as Claypole surveyed him with suspicion. Whether Noah remembered having encountered that grin before, or merely noted, as Charlotte had been too charmed to note, that both boys were wearing identical trousers, is not especially important – what matters is that, after only a few short moments, his eyes now widened with understanding and he cried: 'Wait a minute! 'E's no clerk! 'E's . . .'

'Run for it, Oliver!' shouted the Dodger, dashing past Claypole and out into the yard. No longer hesitant

Oliver tried to hurry after him; but Claypole caught hold of his arm and pulled him back. The Dodger hastily re-entered the room and delivered a sharp kick to Claypole's shin. With a screech of pain, Claypole released Oliver and clutched his injured leg, hopping around the room in his agony. Seeing the two boys make for the yard again, however, he promptly recovered and ran between them and the door, slamming it shut. A chase ensued; chairs were toppled, crockery fell noisily to the floor. These chaotic proceedings came to an abrupt end only when the Dodger snatched a bag of flour from the dresser and hurled it at Claypole; Claypole stepped aside to avoid it, at the very moment that Charlotte chose to intervene by moving towards the centre of the fray; she walked directly into the bag's path; it struck her on the side of the head, bursting open and sending its contents cascading down her dress. Meanwhile Claypole fell suddenly backwards onto the floor, for Oliver had thrust out a leg, tripping him as he had moved out of the way. The Dodger now ran forward and overturned the kitchen table so that it landed face downwards on top of the prostrate Noah. Both boys raced to the door which led to the yard, pulled it open, and sped from the kitchen and up the steps to the street. Scrambling from under the table, Claypole hurried out after them, screaming: 'Stop thief! They've stolen the silver! Stop! Stop thief!'

Poor Charlotte, covered with flour, could only stare down at her clothes, oblivious of everything but her own private tragedy: 'Noah!' she wailed, 'My dress! Look at my dress!'

Noah's irate cries of 'Stop thief! They've stolen the silver!' quickly taken up by others, followed Oliver and the Dodger for some considerable time as they ran through the streets of Pentonville towards the darker area of the city. Both boys knew this locality well, and when they had reached it, they soon found a filthy concealed passageway that was reasonably secure from further pursuit. They stopped at last, panting.

'Well, we beaten 'em. For now,' gasped the Dodger, once the noise of the hunt had subsided.

'For now?' said Oliver.

'You 'eard 'im,' observed the Dodger, 'You 'eard wot he was shoutin'. "Stop thief. They've stolen the silver." You don't think 'e'll let it go at that, do you?'

'But what can he do?' asked Oliver.

' 'E can lay a charge, that's what. With full descriptions, for every peeler in London. An' we're done. Nowhere to go, an' nowhere to 'ide. An' no ol' Fagin now to pertect us.'

'There's someone who might,' said Oliver.

'Might what?'

'Protect us,' said Oliver, 'if we explained.'

'Who?'

'Mr Grimwig, my guardian's friend. He's a magistrate.'

The Dodger looked instantly sceptical. 'Well,' he said, with a sigh, 'we can always try 'im. Though like as not, 'e'll end up tryin' *us*.'

So the two boys returned to Pentonville, by a less obtrusive and more circuitous route, through shaded back streets and alleys, glancing about them as they went, terrified of being apprehended. Grimwig's house was only a few streets from Mr Brownlow's; the nearer they came to it, therefore, the greater was the danger of being recognized and caught. Oliver was convinced, however, that they would both be safe from harm once everything had been explained to his benefactor's best friend, and so, when they had reached the house, he boldly ascended the front steps and knocked on the door. Having explained who he was to the genial maid who opened it, he was ushered inside. The Dodger loitered uneasily in the wide, empty street, looking nervously from one end to the other. Suddenly two gentlemen appeared from round a corner; both dressed in open greatcoats and tall hats, ambling officiously side by side. The Dodger recognized them immediately by their identical red waistcoats, and he darted into a narrow opening between Mr Grimwig's house and his neighbour's. He crouched behind a pile of boxes, not even daring to breathe. The two gentlemen strolled past the opening, glancing down it briefly; there could be no doubt that they were searching for someone; though not in a very meticulous manner. The Dodger waited for a minute or so before re-emerging into the street, gazing in the direction they had taken. A moment later, a hand touched him on the shoulder. He jumped and spun round. 'Wot you tryin' to do!' he barked, realizing that it was only Oliver who had frightened him.

'It's no good,' said Oliver softly, looking very downcast.

'Not much. 'Cept to give me 'eart failure,' said the Dodger. 'All right. Wot's 'appened?'

'It's no good,' Oliver repeated, 'Mr Grimwig's gone to the country, and they don't know when he'll be back.'

'Well I never 'ad much 'opes of it,' said the Dodger philosophically. 'Now, let's go. It ain't safe 'ereabouts, The runners are runnin'. Place is crawling with 'em.' Receiving only a blank stare from his friend, he impatiently continued: 'You forgot everythin'? Runners! Bow Street runners! Magistrate's officers, in their red weskets. Now come on, or we'll be took for sure.'

'Red waistcoats?' said Oliver, 'You mean like . . .' and he pointed to a spot behind the Dodger.

The Artful Dodger swung round. The two gentlemen had reappeared, their red waistcoats ablaze. Seeing the boys, one of them cried, 'Stop thief!' at once and raised a rattle above his head, twirling it frantically.

'Come on!' cried the Dodger, as the runners commenced their pursuit.

Once again the two boys had to tear through a series of streets and passages, twisting and turning, glancing only occasionally behind them, with the ever-increasing noise of the chase baying in their ears. Once again, bent double with exhaustion, they succeeded in reaching a place of passable concealment; on this occasion, a short, narrow alley closed off at one end by a high brick wall against which two empty barrels lay on their sides. Oliver and the Dodger hid themselves inside the barrels and waited for the hue and cry to subside.

'Have they gone?' Oliver whispered from his barrel when silence prevailed.

'Given up,' replied the Dodger, crawling into the open. 'But for 'ow long? One thing's sure, these togs are a dead giveaway. So? We change 'em.'

A nearby clothes stall provided them both with the necessary transformation. At the sight of their comparatively fine school clothes, the stall's owner proved very willing to furnish Oliver with a threadbare jacket, cap and trousers, and the Dodger with a colourful but tattered waistcoat, a frayed tailcoat and breeches, a red-spotted neckerchief and a battered top-hat. Oliver could not fail to be troubled by the sudden change which overcame his friend as soon as he had donned these worn but all too familiar garments.

'Like ol' times, Oliver m'dear, ain't it? Like ol' times,' observed the Dodger, as he swaggered comfortably along, with his thumbs tucked into the armholes of his waistcoat. They were walking down a wide and busy thoroughfare. Evening had descended. 'Fancy a spot of 'andkerchief pullin', Oliver m'dear?' he suggested. Oliver winced. 'Only jokin' o' course,' declared the Dodger, with a grin. 'An' two pennies to the good as well,' for the stall-holder had furnished them with money as well as these outfits in exchange for their former garments. The Dodger chinked the coins in his hand and said, thoughtfully: 'We need somethin' to eat. Pity to waste these on it, though.'

Oliver suddenly came to a halt and stiffened, as he saw the two runners appear once more directly ahead of them. The Dodger stopped too, but instead of turning on his heels and running, he whispered, 'Well now, time to try our luck' and immediately leant casually against the railings of the house they had been passing: he proceeded to whistle softly to himself, adopting a cheerfully innocent countenance. Oliver did his best to look thoroughly unconcerned as well, as the gentlemen advanced; he was so terrified, however, that whistling was quite beyond him.

'Evenin', officer,' said the Dodger cheerily, as one of the runners stopped to examine him in the half light. 'Lovely evenin'.' The other runner had stopped too, and was peering suspiciously at Oliver. 'Gettin' maybe a bit chilly though,' added the Dodger.

For several very long seconds, the two men stood before the boys, inspecting them distrustfully. At last, the one who appeared to be interested in the Dodger snorted and turned away, continuing his journey down the street. The other runner stared at Oliver for a while longer before turning, too, and following his companion.

'And you said *I* gave *you* heart failure!' Oliver exclaimed when the runners had rounded a corner.

'We 'ad to know, didn't we?' said the Dodger.

'I suppose so.'

'Not too 'ealthy on a empty stomach, though,' said the Dodger. He glanced about him. ''Swelp me!' he suddenly announced, '*I* know where we are!'

'Where?'

'Round that corner! Mr Simmons, benefactor o' the poor! Good for a wad o' bread an' a bite o' cheese anytime. Maybe we'll eat after all, Oliver. On the 'ouse, so to speak.'

'He'll give us something? Just for the asking?'

'Well,' the Dodger observed, 'Must be sick o' the sight o' *me*. But you could try.'

'What do I have to do?' Oliver asked.

The Dodger took his friend's arm and began to pull him down the street, furnishing him with his instructions as he did so: 'I'll keep out o' sight,' he whispered. 'You rings the doorbell an' asks for Mr Simmons. When you got 'im – must be 'im, 'imself, no one else – you tell 'im you're poor, which you are, starvin', which you are, an' a orphan, which you likewise are – so no word of a lie – an' can 'e 'elp? Nothin' to it!'

When they had reached the front door of a small but homely residence in a quiet tree-lined street, Oliver obediently ascended the steps and rang the bell. It was answered by a stout and somewhat stern old lady who had presumably been disturbed in the act of making bread, for her sleeves were rolled up and her sturdy arms were covered with flour. Oliver politely inquired if Mr Simmons was at home. The cook surveyed him sceptically and immediately replied that he must have come to the wrong house, for no such person lived there. Oliver, with his experience of servants who were in the habit of preventing him from seeing their masters, wondered if he should believe her, so he persisted in his inquiry, repeating his request to be brought before Mr Simmons, whereupon the cook sharply repeated her assurance that the gentleman in question, whoever he might be, did not reside there, and she quickly shut the door in the boy's face.

Oliver turned dejectedly away and returned to the Dodger, who was leaning against the railings at the front of the house. 'You must have made a mistake,' said Oliver, morosely, 'She had no idea whom I was talking about. None at all.'

'No Mr Simmons?' said the Dodger, 'Ah well, mistakes 'appen. The best of us makes 'em. Meantimes, let's 'op it.' He seemed suddenly eager to leave the vicinity and return to the narrow passage in which they had concealed themselves when fleeing from the runners.

Once they had reached this place, which was only a few minutes walk away, the Dodger glanced about him before exclaiming excitedly: ''Ave a go at *this,* Oliver!' Whereupon he extracted from under his tailcoat a satisfyingly large portion of meat pie, which he broke into two equal parts. Oliver stared at the well-filled pastry which had been handed to him as the Dodger began to eat, ravenously. 'Go on!' said the Dodger, 'Eat up!' Oliver was soon making his way through the delicious pie as hungrily as his friend.

'Compliments o' Mr Simmons,' the Dodger then announced.

'What?' said Oliver, glancing up with his mouth full of pie.

'Compliments o' Mr Simmons,' repeated the Dodger. 'A true benefactor, like I said. Soon as I saw who answered the door – cookie 'erself – well, the kitchen 'ad to be empty, didn't it? So I popped down to the basement an' into the kitchen an' – thank *you*, Mr Simmons!'

Oliver stared at him, open-mouthed. 'You stole it!' he cried, 'And *I* helped.'

'Needs must, as they say,' declared the Dodger, calmly. 'An' whose need is greater 'n ours? I 'aven't eaten for two days. You've only 'ad bread an' water.'

Oliver put the remainder of the portion onto the ground beside him. 'No,' he said, shaking his head, 'I can't.'

The Dodger peered at his friend incredulously. 'Oliver m'dear!' he said, 'Number One! Remember? Look after Number One!'

Oliver did not need to be reminded of Fagin's favourite instruction. 'You're not Fagin,' he said, 'and neither am I. I can't eat it.'

'Oliver!' exclaimed the Dodger, in exasperation.

'Unless . . .,' Oliver continued.

'Unless what?'

'Unless you promise never to steal again. Even if we are hungry.'

'Oh oh all right,' said the Dodger, but he added with a grin: 'Course, if we're *starvin'* . . .' He caught a disapproving glance. 'All right, only joking,' he said. 'We're not likely to for a while anyway.'

'Why not?' asked Oliver.

'Biscuits,' replied the Dodger with a wink, tapping the pocket of his tailcoat.

Night had set in, and it was going to be a bitterly cold one. Both boys had been too active until this moment to notice the rapidly decreasing temperature: but now, as they sat in the damp alley with nothing but a clear and frosty night sky above them, they began to shiver.

'Need a roof over us,' declared the Dodger, glancing upwards.

'Who'd take us in?' said Oliver, miserably. 'We've no money.'

'We 'ave! Two pennies.'

'For a night's lodging? For the two of us?'

The Dodger shrugged. 'It'll be enough,' he said. 'To-night we're beggars, not choosers. Eat up an' we'll be on our way.'

'Where to?' inquired Oliver, considerably perturbed.

The Dodger said nothing; when they had finished their food, however, he led his friend through a complex maze of tiny streets, which grew darker and dirtier by the minute. At last, he halted outside a narrow, low, doorless entrance in a black wall.

'This is the place,' the Dodger announced. 'The Penny 'Ang.' Oliver followed through the entrance into a long ill-lit passageway. They had taken only a few steps when a gigantic, rough, unshaven figure loomed forward and barred their way. 'All right. 'Old it,' he growled. 'That'll be a penny each.' The Dodger extracted the two coins from his pocket and handed them over; the giant inspected them closely for some moments before stepping aside and returning to the shadows from which he had emerged.

'Find yourself a space, Oliver,' said the Dodger. Oliver did not understand him at first, but soon realized what he had meant. Along this narrow, filthy, litter-strewn passage, a thick rope was stretched taut, about one foot from the wall and some five feet from the floor. Leaning against the wall, with their arms and shoulders draped over the rope, were innumerable men and women; they were the human refuse of the city; London's criminals led the lives of princes in comparison to theirs; and this, the cheapest and meanest form of night's lodging known to man, was where they slept, or contrived to sleep.

The two boys had to pass a considerable number of these sorry creatures before they found a space wide enough for themselves. 'This'll do,' said the Dodger, ducking under the rope and swinging his arms over it. Oliver slipped into position beside him. Their immediate neighbours were a slatternly female of indeterminate age, who was mumbling and crying in her sleep, and a twitching drunkard.

'Well, 'ere we are,' declared the Dodger, philosophically, 'The Penny 'Ang. Least we'll be safe for the night. Sleep well.' He settled his lower extremities against the wall and closed his eyes. He was both extremely tired and apparently quite accustomed to this form of rest; and was therefore fast asleep in a very short while. Oliver, however, despite his own thorough exhaustion, remained miserably awake for an age; listening to the chorus of muttering, cursing and weeping that filled the stale air around him.

CHAPTER FOURTEEN

The gigantic keeper of this salubrious institution had an amusing way of rousing his guests from their slumbers in the morning; he would shamble to one end of the long passage and untie the rope, causing the sleepers to tumble onto the straw-scattered floor, crying out in angry protest at being thus so violently awakened; on this particular occasion, the slattern beside Oliver shrieked with terror and began to claw in wild half-conscious abandon at him and the Dodger.

' 'Ere, shove off! ' cried the Dodger.

'I beg your pardon, ma'am,' said Oliver politely, and helped her to her feet. When she had at last become mildly aware of her surroundings, she pushed him away, glared at him briefly, and lurched towards the street, grumbling incoherently.

'I s'pose that's wot they call a rude awakenin,' said the Dodger, retrieving his hat from the floor and putting it on; he sat with his back against the wall and examined the assorted derelicts with whom he had had the pleasure of spending the night, as they shuffled from the passage and out into the street. The drunkard who had been his immediate neighbour was lying in a motionless huddle on the floor. The Dodger stretched himself and said with a yawn: 'Well – the start of another perfect day.' He extracted two biscuits from his tailcoat pocket and offered one to Oliver, who was squatting beside him. Oliver shook his head morosely. 'Suit yourself,' said the Dodger, with a shrug. 'It's all we got,' and he munched hungrily at his biscuit, stuffing the other back in his pocket. ' 'S an undeniable fact,' he now declared, scratching at his chest and watching a man some yards away who was doing the same thing. 'This is the one place you're sure to take out more'n you came in wiv.'

'It's the smell I can't stand,' said Oliver. 'It's horrible.'

The Dodger sniffed the air. 'I never used to notice it,' he said. 'Funny thing. Nothin' I wanted so much as to get back to the old life. But these last cushy months, they've spoilt me for enjoyin' it.'

After a pause, Oliver said quietly: 'I've been thinking, Dodger.'

'Congratulations.'

'No, I'm serious. With nowhere to live and no money . . .'

'We might be led back into a life o' crime,' interposed the Dodger, in a sarcastic tone. ''Ow shockin'!'

That happened to be exactly what Oliver had been contemplating during his hours of restless wakefulness; or one of the things he had considered at least. He had also been thinking about his guardian. 'Not only that,' he now said. 'I have to try to help Mr Brownlow too.'

'Wot could you do?' said the Dodger. 'Best to leave 'is doctor to take care of 'im. E's in a nursin' 'ome ain't 'e? Not even in London.'

'I don't think *we* should stay in London either,' said Oliver.

'Wot d'you mean?'

'We could go to my uncle Harry's place, in the country. He'd know what to do.'

'Very likely,' observed the Dodger, 'but first we 'ave to get there. It's a long ways off, an' if I know Monks an' Bolter, they'll be 'aving the vicarage watched. We'd never reach it.'

'We must do *something*,' said Oliver, desperately.

'All right!' bellowed the giant from the end of the passage. 'Y've 'ad yer money's worth! This ain't a 'otel, y'know!'

'Ain't exactly Buckingham Palace, neither,' declared the Dodger, rising lazily.

'Wot was that? Wot you say?' inquired the giant aggressively, advancing towards the boys. Oliver stood up, frightened; but the man now stumbled over the drunkard who was still lying motionless on the floor.

''Ere! You!' he growled, kicking the prone figure viciously, 'On yer feet! Get up!'

The poor drunkard responded to this attack by remaining mute and utterly limp. The giant scratched his chin and kneeled beside him.

'What's wrong? What's happened to him?' asked Oliver, running forward.

'Best not to know. Come on,' the Dodger whispered, hurriedly pulling Oliver along the passage towards the street. As the two boys emerged into the morning light, Oliver heard the giant call out, in a most irritable manner: 'This one 'ere's snuffed it!'

'Now listen, Oliver,' said the Dodger quietly as they walked side by side down the street. ''Ere's what we do. Find the nearest market, which I 'appen to know is just round that corner, an' you go round the front o' the stalls an' I'll . . .'

'No,' retorted Oliver, shaking his head firmly.

'It's only an orange and a couple of apples!' the Dodger protested, 'They'll never miss 'em.'

'It's still stealing.'

'So maybe you've got a *better* idea.'

'Yes,' said Oliver, stopping, 'I have. There *is* someone we can turn to.'

''Oo's that?' asked the Dodger, stopping too.

'Mr Brownlow's doctor, Mr Hyssop. We can appeal to him. I'm sure he'll help us.'

'I don't see why we need to ask anyone,' said the Dodger irritably, as he resumed walking, 'not when you've got thousands in the bank. Why not just go in and get some of it?'

'It's not like *real* money,' Oliver explained, following him. 'It's all tied up in stocks and securities. What they call a trust.'

'You mean you can't touch it?'

'Not without Mr Brownlow to sign the papers.'

'Blimey O'Riley! An' I thought . . . wot a sell!'

Oliver stopped again abruptly. The Dodger walked on for a few steps and halted, turning. Oliver was examining him in what appeared to be a somewhat injured manner.

'Wot's up?' inquired the Dodger.

'Is that why you came after me?' asked Oliver, sternly. 'Is that why you saved me? Just to get at the money?'

''Course not! Wot makes you think that?'

'It's all anyone seems to care about,' retorted Oliver gloomily.

'Never even entered my 'ead,' declared the Dodger. 'So that's all the thanks I get, is it? Well, I say . . .' His indignation, however, was not very convincing, and he knew it. He decided to sidestep the subject quickly, and said: 'All right, I s'pose there's nothin' else for it. If you're so set on seeing this doctor.'

Oliver presumed that Mr Hyssop's house could not be far from his guardian's, and the two boys immediately set off for Pentonville. The physician proved to be a well-known personage in the locality, and his residence was soon pointed out to them. As Oliver began to advance towards it, he saw that the Dodger was hanging back anxiously.

'Aren't you coming?' asked Oliver.

'Better if one of us stays outside,' murmured the Dodger.

'What for?'

''Case anything goes wrong.'

Oliver laughed, 'You don't trust anyone, do you?'

'*You* maybe,' said the Dodger. 'But only because you don't know any better.'

'Well,' said Oliver, 'I know I can trust someone like Dr Hyssop.'

So the Dodger loitered on the opposite side of the street, as Oliver walked boldly up to the doctor's front door and rang the bell. The maid who opened the door eyed him somewhat suspiciously, and told him to wait there while she fetched the doctor. When this gentleman appeared, he recognized the boy at once and seemed instantly concerned at the sight of his threadbare clothes and pallid countenance. He ushered him into his consulting room. Oliver at once explained how he had had to escape from his guardian's house the previous evening, for he was being kept prisoner there.

'By Mrs Carraway?' the doctor asked.

'And Noah Claypole, the one who calls himself Bolter,' said Oliver. 'They kept me locked in the cellar and wouldn't let me see Mr Brownlow.'

'I did say he was not to be disturbed,' said Dr Hyssop with a frown, 'but that seems unnecessarily severe.' He motioned to Oliver to be seated.

'It wasn't only that, doctor,' Oliver continued, when he had sat down, 'I'd been left some money. Bolter tried to force me to sign it over to him.'

'Good gracious me!' exclaimed the doctor, appalled. 'And Mrs Carraway was a party to this?'

'I'm not sure.'

'I can scarcely believe it of her,' said the doctor, 'although I admit, I find Bolter singularly unpleasant and never understood why she employed him. What a pity your guardian is so ill! He would know how to deal with this.'

'How is he?' Oliver now inquired, anxiously.

'Responding better to treatment now he is in the clinic. You can at least feel easier on that score.'

A warm wave of relief did indeed pass over the boy as he heard this news; he felt happy for the first time in several days, and he sank back into his chair, smiling gratefully. Everything would turn out for the best now, he was certain. There were kind people in the world apart from Mr Brownlow, and one of them was this good doctor.

'My poor boy,' said Hyssop, 'all this must have been very distressing for you. Where did you spend the night?'

'In a Penny Dosshouse,' said Oliver. 'It was horrible.'

'I have no doubt,' retorted the doctor, with a distaste. 'Those places are dens of vice and squalor. What a blessing you came to me!' He promptly went to a cabinet on the wall, and removed from it a small dark bottle and a medicine spoon. 'First,' he said, 'we must make sure that you contracted no intestinal disease. Here – take this,' whereupon he poured out a spoonful of brownish liquid which Oliver obediently swallowed. 'Good – good,' said the doctor, recorking the bottle and replacing it in the cabinet. 'Now, I am, of course only too happy to do what I can,' he continued. 'You have an aunt and uncle in the country, do you not?'

'Yes.'

'Well, I suggest you stay here quietly to recover, while I contact them, and the Police.'

Oliver was very willing to accept this suggestion, for he suddenly felt very tired. This was understandable, for he could not recollect having slept at all during his night at the Penny Hang; his eagerness to contact the doctor however had prevented him from experiencing the effects of sleeplessness until now, when they wafted over him powerfully. But he remained wakeful enough for the moment to remember that his friend was waiting for him outside and would become concerned if he had to wait there too long. 'Thank you, doctor,' Oliver now said, with a yawn. 'I... I have a friend...'

'I think a close relative would be better,' interposed the doctor, busily. 'And of course, the Police must be informed. Though perhaps we should leave that until your uncle or aunt has arrived. But forgive me. You are tired, naturally. Here –' Oliver could barely keep his eyes open or prevent his head from drooping. Dr Hyssop helped him to rise from his chair and led him to a consulting couch in a corner of the room, saying: 'You can lie down for a minute or two, if you wish...'

Very willingly, with the good doctor's help, the boy stretched himself out onto the couch.

'Doctor, my. . . .' he murmured, 'Dodger, my friend. . .'

'Yes, yes,' said Dr Hyssop, soothingly, 'we'll talk again later. You have a little sleep first. Then you can tell me. . . .'

Oliver heard no more, for he had tumbled into the deepest and most well-deserved of slumbers.

The Artful Dodger was pacing impatiently up and down the pavement opposite the house, his hands thrust firmly into his pockets, with a bowed head and a furrowed brow, when he heard the front door open and glanced up, expecting to see Oliver. But the person who emerged was someone whom he had never before encountered and whom he immediately presumed to be Dr Hyssop. Having reached this conclusion, he quickly turned and continued to pretend to gaze at the paving-stones, doing his best to remain inconspicuous. Out of the corner of his eye, however, he saw that the gentleman in question appeared somewhat troubled as he closed the door behind him, put on his hat, and set off briskly down the street. The Artful Dodger hesitated only for a moment before deciding that the thing he had to do next was to follow the good doctor to wherever it was he might be bound. The journey proved to be a short one, for, as the Dodger had already begun to suspect, Dr Hyssop's destination was the home of Oliver's guardian.

'Oliver?' inquired Mrs Carraway, her voice shaking, as she ushered the doctor into Mr Brownlow's sitting room. 'He came to your house?'

'To ask for sanctuary,' explained Hyssop, prompting a low wicked laugh from Noah Claypole, who was with them. 'It is not in the least amusing!' snapped the doctor, glaring disgustedly at him.

'Oh I can see the funny side,' retorted Claypole, softly.

'Where is he now?' asked Mrs Carraway.

'I left him asleep in my study.'

'He may be gone, when you get back!' exclaimed the lady urgently.

'No fear of that,' responded the doctor. 'I gave him a sleeping draught – quite a strong one. He'll know nothing for several hours.'

Mrs Carraway was instantly relieved, and Claypole laughed again. Doctor Hyssop, however, remained agitated, and proceeded to pace up and down the room, saying: 'But what are we to do now? Oh how I wish I'd never become involved!'

'But you *are* involved, Doctor,' observed Claypole, quietly. 'As 'eavily as any of us.'

'Keep your remarks to yourself, Bolter!' Hyssop barked. 'I was addressing Mrs Carraway.'

'Was yer now?' said Claypole, advancing dangerously, 'H'oh was yer? Well, yer'd better start listenin' to *my* remarks, Doctor, 'cos they're wot *goes* round 'ere. Now ain't that right, Mrs C.?'

'Yes, Mr Bolter,' replied Mrs Carraway, in a low, nervous and submissive voice; a voice the doctor had never heard from her before.

'So let's not forget that,' declared Claypole.

Hyssop was thunderstruck. He had supposed, until this moment, for there had been no reason to do otherwise, that the dreadful Bolter was the servant of Mrs Carraway's wishes; he now realized, with horror, that their relationship was quite the reverse. He stared from one to the other. 'I'm washing my hands of this,' he announced firmly, advancing towards the door.

Claypole quickly stepped into his path. 'You supplied the drugs for us to start slippin' into Brownlow's food and drink,' he snarled, 'to make 'im look ill. Yer can't run away from that.'

There was a pause. Dr Hyssop lowered his head. 'I was . . . I was tempted,' he muttered, glumly, 'and I . . . and I yielded to temptation.'

'As I guessed yer would,' declared Claypole.

Dr Hyssop looked up. 'So it was *you* who was behind it,' he said.

Claypole nodded proudly and replied: 'Like I was behind Mrs C. becomin' 'ousekeeper 'ere.'

'The point is,' Mrs Carraway now impatiently interposed, 'what are we to do?'

'Well, there's no call to panic,' said Claypole, 'Nothin's changed. As long as Brownlow stays in that nursin' 'ome, you can stay 'ere, livin' a life o' leisure.'

'And help *you* to draw on his finances,' rejoined Hyssop, with disgust.

'While *you* gets paid reg'lar and substantial doctor's fees!' snapped Claypole, glaring back at him; his face then relaxed into a grin and he said, with a shrug: 'We all 'ave wot we want. The only fly in the ointment was Oliver. Well, now we've got 'im too.'

'But what do we do with him?' asked Hyssop.

'We'll have to give up the idea of getting at his money,' said Mrs Carraway.

'Why?' demanded Claypole sharply.

'It will take too long,' announced Mrs Carraway. 'We must have him put away.'

Noah Claypole was suddenly frightened; villain that he unquestionably was, the list of crimes that he was willing to perpetrate did not include that of murder. 'Put away?' he echoed, shakily.

'Well, that's what you're suggesting, isn't it?' said Mrs Carraway, with a calm expression.

'No, it is not!' Claypole hastily replied.

'I agree,' declared the doctor firmly. 'I will not be a party to murder!'

Noah Claypole winced. 'No need for that kind o' talk!' he exclaimed. 'No need at all!'

'We can't take the chance of him escaping again and giving us away!' cried Mrs Carraway, with extreme impatience.

'Wait!' said the doctor. 'You were planning to hand him over to the Police on some trumped-up charges. We can still do that. If he were discredited, no one would believe him!'

'No,' retorted Claypole dismissively. 'No, it's too late. Too dangerous now. 'E might come up before a nosy magistrate, who'd investigate. Might even send another doctor to look at Brownlow.'

'We can't risk that!' exclaimed Hyssop, truly alarmed.

'No,' said Claypole. After further thought he announced: 'Well, leave it to me. I 'ave a friend who's interested in this 'ole business. 'E'll know wot to do.'

The evil Monks had learnt of Oliver's escape from Mr Brownlow's house and had naturally reacted furiously, threatening Claypole with a most dire series of tortures if the boy was not caught again very quickly. He had declared that he would wait at the Three Cripples tavern until Claypole could furnish him with good news; if there was no news by that evening, or if the news proved to be bad, Claypole could reliably expect vengeance of the most ghastly kind. Noah Claypole was obviously thoroughly relieved, therefore, when he heard that Oliver was lying drugged at Hyssop's house, and he now hurried to the Cripples to relate this happy fact to the waiting Monks, who was seated in the private bar with Ned Fingers.

'We've got 'im!' he announced joyously as he entered the room.

'Safe?' asked Monks, with wolfish delight.

'Safe 'n' sound' said Noah, holding out an open hand and closing it tightly.

'Where is he?' asked Monks.

'At the doctor's house.'

'He can't get away?'

'Not this time.'

Monks laughed quietly. Feeling bold enough to be mirthful too, Ned Fingers also laughed, a little nervously. Monks turned on him sharply, without a trace of amusement in his face. Fingers' little giggle died away.

'So you are pleased too, are you Fingers?' hissed Monks.

'Oh yessir!' replied Fingers anxiously, 'Yes, Mr Monks.'

'Why?'

'Well . . . ,' said Fingers. 'It was Oliver that snitched on Fagin an' Bill Sikes. 'E ought to be taught a lesson.'

'So you'd say he deserved to be punished?'

''Ung!' declared Fingers, 'An' drawn! An' quartered, for good measure.'

'What a bloodthirsty little ferret you are,' said Monks, almost fondly. Fingers grinned at this indication of approval. But now Monks turned away from him again and towards Claypole, saying softly: 'No, I don't want him killed. That would be too easy.'

'Wot's the answer then?' said Noah, 'We can't keep 'im locked up forever – an' 'e knows too much to 'and 'im over to the law. So that's out.'

'Thanks to your greed and incompetence,' observed Monks, coldly.

'I'd say that was the pot callin' the kettle black!' retorted Claypole in a hurt tone. 'Even Fagin an' you came a cropper over 'im, as I remember.'

That was a brave thing for Claypole to do; to remind Monks of his previous failure. He was not sure, however, that he had been especially wise to do it, for the villain now glared at him with a murderous expression. Ned Fingers quite expected him to pounce upon Claypole and strangle him there and then; but Monks suddenly relaxed and nodded in agreement. 'You are quite right for once, Bolter,' he said softly. 'Except that, where you were too crude, we were too subtle. Now I know *exactly* how to deal with my dear little . . . Oliver. Something much more direct.' He smiled his horrible half smile, then sharply turned to Fingers. 'You know the East India Dock?' he demanded.

'Yes, Mr Monks.'

'Get down there. If the brig *Tiger* hasn't sailed, find

the captain and tell him I want to see him.'

'Yessir!' cried Fingers, and rose from where he was sitting. He glanced briefly at Noah for his approval.

'Sharp about it!' barked Monks.

'Yessir!' cried Fingers, and he was gone.

'Wot's the game, then?' asked Claypole.

'You'll find out,' said Monks. 'But listen, Bolter – if Oliver has escaped again—'

''E can't 'ave,' Noah interposed quickly. 'The doctor's got 'im lyin' in his consulting room, drugged, dead to the world.'

'He'd better be,' hissed Monks. 'Or you'll join him. Only *you* won't wake up.'

The reader will no doubt recollect the existence of a tiny window that was fixed high in the wall of this room, through which it was possible to observe, and indeed hear, any conversation that might be occurring therein. The window was curtained on the other side. On this occasion, the curtain was pulled across, so that Monks and Claypole would have seen nothing suspicious, even if they had chosen to glance in its direction. For his part, the Artful Dodger, who was at this moment standing behind the window, had no need to pull the curtain back in order to be able to view the two men, for he knew them by their voices, and could hear every word that passed between them. Having seen Dr Hyssop enter Mr Brownlow's house, he had waited in the street for further developments. After ten minutes or so, Noah Claypole had emerged with the doctor, and both men had set hurriedly off in opposite directions. Assuming that the doctor was returning home, the Dodger had decided to follow Claypole rather than Hyssop, concluding that such a course of action might be the more interesting of the two possibilities. As he listened to the conversation reported above, he knew that his conclusion had been correct.

CHAPTER FIFTEEN

A most ominously curious personage arrived in the private room of the Three Cripples tavern that evening, duly summoned by Ned Fingers. He was a brutally thickset, unshaven, scarred and cruel-faced gentleman with a black eye patch and wild yellow hair which reached to his shoulders; he wore striped trousers tucked into his high, heavy boots and a long-tailed brass-buttoned coat of blue cloth, unfastened to reveal an open necked shirt and spotted neckerchief, under a velour waistcoat; round his middle he wore a broad leather belt, and his huge right hand seldom seemed to stray from the hilt of a long and sinister knife which was thrust through it.

'Ye wanted to see me?' this creature growled, filling the doorway with his immense and vicious form. At the sight of him, Noah Claypole could do nothing but gape in open terror.

'That I did, Captain,' replied Monks, without a trace of fear, rising from the table.

'Yere lucky then,' said the man. 'If ye'd sent tomorrow, ye'd ha' found me gone.'

'You're sailing?' inquired Monks.

'For the Ivory Coast.'

'Couldn't be better,' said Monks, quietly.

'Someone ye want rid of,' growled the man, advancing into the room and glaring with his one eye at Noah. 'Is it this 'un?' he asked, and his fingers curled dangerously round the handle of his knife. Noah could only open and close his mouth repeatedly in a silent panic.

'One day maybe,' said Monks, with a slight smile. 'Not just yet.' The man chuckled. 'Bolter,' Monks continued. 'This is Captain Ketch, master of the brig *Tiger*.' Noah merely mouthed a greeting. Monks turned back to Ketch. 'So, Captain,' he said, 'you're off to Africa.'

'On the dawn tide,' said Ketch.

'Better and better,' mused Monks.

At last, Noah managed to speak. 'Would yer care for a . . .?' he squeaked, then coughed, aware that his voice was unnaturally high, and tried again. 'Would yer care for a glass o' wine, Cap'n Ketch?' he asked, in a lower register, reaching for the bottle before him.

'If ye've no rum at hand,' replied Ketch.

'Fingers!' said Claypole to the boy who was still hovering terrified in the doorway. 'Rum for the Cap'n.' Fingers scuttled away.

'Now then,' said Monks, 'to business.' He motioned to Ketch to sit. 'Do you have a full crew, Captain?' he asked, when Ketch had done so.

'As full as can be mustered these days,' replied Ketch. 'Soon as they hear ye're bound for the Ivory Coast, the yellow dogs turn tail.'

'Cabin boys?' inquired Monks.

'Not so easy to come by as they were. They don't last long, d'ye see. It's the fever.'

'And you work them hard,' said Monks.

'I make sure they earn their keep.'

This was a chilling thought indeed, and Monks smiled at it. 'I'll warrant that,' he murmured. 'Well, Captain, Mr Bolter here can put you in the way of a likely lad.'

'Is that so?' said Ketch, considering Noah. 'Has a hankerin' to go to sea, has he?'

'Well . . .,' Claypole began.

'Or maybe he can't make up his mind,' continued the Captain, with a cruel leer. 'But you, for his own good, want to find 'im a berth, steer 'im into the right profession. Is that right?'

'That's it. That's it, exactly,' said Monks.

'Exactly,' echoed Claypole, as Fingers returned to the room with a large glass of rum on a tray.

'Well,' declared Ketch, taking the glass, 'as Mr Monks knows, I'm always on the look-out for a promisin' lad. Prepared to pay for 'im. And no questions asked.'

Whereupon he tossed back the rum in one gigantic swallow, wiped his mouth with the back of his hand and grinned terribly.

Night had descended fully, and Oliver was still sound asleep under a blanket on the couch in Dr Hyssop's consulting room. He was alone in his slumbers, and the room was dimly lit by a solitary lamp on the doctor's desk. Suddenly the only window, which looked out into the garden, began to inch up, and shadowy figure peered in. With the expertise of a practised housebreaker, he pushed the window slowly open, climbed nimbly onto the ledge and slipped silently into the room. He saw Oliver at once and stealthily approached the couch. 'Oliver! Oliver!' he whispered urgently. Soliciting not the slightest reaction, he reached forward and gently shook the boy's shoulder, whispering more loudly: 'Oliver! Wake up! It's me, Dodger! Wake up! Come on, we're getting out!' Oliver remained infuriatingly motionless; the Artful Dodger reached the conclusion that he would have no alternative but to lift his unconscious friend up and carry him to freedom. He had begun to do this, and had raised Oliver a few inches when he heard voices and the sound of approaching footsteps. In an instant, he lowered the boy onto the couch and ran to the window; realizing, however, that he would not have time to clamber over the sill and into the garden, he decided to dive under the desk. He had just done so when the door opened and three people walked in.

'So that's 'im?' growled Ketch. 'Not sick, is he?'

'No, no,' said Hyssop softly. 'He's just asleep.'

'Best way for 'im to come aboard,' observed Ketch. Ned Fingers, who was the third member of the party, giggled nastily. His mirth vanished abruptly, however, when he saw the boy stir slightly and his closed eyes begin to flicker.

''E's wakin' up!' squealed Fingers, 'Doctor!'

Ketch instantly produced a short heavy cosh from the pocket of his coat. 'No need for that!' said Hyssop firmly. 'Not here.' He rapidly went to the cabinet in the wall, removed the small dark bottle and uncorked it as he returned to Oliver, who was now beginning to raise his head, his eyes opening dazedly.

'All right, my boy,' murmured the doctor soothingly, supporting the boy's head with one hand and putting the bottle to his lips with the other. 'All right now. You're quite safe. Just a sip of this and you'll feel much better.' Oliver sipped obediently and within a second his head had fallen back onto the pillow in a deep sleep. Fingers proceeded to giggle again.

'Belay that, ye bilge rat!' growled Ketch, raising his cosh. Fingers ceased giggling instantly, and the Captain approached Oliver with a view to picking him up.

'No one must see him being taken out!' said Hyssop, nervously. 'He mustn't be traced back to this house!'

Ketch grunted and pulled the blanket up to hide Oliver's face, 'Get his feet,' he said to Fingers. Fingers did so, and they raised the boy and carried him from the room. The doctor followed them out, closing the door.

The Artful Dodger scrambled hurriedly from under the desk, exasperated with himself for being just too late; he did not know where to turn or what to do. At all events, he decided, he had to follow his unconscious friend to wherever he was being taken to next. He was about to move quickly to the window, when he caught sight of the small dark bottle on the desk, which Hyssop in his nervousness had forgotten to return to the cabinet; he put it into his pocket.

The doctor returned immediately to Mr Brownlow's house to report to Mrs Carraway; there was little he could tell her that she would not know soon enough anyway, but he had no desire to be seen walking through

London on a dark winter's night in the company of a youthful thief, a villainous-looking sea-captain and a body wrapped in a blanket, so he took his leave of Fingers and Ketch as soon as they had reached the street, and hurried away. Fingers and Ketch carried Oliver as hastily and as surreptitiously as they could to the Three Cripples, where Claypole awaited them. Monks, as was his habit, had decided to vanish for the moment.

The Captain laid his unconscious captive on the bench in the tavern's private room and proceeded to tie him up, still wrapped in the blanket, with a strong cord, so that he was eventually contained in a thoroughly secure package. 'That'll hold him,' announced Ketch, inspecting his handiwork. 'If he starts to wake up again.'

' 'E won't suffocate, will 'e?' asked Claypole, somewhat anxiously.

'I've left 'is chest free,' declared Ketch, 'I want 'im fit for work, when he gets aboard.'

'Yer said y'd pay for 'im,' said Claypole, ' 'Ow much?'

'Standard,' replied the captain, extracting a handful of coins from his waistcoat and paying them out into Claypole's outstretched palm. 'Five guineas a cabin boy.'

Claypole was delighted to receive this sum. But his fears returned when the Captain now made for the door and said: 'I'll be back to fetch 'im jus' before sailin' time. Keep your eye on 'im.'

'Yer leavin' 'im 'ere?' asked Claypole, nervously. 'Why not 'aul 'im off now?'

'Less people about an hour before dawn,' said Ketch. 'Less chance o' some busybody takin' it into their head he's bein' shanghaied.' He chuckled evilly and left the room. Claypole looked at his watch thoughtfully, and then at the body on the bench.

'I'd sooner be in Newgate prison than sail wiv that one,' declared Ned Fingers with a grin.

'That's a fact, Fingers,' retorted Noah distractedly, 'Well yer 'eard the Cap'n. Keep an eye on 'im,' he walked rapidly to the door.

'Where yer goin', Mr Bolter?' asked Fingers, apprehensively.

' 'Ome, – if it's any o' yer business.'

'Leavin' me alone with him?' said Fingers, with indignation, 'Why?'

'Because yer works for me, that's why.'

'But I works fer nothin'!' protested Fingers. 'An' you walks off wiv five guineas!'

After a pause, Claypole retorted with a sigh: 'I'm disappointed in yer, Fingers. Never thought yer was so greedy . . .' He reluctantly handed the young thief one of the guineas.

' 'S more like it,' said Fingers, after having bitten the coin to test it.

'Now,' said Claypole, 'Listen. Yer not on no account to leave this room, nor let 'im out o' yer sight.'

'Right,' said Fingers.

'If yer does,' said Claypole threateningly, 'yer'll not only 'ave me to deal with, but Monks an' Cap'n Ketch. So, remember.'

'Right,' said Fingers.

When Claypole had gone, Fingers had room to reflect on the seriousness of such a threat; he was no longer so afraid of the great Morris Bolter, for he was beginning to discover certain cowardly traits in that gentleman, but he did not especially relish the thought of suffering at the hands of the mysterious Monks, or, worse still, of the terrible Captain Ketch, should anything untoward now happen to Oliver. He hurried to the door and locked it on the inside; then, after having carefully examined the knots securing the boy, and having satisfied himself as to their tightness, he sat at the table, not permitting his eyes to stray from the body for one moment.

Noah Claypole walked briskly home, well-satisfied with all that he had achieved. Mrs Carraway and Dr Hyssop were waiting anxiously in the sitting-room when he arrived.

'Is everything settled?' asked the lady.

'Everything taken care of?' asked the doctor.

'All ship-shape an' Bristol fashion,' replied Noah, handing his hat to Mrs Carraway, who took it obediently. Master of all he surveyed, he sat himself down in an armchair by the fire, stretched his long legs with a yawn, and said: 'Bring us a glass o' sherry will yer?' Meekly, Mrs Carraway did as she was commanded.

At precisely this moment, Ned Fingers was staring in terror at a section of the floor in the private room of the Cripples; it appeared to be rising, very slowly, creaking as it did so. He soon realized that he was gazing at a trap-door, the existence of which he had previously been unaware. His fear increased as he saw someone emerge from the dark hole. He did not recognize this personage at first, for the room was dimly lit. As the figure climbed out, however, and began to approach him, Fingers suddenly cried, in joy and relief: 'Stone the crows! It's the Dodger!'

'Wotcher, Fingers,' said the Artful Dodger, with a grin.

'I can't believe it,' said Fingers, 'Where d'you come from?'

'Up through there. It's an old bolthole of Fagin's.'

Fingers rose to examine the trap-door and said with a chuckle: 'There all the time, eh? 'Andy, that.' He examined the new discovery for some moments before turning again to his old colleague in crime. ''Ere,' he said, 'I thought yer'd been transported.'

'Escaped, didn' I?' said the Dodger, with pride.

'Might ha' knowed it,' declared Fingers, admiringly. 'Never was a jail could 'old you, eh, Artful? So yer've come back to join us?'

'Looks like it,' said the Dodger.

''Ere,' said Fingers, jerking his thumb in the direction of the body on the bench, 'Yer'll never guess at who's in there. Twist – Oliver Twist, 'im that done for Fagin an' all of us.'

'Get away!' exclaimed the Dodger. 'A goner 'is 'e?'

'Nah . . . ,' replied Fingers, chuckling. 'E's been press ganged. Which ain't 'alf wot 'e deserves. Still – things is all right now, with Mr Bolter in charge.'

'Bolter? Never met 'im.'

''E's your sort,' said Fingers. 'Nearly as good a fence as old Flat'at was. Even meaner.'

The Dodger laughed, 'Well,' he suggested, 'let's 'ave a pot of ale to celebrate, eh?'

'Right!' said Fingers; but he did not move, for he expected the Dodger to be the one would go and purchase the celebratory drink.

The Dodger then said softly, with a wink: 'Only I don't want to risk showin' meself in public, eh? Not just yet.'

Fingers' face fell. 'Well, I'd fetch it,' he said, 'but I promised Mr Bolter I wouldn't leave 'im alone.' He pointed to Oliver.

'No problem, Fingers,' said the Dodger casually, 'I'll watch 'im for yer.'

Fingers hesitated briefly, 'Yer on!' he said, extracting the guinea from his pocket, 'An' the ale's on Mr Bolter!' Grinning, he unlocked the door and scurried from the room. The Dodger took immediate advantage of the boy's absence and ran to Oliver, lifting the blanket from his face and whispering urgently: 'Oliver! Wake up! Come on – for pity's sake! This time *wake up*!' He shook his friend frantically, but there was no response. He then tried to untie some of the knots in the cord, but they were immaculate and stubbornly complex. He was tugging at one of them when he sensed danger; he quickly covered Oliver's face again with the blanket and retreated to the centre of the room, adopting an innocent countenance just as the little thief returned, carrying two tankards of ale.

'That was quick!' declared Fingers, happily.

'That it was,' said the Dodger.

Fingers kicked the door shut and laid the tankards on the table. ''Ere we are,' he said, 'Somethin' to celebrate all right. You back an' Twist on 'is way out for good.'

'Don't 'ear 'im breathin',' said the Dodger casually, seating himself at the table, 'not smothered inside that blanket, is 'e?'

Instantly alarmed, Fingers ran to inspect Oliver, bending down to listen to his chest. It was a fateful move on his part, for in leaving the table unattended, even for such a brief period of time, he unwittingly allowed the Dodger to remove a small dark bottle from his pocket, uncork it with a flick of the thumb, and pour its contents into one of the tankards of ale. When Fingers returned to the table, having satisfied himself that Oliver was still alive, the Dodger was sipping the other tankard innocently.

''E's breathin' all right,' announced Fingers, sitting down opposite the Dodger and eyeing him with admiration. 'I can't wait to see the gang's faces, when they find out yer back,' he said with a chuckle, picking up his tankard. 'It was good wiv Bolter. Now we've got the Artful Dodger's as well, we'll start a reign o' crime such as old London's never seen.'

The Dodger smiled. 'Let's drink to that,' he said.

They clinked their tankards together, and drank. Having swallowed a huge draught, Fingers set his tankard down, grinned at the Dodger, and fell flat on his face on the table top.

Some time later, a good hour before daylight, Monks and Captain Ketch returned to the Three Cripples Tavern to collect Oliver. Monks was surprised, and angry, to find the door of the private room unlocked and no one within, except of course for the wrapped body, which lay safely on its bench.

'Fingers!' barked Monks.

'No sign of 'im,' said Ketch.

'Typical!' snarled Monks. 'Typical! Typical of the riff-raff Bolter uses. Not one you can depend on.'

'No matter,' said the captain, approaching the body. 'The boy's still 'ere. That's all that counts.'

'Want a hand with him?' asked Monks.

'No need,' replied Ketch, swinging the body over his shoulder as if it were no heavier than a sack of feathers.

'You'll be careful?'

'Don't worry. There's no one about at this hour. I won't untie and uncover 'im till we're well out to sea. There's no risk of 'is bein' spotted and rescued.'

'Good. Good,' murmured Monks, in an unholily satisfied tone.

'Now mind,' growled Ketch, gazing dangerously at him. 'we clapped hands to a bargain. I didn't ask no questions. And don't you ask none o' me, whatever becomes o' 'im.'

'Agreed,' said Monks, moving to the door; he peered into the darkness outside, and having concluded to his satisfaction that their exit would not be observed, left the room. Ketch followed him, with the tightly bound bundle over his massive shoulders.

Oliver awoke to find himself in a dirty, straw-floored lean-to that was little bigger than a chicken coop. The early morning light filtered through the gaps between the planks that made up the walls of this tiny and unattractive abode. Still barely conscious, he tried to remember the circumstances of his falling asleep in the first place, and soon recollected that he had been lying on Dr Hyssop's couch when a sudden and uncontrollable drowsiness had overcome him.

'Mornin',' said a familiar voice. Oliver was startled into full wakefulness in an instant, and saw the Artful Dodger sitting beside him with his legs crossed.

'Where ... where are we?' Oliver asked.

'Little place I know,' replied the Dodger.

'But how did we . . .?'

'Last o' the biscuits,' announced the Dodger, a little despondently, breaking it in two and handing one half to his friend.

'But how did we get *here*?' asked Oliver.

'I'll have to begin at the beginnin',' said the Dodger, with a grin. 'You eat up, an' I'll tell yer all about it.' Whereupon he did so, in great detail, leaving until last, the pleasant revelation that little Ned Fingers was perhaps at that moment waking up to discover that he was tied up in a blanket, with nothing but the sound of the rolling sea in his ears, on his way to Africa.

CHAPTER SIXTEEN

That afternoon, in the private room of the Cripples, the great Morris Bolter interviewed two more thieves who were eager to be members of his gang. One of these was a young woman with a hollow-eyed, pinched face and a propensity to breathe somewhat noisily through her nose; her companion was a thin, pale pock-marked youth with teeth as black as his hair. Claypole thought he had never before encountered quite such an unpleasant looking couple; they seemed exceptionally dirty, too, and he, for his part, was feeling particularly fine and clean and impressive this afternoon, for with the four guineas acquired the previous night he had just purchased a sparkling waistcoat and a splendid pair of new boots.

The youth had procured, by mysterious means, a gold snuffbox, ornately decorated with enamel, which he had proudly handed to Claypole for inspection. Claypole appeared to be less interested in the box however, than he was in the snuff that it contained, a pinch of which he now picked up between his thumb and forefinger and put delicately to his nose; fortunately, he succeeded in rapidly extracting a silk handkerchief from his waistcoat pocket and managed just in time to catch the full force of the ensuing sneeze; he had never taken snuff before, and had not realized that it was capable of producing a nasal catastrophe of such turbulent proportions.

'Y'know,' he said, when he had regained his composure, 'I may jus' keep this meself. Snuff – well now – snuff-takin' is – yer might say – hafter all, a gentleman's hoccupation.'

The youth leaned forward, his eyes narrowing threateningly, 'Keep it?' he snarled.

'Oh, yer'll get wot's due!' snapped Claypole, with a scowl.

'I'd like to see it,' said the youth, remaining distrustful. 'In me 'and, Fingers said.'

'Fingers?' exclaimed Claypole quickly sitting up. 'You seen 'im?'

'Day 'for yesterday,' replied the youth. ''E said, if we came to you, 'e'd see we got a fair deal.'

''E did, did 'e?' retorted Claypole, bridling. ''E would, would 'e? Well, 'e ain't 'ere to see nothin', is 'e?'

The youth looked startled, ''E's gone?' he inquired.

'Without a wave of 'is – well, as yer might say – fingers. An' I made 'im me lootenant.'

'Lootenant, eh?' said the youth, his eyes lighting up interestedly.

'Partaker in all me affairs,' said Claypole.

The youth glanced briefly at his snivelling female companion, whose countenance also betrayed a sudden interest; he then adopted an abruptly ingratiating manner and said: 'Ungrateful that, Mr Bolter.' Noah Claypole merely snorted, somewhat despondently.

'Mebbe . . . ,' the snivelling woman tentatively began.

'Now if you was needin' someone, Mr Bolter,' interposed the youth. 'Like, to take 'is place?' Claypole stared up at him.

The woman, however, would not be silenced and, after controlling her snivelling as best she could, she continued: 'Mebbe it'd be worth a little somethin', mebbe, findin' where 'e might've gone.' Claypole now stared at her. *That*, he thought, surveying the both of them, was without doubt the more intelligent suggestion.

Oliver, after listening to the tale of how he had been freed from the evil intentions of Claypole, Monks and Ketch, had fallen asleep again, for Hyssop's potion, whatever it was, had been a powerful one. He now awoke once more to see the Dodger peering at him intently. They were still in the little hut. A low evening light filtered through the slats.

'Mm. You'll do. Over it, I reckon,' said the Dodger.

'I suppose so,' said Oliver. 'If I just wasn't so hungry.'

'Well,' retorted the Dodger with a grin, 'chances are we can do somethin' about that.' He reached into his pocket and produced two pennies with a flourish, clinking them in his palm. 'An' before you say what you're thinkin', I earned 'em,' he announced, ''Oldin' a 'orse for a cabby wantin' a stoop o' ale.' He raised a finger threateningly, 'An' if you says anythin' to anyone about me takin' the straight an' narrer I'll . . .'

Oliver, thoroughly awake for the first time in over a day, burst out laughing. After some seconds of surprise, the Dodger also began to laugh uncontrollably. Their mirth was quickly cut short, however, by the sudden entrance of someone else onto the scene. The small makeshift door of the hut opened noisily, and the person in question was preceded by a battered handcart piled high with large but empty sacks from which there protruded a round-headed, long-handled brush. The Dodger leapt out of the cart's path and proceeded to glance about vainly in search of some weapon of defence; Oliver was on his feet in an instant. The owner of the cart then appeared; he was a tall, broad gentleman with grizzled hair and a pair of eyes that peered redly from a face so black with ingrained soot that its other features were indefinable in the hut's gloom; he wore a low-crowned, curly-brimmed hat and a spotted neckerchief, a drab waistcoat and a shapeless jacket, worsted trousers held up by a broad belt and tied with bootlaces below the knees, and heavy boots with steel toe-caps.

''Ere!' this fearsome individual declared harshly, as he saw two shapes lurking in the shadows of his hut, 'Wot yer doin' 'ere?' Private property this is! 'Oo are you anyway?'

The Dodger, seeing no escape for the moment, decided to step forward and present himself. 'Name o' Dawkins, Jack,' he announced cheerfully, 'an' this is a friend, Oliver . . . Oliver Brown. An' who – if I might make so bold – 'ave we the pleasure of addressin'?'

The man appeared to inspect the boys appraisingly, and to eye Oliver with a particular interest. 'Bold, bold,' he muttered, 'an' a bit big, an' not big enough.' Whereupon he chuckled quietly to himself for a few moments before saying: 'All right, Master Dawkins an' Master Brown, I ain't goin' to chop yer 'eads off. Me name's Samuel Slammett, whose sainted ma called 'er little Samival, but most now just gives Sam'l.' Then he said in a harsher tone: 'An' this 'ere's me shed where I keeps me cart, an' I asked yer already, wot yer doin' ere?'

'Weren't no cart 'ere last night,' said the Dodger.

'Oh wery bold, wery bold indeed!' said Mr Slammett with a sigh. 'Now I asked yer nicely.'

'We were just looking for shelter, last night,' Oliver explained softly.

'Orphans o' the storm,' declared the Dodger, with a grin.

'Orphans!' muttered Slammett incredulously, 'Yer runaways, ain't yer.'

Oliver was about to deny this most fervently, but before he could do so the Dodger said, shamefacedly, 'Not much use tryin' to 'ide it, I suppose.'

''Oo from?' asked Slammett. 'Yer families? Or the peelers?'

'From a life on the ocean wave,' declared Dodger, prompting a stare of even stronger disbelief from the man. 'It's the truth!' he continued. 'They were wanting to ship Oliver off – 'is alf-brother, an' 'is alf-brother's friends – sellin' 'im as a cabin boy, sailin' for the Ivory Coast.'

'An 'alf brother?' exclaimed Slammett, 'An' 'e cut an' run?'

'An' that's 'ow we 'appen to be 'ere,' said the Dodger, 'Shelterin', like 'e said.'

'Well, well,' muttered Slammett. 'Well . . . well, the Ivory Coast! Well, I don't blame yer.'

'And it's all right, then, if we stay?' Oliver now asked

meekly. 'Just for one more night perhaps?'

'Now that's a fing, ain't it?' mused Slammett, scratching the back of his thick neck reflectively. 'Now that's a fing. Me Christian duty, y'know . . .'

'You wouldn't give us up, would you?' Oliver pleaded anxiously.

'To the Ivory Coast?' exclaimed the man, in a scandallized voice. 'Wot yer take me for? Not to the Caribbees, an' all them palm trees, not against yer will! But stayin' 'ere? No, it's me Christian duty not to let yer.'

'Christian!' the Dodger then muttered, disgustedly, 'Come on, Oliver. We may as well go.'

The two boys moved despondently to the door, but the man stepped forward and barred their way. 'Not so fast,' he said. 'Where'll yer go?'

'We can find a Penny Hang,' said Oliver, morosely, 'we've got . . .'

'We've got friends'll slip us a copper or two,' the Dodger interposed, for he did not consider it safe to mention the fact that they had money to a stranger of such cast, however paltry the sum.

'But won't slip yer a corner o' floor to lie on,' declared Slammett. 'No. I couldn't let yer. But as me sainted ma used to say, a 'ome shared is a 'ome warmed, an' that's where yer'll go, you an' . . . Master Brown. 'Ome. Care o' Sam'l Slammett. 'Ome. As long as yer needs it.'

The offer took both boys entirely by surprise. Oliver was delighted at the gentleman's kindness, but the Dodger considered it too abrupt to be anything but intensely suspect. He knew, however, that in their present state, neither of them were in a position to decline it.

'Ome then, such as it is,' announced Slammett. 'An' not too bad, neither, is it? Runnin' water. 'Ow many yer knows got that, eh? An' a cheery fire to keep us cheery.' He had led them to a large and not completely unhomely room, lit by a solitary candle on the single table and the glow from a small coke-burning stove in one corner, which crackled merrily. On the stove, a large enamel teapot hissed a welcome. The room's only other furnishings comprised a narrow truckle-bed, a battered dresser, four stools set around the table, and a high pile of black sacks against one of the walls. The place boasted two sizeable windows, both grimy and incongruously barred, and two doors, one leading to the passage outside, and the other to what the boys presumed to be a cupboard. This latter door was heavily padlocked. There was a sink, too, with a tap. 'Better'n the old shed, eh?' said Slammett, locking the door through which they had just entered, and moving towards the sink.

'It's very good of you to take us in,' said Oliver.

'Christian duty, like I said,' retorted Slammett. 'Eh, Master Dawkins?'

'Like you said,' said the Dodger.

'Coke burnin' in the stove, an' tea brewin' in the pot. Warm outside an' in. Wot we all needs to be, wot we all soon will be.'

Samuel Slammett had turned on the tap and doused his black face thoroughly. He now wiped it dry and comparatively clean with a rag that hung beside the sink, revealing a countenance that no longer seemed sinister, but cheerful and friendly. He went to the dresser and removed from it four cracked plates and four similarly chipped mugs, bringing them to the table.

'Would you like me to pour it? The tea?' asked Oliver.

'No, no, needs a knack,' replied Slammett, returning to the dresser and lifting out a platter bearing a large loaf and a dish of butter. ''Andle gets 'ot. Dob'll see to that.'

'Who?' asked Oliver.

'Dob,' said Slammett, placing the loaf and the butter on the table. ''E's use to it.' He then turned in the direction of the large pile of sacks and called: 'Dob! Hey, Dob!'

There was a sudden convulsion from amid the pile,

and a lengthy fit of raucous coughing; as the noise began to subside, a very thin, very ragged youth emerged; under dirt as ingrained as Slammett's, his features were pale and drawn. Both Oliver and the Dodger noticed, as he slowly approached them, that his skeletal hands were trembling.

'Friends, Dob,' said Slammett. 'Master Dawkins an' Master Brown. Stayin' wiv us a while.' The announcement seemed to solicit a suddenly perturbed look in the youth's hollow eyes.

'Hallo, Dob,' said Oliver, in a friendly tone. Dob appeared to try to reply, but could only embark on a renewed paroxysm of coughing.

'Poor lad can't talk. Can yer, Dob?' Slammet explained. The youth lowered his eyes, and shook his head, still coughing violently. Over this sorry sound, Slammet then continued: 'Like yerselves, an orphan o' the storm. Not much use to 'isself, or anyone, but 'e don't cost much to keep. So, like yerselves, 'ere 'e is. Dob, lad, pour the tea for us, will yer?' Dob moved obediently to the stove and, after blowing on his fingers, grasped the teapot handle firmly and lifted it from the stove. The Dodger assumed that this action must be painful, but there was no sign of agony on the youth's worn features as he proceeded to pour the tea into the mugs on the table. As he was doing this, Slammet returned to the dresser and removed a second platter bearing a slab of cheese and several onions, which he then placed on the table. 'Well, as me sainted ma always said . . . ,' he declared, drawing up a stool and seating himself, 'if wishes were dishes we'd all eat 'earty.' He chuckled. 'Mebbe not that 'earty though, but enough, we can 'ope, to keep us from rumblin'.'

Apologetic though he was for the quality of the meal, both Oliver and the Dodger considered it a banquet, and fell to it, hungrily, prompting a loud roar of mirth from their host. The Dodger became aware, however, after a while, that poor Dob could only pick at the food in a most desultory manner, taking the tiniest mouthfuls, and interspersing each one with a further bout of coughing.

'You've done what?' hissed Monks. It was the morning after the mysterious disappearance of Ned Fingers, and Monks and Noah Claypole were seated in the private room of the Three Cripples.

'Well,' replied Claypole, 'I thought you'd best 'ear it from the woman herself.'

'And you've given her my name.'

'No 'course not! Wot yer take me for?'

'A purblind, bumbling fool,' said Monks, quietly. 'But you invited her to meet me. Someone else to see us together. When it'll be weeks before we can possibly hear from Ketch.'

Noah Claypole began to despair of ever being able to perform an action capable of winning his evil accomplice's approval. The slatternly, snivelling young woman he had met the previous afternoon, in suggesting she might be able to find Fingers for a price, had aroused in Noah a suspicion that she may actually know of the little thief's whereabouts. Further contemplation had led him to realize that Fingers was the only person, apart from Mrs Carraway, Dr Hyssop, Captain Ketch, Monks and himself, who knew of the successful abduction of Oliver Twist, and that it was therefore not safe to allow him to continue to wander about the streets on his own in an independent fashion, wherever he might be. The woman had also hinted that the disloyal little creature could well have joined another gang, under another fence, implying thereby that she perhaps knew this to be the case, even to the extent of knowing who the other fence was. Haunted by these awful possibilities, Claypole had concluded that the woman should be brought as soon as possible before Monks who, with his openly dangerous qualities, would be more capable of extracting the truth from her than he was; probably by merely giving her the benefit of one of his powerfully menacing stares. Accordingly, Claypole had instructed the woman to attend him in the private room of the Cripples that morning, at a time when he and Monks had already arranged a meeting.

There was now a tap at the door and the woman peered into the room. Monks was seated with his back to her and stiffened at her entrance.

'Mr Bolter?' said the snivelling woman.

'Get rid of her,' Monks murmured to Claypole.

'Yer said to look in, Mr Bolter,' said the woman.

'Get rid of her,' Monks repeated, softly, as his hand crept towards the silver handle of his cane. 'Get rid of her, or I'll do it for you. Permanently.' His fingers closed around the handle.

'Mr Bolter?' said the woman.

'We ain't – we ain't ready,' said Claypole nervously. 'Come back – in a 'our. That'll do it. In a 'our.'

'But yer said . . .'

'An' now I'm sayin', come back!' barked Claypole, his voice rising charply. 'Come back in a 'our! Jus' go!'

The woman stared at him in puzzlement for a moment, then sniffed, shrugged, and withdrew, closing the door. In one rapid movement, Monks raised his cane and slammed it down sharply onto the table top. 'And if you ever dare to do anything like this again,' he snarled, 'if you ever presume to plan my meetings for me, it'll be you my cane will tickle.'

Claypole's own patience snapped at this point. 'But Fingers can tie us in!' he protested, loudly. 'Not just with Oliver, but with Brownlow too! An' not just me. 'Yssop an' Carraway an' you as well!'

Monks laughed. 'No, Bolter,' he muttered evilly. 'You and Hyssop and Carraway perhaps, but not me. You'd better change the locks on your storeroom, then go home and lord it over your women. It's all you're suited for.' He rose, and stalked from the room without a backward glance.

Claypole wondered if he would ever see the villain again. He knew, at any rate, that he would have to find out where Fingers was for himself. He now decided to try and do it by winning the woman's confidence. He assumed, correctly, that she would be waiting in the main bar of the tavern, and immediately went there and apologized most profusely to her for having been somewhat curt. She accepted his apology most graciously, and he then invited her to accompany him to what he called his home. As they walked together towards Pentonville, she told him of her attempts since their last meeting to glean some helpful information as to Ned Fingers' whereabouts, but that most unfortunately, and although she had tried very hard, she had learnt nothing new. Claypole merely responded smilingly that he was sure that she had nonetheless done her best.

When they reached Mr Brownlow's house, the woman gazed wonderingly up at it. 'Coo, all this!' she exclaimed. 'An' it's really – I mean, well, really all yer own, Mr Bolter?'

'Every stone an' stick,' declared Claypole, smugly, taking her arm and leading her up the front steps. As if to reassure her that the place was very much his own, he produced a key from his pocket with a flourish and unlocked the door. Bowing most elegantly, he ushered her through and into the sitting room, which, to his great relief, was empty.

'Must be a – stands to reason,' said the woman, in an awed tone. 'Must be a sight o' work for *Mrs* Bolter, keepin' it up, I mean.'

' 'Ere now!' said Claypole. 'Wot yer fittin' me out for? *Mrs* Bolter?'

'Well, I jus' thought, well, all this.'

'Got me own 'ousekeeper, I 'ave,' announced Claypole, impressively. 'Never saw need for a Mrs Bolter.' Whereupon he added, softly with a sly grin, and allowing an arm to slip gently about the woman's waist: 'Least, not till recently. Wery recently.' The woman beamed at him.

'But,' Claypole then said, releasing her, 'speakin' serious, though, reason I asked yer 'ere, I wanted yer to know for sure I ain't just no flash 'Arry.'

'Oh I'd never thought that, Mr Bolter,' said the woman, in a shocked tone.

'No. Well. Listen,' said Claypole. 'The new fence, I need word about 'im, where 'e works from, an' 'ow assumin' – to start with – he does.'

He had hoped to elicit from the woman at this point, an immediate revelation as to who the fence was, if he existed at all, but she was either too clever for that, or she genuinely did not know. She merely replied, mysteriously, 'I've 'eard – we all 'ave.'

''Eard's right,' Claypole interposed. 'Everybody's *'eard*, nobody's *seen*. I want somebody as seen. But more'n that, I want Ned Fingers. I know, I know. Yer tried. Well, try again. An' be sure o' this. There'll be a nice bag o' change – an' mebbe more than money for the right party – when I 'as wot I wants.'

The woman grinned and snivelled most excitedly. 'Yes, Mr Bolter. I'll find 'em, both o' them,' she said. Claypole surveyed her for a few moments, then turned away and concentrated on pouring himself a glass of sherry. Sipping it, he moved to the window, and gazed out into the gardens beyond, very thoughtfully and for a long time. He seemed lost in his musings and was clearly not prepared to share them with anybody, least of all the woman. He had, it appeared, entirely forgotten about her. Understanding this to be the great Morris Bolter's way, and accepting that men of his stature often wished to be left alone with the burden of their own important thoughts, the woman tiptoed respectfully out of the room, shutting the door quietly behind her.

CHAPTER SEVENTEEN

'I don't know,' said the Dodger that evening, 'I don't trust 'im. Nor 'is sainted ma, neither.'

'But he's been kindness itself to us!' protested Oliver. 'And look what he's doing for poor Dob!'

There was a sudden rustle from the pile of sacks amid which poor Dob was lying. It was quickly suppressed, however, as the door opened and Mr Slammett came into the room, looking cleaner than usual and carrying an empty sack over his shoulder.

'Well, that's done,' he said, closing the door and crossing to the cupboard, he unlocked the padlock on the cupboard door.

'Business, Mr Slammett?' asked Oliver.

'As yer might say,' said Slammett, with a chuckle. 'As me sainted – no she didn't, did she?' He opened the cupboard, tossed the sack inside, closed the door, and repadlocked it. 'Some of it done, anyway,' he declared. 'As for the rest? Wery hard. Wery hard. Pour us o' cup of tea, will yer, Oliver me lad.'

Oliver went quickly to the stove, picked up the faithfully bubbling teapot with the end of his cap, which he used as a glove, and brought it to the table. Slammett sat down at the table with a sigh, as Oliver poured him a mug of tea.

'Wot's 'ard then?' asked the Dodger, who was already seated at the table.

'Climbin' boys,' said Slammett. 'Wery 'ard to come by these days. Given a bad name as a hoccupation by some in the trade.'

'What trade, Mr Slammett?' asked Oliver, returning the pot to the stove.

Chimbley sweep,' replied Slammett. 'Wot 'd yer think I was in?'

'Oh,' said Oliver, 'that explains the . . .' He broke off, suddenly embarrassed.

'The dirt and the grime' said Slammett, with a laugh. 'Grime an' dirt yer learns to live with 'em in this perfession.'

'What's a climbing boy then, Mr Slammett?' asked Oliver, returning to the table.

Slammett smiled at him, amused by his innocence. 'Well now,' he explained softly, 'I'm the sweep. I got me brush an' me 'andles, an I sweeps out the chimbleys. But there's always something, some soot as I just can't reach. So? I 'as me climbin' boy.'

'But what does he *do*?' Oliver persisted.

''E climbs up with a sack an' a brush, inside the chimbleys, cleans 'em out, the hard bits.'

'Inside?' said Oliver, in puzzlement.

'There's always 'and 'olds for a lad as knows 'is business. Bricks stickin' out, staples, thinks like that. Some chimbleys even 'as steps cut special.'

'That doesn't sound too difficult', said Oliver, with a bright smile.

'Well it needn't be,' said Slammett, 'if yer knows wot yer doin.' But I won't pertend to you, times it can be 'ard an' dangerous.'

'Like when the chimneys are narrow,' observed the Dodger, quietly, staring into his mug.

'You been climbin'?' inquired Slammett, quite sharply, gazing suspiciously at the Dodger.

The Dodger looked up. 'No,' he said, blankly. Slammett relaxed. 'But I've 'eard about it,' said the Dodger.

Slammett gave him a second troubled glance before saying with a chuckle. 'No, like I said before, a bit big, Master Dawkins, a bit big'. He turned once again to Oliver. 'But as he says, Oliver, when the chimbleys is narrer, then it's elbows an' knees all the way.'

'And when the chimneys are blocked . . .' the Dodger began.

'Blocked?' exclaimed Oliver, with alarm.

'It 'appens' said Slammett, with a shrug. 'Then it's not just a brush yer needs; it's a scraper or even a knife. But enough o' that. As me old ma would likewise say, sufficient unto the biscuits the weevils thereof. Don't concern you, chimbley-sweeping, nor won't it me an' Dob much longer neither. Work'ouse bait we are, Dob an' me, work-ouse bait for sure.' Mr Slammett gave vent to a long mournful sigh.

'A sweep in the work'ouse?' said the Dodger, incredulously.

'A sweep without a climbin' boy?' said Slammett, shaking his head. 'There's no work for a sweep without a climbin' boy,' he shrugged. 'Dob tried,' he murmured morosely, 'but 'e ain't got the breath, poor lad. So it's goodbye, room, an' off to the work'house for me an' 'im.'

Oliver stared at Mr Slammett with a concerned expression, and then towards the sacks where poor Dob lay, so very quietly. The thought of this friendly old gentleman and his sickly assistant being forced to spend the rest of their days in a workhouse filled him with sorrow; he could never forget the terrible days he had endured in such a place himself.

'I'll do it, Mr Slammett' he said, after some thought.

'Do what?' asked Slammett.

'I'll be your climbing boy,' replied Oliver.

Another rustle from the sacks immediately followed this announcement; it was quickly silenced, however, by a sharp glance in their direction from Slammett. The Dodger merely stared in amazement at his friend.

Thus it was that Oliver Twist became a chimney sweep's climbing boy. He and his new master set off early the next morning for his first day's work; it was to be a laborious one, for Samuel Slammett believed that his new employee should be accustomed as quickly as possible to the several varieties of chimney that existed. 'Sooner we starts, sooner yer learns,' he said. 'An' sooner yer learns, easier it'll be.'

The first chimney was a wide one. With his trousers

tied at his knees and a pair of heavy steel-capped boots a size too large for him on his feet – they had belonged to Dob – Oliver climbed it easily, with the aid of a number of bricks projecting from the sides of the shaft at convenient intervals. It was light too, so he could see what he was doing as he brushed the soot from the walls into the sack with a handbrush; and he completed the task quite speedily, for the chimney had not been especially dirty in the first place.

'There now,' said Slammett, when he had finished, 'that weren't too 'ard was it?'.

The second chimney, however, was narrower and darker; the third was narrower and darker still; the fourth was so narrow, so dark, and so very circuitous that the boy had to work in total blackness, inching his way up and supporting himself with his feet, but with his knees and elbows, which became severely grazed in consequence. The dirtier the chimneys were, and they seemed to become dirtier as the day progressed, the more impractical the brush became, and Oliver had to use a scraper to remove the soot. He had not been warned of the manner in which the soot often took its own vicious form of revenge as a result of having been thus disturbed; it would decide, frequently and without warning, to come tumbling down the chimney of its own accord, in great choking cascades, so heavy sometimes that Oliver had to cling desperately to the brickwork to prevent himself from falling with it, coughing, gasping, and blinking as it attacked his mouth, nose and eyes.

The day came to an end at last, and Oliver was so exhausted that he could not remember how many chimneys he had climbed; he thought that it must have been at least ten, perhaps even fifteen. When he returned home with his new employer, the Dodger could do nothing but gaze at him in astonishment, for his face and clothes were as black as night.

'Yer a good lad, Oliver, an' kindly with it,' declared Slammett, going at once to the sink and washing himself.

'Wery kind o' yer – indeed wery' elpin' out.'

'I don't mind,' said Oliver, bravely.

'I knows yer don't,' said Slammett, 'an' it's that as makes it true kindness. Come 'ere an' give yerself a wash.'

Oliver went to the sink and did his best to remove as much of the soot from his face and hands as he could. As he was drying himself with an already very dirty rag, he turned to see Slammett sitting at the table with a large bowl of water before him. Beside the bowl were several rough pieces of cloth and an open hessian bag.

'Right, Oliver, lad,' said the sweep, 'Over 'ere when yer finished.' Oliver approached the table and peered dubiously into the bowl.

'What is it?' he asked.

'Something to 'elp over the bad parts o' the good work yer don',' said Slammett, removing a handful of salt from the bag and stirring it into the water with a wooden spoon. 'Roll up yer sleeves, Oliver.'

'But what is it?' asked Oliver, doing as he was instructed.

'Salt,' said Slammett. 'Ardens the skin. After a while, makes it like leather. Show 'im, Dob.'

Dob rose obediently from the pile of sacks and quietly came forward, rolling up his sleeve and turning his elbow towards Oliver for inspection. It was discoloured and calloused, but dry and hard.

'Come on then, Oliver,' said Slammett, dipping one of the cloths into the water and wringing it out. 'May's well get started. Tell yer wot, Dob, you can take over 'ere. Show Oliver 'ow.' He handed the cloth to the pale, nervous boy, who took hold of Oliver's arm and gently put the cloth to his exposed and heavily grazed elbow. Oliver experienced a sudden, searing pain, and breathed in sharply through his teeth.

'Stings a bit at first. Jus' shows it's workin',' said Slammett. 'Get on with it then, Dob.'

Before Oliver could resist, Dob quickly pushed his elbow into the bowl of salted water. He emitted a howl of such volume and obvious agony that the Dodger, who was lying amid the sacks, sat up abruptly and glared at Slammett with a look of sudden, distrustful hostility.

As time passed, Oliver hoped that he would become more proficient at his new profession and therefore less exhausted at the conclusion of each day's work; but, contrary to his expectations, he grew more and more tired, and every job took longer to complete than the last. He also began to suffer spasms of coughing; not as ferocious as poor Dob's debilitating paroxysms, of course, but painful nevertheless. Samuel Slammett, however, seemed well pleased with him. 'A good team we're becoming, that we are,' he announced, as they were returning home from Oliver's fifth day as a climbing boy. 'Slammett an' Brown, eh? Sweeps by appointment.'

Oliver made an effort to smile. Slammett looked concerned. 'Eh, lad, yer wore out, ain't yer?' he said.

'I'll be all right,' replied Oliver, weakly.

'Mebbe yer will, with some vittles inside yer an' a good sleep,' said Slammett. 'As me sainted ma used to say, a lesson learned is a rest earned. But talkin o' lessons, I've 'ad a thought. When yer tired, y' say, times yer forgettin' which parts o' the chimbley is cleared.'

'It's not as bad as that,' said Oliver.

'No, but there's a way yer could be sure.'

'I could mark the walls' suggested Oliver.

'In that dark? Wot with?' said Slammett, chuckling. 'Luminous paint?' He lowered his voice to a whisper and continued. 'No but easy, really, wery easy. Each room as yer passes, look in, spy for something.'

'Like what?' said Oliver.

'Well, something special. A cabinet fer instance, with some good china, a silver clock, mebbe, things like that, things that catches the eye. Then, when yer down, yer tells me, an' it'd be easy for me to check.'

'Suppose there isn't anything?' said Oliver.

Slammett laughed. ''Ouses *we* go to,' he replied, '*that'd* be something special, anyway! Right. Now it's 'ome, an' vittles, an' bed.'

That same evening, while Oliver was being subjected to the daily torture of having to have his knees and elbows soaked in brine, there was a sudden but timid tap on the door of the room.

'Now 'oo the . . . ,' said Slammett, with obvious annoyance, moving to the door, unlocking it, and opening it slightly. 'Oo is it?', he barked to whoever was standing outside. 'You! Wot yer want?!' Whereupon he quickly stepped out of the room, pulling the door to behind him, and slamming it shut. In an instant the Dodger was on his feet and bending his head towards the door, listening intently. His eyes widened at what he heard. After only a few moments, however, he ran back to the table and sat down again just as Slammett opened the door again and peered into the room. 'Got to go out,' he declared, and continued, chuckling. 'Matter o' the 'eart, as me sainted ma might 'ave put it. Be back in not too long, but yer'll be all right. Lockin' the door 'ill keep yer safe.' He withdrew, closing the door. The boys heard the key turn in the lock.

'Well, well,' mused the Dodger, softly, 'a matter o' the 'eart, eh?'

'Isn't that why he's gone out then?' asked Oliver.

'Not unless 'e's in love with Fingers,' retorted the Dodger. 'Ol' Ned 'isself.'

Oliver stared at him in bewilderment. 'There was a woman out there,' the Dodger continued. '"Yer gets around a lot o' places," she says. "Wot of it?" says Slammett. "I was wonderin' if yer'd seen or 'eard anythin' o' Ned Fingers," she says. "Fingers?" he says. "Wot would I be doin' with 'im?" "There's parties as'd pay quite a bit for findin' 'im," says the woman. "Fingers, eh?" says Slammett, then 'e comes back in, an' now 'e's off.'

'But . . . But how could he?' Oliver protested, unwilling to believe what the Dodger had reported. 'How could he? Someone like that? When he's done so much for us?'

'Which yer knees an' elbows 'ave paid for,' observed the Dodger.

'And Dob?' said Oliver, 'What about Dob?'

'No!' cried Dob, suddenly. It was the first word either of them had heard from him in the five days they had been there. They both turned towards the pile of sacks to see the pale, trembling boy doing his best to stand, and convulsed with the effort he was expending in attempting to speak. 'No!' he repeated, trying not to cough. 'E's not wot yer fink! Not a bit of it! Fings I could tell yer!' Whereupon he collapsed back onto the pile of sacks in a frenzy of coughing more violent than any of the boys had yet seen. They rose from the table, and ran towards him, leaning over him with concern. ''E made me,' the wretched youth continued, when the coughing had subsided. ''E *made* me like this. An' I'm lucky I'm livin'. I *was* 'is climbin' boy, not a little while, a year. A whole year, till me lungs give up. Soot an' burnin' smoke. But I was lucky. Two afore me, they died. Both on' em. One suffocated, up a chimbley. The other, 'is 'eart jus' give up on 'im. Worse 'n lungs. I was lucky. Somefing else, too. 'E aint jus' no sweep. 'E plans fings. Robberies, raids, at the 'ouses 'e visits. Everything laid out neat. Every room, an' jus' wot's to be took in it.'

For the moment, the boy could say no more. 'I've just realized something,' said Oliver.

'Wot?' said the Dodger.

'Just now when we were coming home, he told me – so that I could remember where I'd swept – to look into the rooms I passed. For china cabinets, silver, things like that.'

'An' then to tell 'im,' said the Dodger, with disgust.

'So that he could check,' said Oliver.

'An' there you are,' rejoined the Dodger, with a grin. 'That's 'ow 'e does it. As me sainted ma would surely 'ave said, time we were movin' on, Oliver me lad.'

He rose and was about to move immediately to the door when Dob sat up quickly. He made another supreme effort to speak, and finally succeeded in whispering:

'Yer won't. 'E won't let yer. Wot yer fink them window-bars is for? Wot yer fink that door-lock's for? Keepin' fieves out? No. They're for keepin' us in! 'E won't let yer go till 'e's got yer like me.'

Having explained as much as he found it possible to explain, the trembling, terrified boy fell back on the pile of sacks and closed his eyes in utter exhaustion.

In the darkness of the ensuing night, the Dodger found sleep impossible. Oliver, though troubled by poor Dob's revelation, was too tired to allow it to prevent him from a deep slumber. All three boys, as was their custom, were lying on the pile of sacks. Samuel Slammett, their keeper, was snoring contentedly on his bed. The Dodger decided to attempt an escape. He rose silently and stealthily approached the bed. In the dim light that glowed from the still burning stove, he saw that the keys to the room and to the cupboard were tied to a string about the chimney sweep's neck. Carefully, he bent towards the sleeper and proceeded to work one of the keys free. Thanking his experience as a practised stealer of such items, he succeeded in removing the key at last, and turned to examine it in the stove's light. As he did so, a strong hand shot out and siezed his arm, pulling him back onto the bed. The Dodger struggled to break from the man's grasp, but Slammett held onto him tightly, quickly retrieving the key with his free hand and dropping it into his pocket. He laughed cruelly and, with a neat twist of the wrist, sent the Dodger spinning to the floor. ''Ave it yer own way then!' he growled, 'Where can yer run to?' The noise of the Dodger's fall woke Oliver, and he sat up as Slammett continued: 'Wot were yer after, anyway? A spot o' thievery mebbe? 'Ave a peek in me cupboard, see wot I got laid away fer a rainy day? Got the wrong key, didn't yer? Or mebbe not. Mebbe the right one. Fer cuttin' an' runnin' again . . .' Oliver rose slowly from the sacks. Slammett glanced at him. 'I see', he said, in an abruptly vicious tone. 'Both o' yer. Well yer not goin' nowhere, none o' yer.'

'You can't keep us here against our will,' said Oliver firmly.

'Oh can't I?' retorted Slammett. 'Yer think I believed that tale 'e spun? Sold for a cabin boy?'

'It was the truth!' Oliver protested.

'I've met lads afore a step ahead o' the peelers', said Slammett, ignoring him. He then turned threateningly to the Dodger. 'You listen, you,' he continued. 'If you tries anything, when Oliver, an' me are out, Oliver'll be in 'ere waitin', an' ready for 'andin' over to them as I'm sure'll be 'appy to 'ave 'im.' He grinned cruelly and swung back onto his bed. He was apparently asleep again in an instant. The Dodger resigned himself to having to remain in that place for some time yet, and crawled despondently towards the sacks.

But Oliver was not so acquiescent. The first chimney he had to climb the next morning was one of the wider, more open ones, helpfully furnished with protruding staples; it was not too impenetrably dirty, either. Halfway up, however, as he was brushing away what soot there was he felt something tear at his arm. With a cry of pain, he turned his arm towards him and saw a long rent in his sleeve; with a savage graze beneath it. He examined the wall to his right and noticed a large, damaged staple projecting from the brickwork, with one of its sharply pointed legs twisted outwards. Thrusting his brush under his belt, he tugged at the offending object and freed it at last. Holding it in his hand, he turned it about, and peered at it thoughtfully; then, perching himself on another staple he gazed upwards. He had been sitting there for several minutes when he heard a gruff voice calling to him from below: 'Oliver? 'Urry it up, will yer! There's customers waitin'!' Slammett's unpleasant bark was all the encouragement he needed to make up his mind. He pulled his sack over his shoulder, thrust the damaged staple into his pocket, and proceeded to climb, faster and faster, and with surer purpose at each step. Slammett's commands grew even more distant, 'I'll give yer five minutes, Oliver, if yer not down by then. . .!'

The chimney was topped by a mercifully large hold through which Oliver (having first removed the chimney-pot), managed to squeeze himself without excessive difficulty. He emerged onto a flat roof with a low parapet and a trapdoor in its centre. He ran to the trapdoor and tried to lift it, but it was heavily bolted on the inside. He ran to the parapet and gazed down over it towards the street, four storeys below him. He made a rapid circuit of the roof, and soon reached the conclusion that there was no means of escape over its edge. He hurried back to the chimney and listened. He heard Slammett cry furiously: 'That's it then! I warned yer! Now I'm comin' up for yer!'

Oliver hastened to the trapdoor and tried once more to lift it but it remained stubbornly immovable. He glanced wildly about him, until he decided at last that there was only one escape route available; and he returned to the chimney. When Samuel Slammett arrived on the roof by means of the trapdoor, his assistant was no longer there. He crossed to the roof-edge and peered down over the parapet at the street below. He straightened, scratched the back of his neck pensively, looked round, and then saw that the chimney pot had been removed and that the boy's sack was still lying beside it. He hurried to the chimney and stared down into the darkness. 'Oliver!' he bawled.

*

'Dodger! Dodger!' cried Oliver, breathlessly, knocking violently on the door of Slammett's room with his clenched fist.

'Oliver?' replied the Dodger, disbelievingly, from within.

'I got away from him,' said Oliver. 'Can you get the door open?'

'No 'ope,' replied the Dodger morosely. 'We've tried every which way. 'E's left nothin' we can use.' Then he said firmly; 'Oliver, forget about us. There's only one thing left now. They won't be watchin' yer Aunt's anymore.'

'No. I'm not going without you,' retorted Oliver, removing the bent chimney staple from his pocket.

'If you can reach 'er,' said the Dodger, 'maybe she can manage some 'elp for all of us.'

'No, Dodger,' Oliver persisted, dropping to his knees. 'Listen. I'm putting something under the door. I's the best I can do.'

There was a considerable gap between the door and the floor, and it was through this gap that Oliver pushed the staple. Inside the room, the Dodger picked it up with a grin and showed it to Dob, who was standing beside him. 'Get yer runnin' shoes on, Oliver,' said the Dodger. 'It's a best'll do nicely. We'll be out o' 'ere in no time!' Watched eagerly by Dob, he proceeded to work at the lock with one of the staple's pointed ends, removing it now and then to bend it this way and that. At last, Dob emitted a sudden yelp of delight as he heard the levers within the lock swing up and saw the bolt click back. 'Ready, Oliver?' cried the Dodger, rising to his feet. 'Well, 'ere we're comin', ready or no!' Leaving the staple in the lock, he pulled the door open happily and flung it wide.

His happiness was wretchedly brief; for in the passage outside the door stood Slammett, holding his now helpless friend in his strong grip; 'Ready, were we?' said Slammett, with a short, cruel laugh. 'Ready for leavin' the 'appy 'ome, were we? All of us? Even Dob?' He threw Oliver into the room and followed him in, forcing the Dodger and Dob to retreat backwards. 'Well yer've 'ad yer chance,' he snarled, slamming the door shut behind him. 'Don't look for it again. An' me sainted ma always did say, the fambly as prays together, stays together. Well, you're stayin', oh you're stayin', and yer best – yer best start *prayin'* too!'

CHAPTER EIGHTEEN

A good six weeks had passed since Rose Maylie had received a letter from her nephew; and two since she had written to his friend Jack Dawkins. Unbeknown to her, the Dodger had started to write several letters in reply, but had not once succeeded in completing even the first sentence. Composing letters was not one of his foremost skills; indeed, he had never written one in his life before for he had not previously been called upon to do so. It had not been stubbornness, therefore, that had prevented him from answering Mrs Maylie's anxious inquiry, but mere embarrassment; and now, imprisoned as he was in a chimney sweep's home in London, he was in no position to repair his former negligence.

Naturally, poor Rose was deeply troubled by the silence that had prevailed for far too long. Noting her increasing agitation, her good husband at last decided that he would correspond directly with the one person who had not only a moral, but a legal, obligation to ease their legitimate disquietude; he would write to Mr Stalker. Rose was mildly comforted by this decision on Harry's part, and resolved to wait patiently for the Headmaster's reply.

Meanwhile, in London, Mr Samuel Slammett, her nephew's jailer, was making doubly certain that the boy and his friend Dawkins would not be able to escape from their captivity. Whenever he left the room, with or without Oliver, he would secure the door with a heavy padlock on the outside; and to prevent Oliver from slipping away, as he had previously attempted to do, while he was up a chimney, he attached a long rope to the boy's waist, never allowing the other end to leave his grasp, even for a second. 'One fancy move,' he would snarl threateningly, 'an' I'll bring yer trumblin' down.'

Early one morning, when Oliver and his master were loading the handcart with sacks and brushes in preparation for another day's sweeping, they were approached, to Oliver's considerable astonishment, and perfurbation, by someone the boy knew only too well.

'Hah, Mr Slammett I do believe? said this all too familiar personage cheerily. 'This your 'ouse – er – residence? Almost neighbours, as yer might say.'

Oliver hastily lowered his head in the hope that he would not be noticed but was certain, at the same time, that he would be soon enough. Noah Claypole, however, appeared to pay him no heed whatsoever, and continued to gaze smilingly at Slammett, who now muttered, mysteriously: 'That – er – business we was discussin' . . .'

'Settled,' announced Claypole. He then glanced about him and said softly: 'But I was – er – thinkin' there might be other matters we might discuss, to mutual hadvantage, as yer might say.'

'Oh yes?' retorted Slammett, cautiously. 'Wot 'ad yer in mind.'

'Well,' said Claypole, 'word gets about. An' – well, I 'ave certain contacts 'oo might be – as yer might put it – useful to both our h'interests.'

'Contacts?' asked Slammett. 'Wot Contacts?'

'Collectors, suchlike,' replied Claypole.

'Collectors?' said Slammett. 'Wot of? Soot? Chimbley sweepin's?'

'As yer say, as yer say, chimbley sweepin's,' murmured Claypole, with a thin smile that could not hide his annoyance. 'As yer say, as yer say,' he repeated. 'Well. Good-day to yer, Mr Slammett.' And with a tip of his fine hat, he left them, without so much as a glance in Oliver's direction. The boy was understandably dismayed at having escaped his former tormentor's attention so easily; he concluded that his face and clothes, which were by now thoroughly ingrained with soot, had rendered him utterly unrecognizable; but a cause for even greater dismay at this moment was the strange conversation he had just overheard.

He told the Dodger of the curious encounter at the earliest possible opportunity; which was late that night, when he could be reasonably certain that Slammett would be safely asleep. 'Dodger?' he whispered. 'He knows Noah Claypole. We met him.' The Dodger whistled noiselessly through his teeth. 'He didn't recognize me,' Oliver continued.

'Maybe not,' whispered the Dodger. 'Not this time. But if they should get talkin' to each other, one thief-master to another ... well ...' There was a long thoughtful silence. 'Seems to me, Oliver,' muttered the Dodger at last, 'we really got to find some way out of 'ere, but soon. Or you 'ave.' There was a second lengthy pause. Then the Dodger whispered, 'Oliver?'

'Yes?'

'Most chimneys 'as bends, don't they?'

'Yes. Side-shafts.'

'An' where there's shafts,' observed the Dodger, 'there's hearths, there's rooms, an' in some of them rooms, stands to reason, there'll be people. If you could get shot of that rope, for just a minute ...'

'I could ask for help!'

'Well . . . ,' whispered the Dodger, 'you could 'ope someone'd listen, anyway.'

The following morning's first chimney was dark, but reasonably wide. Climbing upward hand over hand, brush in belt and sack over shoulder, Oliver halted abruptly as one hand grasped at nothing, and he pulled himself up to a ledge where a sideshaft opened outwards from the main chimney. He craned into the opening, laying his sack on the ledge, and saw that the shaft was quite short, slanting downwards to end over a large, empty hearth, beyond which he could discern part of a carpeted floor. He was gazing down the shaft when he felt a sharp tug at the rope round his waist and heard Slammett shouting distantly, 'Wot's 'oldin yer? Oliver?

Yer 'ear me?' Oliver glanced about him urgently, and noticed a brick protruding from one of the shaft's walls. He tugged at the brick with both hands, testing its firmness. 'Answer me!' yelled Slammett, 'or I'll bring yer down faster 'n yer went up!'

'Yes, Mr Slammett!' Oliver called, obediently, and reaching down, he pulled a short length of the rope towards him.

''Ere!' growled Slammett, 'Wot yer tryin'?'

Oliver quickly coiled the rope to form two loops and slipped them in a clove hitch over the projecting brick, crying: 'It's the rope, Mr Slammett!' It's caught!'

'Wot?'

'Between two bricks, Mr Slammett!' I can't free it!'

The rope stretched tight as Slammett gave it a jerk from below. Oliver prayed that the brick would hold fast; and it did. The rope slackened. 'All right! Slip it!' bellowed the sweep. 'But no games! Yer 'ear me? No games!'

'No, Mr Slammett!' Oliver replied, hurriedly untying the rope from his waist, and lowering his legs into the side-shaft.

'Yer got three minutes, an' that's it! Yer 'ear me? Three minutes, an' not a second more!'

Oliver slipped down the shaft into the hearth. A great cloud of soot followed him. He blinked, coughed violently, and peered into the room. It was small and pleasantly furnished, but apparently unoccupied. He was initially disappointed to find himself alone, but he brightened quickly when he noticed an open bureau on the wall opposite the fireplace. On its desk-surface there lay an inkwell and an abundance of pens and paper. Deciding that he must write an appeal for help in the hope that someone would soon enter the room and discover it, he rose and hurried to the bureau.

'Well, well, a young visitor come to see me,' said a kindly female voice from behind him. Utterly startled, Oliver turned to see a little old lady gazing benignly in his direction. She was so very tiny and the wing-backed armchair in which she was seated so very large by comparison, that he had not seen her at first, for the chair was facing away from the fireplace. She had a pleasant gentle face, and was dressed, Oliver noted, in widow's mauve, her small hands were folded over a book lying open on her lap.

Oliver proceeded to apologize for his presence at once: 'I'm sorry to disturb, no that's . . . that's not true. I have to, you see. I need help. My name is Oliver. Oliver Twist.'

'And you're telling me your name! That *is* nice!' said the little old lady, continuing to smile, and bewilderingly untroubled by the sudden arrival of this soot-blackened stranger in her sitting room. 'I am Euphemia Martin; Mrs Euphemia Martin. Actually, my given names are Euphemia Hortensia Venetia. Most silly, are they not? I have always thought them silly; they sound like a bunch of botanical specimens.'

'Mrs Martin,' Oliver interposed, 'I do honestly need your help, and I have so little time to explain.'

'Oh my, things do seem so . . . pressing at such an age, do they not?' continued Mrs Martin, sympathetically. 'My first young visitor in – oh goodness! ! I cannot remember how long. And so *earnest*! Dear *Mr* Martin . . .'

'Mrs Martin,' Oliver interposed again, still more desperately, 'there are people who would help, I'm sure, if they understood . . .'

'Dear me!' cried the lady, 'I am becoming forgetful!'

Oliver did not trouble to fathom the reason for this sudden observation and persevered in his attempt to persuade her to help him. 'Mrs Martin, if you could see them for me, or write, to explain that . . .'

'I truly am becoming forgetful. And neglectful! A young visitor, and I have not even rung for tea! You will stay for tea, of course, and cakes?'

It was at this point that Oliver at least understood that his hostess was entirely deaf and had not heard one word he had said. He therefore declined her invitation to tea with a wild, and possibly somewhat impolite, shake of his head, and ran once again to the bureau, scribbling a hurried missive, which he then handed frantically to the puzzled but still smiling old lady. Prevented by the urgency of his circumstances from spending a moment more in her company, much as he would have liked to, he hurried to the door and out of the room without offering her even the briefest of farewell bows, reporting at once to Mr Slammett, who was waiting impatiently for him two floors below.

The note he had so hastily written was addressed to his guardian's old friend Grimwig and read as follows:

'Dear Mr Grimwig, your friend Mr Brownlow is held by villains. I too have suffered at their hands and am at present being kept captive by Samuel Slammett, a chimney sweep. Please help us both. Oliver Twist.'

Late that night, Oliver reported his encounter with the curious Mrs Martin to the Dodger and Dob, as they lay amid the sacks in Slammett's room; when he had told them that he had written to Mr Grimwig in the hope that Mrs Martin would deliver the message to that old gentleman, the Dodger seemed doubtful, referring to the lady as a 'fruit-cake', and expressing his conviction that she would almost certainly have been too perplexed by the note to have done anything with it; if she had read it at all.

As it happened, Mrs Martin *had* read the note, and was certainly baffled by its contents; but the Dodger's scepticism proved to be unjustified, for the next morning, having noted the address that Oliver had scribbled on the back of the piece of paper, she put on her bonnet, stole and gloves and set off for Mr Grimwig's house, which happened to be not very far from her own.

'Fry me and fritter me!' declared Grimwig, once he

had read the soot-smudged message, which Mrs Martin had handed to him. 'Upon my soul, it is a most extraordinary occurrence. Most extraordinary! Will you not agree, ma'am?' He looked up at the little old woman seated opposite him, who, in response to his enquiry, merely smiled sweetly. 'Will you not agree ma'am?' Mr Grimwig repeated, more loudly. 'Extraordinary, ma'am. And a sweep's boy, you say?' Mrs Martin continued to smile, and nodded encouragingly. 'Yet here they are,' observed Grimwig, returning his attention to the note. 'My name, my address, my old friend's name, and the boy's signature. It must be! It cannot be otherwise! Oliver Twist, or I'll eat my head! But a climbing boy?' He shook his head mistrustfully, and, dropping the note onto the desk in front of him, he extracted a large handkerchief from his pocket and proceeded to wipe his soot-soiled fingers with considerable vigour.

'You can see of course, Mr Grimwig,' said Mrs Martin, 'why I felt impelled to call upon you. Extraordinary, do you not agree?' The old gentleman stared at her irritably, for he had just asked her exactly the same question. 'One of dear Mr Martin's favourite quotations,' the lady continued blandly. 'By their works shall ye know them. Or was it fruits? Is it by their *fruits* shall ye know them? I cannot remember. I *think* it is . . .'

'Mrs Martin!' Grimwig interrupted irascibly, and loudly enough to silence her in an instant and cause her to gaze at him in surprise. 'I shall endeavour,' he said, for he had by now understood that the woman was deaf, 'to enunciate very clearly for your benefit.' Whereupon he pronounced each word carefully as he continued: 'The boy claims, ma'am, that his guardian – my old friend – is held by rogues and that he himself is equally a victim of their machinations.' He was not sure how much of what he had said the old lady had understood; if she had indeed comprehended anything at all, so he now repeated, in a thundering voice, *'Held by rogues, ma'am!'*

Mrs Martin suddenly appeared startled and cried: 'That poor boy? Held by . . .? Oh we must save him, Mr Grimwig! Mr Martin would never have countenanced . . .'

'Please, ma'am!' barked Grimwig, raising his hand to silence her once again. 'My friend Brownlow is indeed under care, but his attendant is a medical gentleman known to me, and respected in his profession. And if Twist truly seeks my aid, why did he not approach me directly? No, ma'am, no! That unhappy boy, ma'am, is a known criminal . . . *A known, criminal, ma'am!*' And I can only believe that – with or without the connivance of this Slammett – his purpose in your sitting-room was, robbery . . . *robbery, ma'am*!'

'Robbery, Mr Grimwig?' exclaimed Mrs Martin, who had clearly understood that much. 'But that note . . .'

'A device, dear lady, nothing more,' declared Grimwig, 'No doubt to alloy your suspicions; perhaps even to lure you from home.' Whereupon he leaned forward and shouted: *'Look to your silver, ma'am,* look to your silver. Twist is after it – *or I'll eat my head*!' The gentle little lady was terrified, not merely by the nature of what she had been told, but by the furious violence with which Grimwig now stuck his stick upon the ground. She decided to remain in his presence not a moment longer, and hurried home; only to find, much to her relief, that her collection of silver remained, for the moment, untouched.

For his part, Mr Grimwig decided to visit Brownlow's house immediately, Mrs Carraway answered the door and showed him into the sitting-room, and the first thing he did was to ask, very naturally after his friend. He was understandably agitated by the news that Mr Brownlow had been removed to a sanatorium in the country; but Mrs Carraway, after apologizing for not having informed him of this before, assured him that such a course of action had been firmly recommended by the very reputable Dr Hyssop, who now had strong hopes for a recovery, although, it would probably only be partial, she announced sadly.

'And Twist?' Mr Grimwig inquired. 'Young Oliver. What news of him.'

'News, Mr Grimwig?' said Mrs Carraway, somewhat nervously, 'of Oliver Twist?'

'Know where he is, do you?' said Grimwig, 'Seen him, have you?'

The lady made a very tentative reply: 'I have no idea where he might be, sir. Should I have?'

'Wouldn't expect you to, ma'am,' retorted Grimwig, gruffly. ''Pon my soul, I'd be surprised if you did!'

Mrs Carraway relaxed at once and declared with assurance: 'No, sir, I have not seen Oliver Twist.'

'Gone back to his former companions, or I'll eat my head!' said Grimwig. 'Perhaps it's as well my poor friend should be as he is, before his plans for adoption could be completed.'

'That is another matter concerning which I should, of course, have informed you, Mr Grimwig,' said the lady diffidently. 'I have, in fact, taken the liberty of halting the legal process.'

'Of Twist's adoption?' said Grimwig startled.

'Until Mr Brownlow can act on his own behalf.'

'Capital, ma'am! Capital!' declared Grimwig, beaming broadly, whereupon he rose from his chair and said; 'Meantime, if you hear from the boy, let me know.'

'Of course, Mr Grimwig,' said Mrs Carraway, softly.

'Had the impertinence to communicate with me, the jackanapes!' Grimwig announced, as he was being shown to the front door. 'Working for a sweep! And using his position to plot robberies, and his acquaintance with me to lull his victims. Jackanapes! Well, good day to you, ma'am.' He raised his hat, descended the steps to the street, and walked off briskly, muttering, 'Jackanapes! Jackanapes!' without a backward glance; he did not notice, therefore, that Mrs Carraway's steely countenance had suddenly turned quite white.

At this moment Noah Claypole was in the private room of the Three Cripples tavern with Samuel Slammett. On the table between these two gentlemen there lay an impressive collection of goods, which comprised a silver candelabrum, an ormolu clock, a number of gold spoons, three or four watches, several rings and various other items of precious jewellery.

'That's yer top offer?' said Slammett with a fierce scowl. 'That's good that is, an' 'igh carat. Blow on it an' it bends.'

Noah Claypole shrugged dismissively and replied: 'I named yer a price. Blow on it, if yer like; it won't bend. Yer won't get a better.'

'I came 'ere at your invitation,' protested the sweep. 'I expected a honest discussion o' values as between gennelman an' gennelman.'

'Hinvitation?' retorted Claypole derisively. 'As I recalls it, Mr Slammett, I suggested – wery casual-like – that yer drop by, if in the vicinity. As for honest; well, as always, that's a word as takes its meanin' accordin' to 'oo's speakin', an' to 'oom.'

'Yer uses a lot o' words, Mr Bolter, a lot o' words. With meanin's accordin' to need,' said Slammett, returning the articles to his sack. 'But as me dear departed ma used to say, never look a gift-'orse in the mouth; like as not it'll spit in yer eye.'

'Wot's that supposed to mean?' said Claypole.

'As yer takes it, Mr Bolter,' replied Slammett, rising and throwing his sack over his shoulder. 'But yer ain't the only stall in the market.'

Claypole straightened, suddenly attentive. 'There's a new dealer?' he said. 'You've met him?'

Slammett surveyed him with narrowed eyes before replying: 'No, but I knows where to find 'im. Tell yer wot,

Mr Bolter, me ma taught me, never be 'asty. Yer 'as until termorror lunchtime. I'll send me new boy round. No I won't! Not that one, 'e ain't to be trusted. But yer knows where to find *me*.' He grinned maliciously and left the room. Noah Claypole stared after him, deeply troubled. So a rival existed, he thought. Whoever he was, and whether Fingers worked for him or not, he existed, and that was cause for considerable concern.

What Mr Grimwig did next was to summon a Bow Street officer to his house. When called by a magistrate, and Mr Grimwig was one such, the runners were prompt in their attendance, and this one was in the old gentleman's study before five o'clock that evening. Grimwig handed him the soot-covered note written by Oliver, explaining how he had come by it; and the circumstances of its delivery to Mrs Martin; and declared that he considered all this to be proof of the boy's certain guilt as a thief, or at least as an accomplice in thievery. The runner, after examining the piece of paper and its message, had to admit that he considered that debatable.

'Debatable? Debatable?' said Grimwig, irritably. 'Depend upon it, sir, I speak upon consideration; I act upon decision!'

'I don't doubt it, sir,' observed the officer, placatingly, 'I don't doubt it in the least. I was merely suggestin' that whereas the h'occurrences you describe may *prove* to be of criminous h'activity, they are not *as yet* h'incriminatin' in themselves. Hearsay an' supposition, sir.'

Mr Grimwig appeared to be slightly mollified. He grunted and muttered: 'I suppose, it's true, I suppose. But what of this Slammett?'

'Very respectable, sir,' the runner announced, 'in the business for years! Drives his boys perilous hard perhaps, but otherwise never a complaint. No criminous h'association.'

'I fear nevertheless, sir,' said Grimwig, 'that – evidence

or not – all the reports bend but one way. Oliver Twist is fast becoming – if he has not already become – a hardened criminal. A thief, sir, or I'll eat my head!'

He then recounted something of the boy's past history, dwelling particularly on his association, as a child, with the notorious thief-master Fagin and his gang. Naturally enough, this information proved to be extremely interesting to the Bow Street officer, who after some reflection, said: 'Well, sir, we'll h-investigate, of course. We'll pick the lad up for h'interrogation, let the axe fall as it may.'

Mr Grimwig was amply satisfied by such a decision, and instructed the officer to arrest the boy at the earliest opportunity.

While Mr Grimwig was interviewing the runner, Noah Claypole was being informed, in Mr Brownlow's sitting-room, of something that troubled him even more than the knowledge that there was a new fence about.

'Grimwig?' he said, 'Old Grimwig? . . . 'E's 'eard from Oliver?'

'He said so, in so many words,' replied Mrs Carraway.

Noah glanced at Charlotte, who was standing morosely by the door. 'It don't make sense!' he said. ''Ow can 'e 'ave? Oliver's on 'is way to the Ivory Coast!'

'Mr Grimwig was quite definite,' said Mrs Carraway. 'Twist is working as a sweep's boy, and using his acquaintance with Grimwig to . . .'

''Old it!' said Claypole, suddenly, 'Wait a bit! A climbin' boy, eh?'

'Yes,' said Mrs Carraway.

'No,' muttered Claypole, stroking his head. 'No – can't be!'

'What can't be, Mr Bolter?' asked Mrs Carraway.

'Sam'l Slammett,' said Claypole. 'Acquaintance o' mine. E's a sweep an' 'e's got a new boy. Mentioned 'im special. Not to be trusted, 'e said, jus' like – No, couldn't be! Couldn't be!'

'Mebbe it was Ketch!' said Charlotte, in an effort to be helpful. 'Mebbe Ketch let Oliver go!'

Claypole made her feel small and unimportant again in an instant by snarling and saying: 'Yer thinks *that*, yer doesn't know Ketch!' But he added thoughtfully, 'Still, wouldn't do no 'arm to check.' He certainly did not wish to visit Samuel Slammett so promptly, for that gentleman would interpret such a visit as a clear sign that he was worried about his rival dealer; but the possibility of discovering that Oliver, far from being on his way to the Ivory Coast, was by some unaccountable means still in London, outweighed all matters of pride, and he resolved to call on Mr Slammett immediately.

CHAPTER NINETEEN

Oliver's spasms of coughing were by now quite lengthy and disquietingly violent; indeed they had become almost as savage and debilitating as Dob's had been when the two boys had first arrived in Samuel Slammett's home. Conversely and ironically, Dob's health had begun to improve since he had been replaced as a climbing boy by Oliver, and he watched his new friend's deterioration with increasing sympathy and concern.

'Yer knows what that is, don't yer?' he said to the Dodger, as Oliver was undergoing yet another distressing attack.

'Wot wot is?' asked the Dodger.

'That coughin',' said Dob. 'It's the start of the fever; climbin' boy's fever. The soot an' the dust, they clogs up yer lungs.'

'I'll get over it,' said Oliver, managing to control the paroxysms for a moment.

'No yer won't,' said Dob. 'Not while yer climbin', yer wont.' He turned to the Dodger as Oliver recommenced coughing. 'Yer got to get 'im out, 'fore it's took 'old proper. Don't matter 'ow, just 'ow soon.'

The three boys were locked, as usual, in Slammett's room; it was early evening, but their jailer was not at home. Oliver was at the table, coughing incessantly; Dob was lying on the pile of sacks, and the Dodger was pacing back and forth impatiently. 'Maybe if we all three of us jumped Slammett,' he now suggested.

'We'd land in three corners of the room, with Slammett unbucklin' his belt,' said Dob, dejectedly. The Dodger was forced to admit that such would almost certainly be the case, and continued to pace from one end of the room to the other, thinking hard.

Oliver now controlled his coughing long enough to

say, suddenly: 'There's one place we haven't tried . . .'

'Wot's that?' said the Dodger.

'The cupboard,' said Oliver. 'You could open it couldn't you. Dodger?'

The Dodger crossed hurriedly to the cupboard and examined the padlock, which was a thick, strong one. ''Ere! try this!' said Dob, producing from his pocket the twisted staple which Oliver had torn from the chimney during his first attempted escape. 'Slammett threw it away when 'e fixed up the padlock out there.'

The Dodger grinned and took the staple; watched eagerly by his two companions, he proceeded to pick at the padlock, muttering softly as he worked. 'You can do it, Dodger, you can open it – a twist 'ere, a twist there. Not as you can see much point in it – Turn, will you! – when all it'll get you is a slammin' with Slammett's belt – Move then! But you can do it, can't yer? You can open it, can't you!' The lock clicked open, and the Dodger turned beaming to his friends. Oliver smiled, tiredly, and embarked on another spasm of coughing. Dob laughed with delight. 'An' now wot?' asked the Dodger.

'Look inside,' said Oliver, suppressing his cough momentarily. The Dodger pushed the door open and gazed into the near-darkness letting out a long whistle of astonishment. 'It's the takin's!' he announced. 'Slammett's loot! All of it!' Oliver and Dob scampered forward and saw what the Dodger saw; the cupboard was lined with shelves and upon every shelf there lay a collection of items worthy of the finest of homes, glinting in the light which now shone on them from the room; items of silver and gold, some of them studded with gems of many colours: clocks, watches, plates, serving-dishes, teapots, vases, spoons, bracelets, necklaces, brooches and rings; all of them without exception both exquisite and costly.

The Dodger and Dob were understandably impressed by the sight before them, but Oliver was disappointed, for his mind was solely concentrated on the idea of escaping, and he could discern within the cupboard no means by which this could be accomplished. 'Nothing else?' he asked, morosely.

'No, not as I can see,' said the Dodger, stepping into the cupboard to examine the stolen articles more closely. Then he suddenly cried: 'Wait! It's a fireplace! Behind the shelves! A fireplace! It's got boards in front of it!'

'I thought there had to be,' said Oliver. 'I couldn't imagine them building a room as large as this without one.'

Without a moment's hesitation, the Dodger cleared the shelves before the fireplace of the items they carried, and tore them down, he then tugged at the boards, which had been nailed to the wall in a careless manner and came away quite easily. Once the fireplace was fully visible, Oliver entered the cupboard and peered up into the chimney. 'It's narrow enough,' he said, 'but it'll do, I think.'

'Narrow?' said the Dodger, with concern. 'Fine for Dob an' you, then, but what about me?'

'It's the only way, Dodger,' said Oliver. 'You'll have to try it.'

Suddenly Dob, who had very sensibly been listening at the door of the main room for the sound of anyone approaching, ran to the cupboard and whispered urgently: 'Slammett! It's Slammett! 'E's coming! I could 'ear 'im! Go quickly, both of you! I'll see wot I can do, 'oldin' 'im up.'

'We ain't leavin' you, Dob,' said the Dodger.

'No option,' said Dob, 'I 'asn't the breath. Go now, before it's . . . There was a loud rattling of chains outside the main door; Slammett was clearly unlocking the padlock. 'Too late!' whispered Dob. 'Quiet as quiet, now! See wot I can do!' And before either Oliver or the Dodger could protest, he had shut the cupboard door on both of them, throwing them into utter darkness.

Dob had just succeeded in closing up the padlock again, and had lain down in his familiar position amid the sacks, when the main door of the room opened and Samuel Slammett entered. Naturally he was startled by the immediately apparent absence of Master Dawkins and Master Twist. Dob did not allow him to express his astonishment verbally, however, for he quickly said: 'Gone, they are, Mr Slammett. Gone an' left me 'ere. *'E* came for 'em, picked the locks an' all.'

''Oo?' demanded Slammett. ''Oo come?'

'Bloater, was it?' said Dob, 'Bloater, something like that'.

'Bloater? Wot would 'e want with . . .?' Slammett's red eyes widened abruptly, and he crossed hastily to the cupboard, testing the padlock. Once he was satisfied that it was secure, he returned to the door of the room, muttering: 'Right, Mr Bolter, wotever it was!' He paused briefly at the door to say, 'Dob – leave 'ere, an' I'll find yer an' break yer back!' He was about to leave the room when, most inopportunely, the sound of a very recognizable attack of uncontrollable coughing emanated from the direction of the cupboard. Slammett turned again to stare at Dob, his lips curling into a vicious scowl. 'Gone, are they?' he snarled. 'Took by Mr Bloater, was they? I'll deal with you later!' He hurried back to the cupboard, extracting the key from his pocket, and unlocked the padlock. To his understandable fury, the door refused to open. He pushed it, hit at it with his fist, and finally lent it all the weight of his considerable bulk by running at it with his shoulder, but it remained stubbornly shut. 'Dawkins! Twist! You 'ear me?!' he thundered. 'Open up, I knows yer there! Longer yer leaves it, worse it'll be for yer!'

Within the cupboard, rendered impenetrable for the moment by one of the removed shelves which had been wedged tightly under the door's handle, Oliver had already wriggled a few yards up the chimney, and the Dodger was doing his best to follow. He had managed to ascend no more than a couple of feet however, and his legs were still dangling into the hearth, when he cried, 'Oliver! Oliver! I'm stuck! You go on! I'm finished!'

'You can't be!' Oliver called from above him. 'Reach up one arm! Keep the other by your side! It'll make you narrower!'

'It's no good! I can't make it!'

'You can!' cried Oliver, firmly. 'Reach up, there's room enough! Reach, and I'll take your hand!'

Meanwhile, Slammett was continuing his assault on the cupboard door with ever increasing fury, until, with the sound of rending wood, the shelf snapped and the door fell inwards, torn from its hinges. The sweep threw himself across it and into the cupboard. He was just in time to see the Dodger's heels disappearing into the chimney. Quickly kneeling before the hearth, he thrust an arm wildly into the shaft, in the hope of catching hold of one of the boy's feet; but his hand returned empty. 'The roof! I'll get them on the roof!' he bellowed, hurrying out of the cupboard.

He halted before the cupboard in dismay. There were now four people in the room; Dob, still lying on the sacks, two policemen, and a gentleman in a tall hat, whose red waistcoat immediately identified him as an officer from Bow Street.

'Mr Slammett?' said the runner, quite calmly, 'I have reason to believe you know the whereabouts of one Oliver Twist, a climbin' boy.'

Samuel Slammett regained control of himself with remarkable speed. 'Twist?' he declared. 'Never 'eard of 'im. *That's* my prentice, there. Dob. No other boy 'ere.'

The runner glanced at the boy on the sacks, who now abruptly exclaimed: 'Don't believe 'im, officer! Oliver's in the cupboard! Along with everything else!'

'H'everything else?' said the runner, inquisitively, advancing towards the cupboard.

Slammett glared briefly at Dob before stepping backwards and stretching himself across the cupboard's doorway in an attempt to prevent the officer from seeing what it contained. 'Yer ain't goin' in there!' he cried. 'This is my 'ome! A private 'ouse! Yer ain't got a warrant!'

As it happened, the officer, being a tall gentleman, did not need a warrant, for he already had a clear view of the cupboard's valuable contents over Samuel Slammett's shoulder. 'Well, Mr Slammett!' he said. 'Well, well, quite a haul!' Acknowledging defeat momentarily, Slammett stepped aside to allow the officer a closer inspection of the stolen articles. As the officer moved past him, however, the sweep decided to attempt an escape, and ran for the door of the room, only to be intercepted, inevitably, by the two policemen, who each caught hold of one of his arms and swung him round to face the runner, who now emerged from the cupboard. 'As I said, quite a haul, Mr Slammett,' this gentleman observed. 'You h'amaze me.'

'Yer 'asn't . . . no right . . . ,' muttered Slammett, thoroughly downcast.

'Oh haven't I?' said the runner, with a short laugh. 'Your h'accomplice, Oliver Twist, may 'ave h'escaped, but we'll pick him up, sooner or later. For the moment, you'll do nicely, thank you.'

'No right,' murmured Slammett, 'No right . . . as me . . . sainted ma . . used to say.'

'If I were her,' declared the officer, 'or if I was yourself, I'd be very careful what I say. H'indeed, in your own best h'interests, I'd be careful to make it nothing at all.'

As it happened, Noah Claypole was approaching Slammett's tenement house at this moment. In a juster world, he would have arrived at the house a few minutes earlier; for if he had done this, he would have been in Samuel Slammett's company when the guardians of the law arrived. But, the world being less just than it should be, he was just in time to glimpse the gentleman whom he was about to visit emerging from the house between two policemen, and handcuffed to both of them. Noah darted into the shadows of a small passage in the tenement yard and watched, not without a certain feeling of pleasure, as his unhappy fellow-criminal was hauled away to justice, followed by a magistrate's officer and a thin, weak-looking, soot-stained boy, who was, to Claypole's considerable relief, most definitely not Oliver Twist. But then neither was this boy the one he had briefly noticed in Slammett's company on his last visit to this tenement two days previously. *That* boy could have been Oliver, Noah mused; he could well have been Oliver, merely rendered unrecognizable by the blackness of his countenance and his clothes. Reaching this conclusion, Claypole was severely troubled once more.

That morning, the Reverend Harry Maylie had received a somewhat curt communication from Mr Stalker, in reply to his anxious inquiry as to the reasons for Oliver's apparent reluctance to write any letters to his aunt.

'My dear?' said the good clergyman to his lovely wife, 'I have heard from Mr Stalker. I have, I fear, grave news. The boys are gone from school, both your nephew and Dawkins.'

'Harry, no!' exclaimed Rose. 'How could they be?'

'Indeed, my dear, how could they be?' said her husband. 'But I must tell you, Rose, I am not satisfied. I have faith in both boys, and I shall take this matter further.'

'We must pray for them, Harry,' said Rose Maylie, softly. 'Now and always; wherever they may be.'

CHAPTER TWENTY

''Ere we are again!' said the Dodger. 'Or if we aint', we might as well be! One street's much like another when yer ain't got no place to go'. The two boys had run into an alley-way no different in its darkness and dirtiness from the others they had hidden in now and then since their arrival in London. They were both sitting on the damp ground with their backs against a wall, fighting to regain their breath. It was snowing.

'We could try to reach my uncle's,' suggested Oliver.

'In the country? 'Ow far d'yer think we'd get? With our description posted up in every police station by now?' The Dodger shook his head wearily. 'No, we're safer 'ere in the smoke, where they just might not spot us. At least we ain't got Monks an' Claypole to worry about. They think they shipped you off to Zululand.'

Oliver seemed concerned nevertheless. 'There's the letter I gave the old lady,' he said. '*She* knows I'm still here.'

'She'd not 'ave gone to *them,* would she?' retorted the Dodger. 'The runners maybe, or your friend Mr Grimwig, but not *them.*' Oliver agreed that such an action on her part was highly unlikely; but he remained anxious; for he would, at that moment, have felt easier in his heart if *nobody* had known of his presence in London, not even Mrs Martin.

'But no sign of Twist?' inquired Mrs Carraway.

'They brought out Slammett an' a boy,' said Claypole, 'but not the one I saw. Whoever 'e was, 'e'd gone before the coppers arrived.' Noah had returned immediately to Mr Brownlow's house from Slammett's tenement, and had reported what he had seen there to Mrs Carraway.

'So the one you saw might still have been Twist,' observed this lady.

'I told yer! I don't know!' exclaimed Claypole impatiently. 'I never looked at 'im close!' He quietened. 'It could 'ave been,' he said.

'You'll have to tell Mr Monks,' declared Mrs Carraway.

'I know, I know,' said Noah, not relishing the thought in the least. 'Like it or not, 'e's back in this, till we know for sure wot's 'appened.'

'And in the meantime?' Mrs Carraway asked.

'Meantime,' replied Claypole, sternly, 'there's too much at stake – for all of us – to risk a slip-up now. Au' 'ere's where yer start earnin' yer keep, Mrs C. We need to find out more about that letter to old Grimwig, an' 'e won't deal with neither Monks nor me. So, it's clear who it's up to, ain't it?'

Mrs Carraway understood him perfectly and said she would call on Mr Grimwig the following morning. For his part, Noah Claypole decided to try and visit Slammett in Newgate Prison, to which place he presumed, the sweep had been taken. After that, distasteful though the prospect was, he would have to contact Monks and acquaint him with this new development, although he had no idea where the villain might be, if he was in London at all.

Another cloudlessly cold night had descended on London, and once again Oliver and the Dodger had nothing to protect them from the air's bitterness. It had stopped snowing, but the snow lay in a frozen crust upon the ground, and a sharp, icy wind rushed mercilessly down the alley-way. Nevertheless, propped against the wall and each other the two boys tried to sleep. The Dodger soon fell into a deep and satisfactory slumber; but Oliver remained fitfully wakeful, troubled both by his thoughts and frequent bouts of terrible coughing. In the darkness and silence that had now fallen upon the city, he suddenly thought he heard a cry and the sound of scuffling nearby. He quickly stood up. With his support gone, the Dodger fell sideways, woke up, and peered about him blearily. 'Wot is it? Wot's up?' he demanded.

'Shh!' whispered Oliver. 'Listen!' The Dodger did as he was told; there was the sound of several pieces of wood clattering onto stone, and a sorry voice was heard to plead 'No . . . No . . . No!' repeatedly. 'Someone's in trouble!' said Oliver.

'Who isn't?' said the Dodger, laying his head on his arm and closing his eyes again. 'Wake me when . . .'

'Oh, come on, Dodger!' Oliver interrupted, 'We can't just leave it.' There was now a squeal of real terror from the direction of the street into which the alley led. 'Come on!' said Oliver firmly, and ran off. With extreme reluctance, the Dodger sleepily rose to follow him.

As Oliver emerged from the alley into the street, he saw two figures under the light of a streetlamp some twenty yards to his right. One of the figures had backed into a corner, his arms raised defensively; the other was threatening him with a club. Scattered on the pavement between them was a collection of small wooden objects of various shapes, which had clearly spilled from a dropped sack. Oliver ran towards the two figures, and before the person with the club had even registered his approach, he had launched himself at the villain, catching hold of his raised arm. The attacker, who was a large, strong, thickset man, threw Oliver off in an instant, causing the boy to stagger backwards and onto his knees. Oliver caught a brief glimpse of the attacker's scarred, brutal visage, and a set of broken, scowling teeth, before he closed his eyes, certain that he was about to be beaten to death for his bravery; but he then heard the sound of running feet behind him and the Dodger calling: 'Come on, Bob! Come on, Charley! Bring the dogs!' When he opened his eyes the man with the club had vanished, and the Dodger had reached him.

'Don't you ever do that again!' said the Dodger, quite sharply, and he turned to the person who was still cowering in the shadows. 'All right, Grandad?' he asked.

''E was going to break them,' squeaked the figure. When I said I 'adn't no money.'

'Looked more as if 'e wanted to break *you,*' said the Dodger. Both boys now looked down at he scattered objects that lay on the pavement and discovered, to their astonishment, that they were wooden toys, manufactured with great affection and care; there were soldiers, and tiny buildings, and horses, and clowns, and monkeys on sticks, and a whole variety of other fascinating playthings.

'Are they all right?' said Oliver, surveying the toys with considerable concern.

'I think so,' said the man who owned them, as he bent down to pick them up.

'Everything is, then,' said the Dodger. In the light from the street-lamp, the person they had saved from attack now revealed himself to be a short, and stocky old gentleman with a great grey shock of wild wispy hair, a kindly, whimsical face and a pair of eyes that seemed permanently afraid. 'Toys ...' said the Dodger, when they had all been collected and returned to the sack from which they had tumbled. 'Make 'em yerself, do yer?' The man nodded. 'Dan, Dan, the toy-makin' man,' the Dodger muttered.

The man straightened abruptly and stared at him. ''Ow'd you know my name's Dan?' he asked, nervously.

The Dodger merely shrugged and grinned as the toymaker surveyed him suspiciously.

'We didn't,' Oliver explained, laughing. 'It's just a rhyme from school. My name's Oliver – Oliver Twist. And this is Jack Dawkins.'

The Dodger gave him a quick anxious glance, indicating that he considered such a revelation of their true names to have been far too hasty. But the toy-maker named Dan shook his head and chuckled reassuringly; 'An' mine's Dan Posset,' he said, smiling. 'Possett as may 'ap yer ma made yer as a nipper. Milk an' spice. But whisper it, lad, whisper it, up a chimbley at midnight. Give yer name to all an' sundry, yer givin' part of yerself, an' who's to tell wot use might be made of it?'

Oliver was not entirely sure that he understood the full meaning of these remarks, but the Dodger comprehended them immediately and nodded in complete agreement. 'An' that's the truth, Grandad,' he said, turning away, eager to leave Mr Possett to his own devices as soon as he could. Just then, however, Oliver was unable to prevent himself from undergoing a renewed spasm of painful coughing.

'What's the matter?' asked Dan Possett.

'A touch o' fever,' explained the Dodger, still keen to escape. ' 'E was climbin' for a sweep for a while.'

'An' eatin' not much more than soot, by the looks of him,' said Dan, gazing at Oliver sympathetically. 'Well, maybe we can do somethin' about that.' Whereupon he suggested that both boys come and dine with him in his own lodgings. The Dodger remained hesitant, for in accepting a not dissimilar invitation from an apparently friendly stranger a fortnight previously, he and his companion had found themselves the prisoners of someone who had turned out to be far from friendly; but at the sight of the fervour that had entered Oliver's tired eyes at the mention of nourishment, he knew at once that he would have to accept the toy-maker's offer. The night was frosty; they were tired and hungry and they could not refuse.

Daniel Possett lived in a single room on the ground floor, that faced a street only a quarter of a mile from the one in which the boys had rescued him. It was not only where he lived, but where he worked, and was cheerfully filled with toys like those they had seen scattered on the pavement. There was a large bay window which looked out onto the street but which was heavily curtained with sacking. Before this window stood a long trestle table, littered with carpentry tools, pieces of wood, lengths of twine, a gluepot, and more toys in various stages of completion. There were two doors in the room, one leading to the street, the other to a scullery; and a hearth in which a small fire burned. Against the wall opposite the window stood a truckle bed, and next to that, a tall dresser. In the centre of the room there was another trestle table, with two stools and a rickety wooden armchair.

Welcoming his new friends to his home, Dan Possett bade them sit at the table while he disappeared into the scullery for a moment or two and brought them their supper; a veritable feast, in their eyes, far grander than anything Samuel Slammett had provided them with consisting as it did of bread, cheese, as much cold meat as they could manage, which was a great deal, and a glass or two of gin-and-water to warm them.

'Well,' declared the Dodger, when he had eaten his fill, tapping his chest and exhaling loudly, 'better than all right that was!'

'Did me good to see you eat so 'earty,' said the toymaker, gathering up the plates.

'Thanks, Mr Possett,' said Oliver, who had also eaten ravenously.

'None needed, Oliver,' retorted Dan Possett. 'But for you, I might've 'ad me brains bashed out. Wot there is of 'em. Now – seein' as 'ow you're out so late, I take it you've no place to go.'

The Dodger glanced up at him, suddenly suspicious again. 'Not bein' nosy, Jack,' Possett continued placatingly. 'But if that's the case, yer welcome to a shakedown 'ere. You think about it, while I wash these out.' He carried the plates into the scullery.

'Can we help, Mr Possett?' Oliver called after him.

'No, you rest comfortable,' replied the amicable voice from the scullery. ''Ave a look at the toys, if you've a mind to.' Dan Possett whistled heartily as he rinsed the plates.

'Why d'you 'ave to go and give him our names?' The Dodger whispered to Oliver.

'We can trust Mr Possett,' Oliver replied.

'That's wot you said about Slammett,' said the Dodger.

'Mr Possett isn't like *him*!' Oliver protested quite loudly. The Dodger put his finger to his lips and glanced warily towards the scullery. 'Maybe not,' he whispered. 'But Mr Dan Possett ain't all 'e seems to be. Leastwise, I don't think 'e is. Or to put it different, I don't think 'e's *just* all 'e seems.' His friend appeared not to understand this at all, so he added: 'If I'm wrong, I'll apologize. Right? So wot do we do?'

'I can't go any further tonight,' said Oliver, with a weary sigh.

'That's a fact,' retorted the Dodger. 'You need time to rest up, an' get that soot out of yer lungs.' He thought for some moments before suggesting: 'If old Dan's willin,' we could kip 'ere for a night or two.'

'We could help him make his toys!' Oliver declared, with sudden enthusiasm.

'If that's wot 'e wants,' said the Dodger, uncertainly. 'Anyway, we'll stay 'ere till you're fit. Then, we'll find someone to listen to our side of things.'

The proposal was accordingly put to the toy-maker, who was more than willing to accommodate his rescuers; saying that they could stay as long as they wished; and when they wanted to leave, they could do that as well. When Oliver asked if he could help him in the manufacture of his toys, he replied that he thought it a splendid idea, and would begin to instruct him in the finer arts of toy-making the very next morning. For the moment, however, what the boy needed most, he declared, was a long sleep. He produced two very inviting straw mattresses from underneath his work-table, laying them out on either side of the hearth, and furnishing each one with a threadbare blanket. Oliver slept deeply and contedly that night, by Daniel Possett's warm and friendly fire, as the winter wind howled outside.

'It is not possible!' said Monks, 'Not possible. I was here when Oliver was carried out.' The villain was pacing up and down the private room of the Three Cripples Tavern, in the manner of a caged beast. He stopped and glared at Noah Claypole, who was eyeing him nervously from behind the table. 'This Slammett?' Monks inquired. 'You questioned him?'

'With 'im 'andcuffed to a Bluebottle?' retorted Claypole. 'An' now 'e's in Newgate,' he added, dejectedly, as Monks began to pace again.

'Can you get to him?' asked Monks.

'I've tried,' said Claypole. 'But 'e won't talk. Not to nobody, in case it gets 'im in deeper.'

Monks muttered: 'So all we have to go by is this note Grimwig's supposed to have had.' He suddenly stabbed at the air with his cane and howled: 'It was over! Oliver was gone! *Out of my life* forever!'

Noah had never before witnessed such a show of evil despair, as that which appeared in his accomplice's half-concealed face at that moment. He controlled his terror at the sight, however, and said bravely; 'Well it was you that arranged for 'im to be shipped off with Captain Ketch.'

Monks stopped in his tracks again and gazed at him. 'And it was your fool of lieutenant, Fingers, who was supposed to watch him!' he snarled. Then a thought struck him. 'Could he have been bribed to let Oliver go?' he asked pensively.

'Wot d'yer think?' replied Claypole. 'Course 'e could've been. 'Cept for one thing. 'E's mortal scared of me is Fingers – an' even more of you.'

'Then where *is* he?' said Monks. 'You're sure the police haven't picked him up?'

'I'd 'ave 'eard,' said Claypole, 'through my professional contacts.'

'Calmly – we must think calmly,' Monks murmured, seating himself at the table and attempting to do just that. 'And clearly. That other boy – the one who helped Oliver get away from you. Who was he?'

''Ow should I know?' Noah replied.

'Where is he?'

'Why keep askin' *me*?' said Noah indignantly.

'Oliver was drugged,' Monks continued, his thoughts racing. 'If he did escape, he must have had someone to help him.'

''E was alone when 'e went to Hyssop's,' said Claypole.

'Yes . . . yes . . .' said Monks. 'Confound it! All we have is *questions*! And no *answers*!'

'Well anyway,' said Claypole, 'I've got Mrs Carraway to visit Grimwig in the mornin'. You come along about noon, an' we'll both 'ear wot 'appened.'

Monks surveyed him with distaste. 'Both?' he snarled. 'My main regret about this presumed letter is that it has compelled our meeting again.'

Noah Claypole glanced at him suspiciously; he experienced a sudden fear that Monks might be intending to vanish, and leave him alone with the problems that would almost certainly arise if Oliver Twist was still about. He had had difficulty enough in tracking his accomplice down on this dark winter night, hurrying desperately through the snow-covered streets and alleys around Saffron Hill, asking all those he passed if they had seen an evil-looking gentleman with an unmistakable silver-topped cane. At last, after searching for over two hours, he had seen him, standing in a dark doorway, to no purpose apparently except to gaze maliciously at anyone who happened to be walking by. Now that Claypole had found him again, he was determined not to let him slip away; so he summoned up the courage to remark: 'We're partners, Mr Monks, like it or not. Leave it or lump it, we're partners, till this is done.'

Whether this statement of complicity impressed the villain or not, Noah Claypole had no means of telling, but Monks turned up obediently at Mr Brownlow's house the next day at noon, as he had been instructed; and both he and Noah Claypole were in the sitting-room when Mrs Carraway returned from her visit to Mr Grimwig. She informed them that she had managed to bring the conversation round to the subject of Oliver quite speedily; the old gentleman had, in fact, shown her the letter.

'It was addressed to Mr Grimwig,' she announced, 'and apparently written by Oliver. Smudged with soot, but legible.'

'So 'e *was* with Slammett!' exclaimed Claypole.

'Yes,' said Mrs Carraway, 'Mr Grimwig was positive about the name. A reputable tradesman, he assured me.'

Claypole snarled. 'Reputable tradesman . . . ,' he muttered.

'Whom Grimwig is convinced Oliver was using to promote robberies,' the lady continued.

'We must keep him believing that,' said Monks. 'So now we know the worst. Somehow or other, my little brother got away.'

'No,' said Claypole, 'I don't credit it. 'Ow could 'e?'

'Who else could it be?' said Monks.

'That other boy,' Mrs Carraway suggested. 'The one who came to the house.'

'Whoever it is,' said Monks, with a deadly gleam in his eye, 'he must be found; and silenced.'

'To set our minds at rest, it might be possible at least to obtain a description,' Mrs Carraway suggested, eliciting a sharp look from both men. 'The lady who brought the letter to Mr Grimwig. She certainly met the writer. The note was written in her house, and in her presence.'

'Where do we find 'er?' said Claypole.

Mrs Carraway permitted herself a small tight smile of pride. 'Mr Grimwig was most sympathetic to my natural anxiety for assurance, and he provided me with the lady's name. Also with her address.'

'S.R.C.B.?' declared the little old lady inquisitively.

'Sociey for the Relief of Climbing Boys,' explained the strange gentleman seated opposite her, with an ingratiating smile.

'I am so sorry Mr . . . Mr Leeford, is it? But I am, I fear, just a little hard of hearing,' said the lady sweetly.

The strange gentleman appeared to suppress a spasm of anger before smiling again, and saying, more loudly and distinctly, 'A charitable organization, ma'am founded to relieve the plight of *climbing boys*.'

'Ah!' exclaimed the lady, nodding, 'Climbing boys! Sweep's boys.'

'Yes, ma'am,' said the gentleman, with great patience.

'I met one only recently,' the lady announced.

'Yes, Mrs Martin, it's about *that* boy that I . . .'

'Such a sweet young man! And so well spoken. Why, if you did not see him, you would never believe his occupation.'

'I did *not* see him, ma'am,' declared the strange gentleman, quite violently. '*That* is why I am here!'

'Oh dear, oh dear, I do not understand it,' remarked Mrs Martin shaking her head sadly. 'Everyone, recently, seems to regard life as so very . . . pressing.' Whereupon she proceeded to gaze distractedly out of the window. 'Now dear *Mr* Martin,' she continued, 'dear Mr Martin always said, the man who runs towards tomorrow – and I am sure he included in this the woman as well – loses sight of the beauty of today. Such a wise thought. Will you not agree, Mr Leeford?'

'I will, ma'am,' said the gentleman, toying with the silver top of the cane he carried. 'But I would be obliged if you would at least describe this sweet young man, this boy who called himself *Twist*. This – is what I have to know.'

To his great relief, the deaf old lady seemed to have understood the main burden of his request, and said immediately and with delight: 'Why certainly, Mr Leeford! Why did you not ask at once? So that you may seek for him, of course, to rescue him from those rogues ...' The strange gentleman smiled thinly. 'Now let me see,' Mrs Martin continued, 'Not very tall – in fact, I would say short for a boy of some fourteen years; and slight, thought not delicate, of build.'

'And his features, Mrs Martin? His hair and eyes?'

'Oh beneath that layer of soot, the finest of countenances; sensitive; intelligent. His hair, as far as one could tell, fair. His eyes? Pale, I think; I regret I cannot be certain. But there, Mr Leeford, is this the boy you seek?'

The strange gentleman appeared to brood in a curious manner, before nodding slowly and mouthing something which the kindly old lady could not begin to comprehend. If her hearing had been good, she would have heard him whisper dangerously: 'Yes, ma'am, yes. You have, to the life, pictured Oliver Twist.'

When the Reverend Harry Maylie arrived at Stalker's Academical Establishment and was ushered at once into the presence of the Headmaster, his first mention of the name 'Twist' prompted a spasm of spluttering fury in Mr Stalker. His lips tightened, his face turned scarlet and his eyes looked as if they might pop from their sockets.

'A wolf!' he barked. 'Do I say so, sir? Do I? I do! A wolf, a tiger, an afreet, a spirit of evil!' Harry Maylie stared at him incredulously as he continued: 'Why, sir, was he here a day before he engaged in the foulest abomination?'

'Surely not ...,' Harry began.

'Do I lie, sir?' interposed Mr Stalker. 'I? I do not! Gaming in class, casting dice while others laboured! Did he not only indulge in fisticuffs himself, but incite his fellows to riot, uproar and insurrection?'

'Incredible . . . ,' said Harry, stroking his head.

'And was that not enough? No it was not!' the Headmaster thundered. 'Finally, unwilling to accept his punishment like a gentleman, did he not flee the hand of justice, slipping away like the proverbial thief, and bearing in his pocket . . .'

'Not theft as well!' Harry interrupted.

'Worse, sir, worse!' declared Stalker. 'Oh how sharper than a serpent's tooth! The reputation of this establishment, this abode of learning; unsung mayhap, but unsullied till the coming of – I can barely utter the name – Twist!'

'It sounds . . . so unlike the boy,' said Harry, softly. 'And Dawkins?'

Mr Stalker shook his head gravely. 'Do I blame myself, sir?' he said. 'The day Twist darkened these portals, in all innocence did I not give the one into the care of the other? How sorrily these roles were reversed!'

Harry gazed at the incensed gentleman for a few moments. Difficult though it was to believe that Oliver could commit the crimes attributed to him, he could see no reason why Mr Stalker should be lying about such things; and perhaps the boy's misdemeanours were entirely the result of Dawkin's influence. 'No, Mr Stalker,' he now said with a sigh. 'You must not blame yourself. They knew each other before, both corrupted by the same villain. Alas, you must blame *me*. *I* was the cause of Dawkin's reprieve from transportation. *I* was the cause of the arrival of both boys here; the cause of all that has followed.' He rose despondently from his seat. 'I thank you for your time, sir,' he said, 'I shall not trouble you further.'

Mr Stalker stared at him in blank astonishment for a second or two, before reaching for the handbell on his desk and giving it a sharp ring. A moment later the door to the study opened and a short but very fat boy, of about Oliver's age, with a chubby but pleasant face, entered. 'You will kindly see this gentleman out,' said the Headmaster to the boy, before turning to the clergyman and remarking mournfully, 'Alas, sir, yes. We cannot always determine how our best-laid schemes may be answered. Shall we meet again? I fancy not. But if you should discover the fates of your nephew and Dawkins, I should be obliged for a brief communication on the matter.'

'Certainly, Mr Stalker,' said Harry Maylie. 'And once more, my thanks.' The Headmaster nodded and waved him, rather rudely, from the room.

'Excuse me, sir,' said the fat boy to Harry, once the study door was closed behind them. 'Are you – I mean is Oliver your nephew? Oliver Twist?'

'Yes,' said Harry.

'You see,' said the fat boy, 'I was his friend, and – well I don't think Mr Stalker could tell you everything about what happened.'

'What is your name, boy?' asked Harry, with a frown.

'Rice, sir. Tommy Rice. You see, he couldn't really know why Oliver ran away. After Dawkins got the letter –from Oliver's aunt . . .'

'After . . .? Harry began, thoughtfully. 'Go on.'

'It was the first he'd heard about his guardian's illness. And then Dawkins worked out about the letters, how the Porter must have stolen them . . .'

'The School Porter?'

'Yes, sir, Mr Bumble, sir.'

'Bumble? The name caused a sudden pang of concerned horror in the clergyman's heart. 'Bumble?' he repeated. 'Bumble is the School Porter?'

'Was, sir,' said Tommy.

Harry Maylie glanced briefly at the door of Mr Stalker's study before putting an arm around the boy's shoulder and saying: 'Come, Master Rice, was it not? We have much to discuss.'

'Yes, sir,' said Tommy, and obediently proceeded to explain everything as the two of them walked down the corridor together.

CHAPTER TWENTY-ONE

On his first day in Daniel Possett's lodgings, Oliver had proved himself an eager pupil in the practice of toy-making. He was too frail, however, to spend more than a few hours at the work-table, cutting the wooden parts and stringing and glueing them together, before he felt the need to return to his mattress by the fire.

'Sleepin' sound, ain't 'e? Like a babe,' observed Daniel Possett that evening, gazing fondly at the boy.

'Oh, Oliver's a babe,' said the Dodger with a chuckle. 'A babe, 'e is. Innocent an' trustin'.' He and Dan were seated at the table in the centre of the room, having both enjoyed another hearty supper.

'Learns quick, though,' said Dan, pointing to the toys on the work-table. 'Cut some o' them up a right treat.'

'Other things 'e might not be so quick with,' the Dodger retorted casually. 'Things I don't doubt *you* could teach him, Dan Possett.'

Dan was suddenly wary. 'Like wot?' he asked sharply, his eyes narrowing.

The Dodger grinned and stared into his mug of gin-and-water. 'Well,' he said, 'let's say, just for instance ...' 'Ow about the three card trick? I'm sure, if anyone could teach 'im that it'd be Three Card Dan.'

There was a long pause. ' 'Ow d'yer know?' whispered Dan.

'You could say, I been around a bit longer 'n Oliver,' said the Dodger, still without looking up from his mug. 'I knew you straight off. I've 'eard stories, 'undreds of 'em, about Dan the cardsharp who uses toy sellin' as a cover. The best trickster in the country, I've 'eard.' Dan sighed. 'Don't worry,' the Dodger added, glancing up at last. 'I ain't likely to split – not even to Oliver.'

'Never thought yer would,' said Dan, with considerable relief nevertheless, and sighed again. 'That's not the trouble,' he muttered dejectedly. 'Yer talkin' of the past, Jack, an' me 'ands went with it . . .' He held them up for the Dodger's inspection. They were gnarled and bent with age. 'I was best,' he continued. 'The best. But me speed's gone, an' me eyesight's goin' an' without both . . .? I'm finished, Jack. Finished.'

There was another pause before the Dodger said, hesitantly, 'I was wonderin'. You in a place like this. It needn't be so bad.' Dan gazed at him inquisitively. 'Wouldn't be, if . . . well . . .,' the Dodger said, 'suppose you 'ad an apprentice, someone you'd trained yourself?'

'You?' said Dan.

'Why not? You teach me the trade, an' we work together, 'alf an' 'alf, on everythin' took . . .' Dan glanced at the sleeping boy on the mattress. 'Oh, just so *'e* dont' know,' the Dodger added quickly, sensing his doubts. 'Just so *'e* don't ever know.'

Dan thought for some while. 'Might work . . . ,' he muttered at last. 'Might. All right,' he then declared. 'But we start slow – an' it'll take practice. Not the Three Cards. That's well, that's more'n just a trick, an' it ain't somethin' you can do on yer own. No, we'll start with thimble-riggin'.'

'Thimble-riggin,' the Dodger mused. 'Never could see 'ow *that* was done.'

Dan chuckled and went to the work-table, rummaging among the half completed toys. 'Magic, that's all,' he said with a grin. 'Just magic.' He returned to the centre table with three wooden thimbles, each painted with the face and wings of an angel. 'Touch o' class,' he explained, showing them to the Dodger. 'Not just three thimbles; three angels. But just you watch an' see 'ow sometimes even they can't be trusted.' He laid the three thimbles down in a row on the table, and tore a tiny pellet of bread from a loaf they had been eating. He then placed the pellet under the middle thimble and moved the thimbles around the table-top, across and behind each other for some time, as the Dodger tried to keep his eye on the one containing the bread. 'Now then,' said Dan, as the thimbles stood in a neat row again, 'Which one?'

'The middle one,' said the Dodger.

'Lift it.'

The Dodger lifted the middle thimble but the pellet was not there. He set it down again and picked up the other two in succession but neither of them contained the pellet, which had vanished into thin air. 'I told yer,' said Dan, with a wink, 'Magic!' and he produced the pellet from the Dodger's ear.

'Do it again' said the Dodger. 'I'll watch yer more careful.' Dan repeated the trick, five more times indeed, but the Dodger remained baffled.

'Now watch,' said Dan at last, revealing the pellet in his palm, 'this time I'll show yer.' He proceeded to explain, matching the actions to his words as the Dodger watched intently. 'Well then, yer puts down the pea – or bread pellet, or wotever. Yer picks up an angel an' puts it down over the pea. Yer takes away yer 'and; ring an' little fingers closed. Yer moves the angels about with both 'ands, an' invites the mark to choose 'is lucky angel. Go on then, choose!'

The Dodger lifted a thimble, certain that it contained the pellet; but the pellet had disappeared once more.

'An' o' course, the pea ain't there! Couldn't be, you see,' said Dan, opening his palm to reveal the pellet, 'since it's 'ere, where you nipped it up with yer nail to start with ...'

'But I didn't see yer do it!' the Dodger protested.

'That's the magic,' said Dan, adding with a grin, 'or the skill. Now you try.'

As a former pickpocket, once the envy of his fellows for the nimbleness of his fingers, the Dodger acquitted himself comparatively well his first attempt to pick up the pellet from under the thimble without being seen. 'Not bad,' observed Dan admiringly. 'For the first time.

Least yer got the pea up from under. 'Ave another go.'

The Dodger repeated the trick successfully. '*Now* wot yer got to do,' said Dan, 'is the 'ard bit. Yer got to put it back.'

'Wot?' said the Dodger.

'Yer got to put it back under another angel, the angel wot the mark 'asn't picked, as yer lifts it up. Otherwise there's no winnin's in it, is there?'

The Dodger grinned knowingly. 'Teach me 'ow,' he said.

So Daniel Possett taught him. The Dodger remained seated at the table for most of the night, perfecting the trick. Simple though it was in essence, it required considerable skill and practice to be rendered capable of deceiving the eye of the most discerning stranger. As morning approached, however, the Dodger considered himself adequately proficient and Daniel Possett had to agree. He decided to put his new partner to the test under the gaze of the world at large that very day.

The toy-maker lived in an area of the city known as Cheapside, which lay beneath the eastern shadow of St Paul's Cathedral. He chose to sell his wares, however in a busy street market called Leadenhall, which was still further east, about half a mile from his home. It was to this place that he and his two new friends sallied that morning, after a nourishing breakfast, with two sacks of toys. Oliver was cheerfully awake by now, much refreshed from his long rest. He remained pale, however, and still could not avoid succumbing to the occasional bout of coughing, although the attacks were becoming less frequent and not so painfully debilitating. As Dan erected his stall and began to arrange the toys, Oliver asked if he could help to sell them. His request was willingly granted. The stall was soon attracting custom, and the boy proved to be a very successful salesman; so successful, indeed, that Dan felt he could leave him to mind the stall alone while he and the Dodger removed themselves to another corner of the market. There they set up a small table, upon which the Dodger laid the three thimbles, a dried pea, and a pile of coins.

'First,' Dan explained, 'Yer makes *me* yer mark, Jack, an' yer lets me win.'

' 'Ow long for?' asked the Dodger.

'Until we've got a nice crowd,' said Dan, with a wink. 'Tuppence a game, right?'

'Right,' said the Dodger, and they began to play. In only a few minutes they had attracted a large number of interested spectators, for every time Dan lifted a thimble to reveal the pea, which the Dodger had remembered not to pick up, he let virtually the whole of Leadenhall Market know the happy fact, by calling out in a loud, gleeful voice, 'I won! I won! I won again!,' and the Dodger would emit a doleful sigh, handing him two pennies from the pile.

'An' there we are, an' there they go,' cried the Dodger, moving the thimbles rapidly and confusedly about on the table. 'The dancin' angels, round an' round. But which one 'as the pea?'

'The end one,' declared Dan.

'Tell yer wot, sir,' said the Dodger, 'So's I can't cheat no way, you lift it yerself.'

Dan lifted the thimble and once more the pea was revealed. 'I won! I won again!' he cried.

'I'm afraid, sir, yer just too good for me,' announced the Dodger, handing over two more pennies. 'Need to give someone else a chance, or I'll be ruined. That's if anyone else is interested in dancin' angels,' he added, glancing round him at the throng. Several eager people moved forward immediately. 'One at a time, please, ladies an' gennelman!' exclaimed the Dodger. 'One at a time! You, sir. Tuppence a game, right?' The gentleman in question laid two pennies on the table-top. He lost them quickly, for now the pea was suddenly proving to be more recalcitrant.

Grinning knowingly, Dan Possett returned to the toy-stall, which to his surprise, was now entirely encircled by an equally large crowd of customers, some of whom were coming away with toys in their hands. To his further astonishment, Oliver was selling the toys and very successfully, for anything up to sixpence each; a price which Daniel Possett, in all his years as a toy-maker, had never had the temerity to demand. 'A dancing monkey?' the boy was saying. 'Certainly, sir. That'll be sixpence, if you please.'

Dan chuckled. At this rate, he thought, he would be a rich man in no time at all, and he thanked the fates for sending him two such valuable assistants.

'Very 'ealthy. Very 'ealthy indeed', he declared that evening, as he counted out the day's earnings on the table in his lodgings. 'For a first day's takin's, more'n' twice wot I usually looks for.'

'That sounds promisin',' said the Dodger, with a grin.

'An' almost all of it not from you, Jack,' said Dan, 'but from Oliver. Dancin' monkeys I been selling for a penny, 'e sold for sixpence.' He gazed admiringly at Oliver, who was sitting opposite him at the table.

At that moment, the Dodger decided to blow his nose; but in extracting a handkerchief from his pocket, two of the thimbles emerged with it, and tumbled onto the table. He tried to retrieve them quickly before Oliver's interest was aroused, but he was too late. 'I haven't seen these before,' said Oliver, picking one up and examining it curiously.

'Thimbles!' the Dodger announced sharply. 'That's what they are! You can see.'

Oliver was surprised by the apparent hostility in the Dodger's voice. It was only an attempt to cover considerable confusion and embarrassment, but he was not to know that, and seemed, mildly pained. To placate him, Dan Possett shook his head and smiled. 'E's playin' games, Oliver,' he said kindly. 'They ain't thimbles, they're part of a trick.' The Dodger gave Dan a shocked glance, for he had understood that this side of the business was on no account to be revealed to his friend.

'What sort of trick?' asked Oliver, innocently.

'A trick for little 'uns,' Dan replied. 'I was showin' Jack at the market. Wasn't I, Jack? 'Ere, let me 'ave them ...' Oliver handed him the thimbles. 'Jack likes it,' Dan continued, chuckling. 'Appeals to 'is underdeveloped mind.' The Dodger scowled, but Dan Possett ignored him and placed a thimble on the middle finger of each hand, closing his fingers over his palms and holding out his fists towards Oliver. 'Right then, 'ere's 'ow it goes,' he said, and he began to recite a rhyme: 'Two little angels, in a golden hall; one named Peter . . .' whereupon he raised one middle finger, revealing a thimble; 'One named Paul.' Whereupon he raised the other middle finger, revealing the second thimble. 'Fly away Peter,' he said, quickly folding down the left middle finger and flicking up his index finger in its stead. 'Fly away Paul,' and he did the same with his right hand. 'Come back, Peter, come back Paul,' and the index fingers were replaced by the middle fingers in the twinkling of an eye. 'An' that's it,' he declared.

Oliver laughed and applauded delightedly. The Dodger laughed too, but out of relief rather than for any other reason. Dan Possett smiled in a sheepish fashion and handed the thimbles back to the Dodger, who pocketed them hastily.

The next day trade was just as brisk, if not more so. It was interrupted, however, or at least the Dodger's side of it was, by the sudden appearance of two top-hatted policemen in the market. Dan spotted them first, strolling interestedly amongst the stalls. He pushed his way hurriedly through the throng that surrounded the Dodger, and whispered urgently in his ear. 'Clear up, Jack, or we're nabbed! Coppers!' The Dodger scooped his takings and the thimbles from the table; his immediate reaction was to start running, but Dan caught his arm and said sharply: 'Steady! You'll give us away for sure!'

By this time Oliver, who was at the toy-stall, had also

caught sight of the policemen. He too felt like deserting everything and fleeing from the market as fast as legs would carry him, not because of what he was doing was in any way illicit, but because if, as the Dodger had said, his description was by now posted up in every police station in London, he would surely be recognized. He did not run away, however, for he calculated that such an action would attract too much attention and lead to certain capture; whereas if he were to remain where he was, the policemen might not even approach the stall; so he did so, eyeing the guardians of the law warily as he continued to demonstrate the articulated toys to his fascinated customer.

'All genuine handmade, by one of the finest craftsmen!' he cried. 'Possett's Mechanical Toys! All jointed! All moving! A bargain at twice the price! The soldier's tuppence, sir. Thank you very much.'

The policemen had reached his stall, and were watching him. He did not dare to wonder whether their obvious interest was directed at the climbing monkey he held in his hand, or merely at him, Oliver Twist. He swallowed hard, made a determined effort to smile, and proceeded to work at the string on the monkey, making it jump. 'The latest novelty, officers? Watch the monkey dance! Hear the children laugh! The most welcome gift you could ever take home! Sixpence a monkey! A bargain at twice the price!'

One of the policemen was smiling now. Oliver did not dare to consider why; was it out of recognition? Was his brief career as a seller of toys about to come to a brutal end? 'Watch the monkey dance! Hear the children laugh!' he cried again. The smiling officer picked up a monkey from the table; then to Oliver's astonishment and immediate relief, he handed him sixpence, without saying a word, and turned away, working the monkey as he wandered off with his companion.

Daniel Possett, who was now beside the stall, had

watched the scene in utter amazement, for he had never, in his long life, sold a toy to a policeman.

That evening, Noah Claypole interviewed a most brutish looking individual in the private room of the Three Cripples. He was a housebreaker; a good friend, once, of the late Bill Sikes, the most notorious of housebreakers; a grizzled balding, scarred, hulk of a creature whose name was Kags. In earlier days, Noah Claypole would have turned and fled for his life merely at the sight of such a monster; he was not exactly unafraid now, but he knew that he had the upper hand for the moment.

'You'll do what I say, Kags.' he announced. 'Yer'll go where I send yer, an' take wot I pay yer. Transportation for life, weren't it? But yer sneaked 'ome, didn't yer? Well, one word from me an' it'll be back to the Antipodies for you, on the next convict ship.'

'Yer drives a 'ard bargain, Mr Bolter,' growled the monster. 'An' I got no way to argue it, 'ave I? But mebbe one day,' he added, with a vicious scowl, 'We'll 'ave a chance to discuss fings further – eh? – up an alley somewhere, mebbe?'

Claypole could not prevent himself from turning slightly white at the threat. 'Just get it done!' he snapped, controlling his terror. 'You've got the address!'

'Yes, sir, Mr Bolter sir,' said the brute, sneering, 'Right away, sir, Mr Bolter sir!' He turned to the door, opened it, and left the room.

'Interesting,' said a familiar voice, pensively, in the darkness beyond the open door. A moment later, Monks appeared.

'Who?' asked Claypole.

'That man; if he *is* a man, and not a creature from the deep.'

'Kags? 'E's a cracksman, a 'eavyman, used to run with Bill Sikes. But I got 'im where I want 'im.'

'How have you managed *that*?' asked Monks, incredulously.

'Transported for life,' Claypole explained. 'Then someone saw 'im back in London an' told me. Workin' 'ere for me, or for the Crown in Australia, 'e takes 'is choice.'

'Interesting,' Monks repeated. 'And useful. We could need someone like him before we've done with each other.'

'So what's the news?' said Claypole. 'You talked to 'er?' Monks nodded, still gazing out into the darkness beyond the door. 'An' it was Oliver?'

'I'll stake my life on it,' said Monks.

Claypole gasped. 'I'd never 'ave believed it! 'Ow aggravatin'! But 'ow?'

Monks surveyed him blankly. 'Who was it you saw carried out?' Monks gazed briefly heavenwards, unable to credit his accomplice's stupidity. 'Fingers!' Claypole suddenly cried.

'It came to me rather suddenly, too,' declared Monks, smiling thinly.

'Wot a sell!' exclaimed Claypole, unable to avoid laughing, despite his shock and disbelief. 'Poor old Fingers . . .'

Monks quickly approached the table and leaned towards him, no longer smiling. 'And now,' he snarled, 'it is certain that my half brother is still in London. And this time, when we find him, we may let your friend Kags deal with him.'

Noah Claypole shuddered involuntarily; for he was not sure that he relished the idea of anyone being the victim of that creature's brutality; not even Oliver Twist.

'Four days!' cried Daniel Possett, having counted out the money on the table in his lodgings. 'Four days takin's in one!' Oliver beamed with pride and pleasure; the

Dodger grinned with satisfaction. 'An' it weren't from nothin' but the toys!' Dan continued. 'I was sellin' them too cheap. I tell yer, I just realized wot it means! By now, I could've been rich, instead of spendin' 'alf me time 'avin' to dodge the police an' risk bein' sent to jail.'

Oliver stared at him in surprise; the Dodger stared too, anxiously. Dan lowered his head in shame, and announced: 'Yes, Oliver, I 'ave a confession. The toys – oh I made 'em! – but they was a cover for other things, you see. An' 'ere I am, in the autumn of me life, realizin' that all the time I was bein' a poor an' miserable rogue. I'd 'ave been better off, comfortable an' 'appy, just by sellin' the toys I made, than by sharpin'. An' now it's too late. Too late.'

Oliver was both shocked and sympathetic, for the toy-maker, having confessed his wickedness, looked so genuinely remorseful that the hardest heart would have felt some pity for his state. 'Why is it too late?' the boy asked, softly.

'E's right!' said the Dodger. 'Who's to say it's too late?'

'Wot can I do?' Dan wailed. 'Oh wot can I do?'

'Ask Oliver,' said the Dodger. 'Seems 'e's the one with the 'ead for business.'

'There is one thing we could try,' said Oliver, after thought.

'Wot?' said Dan.

'We could sell your toys here. We could turn this place into a shop.'

'I don't see that,' said Dan sceptically. 'I mean, who down 'ere's goin' to be buyin' toys, even if they notice there's a shop.'

'You might be surprised, Dan,' said the Dodger, brightly. 'We could pull the sackin' off the window there and lay the toys on the table, all neat an' with prices on them, to catch the attention of anyone wot 'appens to be walkin' by, like a real shop front.'

There was a long pause as Dan surveyed the window. 'Costs nothin' to try, I s'pose,' he announced at last, retaining a doubtful tone, but unable to mask his interest in the idea.

The next morning, a group of sharp-eyed children who were passing the bay window of Dan Possett's home and work-shop could not fail to notice, through the gaps in the sacking, a frenzy of activity within; a funny old gentleman and his youthful assistant were busily laying out a variety of mechanical wooden toys on the long table immediately behind the window. At a second table, in the centre of the room, another youth was industriously writing on a number of slips of cardboard.

''Ow's the prices comin', Oliver?' asked Dan.

'I've done the pennies and sixpences,' Oliver replied. 'I'm doing a few shillings now.'

'Shillin's?!' Dan gasped in horror. 'There's nothin' 'ere worth a *shillin'*!'

'Leave it to Oliver, Dan,' the Dodger said softly. 'You told 'im, ask a penny for a monkey on a stick. 'E took six times that – a tanner – off that peeler. I always said that's wot made Fagin the crook 'e was. 'E 'as a 'ead for business as well.'

Dan could not resist a chuckle of glee as he continued to arrange the toys.

'They're ready,' declared Oliver, rising from the table and coming over with the price cards.

'Well,' said the Dodger. 'Time you did the honours, Mr Possett sir. Time you declared this establishment truly truly established an' duly open . . .'

A ceremonious solemnity descended on the scene as Dan glanced briefly at his two friends and moved proudly to the window to remove the sacking. As he took it down, he did not know whether to be frightened or pleased at the sight of the sizeable and fascinated throng that had already gathered outside. It consisted mainly of children, who now pressed forward eagerly to gaze at the toys beyond him.

'Better get these price cards down quick,' said the Dodger, and the two boys set about pricing the display. A moment or so later, there was a timid rap at the door. Dan stared in open terror at his friends.

'Well go on, Dan, open it. It's yer first customer!' cried the Dodger. Oliver laughed.

Dan moved nervously to the door, as the knock was repeated, and after still further hesitation, he opened it. A poorly dressed young woman was standing outside, with a kind face and a diffident smile. Two small children, both very ragged, stood on either side of her, clinging to her skirts and peering up shyly as they sucked their thumbs. Daniel Possett smiled. 'Enter, madam, enter. Welcome to Daniel Possett's Toy Emporium,' he said with a flourish.

As it happened, a peculiarly stout personage was passing through Cheapside that very morning, to no particular purpose except that he felt he might as well be there as anywhere, since he had nowhere to go and nothing better to do. It was a bright, cheerful day, although the air was frosty, but the gentleman in question was waddling along with a most melancholy expression on his podgy brow. Those whom he passed could not fail to take note of him for he was really quite exceptionally fat; and despite his obvious dejection and somewhat threadbare appearance, there was a pompous self-importance in his gait which no amount of despondency could overcome.

As this extraordinarily corpulent individual turned into a side street, he noticed a crowd of people, consisting of children for the most part, gathered about a large bay-window and peering excitedly through it. Out of boredom, if for no other reason, he decided to investigate what it could possibly be that they were gazing at with such enthusiasm, and began to move towards them.

'Call again any time madam,' said Daniel Possett, ushering the woman and her two children to the door. 'Special discounts, o' course, to special customers,' he added with a wink. The woman smiled, as did the children, who were both very happy with the toys that had been bought for them.

Dan closed the door behind his first customers; but then, after a moment's thought, he opened it again, flinging it wide with an expansive gesture. Leaving it open, he walked back into the room and sat at the table in the centre, on a chair facing the door, sitting back comfortably and tucking his thumbs into the pockets of his waistcoat, as if he was a millionaire already.

Oliver and the Dodger had been watching, and they now laughed happily. It was very fortunate that they had their backs to the window at the moment, for if they had chanced to turn, they would have seen the familiar figure of Mr Bumble, staring interestedly and incredulously in at them.

CHAPTER TWENTY-TWO

''Ere we are, lads,' said Dan, bringing two steaming mugs from the scullery and placing them on the table, 'cup o' tea.'

'Thanks, Mr Possett,' said Oliver, who was busy painting the tunic of a toy soldier.

'Yer a mind-reader, Dan,' said the Dodger, who was industriously attaching an articulated arm to another toy soldier.

'We'll 'ave a spot o' supper in a minute,' announced Dan. 'Oliver, you've done more'n enough for today. You still 'ave to take it easy, y' know.'

'I've nearly stopped coughing,' said Oliver.

'Shame really,' observed the Dodger, grinning. 'I thought, if all else failed, we could 'ire 'im out as a fog 'orn.'

'No need for that, Dodger,' said Dan, laughing. 'Not now we're doin' well. I'll soon 'ave enough to keep my promise. Buyin' seats for all three of us in a coach that'll take us to Oliver's uncle's place in the country.'

Oliver and the Dodger looked up at him in delighted surprise. 'To get you to safety, lad,' Dan continued, now gazing seriously at Oliver. 'Then you can explain everything an' get everything sorted out'.

It was the evening of the second day's trading at the shop. The previous night, certain by then that Daniel Possett was too good a person to be capable of betrayal, Oliver had recounted to him his entire history, and had explained his present sorry situation. Dan had expressed immediate sympathy for his plight, and had declared that he would do everything in his power to free him from it; he had decided, during the ensuing day, that the only possible course of action would be to accompany the boy to his uncle's, in a manner which would keep him concealed from the prying gaze of both policemen and crooks.

Money had to be made, however, for coach-travel was expensive, and it had to be made as quickly as possible. In order to accrue it with the necessary speed, Dan concluded that he would have to retain his stall and the shop. He initially thought of allowing Oliver to run the shop single-handed, while he and the Dodger worked in the market; but on further contemplation, he did not consider it wise to leave the shop, which was his home and work-shop as well, under anybody's care but his own; a single thief would not have to be especially enterprising or strong to overpower Oliver in an instant, and run off with his toys and the money that had been made from selling them. He then considered sending the Dodger off to Leadenhall while he remained in the shop with Oliver; but he was not sure that he entirely trusted Jack Dawkins, likeable as he was, He trusted Oliver absolutely, though finally reached the conclusion, having weighed up all the alternatives, that he, Dan Possett, would run the shop, while the Dodger and Oliver ran the stall in the market. Oliver's innate honesty would prevent the Dodger from being tempted into trickery; and the Dodger for his part would be able to keep a wary eye open for the approach of any of the many individuals in London who seemed so determined to make poor Oliver suffer.

That same evening, however, two more gentlemen were expressing a mutual concern for Oliver's state, though neither of them had the slightest idea where the boy might be; which fact made their anxiety even greater. One of these gentlemen was the Reverend Harry Maylie, who had never for a moment thought his nephew capable of wickedness of any kind. The other was the irascible Mr Grimwig whose sceptical temperament, it is true, had only recently led him to think the very opposite; but who now, having heard most of what the good clergyman had learnt during his visit to Mr Stalker's

Academy, was beginning to admit that had been very wrong indeed.

'And so,' said Harry Maylie, as he sat in Mr Grimwig's study, 'with Mr Brownlow in that nursing home, all I could think of was to come here.'

'But of course, sir! Where else?' declared Grimwig. 'How long do you plan to remain in London?'

'Until I have some word of Oliver,' replied Harry.

'Of course. Of course,' muttered Grimwig, with a mildly irritable grunt. Prepared though he was to acknowledge the error of his former opinions, he could not derive great pleasure from having to do so, for he had a very contrary nature.

'And you, sir,' said Harry. 'You have had no further news yourself, I suppose?'

'None but what I wrote to you,' replied Grimwig. 'Although, since then, I have learned that a boy who could only have been Oliver called here, at this house, shortly after Mr Brownlow was taken to hospital; while I was out of town.'

'What a pity you didn't see him!' exclaimed Harry.

'Upon my word, sir, it is indeed, it is indeed. Much might have become clear. Then, when I received that letter from him, I should have investigated it myself, instead of reporting him to the Magistrate's runners.'

'At least you would have spoken to him and heard his own story,' said Harry, not without a touch of reproval in his voice.

'Quite so,' retorted Grimwig, somewhat peevishly, for he did not like to be reminded of his mistakes. 'I acted too hastily, sir, I admit. But,' he added with a dejected shrug, 'I am a hasty man, sir. My chief fault, as my poor friend Brownlow used to say. But did they give you any indication at the school as to why the boy should run away?'

'None,' replied Harry. 'Except that he appears to have been driven to it by the man Bumble.'

Mr Grimwig's eyes widened in astonishment. 'Bumble?' he gasped. 'What has Bumble to do with this?'

'He was Porter at the school,' Harry explained. 'Apparently sent there, for some reason, to spy on Oliver.'

Mr Grimwig's brow furrowed. 'If that creature Bumble is involved, then there is more to this than meets the eye, sir, or I'll eat my head!'

'Send in the next!' barked Noah Claypole, curtly dismissing an old woman who had just presented him with a meagre pile of handkerchiefs and a tin turnip watch, for which he had grudgingly paid her a few pence.

'I dunno,' he complained, when she had left the room. 'Where's all the best stuff goin'? There 'as to be another fence feloniously poachin' my business. I'm sure of it. When I find 'im, I'll break 'im in 'alf.'

'Yer mean *I* will,' growled Kags, with a mirthless laugh. This creature was leaning against the wall beside Claypole. Monks was also present in the private room of the Three Cripples that afternoon, seated in the darkness of a corner, sipping at a glass of liqueur.

'Well, look 'oo the cat's brought in,' declared Kags, as the door opened and a chop-haired large-eared person of no more than twenty years ambled into the room, grinning somewhat stupidly from ear to ear.

'Wotcher, Bister Kags; Bister Bolter,' said this adenoidal youth, who was in the habit of speaking through his nose and not, like most other people, through his mouth.

'Barney!' exclaimed Noah. 'It's Barney, ain't it?'

'That is it, Bister Bolter,' replied the youth, grinning still more widely.

'The same as used to be contact man for old Fagin, rest 'is soul,' said Noah, adding softly, 'If 'e 'ad a soul.' Kags laughed viciously, and Barney grinned. 'An' wot brings you 'ere, Barney?'

'Tibes is 'ard, Bister Bolter,' said Barney, suddenly morose. 'Wery 'ard. I were wonderin', if baybe you 'ad a place for be? Course, if you're dot interested,' he added with a shrug, as he saw that Claypole was not especially thrilled at the suggestion he had made. He sighed and turned to the door casually pulling from his pocket, as he did so, an item which both Claypole and Kags at once recognized as being of practically inestimable value; it was a heavy necklace, made almost exclusively of diamonds.

''Old on! 'Old on, Barney!' cried Noah, suddenly very excited indeed. 'Did I say I wasn't interested? Did I?'

Barney turned back and handed him the sparkling object.

'I'd say I was fascinated,' muttered Noah lifting the necklace to the light. 'Yer 'aven't lost yer touch, I see.'

'Bister Fagin's right 'and ban I was,' said Barney, grinning hugely again.

'Exactly,' said Noah. 'An' wot yer did for old Flat 'At, yer can do for me.'

'Be a pleasure, Bister Bolter.'

'Mutual, I'm sure,' said Claypole, with a smile, bending over the necklace to examine it in greater detail.

Just then, as his head was bowed, yet another individual entered the room. ''Ere! Where d' yer think yer goin',' growled Kags, stepping threateningly towards the door.

'I think I am h'entering the Snug Room of this 'ere h'inn,' said a voice which Claypole knew in an instant. He glanced up in the hope that he might be wrong, and immediately turned his head away again when he realized that he most certainly was not. The personage who was at that moment filling the doorway with his massive bulk was none other than Mr Bumble, once the beadle of the parish in which Noah, in distant, less fortunate days, had worked as an undertaker's apprentice.

'Well then, 'Umpty Dumpty,' snarled Kags, 'yer can just roll out again, can't yer?'

''Umpty-Dumpty?' retorted a pompously indignant Bumble. 'I'll 'ave you know, I am 'ere on business.'

''Oo with?' inquired the monster.

'Not that it's any concern of yours,' replied Bumble, 'but I h'am reliably h'informed that I shall find 'ere a certain Mr Monks.'

The gentleman referred to had already recognized Bumble and now rose from his chair, stepping forward into the light. 'How dare you come here!' he hissed. 'Any business I had with you is over, you incompetent fool. Now get out!'

'You 'eard 'im, 'Umpty,' said Kags.

'I advise you to listen to me, Mr Monks,' said Bumble, attempting to retain a dignified posture, although he was not entirely unafraid of the scowling brute who continued to bar his way.

'An' I advise *you* to 'op it!' said the brute, stepping forward menacingly, thereby forcing Bumble to retreat a few inches.

'You'll regret it! You'll regret it!' cried Bumble.

'Throw 'im out!' Claypole now barked, still without turning his head.

'Don't you raise your voice to me, Noah Claypole!' snapped Bumble.

There was a sudden silence. None of the individuals in that room, with the exception, naturally, of Mr Bumble, and of course the person he had just rebuked, had heard that name before. To Monks, Barney, Kags, and indeed to several other members of London's Criminal Community, the young man who was now openly attempting to cover his embarrassment at being thus addressed, was known as Morris Bolter, and by no other name.

'Claypole?' said Noah, doing his best to affect incomprehension. 'Claypole? Noah? Don't know what you're talking about friend. My name's Bolter; Morris Bolter.'

'Bolter, all right!' retorted Bumble. 'You *bolted* with the money out of Mr Sowerberry's till! A little sneak thief apprentice, that's all you are! An' if I tell wot I know . . .'

'Throw him out!' said Monks. 'He can't threaten us without incriminating himself!'

'Out!' snarled Kags, grasping Bumble's collar and pushing him into the passage, a feat that would have seemed quite remarkable if performed by anybody less monstrously strong.

'No, wait!' cried Bumble. 'Wait! Wait! I've something to sell! Something valuable! I know where you can find Oliver Twist!'

Within half a second, Monks had laid a hand on Kag's shoulder, and Kags had released the corpulent intruder, who now turned and saw, to his considerable pleasure and relief, that the three men – Monks, Barney, and Noah Claypole – were staring at him with sudden astonished interest.

He was allowed to re-enter the room, and was even offered a seat and a mug of ale; which he declined, declaring that he preferred port. A large glass was duly brought; the door to the private room was closed, and a whispered counsel commenced, which naturally began with a fair amount of negotiation as to how much the informer was to be paid for his information. When a price had been agreed, to everyone's satisfaction, Mr Bumble told his eager listeners what he knew; which was, quite simply, that Oliver Twist, in the company of his school-friend Jack Dawkins, was living with a certain manufacturer of toys in Cheapside called Daniel Possett; and was spending his days selling those toys from a stall in Leadenhall market; Mr Bumble remarked that he had espied the boys in the shop two days ago, and then again in the market only this morning, having followed them there.

'All new! All workin'!' cried the Dodger. 'Possett's 'And-made Meckanickle Toys! See the monkey dance!

See the dog wag 'is tail! Step right up! Only a tanner! Meckanickle Toys!'

'Thank you, sir. Thank you very much,' said Oliver, to a gentleman who had just bought a painted soldier for his son.

'Best buy in the market!' cried the Dodger, 'Possett's Meckanickle Toys! One for a tanner, two for a shillin'! Step right up, ladies. No charge for lookin'!'

Oliver yawned, for the day's hurried and satisfactory trading had exhausted him. It would soon be time to go home, however; quite apart from the fact that it was late in the afternoon, and the market was beginning to empty, there were scarcely any toys left to sell, although they had brought an ample supply with them that morning.

'All new! All workin'!' cried the Dodger again. 'Possett's Meckanickle . . .'

He stopped abruptly, gazing in sudden surprise and anxiety over the heads of the two ladies who were standing before him and bending forward to examine the toys more closely. Three familiar figures were approaching the stall, pushing their way through the crowd. One was Noah Claypole; the second was Barney, whom the Dodger remembered from his days as a member of Fagin's gang; and the third, unmistakably, and of all the people he had least expected to see again with the possible exception of Fagin, was Mr Bumble.

At almost the same moment, Oliver, for his part, saw two more figures advancing towards the stall from another direction; one was an exceptionally brutish creature whom he had never seen before; the other, immediately recognizable because of his half-concealed face, his sunken eyes, and the silver-topped cane he was carrying, was his half-brother Edward Leeford, better known, to the few people in the world who cared to know him, as Monks.

The two boys glanced at each other simultaneously, realizing as they did so that they were trapped. The

Dodger looked quickly from one approaching party to the other; then, suddenly pointing directly at Noah Claypole, who was now only a few yards from the stall, he cried: 'Stop thief! Stop thief! 'Im! The one with the strawberry 'air! He stole that gennelman's watch!'

The gentleman in question, whom Claypole had just passed, declared in outrage: 'My watch? You scoundrel!' Whereupon he seized the protesting Noah and proceeded to shake him heartily.

'Lemme go! I didn't take nothing!' squealed Claypole. Naturally, the scene attracted an immediate and interested throng of spectators, who came running from all corners of the market to surround the incensed gentleman and the apparent thief. Bumble, Barney, Monks and Kags found themselves in the midst of a jostling and impenetrable mass of people.

'Give me back my watch!' demanded the man.

'I didn't take yer blessed watch!' replied Claypole. 'Let go of me!'

'Give it back!'

'I ain't got it!'

'Then where is it?'

''Ow do I know? Look in yer pocket!'

'Don't be ridiculous! exclaimed the man; but he nonetheless put his hand to his waistcoat pocket. He found, to his understandable astonishment, that his watch was there, unharmed. 'Well I'm hanged!' he declared. 'It was there all the ... *He* said you stole it!'

'Did 'e now?' snarled Claypole, thrashing through the chattering crowd towards the toy-stall. At the same time, Monks and Kags succeeded in extracting themselves from the throng at last and also hurried to the stall. It was unattended. A few wooden soldiers and monkeys lay scattered on the table-top; but Oliver Twist and the Artful Dodger had vanished. The three villains stared at each other in baffled fury.

*

The two boys ran south; stopping for breath only when they had reached a deserted and muddy path between two wharfs on the banks of the river.

'Lost 'em,' announced the Dodger, panting. 'Well, that's it,' he declared, once he had found sufficient breath to do so. 'We're on the run again.'

'What can we do?' Oliver asked.

'Well, we can't go back to old Dan's,' said the Dodger. 'They'll be watchin' 'is shop, that's for sure. We'll 'ave to find somewheres else.'

'Where?'

''Ow do *I* know?' retorted the Dodger, irritably. But moments later his face lit up with a grin; he snapped his fingers, and exclaimed: 'That's it! That's where we'll go!'

'Where?' said Oliver.

'Back where we started! Why didn't I think of it before? Fagin's old 'ideout!'

Oliver was instantly startled, and shook his head firmly. 'Anywhere but there,' he said.

'There's nothin' to be scared of,' said the Dodger. 'Nobody lives there anymore.' Seeing his friend remain silently dubious, he persisted: 'All we 'ave to do is keep out o' sight till it's dark. Then it's over to Saffron 'Ill. You got a better idea?'

Oliver made a great effort to think of one but could not; so it was agreed that they would return, under the cover of darkness, to the unhappy vicinity in which Oliver had first embarked on an earlier life of crime, under the care of the thief-master Fagin.

Once darkness had descended, they struck north and west through the city avoiding all the larger thoroughfares. They had walked a good mile and a quarter before they reached the shaded complex of tiny streets and passages known as Saffron Hill. It was not possible to be unobserved in this locality, for even in the dead of night every filthy alley and yard appeared to be filled with a mass of low humanity, most of whom had no choice but to remain in the open having no homes to hide in. The Dodger and Oliver were unapprehended, however, and at least reached the decrepit house near Field Lane in which Fagin had once lived, and from which he had masterminded many of the finer acts of criminality in London's history. The Dodger pushed open the door, and the boys ascended the familiar broken stairway for two flights until they arrived at what had previously been Fagin's room. Poor Oliver's heart was pounding; more in dreadful recollection than in fear. The room was absolutely dark.

The Dodger groped forward in the blackness, searching for the table, as Oliver shut the door cautiously behind them. 'Watch your step!' whispered the Dodger. 'The 'ole place is fallin' to pieces.' He found the table and felt over its surface. ''Ere,' Oliver heard him exclaim. 'Wot a bit o' luck! There's a bit o' candle left. An' a couple o' lucifers'. He struck a match on the table-top and lit the stub of the candle. He turned to Oliver and grinned; but his smile disappeared rapidly as he saw that Oliver was staring in astonished dread at the fireplace. The Dodger followed the direction of his friend's gaze.

Seated in the room's only chair beside the broken fireplace sat a very old gentleman with a long nose, a bloodless face, and a matted red beard. His shrivelled hands rested in his lap, and he wore a flat, wide-brimmed hat. He was dressed in a greasy flannel-gown.

Fagin chuckled. 'Well, if it ain't the Artful Dodger, an' my own dear, little Oliver. Welcome home, Dodger. Welcome home, Oliver.'

CHAPTER TWENTY-THREE

Fagin eyed his two former charges with a faint, oddly benevolent smile. The boys, for their part, were so astonished that they could not speak for a full minute. As they stared at him, they noted that, although he was dressed as he had always been, and although his red beard was as dishevelled as it had always been, there was something about his countenance and general manner of sitting that betokened an altogether less evil, less villainous air than that which they had previously known. Perhaps, thought Oliver, it was merely that he seemed smaller and more emaciated.

'I can't believe it!' exclaimed the Dodger at last.

'Why not?' inquired Fagin.

'Well . . . *you* . . . ,' said Oliver. '*Here*, Mr Fagin.'

'Where else should I go, my dear?'

'They said – everybody said – you was paralysed,' declared the Dodger.

'And so I am, Dodger,' said Fagin. As if to demonstrate this sorry truth, he raised his right hand with obvious difficulty an inch or two and it fell limply back into his lap. 'A poor, broken old thing,' he continued. 'As anyone can take advantage of; even two boys, if they'd a mind to it.' He gazed mournfully at them.

'We wouldn't 'arm you, Fagin!' protested the Dodger, openly hurt by the suggestion. 'Would we, Oliver?'

'Of course not,' said Oliver, not with absolute conviction.

'There's my good boys,' said Fagin, smiling. 'But then, I always treated you well, didn't I? Whatever else they say I might have done, I always looked after my boys well.'

'Well enough,' said the Dodger.

Fagin sighed. 'Times was,' he said, 'when I'd wake

here in the mornings to see ten or twenty smiling, young faces. Now there's no one. No one. Whole days when I despair for the sound of a human voice.'

'You really can't do nothin' for yourself?' asked the Dodger, with considerable concern.

'Not a thing,' replied Fagin, morosely, indicating his incapacity once more by lifting his right hand slightly and allowing it to drop back.

'But how do you manage, Mr Fagin?' asked Oliver, who was finding it difficult not to feel sorry for the old man by now, in spite of his memories.

'Ah,' Fagin replied. 'Thanks to Betsy, pretty little Betsy that used to be poor Nancy's friend, you remember?'

Oliver nodded, though the recollection was painful.

'She looks after me,' said Fagin. 'Calls in with a little food, every day or two.'

'So she was that daughter, was she, who said she'd take care of you,' said the Dodger, 'when you 'ad that stroke?'

Fagin's eyes narrowed quickly; but then he chuckled. 'You're the sharp one, Dodger,' he said. 'Yes, but for Betsy, I'd have rotted out my last days in Newgate. Cheated the rope, they said. Escaped punishment. But what greater punishment could I suffer than to be as I am? Alone. Everything taken from me. Still,' he added, with a sudden smile, 'that's all forgotten, in the pleasure of seeing you, my dears. Still again – you didn't come lookin' for me did you?'

'Well – not exactly,' replied the Dodger. 'We're on the run.'

Fagin nodded. 'I thought as much. Who from?'

'Mostly from Monks,' said Oliver, 'And Claypole; the one you know as Morris Bolter.'

Fagin's voice abruptly descended into a hiss. 'Yes, ah yes,' he muttered. 'Bolter.'

'The one who informed on you,' Oliver continued.

'Yes, ah yes,' said Fagin, as his half paralysed hands

tightened into claws on his lap. For a moment, his face betrayed hate and malignancy. 'Why so he did, my dear, so he did,' he snarled. Promptly cheerful again, however, he then announced: 'But all in the past now. Bygones. Revenge is for the powerful. I can only endure . . . and forget.'

'Oliver can't,' remarked the Dodger. 'Monks is still after 'im.'

'Ah, such vindictiveness,' observed Fagin, shaking his head. 'To his own half-brother.'

'You knew?' Oliver exclaimed in surprise.

'There's not much I don't know, my dear,' replied Fagin. 'Or didn't, when I was ensnared in wickedness. It grieves my heart to think of all the evil I committed – not least to you, my dear, not least to you. I can't ever expect your forgiveness.'

Oliver, by now thoroughly convinced that the former villain's disability and suffering had made him alter his ways and become genuinely repentant, was all too willing to offer what Fagin said he could not hope to receive.

'You couldn't . . . help your nature, Mr Fagin,' he declared quietly.

'You're a philosopher, my dear,' announced Fagin admiringly. 'My only wish now is to make amends for the past. But there's little I can do. You're both welcome to stay here for as long as you think it's safe.'

The boy's gratitude was instant and unbounded. The immediate problem, the Dodger now remarked, was nourishment. Fagin indicated a small canvas sack at his feet, from which the Dodger extracted a thin wedge of cheese and the end of a stale loaf. He was not altogether overjoyed at the sight of such a meagre repast. 'I wish it were more,' said their new host, sorrowfully, 'but we'll share what we have, as long as we have it.' He smiled at his guests endearingly, and Oliver found himself returning the smile.

*

Daniel Possett the toy-maker soon began to suspect the worst when his two friends failed to return at their usual hour that evening. Nonetheless, he set about laying out supper for three, hoping against hope that his fears might be groundless. He had just placed the plates, knives and mugs on the table when he heard the door-latch lift and turned round smiling in relief; his expression turned to one of disappointment, however, when he discovered that the person who entered was neither Oliver nor the Dodger, but a strange gentleman in a hat and cape, carrying a silver-topped cane.

'Oh, sorry sir,' said Dan to the stranger. 'The shop's closed for tonight.'

The stranger did not reply, but, leaving the door slightly ajar, began merely to glance keenly round the room.

'O' course, if there's somethin' you wants special . . .' Dan said.

The stranger moved forward, still gazing about him, and still saying nothing.

'How can I 'elp you, sir?' asked Dan, more than mildly puzzled by the gentleman's silent and somewhat disconcerting manner. 'Are you lookin' for something?'

'Oliver Twist,' replied the stranger, sharply.

In an instant, Daniel Possett knew who the person was; not exactly, of course, but he realized that he was one of those many pursuers that Oliver had spoken of; perhaps even a police officer, although his malicious countenance rendered that doubtful. Dan decided that his safest course of action in the interrogation that was certain to follow would be to tell the truth.

'He's been living here, hasn't he?' inquired the stranger.

'Well, he 'as been 'ere. But 'e's . . . gone now.'

'But you are obviously expecting him back,' observed the stranger, looking pointedly at the table laid for three. 'Him, and the other one.'

'I – I was wonderin' where they'd got to,' said Dan, nervously. 'I – I ain't seen them all day.'

'So where do you think they are?'

'No idea,' said Dan.

The stranger's hollow eyes rose briefly heavenwards. A monstrous personage now stepped into the room from the street, shutting the door behind him and leaning his brutal bulk against it; he was grizzled and balding and smiling grimly. Dan glanced at him in terror, and then at the gentleman, who now said with affected patience: 'We'll start again. Where have they gone to; or where might they be?'

'I've told you!' Dan pleaded. 'I've no idea. I wish I 'ad! I can't think!'

'Then,' declared the stranger softly, raising his cane and tapping it menacingly on the open palm of his free hand, 'perhaps we can help you.'

The brute by the door folded his arms and laughed gutturally.

I shall spare the reader from a precise description of the agonies meted out to the innocent Daniel Possett by Monks and Kags, and speedily transport him to the private room of the Three Cripples Tavern, to which Noah Claypole, Mr Bumble and the adenoidal Barney had repaired, once they had resigned themselves to being unable to find the two boys for the moment, after a frantic search. It was not until they had reached the tavern that Barney, who was not the most fast-witted of individuals, revealed the identity of Oliver's friend. He had pondered for a good while, he announced, on the fact that he had seemed to recollect that face on first seeing it, and now, at least, it had come to him; the boy with Twist was none other than the notorious Artful Dodger. Claypole, we must remember, had never met this celebrated personage when at the height of his fame; but he had most certainly heard of him.

'The Dodger?' he gasped; 'the Artful Dodger? Are yer sure?'

'Sure as I'b speakin' to you, Bister Bolter. 'Ow could I bake a bistake? There 'e was – Jack Dawkids, large as life.'

'Dawkins,' mused Bumble self-importantly. 'I always suspicioned there was somethin' about 'im. As I said to my late 'Eadmaster . . .'

'Will yer slow it about yer school!' barked Noah. 'If yer so clever, why didn't yer warn us 'e was there?'

Bumble, retaining his dignity, replied: ''Ow did I know who 'e was? You forget, Claypole, that I 'ave 'ad no h'opportunity of formin' a acquaintance with the criminal h'element.'

'No?' said Claypole. 'Well, yer makin' up for it now. An' stop calling me Claypole!'

'No sign of them,' declared Monks, entering at that moment. 'And the old fool Possett knows nothing.'

''E must!' exclaimed Claypole. 'They must've told 'im wot they was plannin' to do!'

'I assure you,' Monks said softly, 'if he had known, he'd have told us.' Whereupon he looked at the hulk Kags, who had followed him into the room, for confirmation of this face.

'I guarantee it,' announced the monster with a mirthless ugly laugh which caused a shudder to pass through all the occupants of the room except Monks.

'Well?' said Claypole, helplessly. 'Wot do we do now?'

'We keep looking,' replied Monks, 'only now we step up the hunt! Get all your people out onto the streets, Bolter. You, Kags and I will be with them. You, Barney – you'll search all Fagin's old haunts, everywhere the Dodger might know.'

'Right-oh, Bister Bunks,' said Barney, with a grin.

'An' 'Umpty-Dumpty 'ere,' suggested Kags, staring maliciously at Bumble, 'can keep an eye on old Possett's shop.'

Mr Bumble straightened indignantly: 'I resent your

continual use of that h-appelation,' he said. 'Kindly desist!'

'Beg yer pardon, I'm sure, yer worship,' said Kags. 'All right, *Roly-Poly* 'ere can keep an eye on old Possett's shop.'

This occasioned much mirth amongst the assembled company, with the exception, naturally, of Mr Bumble, who spluttered and fumed and turned quite red.

As it happened, Daniel Possett had not been subjected to a great deal of physical injury by the villainous stranger and his brutish companion; but the same could not be said for his shop or, more importantly still, for his toys, every single one of which had been trampled upon or pulled apart and rendered irreparable. That sorry fact caused the toy-maker more wretchedness than if he had himself been torn limb from limb. As he sat morosely amidst the havoc that had been wreaked upon his livelihood, however, he found himself all the more determined to do what he could to clear poor Oliver Twist's name. Initially, he thought of leaving London that very night and embarking on the long journey to the vicarage in which the boy's good uncle lived; he would walk all the way, if necessary, however exhausting the prospect. Then he recollected that Oliver had mentioned another personage, a friend of the boy's guardian, named Grimstone or Grimble or something very similar, who lived in Pentonville, and to whom Oliver had written via a certain old lady, but to no apparent avail. He would, he decided, endeavour to contact Mr Grimthorpe the next day.

Oliver awoke the following morning to see Fagin watching him from his chair by the fireplace, from which he had presumably not moved all night. In his still slumberous state, Oliver was immediately filled with perturbation at the sight, and the memories it evoked. Then, more wakeful, he recollected that the old gentleman appeared to have undergone a change of heart since the bad days; and he was doubly reassured when, seeing him stir, the former thief-master smiled benevolently at him. The Dodger, lying in another corner of the room, was also waking.

'Sleep well, my dears?' inquired Fagin, solicitously.

'I've know' 'arder floors,' declared the Dodger with a yawn. 'But not *much* 'arder.'

'Better safe than soft, Dodger,' remarked his host.

'Right as usual,' observed the Dodger.

A dim morning light was creeping through the shuttered windows; and the room was bitterly cold. The Dodger rose from the floor, shivered, and wrapped his arms about himself. Oliver did the same.

'There ain't nothing to make a fire with,' said the Dodger, glancing at the empty grate and then around the room. 'An' nothin' left to eat neither, I suppose?'

'The great virtue that poverty teaches is patience,' said Fagin in a philosophical tone. 'You must both learn it, my dears, like I have.'

'I keep rememberin' all the gelt I left lyin' on the stall in the market,' muttered the Dodger, seating himself at the table and resting his chin dejectedly in his hands.

'I have a shilling,' said Oliver, brightly.

The effect of this announcement was as if a shower of gold had fallen from heaven at that moment. The Dodger gazed in wonder at his friend, and Fagin, after opening his tiny eyes as wide as they would go for a moment or two, chuckled admiringly.

'You're a wonder, Oliver, my dear,' he said. Then he sighed pensively. 'There was a time,' he mused. 'There was a time when the Artful Dodger could've parleyed a shilling up into . . .' The Dodger looked at him, but he had bowed his head. 'But no point . . . No point. Not now Oliver's made you promise to go straight, Dodger.'

If Oliver had been more attentive he would have noticed a glance pass between Fagin and the Dodger at that moment, accompanied on the amiable old gentleman's part, by the slightest of smiles, which disappeared as quickly as it had arrived, and was followed by a look of supreme innocence, as if he had not dropped the profoundest hint. The Dodger guessed its meaning at once, and looked quickly at Oliver, who had gathered nothing.

'Oliver,' said the Dodger sharply. 'Come with me. You and me, we're going to spend that shillin' now.'

'On food?' asked Oliver, eagerly.

The Dodger glanced once again at Fagin, who did not return the look, but gazed about him, as if following the flight of a fly. The Dodger opened the door, grasped Oliver by the arm, and pulled him from the room. Only when the door was safely shut, did the former thief-master permit his countenance to break into a broad, satisfied grin.

No, the Artful Dodger did not purchase nourishment with the shilling; but, to Oliver's understandable astonishment, a battered old fiddle; which the Dodger espied on a stall only a few yards from the entrance to Fagin's home. Oliver became even more bewildered when his friend instructed him to take the fiddle at once to a pawnshop across the street, to take whatever sum of money the pawnbroker offered him for it, and to inform the gentleman that he would return to collect it again by noon at the latest. When Oliver questioned the purpose of such a course of action, the Dodger told him, not a little impatiently, to refrain from being too inquisitive and to do as he was bid. So Oliver entered the pawnshop with the fiddle while the Dodger waited outside. He emerged a minute or two later without the fiddle, but with four pennies and a ticket.

'All right?' asked the Dodger.

'He gave me fourpence on it,' said Oliver, 'but there's sixpence on the ticket.'

'Very good,' said the Dodger.

'Dodger?' said Oliver. 'I don't understand. You spent a shilling on the fiddle, didn't you?'

'Yes,' replied the Dodger.

'And I've just pawned it for fourpence.'

'Yes.'

'And now we don't have the sixpence to get it back.'

'Tell you wot,' said the Dodger, by way of reply. 'You wait 'ere an' I'll 'ave a word with 'im. 'Old on to that ticket now. 'Old on tight.' Whereupon he disappeared into the shop.

Oliver remained thoroughly mystified, but the Artful Dodger knew only too well what he was doing. Behind the long counter of the shop stood a pinched, sharp-eyed gentleman in a quilted dressing gown, with a pair of fingerless knitted mittens on his hands, and a greasy flannel nightcap on his head, from which protruded a mass of dirty white hair. His name, or so the sign above the pawnshop door declared, was Mr MacIsaac. The Dodger merely nodded a greeting to this gentleman as he entered and proceeded to look round the shop; he noticed at once that Mr MacIsaac had already placed the fiddle in the shop-window.

'D'ye want tae pop something?' the pawnbroker asked, in a marked Scottish accent.

'Just the opposite,' said the Dodger.

This mysterious remark aroused the wary gentleman's suspicions at once, and his eyes narrowed as he surveyed the youth.

'My guv'nor,' declared the Dodger, 'deals in antiques, bricky bracks an' stuff.'

'Oh aye?' remarked MacIsaac, scratching his chin and remaining suspicious.

'Pays top prices, my guv'nor,' said the Dodger.

'Oh aye?' the pawnbroker repeated, revealing a hint of interest. He sniffed and nodded in the direction of a shelf behind him; 'Well, that's the retail shelf,' he said.

The Dodger ran his eye quickly along the shelf as if sizing up the value of the items displayed there. He even allowed himself a mildly dismissive snort as he shook his head. 'Nothin' in our line, sorry,' he said, and turned to the door. He paused, appearing to notice something in the window. ' 'Ang on, though,' he now said. 'Let's 'ave a look at that fiddle.'

'No for sale,' announced the pawnbroker. 'It's a pledge.'

'Oh . . . ,' said the Dodger. 'Pity. No 'arm, though, 'avin a look, I suppose, is there?'

Mr MacIsaac narrowed his eyes once more before shrugging and approaching the window, from which he lifted out the fiddle and handed it to the Dodger. It was a decrepit thing indeed; most of the varnish had disappeared, as had all but two of the strings, the bridge, and one of the pegs. Nonetheless, the Dodger appeared to examine it with considerable interest and an experienced eye. He turned it this way and that, frowning; he plucked at one of the slack strings, scowled, and ran his hand across the fiddle's rough back; he grunted thoughtfully; he raised it to his eye and gazed along it from the rounded end to the neck, then reversed it to gaze along it in the other direction. 'Well, now . . . well . . . well . . . well . . . ,' he muttered.

'What?' said the pawnbroker, who had watched this examination in puzzled fascination.

'Just a feelin' . . . ,' murmured the Dodger. 'Just a . . .' He tapped at the soundboard, listened, and tapped it again, allowing himself to show signs of increasing excitement; angling the fiddle to the light, he peered through the S-shaped openings into the soundbox, and whistled to himself, apparently unable to control his enthusiasm any longer. 'I'll bet it is! I bet it!' he said.

'What?' said Mr MacIsaac, intrigued.

'I'll give you ten pound for it,' said the Dodger, in an abruptly business-like manner, laying the fiddle on the counter.

'Ten what?'

'Pound,' said the Dodger.

'For that old . . . ?' The pawnbroker was visibly shaken

by the extraordinary offer, but nevertheless shook his head. 'It's not for sale,' he announced.

'Fifteen,' said the Dodger.

Mr MacIsaac gasped in astonishment. 'Fifteen? Fifteen pounds? For that? Why?'

The Dodger seemed deeply reluctant to reveal the reason, and paused for some time before wincing and announcing resignedly: 'I see there's no point in tryin' to fool you, Mr MacIsaac. I'd bet – dunno for certain mind – but I'd be prepared to bet that that's a genuine stradivarinny.'

'Stradivarinny?' exclaimed Mr MacIsaac.

'Genuine,' said the Dodger, pushing the broken fiddle towards the old gentleman and inviting him by a gesture to examine it for himself. Mr MacIsaac, being no expert in the finer kinds of musical instruments, but deeply impressed nevertheless by the awesome ring of the name this particular fiddle had been given, picked it up and, much as the Dodger had done, peered squinting into the sound-box, as if all would be revealed therein.

'The signature's faded,' the Dodger explained. 'But a touch of the amber-sal volatile treatment should bring it up a treat. All right? Fifteen pounds.' Whereupon he reached into his pocket.

The old pawnbroker, agonized by the dilemma he was now undergoing, exclaimed: 'No, no! I canny sell it! It's a pledge!' But he added hesitantly: 'Mind ye – it's a short-term loan. The boy said he'd be back by midday.'

'Right,' said the Dodger briskly. 'Don't let 'im go till I've seen 'im. I'll just nip back for a word with my guv'nor. Twenty five pound is top offer, though. 'E never pays more than that.' And he was gone, slamming the door behind him.

'Is that a fact?' murmured Mr MacIsaac to himself. 'Is that a fact?' A cunning glint now appeared in his eye. 'An' if it's worth twenty-five pounds tae you, laddy, how much is it *really* worth?' he mused, gazing at the fiddle and carressing it lovingly.

Only a few minutes later, the doorbell jangled again and Oliver entered the shop. The pawnbroker was still gloating over the item that he was now convinced would make his fortune. He glanced up. 'Back sae soon?' he inquired.

'Mr MacIsaac,' Oliver began, 'I'm afraid I can't redeem the...'

'Never mind. Never mind!' Mr MacIsaac interrupted. 'I'll buy it off ye.' Oliver stared blankly at him. 'I'll buy it off ye... for... for... five pounds?'

Oliver could only gaze in growing astonishment as the kindly gentleman took a key from his dressing-gown pocket, unlocked a drawer and extracted five pounds, which he placed on the table.

'But it's...,' the boy began.

'Five pounds is ma highest offer,' said the pawnbroker. 'Tak it or leave it, laddy.'

Oliver took it; he clearly had no choice; and left the shop. Mr MacIsaac chuckled contentedly and put the fiddle under the counter, waiting for the Dodger to return. He would, he decided, inform the youth that the owner of the fiddle had been most insistent on reclaiming the item, and would on no account allow himself to be detained. But such scheming was to no avail, for the Dodger never came back.

'I couldn't understand why we'd pawned it,' Oliver explained, 'until Dodger said that if I told the man I couldn't redeem it, he might offer to buy it.' He was recounting the story to Fagin putting sticks and coal into the fireplace as he did so. The Dodger was setting out bread, butter, eggs and sausages on the table. Fagin grinned as he listened.

'Yes, yes,' he said. 'Go on.'

'So I went back to the man,' Oliver continued, 'and told him I didn't have the money, and he said he'd buy it straight away. I didn't even have to ask him.'

'Better that way,' muttered Fagin. 'Much better.'

'But I was surprised when he gave me five pounds.'

'I can imagine,' said Fagin, glancing up at the Dodger, who was struggling to control his amusement.

'Maybe he was just being kind,' opined Oliver.

'A pawnbroker? I suppose it's possible,' retorted Fagin.

The Dodger could restrain himself no longer and exploded into an outburst of laughter. Fagin chuckled too. Oliver glanced from one to the other, smiling brightly, but unable to comprehend the cause of such mirth.

After several inquiries in the area of Pentonville, Daniel Possett was led to understand that the name of the person for whom he was searching was not Grimble or Grimshanks or Grimthorpe; but Grimwig, a local magistrate. Further consultation amongst the inhabitants of the locality directed him to the person's house. Relaying briefly the nature of his business to the maid who opened the front door, he was hurriedly ushered into the study. Two individuals were seated there, one of whom was a clergyman; the other, a stout but somewhat formidable gentleman with a lame leg, dressed in a blue coat, striped waistcoat, nankeen breeches and gaiters. This last, Daniel Possett presumed, was Mr Grimwig; and it was to him that the toy-maker addressed himself. At the first mention of Oliver Twist, Mr Grimwig introduced the clergyman as the boy's uncle, the Reverend Harry Maylie, who by good fortune had come to London to seek out his nephew, but was now on the point of giving up and returning to the country, with a heavy heart. Dan remarked that it was indeed a happy circumstance that he had arrived at Mr Grimwig's house to prevent him from departing too hastily for he had news of the boy. Harry and Grimwig listened eagerly as he told them all that he knew; all that Oliver had explained to him, and all that had occurred since.

'I have never heard anything so astounding!' declared Grimwig, when Dan had finished. 'Never! Or I'll eat my head!' He struck his stick upon the ground with extreme force, causing the toy-maker to start in fright.

'We are profoundly grateful to you, Mr Possett,' said the clergyman gently.

'As long as I been of some 'elp, sir,' said Dan.

'Of the most sterling kind!' announced Grimwig, rising from his chair with the aid of his stick. 'You shall not go unrewarded.'

'Oh no, sir!' Dan interposed. 'I couldn't take nothin'! Wot I done, I done out of friendship.'

'Then you are also Mr Grimwig's friend, sir,' declared the old gentleman. 'And here's my hand on it!' He clasped Dan's little hand in his own large one, and shook it violently and at some length.

'If only,' said Harry, 'if only we had some idea of who the villains are who are chasing them. Who attacked you, Mr Possett?'

'I wouldn't know, sir,' replied Dan. 'It was a big, 'ulkin' fellow, with a scarred face. 'E called the other one – the younger one – wot was it? Mr Manse, was it? Or Munce?'

Grimwig and Harry Maylie glanced at each other anxiously; mispronounced though the name had been, it was instantly recognizable and struck terror into their hearts.

'Could it be . . . Monks?' inquired Harry, nervously.

Daniel Possett nodded. 'That's it, sir! Monks! Yes. Mr Monks.'

Mr Grimwig returned slowly to his chair, and lowered himself into it. Harry Maylie moved to the window and stared out into the street. The toy-maker could not fail to note that both gentlemen had turned quite pale.

At that very moment, the personage referred to was walking slowly through the city's tangled alleyways, gripping his silver-topped cane, and peering intently about him for any sign of the two fugitives. Claypole and Kags were doing much the same; as were a host of other dubious-looking creatures, on Morris Bolter's instructions. Mr Bumble, former Parish Beadle and School Porter, was surveying Daniel Possett's shop from a place of inadequate concealment across the street; he had arrived there too tardily to observe the toy-maker emerge from his door on his way to Pentonville early that morning. Barney, for his part, was ambling somewhat lazily towards Fagin's former hiding-place near Field Lane; there seemed to be precious little urgency in his countenance and gait, for some reason; as if his heart was not in the search.

In the room that was his destination, Oliver and the Dodger, naturally ignorant of his approach, were about to settle down to a hearty breakfast. The fire was now blazing, and Oliver was frying sausages in a pan above it. The Dodger was buttering several slices of bread. Fagin, seated as always by the fire, was giving both boys the benefit of his somewhat morose reminiscences; pausing only intermittently to emit a long dejected sigh.

'A chain of accomplices,' he muttered, 'a chain, from the Docks to Westminster. But that's all behind me. And to tell the truth, my dears,' he added, a touch more cheerfully, 'to tell the truth, I'm glad of it. I've lost the heart and the stomach for crime. No more use than your poor guardian, Oliver, lying in that Nursing Home.'

'How did you know about that?' said Oliver, looking up in surprise.

'Oh I hear things, I hear things,' murmured Fagin, mysteriously. 'Wickedness, my dear, wickedness. You must do what you can for him; and so shall I, to make amends.'

As Oliver carried the cooked sausages to the table, the old gentleman appeared to become despondently distracted, lost in his own thoughts. The boy glanced at him briefly before whispering to his friend. 'Dodger? Will you promise me something?'

'What?' asked the Dodger, softly.

'Will you promise not to tell Mr Fagin about the money that's in trust for me. I know he's changed. I just don't want him to be tempted.'

' 'E'd be tempted, all right,' observed the Dodger, with a grin.

It was at this moment that Barney entered the room. Seeing the boys, he stopped in the doorway, staring at them. 'I might've knowed you'd be 'ere,' he snarled.

The Dodger had risen from the table in an instant, taking the now empty frying pan from Oliver and holding it tightly and threateningly in both hands. Oliver, too, was quite ready for a fight.

'Saw you, yesterday, didn't I? With Bolter,' said the Dodger.

Barney did not move from the doorway. 'I'b workin' for 'ib now,' he announced. ' 'E took be on, to cut out a new fence that's ruinin' 'is business. And,' he added sharply, 'to find you.'

'Well,' said the Dodger, advancing menacingly towards him, 'now you found us, wot you goin' to tell 'im.'

He stopped a pace or two before Barney, waiting for a reply. It was Fagin, however, who now supplied it. 'Nothing, my dear. Nothing. Barney wouldn't dream of telling him anything, would you, Barney?'

Both boys turned to look at him in amazement.

'Dot likely,' said Barney, resuming his familiar grin and closing the door.

'Barney, you see,' Fagin explained, 'joined Bolter at my suggestion, to find out what wickedness he was planning.'

'So yer safe,' said Barney, eyeing the food-laden table greedily. ' 'E won't come 'ere, if I tell 'im it's clear.' He moved to the table, picked up one of the sausages, and proceeded to eat it.

''Elp yerself,' said the Dodger.

'Ta,' said Barney, with his mouth full.

'You can have mine, too,' said Oliver, gratefully.

'Ta,' said Barney, picking up a second sausage, chuckling as he did so.

'Er – 'Ow about brewin' up some tea, Oliver?' the Dodger suddenly suggested.

Obediently, Oliver picked up a small kettle from the table, saw that it was empty, and left the room to fetch some water. As soon as he was gone, the Dodger moved quickly towards Fagin, who was smiling at him benevolently.

'Turned over a new leaf, 'ave yer?' said the Dodger sharply. 'Reformed, 'ave yer? Pull the other one, Fagin. *You're* that new fence Bolter's so worried about!'

Fagin's smile vanished instantly. His eye took on a dangerous glint as he stared up at the Dodger for a long, menacing moment. The Dodger turned to look at Barney, who had picked up a knife from the table, and was watching him tautly. Then the old gentleman relaxed and laughed softly.

'You're the cleverest, my dear,' he whispered. 'The cleverest, the sharpest of them all, Dodger. You always was. Yes, my dear, I'm back. And doing better than ever.'

'Do word of a lie,' rejoined Barney, admiringly, putting the knife down.

'So you're goin' to take over Bolter's gang, are you?' asked the Dodger.

Fagin snorted with distaste. 'Take them over?' he muttered. 'Take them over? Monks, who ran away and left me to face the music? Bolter, who turned state's evidence and led me to the very foot of the gallows? I'm going to do more than take them over, my dear, much, much more.'

'You said you'd forgiven them,' remarked the Dodger.

'Forgive?' said Fagin, his face hardening into an expression of consuming hatred. 'Forgive?' His shrivelled hands tightened on the arms of his chair; his small red eyes became wild with malice; his mouth curled into a terrible scowl. 'Forgive?' he repeated. 'Never. I'm going to be *revenged,* my dear. I'll be revenged on – on the *whole pack of them*!'

CHAPTER TWENTY-FOUR

Except for the fact that he was prevented by his paralysis from ever moving from his chair beside the fireplace, Fagin appeared to become more and more cheerful as the days passed in the company of Oliver, the Artful Dodger, and, occasionally, of Barney. He was soon quite the merry old gentleman of former times. A touch of colour returned to his pale cheeks; his eyes took on a blithesome look, and his mouth seemed permanently fixed in a carefree smile. The boys did their best to keep him in good spirit; as did Barney, when he was there. This young man proved to be adept at playing the penny whistle, and he would often sit cross-legged on the table, blowing his way through a sizeable repertory of hornpipes, while the Dodger danced and Oliver clapped his hands.

On one occasion, Barney had been playing for well over an hour when he found himself having to stop for lack of breath.

'I'be lost be puff,' he announced.

'He's lost his puff, Oliver,' said the Dodger. 'We sybpathize, dod't we?' Oliver laughed.

'Ah, my dears,' observed Fagin. 'We've all lost something – since there was last dancing here.' Oliver tensed slightly at this, and Fagin, noticing him do so, had to add quickly: 'Not that that's a matter for regret. But the world has changed, and all of us with it.'

'Speak for yourself, Fagin,' said the Dodger. 'I ain't changed.'

'Oh, but you have, Dodger!' retorted Fagin, blandly. 'Turned over a new leaf, haven't you? An honest leaf?'

The Dodger's grin faded and he glanced briefly at Oliver, who smiled innocently, unaware of the conversation's deeper meaning.

'Like we all 'ave,' said Barney, with a laugh.

'As you say, Barney, as you say,' said his mentor, with a sigh. 'But wickedness marches on. And some of its darker angels might be wondering where you are.'

'You're right, Bister Fagid,' declared Barney slipping down from the table and crossing to the door. 'I'd best be gettid' back, before they biss me. Bye bye for dow.' He left the room, closing the door behind him.

'Sooner or later,' said the Dodger, 'someone's goin' to see 'im leavin' 'ere, an' start askin' questions.'

As it happened, Barney had reported to Fagin earlier that he already sensed a certain degree of suspicion in Monk's attitude towards him; and Bolter did not seem entirely confident of his trustworthiness. They were beginning to ask where and how he spent the hours during which he was not in their company. He had lied, of course, but he was not at all sure that they believed him. When Fagin now pointed this out, Oliver asked: 'But why should they suspect Barney?'

'It's nacheral enough,' announced the Dodger. 'Even with an army out lookin' for us, they ain't found us. They must've twigged that somebody's 'idin' us.'

'Some busy bee,' said Fagin. 'And where more obvious to search for that bee than amongst themselves?'

'"B" for Barney,' said the Dodger, with a nod.

'It could just as easily be "B" for Bumble,' said Oliver, thoughtfully.

Fagin and the Dodger gazed at him with expressions of mingled admiration and astonishment. Neither of them, in their concern for Barney, had thought of Bumble as a possible object of suspicion. Oliver's remark now set Fagin thinking as to how they could take the scent off Barney and place it firmly on Bumble's back. The Dodger, however, on further reflection, found the idea of Monks and Claypole suspecting the burly and incompetent Bumble so ludicrous that he could not prevent himself from bursting into laughter.

'Never!' he declared. 'No, we couldn't. I mean, 'ow

could we make 'em believe that? Bumble? Out to get Monks *an'* Bolter? They'd never swaller it!'

'Oh I think they might, Dodger, I think they might,' said Fagin quietly. 'Given the right bait.'

'Like wot?' said the Dodger.

'With a little help from your old friend, Oliver. The magistrate Mr Trimfit, was it? Or Dimwit?'

'Mr Grimwig,' said Oliver, with a smile.

'Some 'opes 'e'd 'elp,' said the Dodger dismissively. 'It was 'im that sent the runners after Oliver.' This information had been relayed to them by Barney.

'I couldn't risk going to see him,' said Oliver.

'Of course not, my dear,' said Fagin. 'But if someone else did . . .' he mused, causing the boys to look at him in puzzlement. 'That woman,' he continued pensively. 'Mrs Carraway. What did Barney tell us she'd said to your friend, Mr Thingamijig? She said if I recall correctly, that she had never seen you; that you had never been to your guardian's house. So if someone were to ask that upright gentleman Mr Thingamijig how it happened, then, that Bolter could lodge a complaint of theft against you, Mr Thingamijig . . .'

'Grimwig,' said Oliver.

'Mr Grimwig, being an upright and sensible gentleman, might begin to wonder if Mrs Carraway was hiding something from him. Do you see, my dear?'

Oliver was not all sure that he did see. But the Dodger did; and now said: 'Don't worry, Fagin. I'll pick someone as can do it neat.'

'I'm sure you will, Dodger, I'm sure you will,' said Fagin with a chuckle.

Noah Claypole's consuming concern over the whereabouts of Oliver Twist had rendered him somewhat slack in his role as a thief-master. Monks was almost permanently in his company now, and had no interest in his other dealings, but kept him firmly to the matter in hand. In order not to let business slip, however, Noah had told Barney to concentrate on receiving the stolen articles that were still being brought to the Three Cripples. Barney had accepted this new appointment with unbounded eagerness, and was apparently doing his best to please the great Morris Bolter; not without success, indeed, for under his discerning eye, trade was continuing profitably, despite the certain existence of another dealer. As a result, Claypole's initial doubts as to his loyalty were beginning to fade; and, to ensure that fidelity further, he offered the youth a sizeable cut in the profits, causing Barney to swear to an unswerving allegiance, and to declare that he would do anything and everything that Mr Bolter required of him.

'Barney's fillin' 'is pockets 'ere,' said Claypole to Monks, who remained suspicious. 'Wot would 'e get out of 'elpin' Oliver and the Dodger?'

'It must be him,' said Monks. 'There's no one else.'

It was at this point that Claypole was struck by a thought not dissimilar to that which had struck Oliver in Fagin's hide-out; only a short while previously as it happened. 'There is though,' he announced. 'Wot about Bumble?'

'That fat fool!' snorted Monks. 'He has no motive to cross us.'

'Why not though?' mused Claypole. ''E could be 'opin' for a reward. 'E thinks you've cheated 'im. Fool 'e may be, but if 'e's in with them, 'e's got the Dodger to do 'is thinkin' for 'im.'

Monks snorted once more. On reflection, however, he did not consider it such a foolish suggestion, and admitted that Bumble would have to be watched. He told Claypole to order Barney to think of someone reliable amongst his vagabond acquaintances who would perform this task. Claypole did this, and Barney suggested a thief who had come into the Three Cripples with a rich collection of pickings only that morning.

'Find 'im,' said Claypole, 'an' tell 'im to get down to Possett's shop now.'

'Right you are, Bister Bolter,' said Barney; and left the room.

'*Quis custodiet custodes?*' muttered Monks pensively.

'Wot?' asked Claypole, who was not an expert in ancient languages.

'Meanwhile,' said Monks, 'Kags can keep a sharp eye on Barney himself. Can't you Kags?'

The creature, who was with them, chuckled maliciously, and immediately set off in pursuit of the suspect.

It did not take Barney more than five minutes to understand that he was being pursued by Kags; it was very difficult for such an exceptionally large monster to remain unnoticed for long, and Barney was a vigilant young man. He obediently found the thief he had been told to find, however, and instructed him to keep an eye on Bumble, who was still devotedly posted outside Daniel Possett's shop, as he had been commanded. The toy-maker himself had not failed to register the presence of the portly personage who had been observing his shop for some days now; and he naturally presumed that the gentleman was waiting to catch a glimpse of Oliver and the Dodger. He decided, however, that for the moment he had done all he could do for the boys, by reporting their circumstances to Mr Grimwig and Oliver's uncle, and that he would wait patiently for any further developments; keeping a wary eye on Bumble nevertheless; just as Bumble was keeping a permanently wary eye on him.

Having done his duty by dispatching the thief, Barney now resolved to give Kags the slip; if only for a short while, so that he could inform Fagin of the fact that he was being followed, and that therefore, if Fagin was going to do anything at all, he had better do it quickly, for he was certain that the net was closing in on him. He managed to escape Kag's scrutiny quite easily by side-stepping quickly into an almost unnoticeably narrow passage half-way along a very short street; Kags had not yet entered the street when Barney disappeared, and lumbering into it now, he gazed wildly about him and hurried down the street as hastily as his thick legs could carry him, passing the passage without even a glance in its direction; Barney then emerged from the passage and darted along the street in the opposite direction, away from Kags. He ran with all possible speed to Fagin's hide-out.

'They're on to be!' he cried as he entered the room. 'They're on to be, Bister Fagid! I 'ad to give Kags the slip to get 'ere!'

'No, not yet Barney,' said Fagin patiently, shaking his head. 'Not yet. They can't be, yet. But getting closer, perhaps.' He gazed at the Dodger.

'Right,' said the Dodger, comprehending Fagin's look. 'Time I was movin'. Fancy a stroll, Oliver?'

Oliver was understandably surprised by this unprovoked suggestion; as indeed was Fagin, who narrowed his eyes.

'With the whole of Bolter's gang out looking for him?' he said.

'They don't know the back alleys like I do,' retorted the Dodger, confidently. 'Besides, Oliver's lookin' pale. Needs some air. Comin', Oliver?'

Oliver glanced at Fagin, who was staring suspiciously at the Dodger, but who now turned to Oliver, smiled, and nodded. 'Yes, my dear, why not? You do look a little pale,' he said.

'Cheers, Barney,' said the Dodger, brightly, as he and Oliver made for the door.

'Wotcher, bate,' said Barney.

'Clever Dodger,' muttered Fagin, when the boys had gone. 'Clever, clever, Dodger. Now what has he in mind?'

*

The Dodger had three things in mind. The first was to find someone who could help to incriminate Bumble in the eyes of Monks and Noah Claypole; the second was to instruct this individual to visit Mr Grimwig with a message, purportedly from Bumble, informing the old gentleman that a charge of theft had been brought against Oliver by Claypole. The Dodger informed Oliver of these two intentions as the boys hastened warily through the streets. He decided not to let his friend know of his third intention – a plan of which Fagin was not aware either – until the first two had been fulfilled.

The individual he had chosen was a young woman who claimed to be an actress; she had once known Betsy, and the unfortunate Nancy, and most of the members of Fagin's gang, so she also knew Fagin and the Artful Dodger. She had the habit, the Dodger remembered, of spending most of her time in a tavern not far from Covent Garden market; and it was to this place that the two boys now made their careful way. Once there, the Dodger instructed Oliver to wait outside while he asked the landlord, whom he knew, if the lady was within, and to tell her, if she was, that the Artful Dodger requested a brief audience with her, in an alleyway across the street.

Happily, the woman was there, and within less than a minute she was scuttling across the cobblestones to the appointed meeting-place. She was a pretty girl; or would have been; if she had not chosen to cover her face with such an abundance of paint.

'Dodger!' she exclaimed. 'Wot are *you* doin' in London?'

''Allo, Mary,' said the Dodger, with a grin. ''ow's business?'

'Terrible,' said Mary. 'What are you doin' ...'

'Never *mind* wot I'm doin' in London,' retorted the Dodger. 'Will *you* do somethin' for me?'

'Depends wot it is, don't it?' said Mary. ''Oo's this?' she added, glancing at Oliver.

'Never *mind* who that is,' said the Dodger impatiently. 'There's money in it, Mary.'

''Ow much?' said Mary.

The Dodger quietly explained how much she would be paid and then what it was he wanted her to do. When he had done so, she looked doubtful.

'Now it ain't Drury Lane, Mary,' said the Dodger, 'but at least yer bein' paid.'

Mary had to admit that being paid anything at all was becoming something of a novelty in her life, and announced that she would carry out the Dodger's instructions with all the grace she could muster.

'Good,' said the Dodger. 'Just so long as yer makes it plain you was sent by a large fat man, who 'opes to be kindly remembered.'

'A large fat man, who 'opes to be kindly remembered,' Mary repeated, to keep the words in her mind. 'Oo's that then?' she asked.

'Never *mind* who it is,' said the Dodger. 'Just do it.'

Mary nodded.

'Sooner the snappier, then,' said the Dodger.

Mary gave both boys a brief, flirtatious smile, and was gone.

'Do you really think Mr Grimwig will become suspicious and go to Mr Brownlow's house?' asked Oliver, uncertainly.

'If 'e don't,' observed the Dodger, 'things is goin' to get rough. And now,' he declared. 'There's you.'

'What do you mean there's me?' asked Oliver.

'You got to get away, Oliver,' the Dodger explained urgently. 'You got to risk goin' to yer Aunt's place. Soon, for sure, Monks is goin' to come knockin' on Fagin's door. I can take care of meself, but . . .'

'But not both of us,' rejoined Oliver, eliciting a silent nod from the Dodger. 'How can I get there? With no money?'

'Listen,' said the Dodger, 'Covent Garden market'll be

packin' up soon. We'll beg a lift for you from one of the carters – part of the road, anyway.'

Oliver seemed reluctant to leave his friend, but the Dodger was firm and he at last agreed to go. The Dodger had little difficulty in persuading a friendly carter who was about to head west to take Oliver with him; or perhaps it was Oliver's concerned countenance that did the persuading. At any rate, Oliver was soon clambering up into the pile of empty sacks on the cart.

'Just one thing more,' said the Dodger softly once Oliver was safely installed amid the sacks. 'You could still get caught, Oliver. An' if it should happen, don't give Fagin away, will yer? You won't, will yer, Oliver?' His countenance adopted a most earnest expression as he said this.

Oliver looked shocked. 'I wouldn't!' he protested with vehemence. 'You *know* I wouldn't, Dodger!'

''Course I knows yer wouldn't *mean* to, but . . . well . . .'

The carter was already seated at the front of his cart and now pulled the reigns of the mule that was about to pull Oliver – or so both boys very much hoped – to safety and contentment.

'Goodbye, Dodger,' said Oliver, as the cart began to move off, weaving its way through the market stalls.

'Bye, Oliver,' said the Dodger, waving a little sadly.

'We'll meet soon,' called Oliver.

'Yes,' said the Dodger, uncertainly. 'Soon.'

His third intention had been carried out; he would now have to report to Fagin what he had done, and was not looking forward to that in the slightest. But he had been right; he knew he had been right. Oliver *had* to escape, not simply from London and his pursuers, but from Fagin's evil influence. The Dodger knew Fagin too well to believe that he could ever undergo a change of heart, or be capable of a single act of kindness, if it even faintly threatened to conflict with his own malicious interests.

CHAPTER TWENTY-FIVE

Barney had been very unwise to escape from Kag's watchful eye; even for the short time that he had intended to do so; for no sooner had Kags lost sight of him than he returned at once without pausing to search a single passage or alley, to the private room of the Three Cripples, in order to report the fact of Barney's disappearance to Monks and Mr Bolter.

'He got away?' Monks snarled furiously. 'You let him get away?!'

'Well, mebbe 'e spotted me, I dunno,' said Kags, somewhat shame-facedly.

'You don't *know*!' hissed Monks. 'Why do you think I told you to be careful, you thundering oaf! How you survived with Bill Sikes I'll...'

Now the monster was not partial to criticism of any kind, and his mildly apologetic countenance transformed itself into one of extreme menace in an instant. 'Bill never 'ad to complain of *me*!' he growled, looming towards Monks, who recoiled despite himself at the possibility of being beaten to death there and then.

'No, 'course 'e never, Kags,' said Noah Claypole, in a hurriedly soothing tone. ''Course 'e didn't. Yer couldn't 'elp it, Kags, could yer? Why'd'yer think I took Barney on? 'E's like Fagin an' the Dodger, is Barney. Eyes in the back of 'is 'ead.'

Claypole's placatory manner appeared to have the required effect on Kags, who relaxed, retaining nevertheless a mildly injured expression.

'Very well then,' said Monks, once all was deemed calm again. 'But if he did lose Kags deliberately, what was his reason? And where was he making for? He would bear questioning, would your friend, Barney.' He picked up his cane and rose from the table. 'You'll remain here, Bolter,' he declared.

'Wot?' said Noah. 'Why should I?'

'Because, Bolter,' said Monks, softly, as he made for the door, 'when Barney returns – assuming he does – Kags may need some help. May you not, Kags?'

The monster nodded slowly and maliciously, pleased again to be called upon to do what he was unquestionably best at.

'Oh and you may as well call off your watch on Bumble, Bolter,' Monks continued, opening the door. He turned back briefly to glance at Kags, and said: 'Look to it, Kags. Don't let him slip past you a second time.'

'I won't, Mr Monks,' said Kags, with a most evil grin.

'Good,' said Monks; and he was gone.

Meanwhile, the actress Mary had found her way, as instructed, to Pentonville, and had been shown into Mr Grimwig's study, where she relayed to Mr Grimwig and to the clergyman who was with him the message that the Dodger had given her; informing the old gentleman and his companion that a large, fat man, who wished to be kindly remembered, would like them to know that the boy Oliver Twist had arrived at the home of Mr Grimwig's particular friend Mr Brownlow some weeks previously; the fat man knew of this because he had been told of it by one Mr Bolter, who was one of Mr Brownlow's servants, and who had laid a charge of theft against the boy.

The effect of this information on the two gentlemen seemed curious in Mary's eyes, for while she had no idea of what the message she had obediently conveyed could possibly mean, there was no doubt that Mr Grimwig and his priestly friend understood its implications immediately. The old gentleman snorted and puffed for a good while, lifting his eyeglass and surveying the woman out of the corner of an eye. The clergyman, for his part, reached for a chair and sat down very slowly, staring into the fire in a most contemplative manner.

'Well,' said Grimwig. 'Well, well. Thank you, my dear. Thank you for coming.'

Mary curtseyed very elegantly.

'And ... um ...,' Grimwig continued. 'And pray accept this for your pains.' Whereupon, to Mary's considerable delight, he produced a shining sovereign from his pocket and pressed it into her palm.

'Thank *you*, sir,' she said.

'A large, fat man, to be kindly remembered,' muttered the old gentleman as he accompanied her from the room and to the front door. 'A large, fat man, to be kindly remembered,' he repeated, as he closed the front door behind her and returned to his study. ''Pon my soul. 'Pon my soul!'

'We should have thought of that,' said Harry, looking up as Grimwig re-entered.

''Pon my soul, yes indeed, we should have, sir, indeed we should,' murmured Grimwig. 'A large, fat man who wishes to be kindly remembered,' he repeated a third time. Suddenly he struck his stick forcefully upon the ground, and bellowed: ''Pon my soul, sir, Bumble, or I'll eat my head! Bumble, sir! It can be no-one else!'

Harry Maylie smiled patiently, for he had already reached that conclusion.

'But why,' Mr Grimwig then reflected, 'would he seek to aid Oliver?'

'Conscience, perhaps?' suggested Harry.

'Conscience?' said Grimwig, with a snort. 'Guilt, more probably. Hoping we'll take it into account when he and the others are brought to book.'

'Whatever the cause,' said Harry, rising from his chair, 'it clearly calls for some action on our part.'

''Pon my soul, indeed, it does, sir,' muttered Grimwig. A further thought now struck him, 'That Carraway woman!' he exclaimed. 'She told me, in plain words, that

Oliver had not been to the house! Fritter me, why did I not notice that? Oh hasty, hasty again,' he added with a sigh. 'Oh, Brownlow, my old friend, I have much to answer for!'

'Don't torture yourself, sir,' said Harry, laying a gentle hand on the old gentleman's shoulder. 'You were not alone in failing to observe the obvious. And perhaps we may all make amends now.'

'We shall, sir,' declared Grimwig, with stern determination. ''Pon my soul, we shall! We'll see Mrs Carraway once more and this time – this time, sir, we will have answers, or I'll eat my head!'

As Monks had commanded, the watch on Bumble was now called off. The thief who had been observing him for the afternoon was instructed by a messenger sent from Noah Claypole that he had done all that was required of him and could return to his everyday business. He had gone, therefore, by the time Mr Bumble took a decision which was to prove to be a foolish one. He had, understandably, grown rather bored with the task that had been allotted him; he had been watching Daniel Possett's shop for several days now, without perceiving anything capable of arousing his suspicions, and was beginning to reach the conclusion that Oliver Twist and Jack Dawkins had no intention of appearing. He had not received instructions, however, to leave his post; and proceeded to wonder if he had in some way been forgotten about entirely. At the same time he felt he could not move until commanded. But he now concluded that if he were to take a certain action on his own initiative, and perhaps even receive further information thereby, he would have the perfect excuse for deserting his post and returning to the Three Cripples Tavern. This action was to waddle across the street and knock upon Daniel Possett's door. It was an authoritative knock, as became such a grand personage. After several moments, during which

Mr Bumble felt he was being observed from the shop's bay window, the door opened, only slightly, and Mr Possett's head emerged from within.

'Well?' said the toy-maker, somewhat curtly.

'Mr Possett?' said Mr Bumble.

'Yes.'

'If I might just step h'inside for a minute or two?'

'We can talk as easy out 'ere,' said Dan, stepping into the street and closing the door behind him, forcing Bumble to take a pace backwards.

'Well – er – if you h'insist, sir,' said Bumble.

'I do,' declared Dan.

'H'allow me to h'introduce myself, sir,' Bumble continued. 'My name is Stalker.'

Daniel Possett's eyes widened momentarily. 'Mr Stalker?' he exclaimed, making it abundantly clear that he recognized the name only too well; but giving not the slightest indication, at the same time, that he was in the least bit impressed by it.

'Ah you 'ave – *have* heard of me, then?' said Bumble. 'Lately Headmaster to that misfortunate boy Oliver Twist, 'oom I believe you are h'acquainted with?'

There was a mysterious pause. 'Oh I know Oliver!' declared Dan at last, in a cheerful tone. 'Funny though, 'e didn't speak about you that much, Mr Stalker, sir. More about the – School Porter, I think 'e was a right villain. Name o' Fumble.'

To Dan's delight, Bumble bridled noticeably at being thus mis-named, but he managed to control his indignation before announcing, with great panache: 'Ah, you mean Mr Bumble! School Porter. Yes. Or was, until I had the sad h'occasion to dismiss 'im. Did I not? I most certainly did!'

'Yes well,' said Dan impatiently. 'Wot can I do for you, Mr Stalker?'

'Ah, Mr Possett,' declared Bumble, with a dolorous shake of the head. 'Your name 'as – *has* been h'intimated as one who just might know the whereabouts of that . . . h'afflicted lad . . .'

' 'Oo? 'Oo intimated me?' asked Dan, sharply.

' 'Oo?' said Bumble. ' 'Oo? Ah well. Oh,' he mumbled, waving a hand in the air. 'Oh . . . various parties, various parties.'

Dan nodded. 'I see,' he said softly. 'An' yer wants me to take yer to 'im.'

Bumble tensed. 'That – that was . . . er . . . the h'idea, yes,' he said.

'Well, o' course, Mr Stalker, sir, I'd be 'appy to only . . .' Dan broke off, peering cautiously up and down the street in a conspirational manner.

'Only?' said Bumble, eager for him to continue.

'Only I can't, not at the moment,' whispered Dan.

Bumble's face fell.

' 'Owever,' Dan added, 'if you was to come back later – when it's dark, say . . .'

'I will! I shall!' announced Bumble urgently.

'Then we just might see wot we just might see, mightn't we?' declared the toy-maker. He winked, turned to the door, opened it, and disappeared into his shop; not even stopping to observe the triumphant glow that was now spreading across Mr Bumble's fleshy features.

'I am not given, sirs, to lying,' Mrs Carraway remarked in an icy tone. She was seated, in a somewhat prim and indignant fashion, in Mr Brownlow's sitting room, facing the Reverend Harry Maylie, who appeared disturbed, and Mr Grimwig, who appeared merely perplexed as he leaned heavily on his stick. 'It may be,' the lady now continued, 'indeed, from what you have told me, it *must* be; that Oliver did arrive here, while Mr Brownlow lay ill upstairs. I can only plead, as housekeeper, that throughout those days most of my waking hours were passed in the sick-room. I assume that, for reasons of his own, Bolter chose not to inform me.'

'Summon the fellow then, ma'am!' exclaimed Grimwig. 'Let him answer for himself.'

'Alas, sir,' replied Mrs Carraway, thinking quickly, 'Alas, I cannot. I – I dismissed him soon after your last visit, Mr Grimwig. I had cause to adjudge him untrustworthy.'

'We can believe that,' observed Harry Maylie, making for the door. 'Thank you, Mrs Carraway.'

'May I ask, sir,' the lady inquired hurriedly, 'how you came by this information?'

'Certainly,' replied Grimwig. 'Our reminder came from – well, a most improbable source. No one ye'd know, Mrs Carraway, and as untrustworthy as you found Bolter. A Porter at Oliver's school, and one time Beadle, name of Bumble.'

Mrs Carraway's reaction to this revelation was one of astonishment and concern; but she was saved from having to display her feelings too openly by a knock on the door and the timely entrance of Dr Hyssop. Naturally this gentleman was startled by the presence in the room of Mr Grimwig and a clergyman whom he had never met before. Mrs Carraway, however, took the situation calmly in hand.

'Ah, Doctor,' she said. 'You know Mr Grimwig of course ...' The two gentlemen nodded to each other. 'And this is the Reverend Maylie, Oliver Twist's uncle.'

Harry bowed and Hyssop returned the bow rather nervously. 'And Mr Brownlow, Doctor?' the clergyman inquired. 'How is he?'

'Happily, sir, no worse,' Hyssop replied. 'Unhappily, also no better.'

'I should very much like to visit him, before returning to the country,' said Harry. 'At the least, to be able to tell my wife that I had seen him.'

'Ah,' declared the doctor, with a rapid glance in Mrs Carraway's direction, 'unfortunately, his condition is still too delicate to allow visitors.' He gave his head a despondent shake.

'Well, sir,' muttered Grimwig sorrowfully, 'in matters like this we must bow to you. Clearly, you have business with Mrs Carraway. We'll leave you both. Good day, ma'am. Good day, Doctor.'

When Mr Grimwig and the clergyman had left the room, Mrs Carraway hurriedly put a finger to her lips and waited until she had heard the front door slam, before speaking.

'They're onto something,' she said. 'Just what I'm not sure. Through one of Bolter's people, or at any rate someone he's mentioned. I'll have Charlotte fetch him.'

She rose from her chair, and made for the door; but the doctor stopped her.

'No!' he said. 'If they are onto something, for all our sakes, surely it would be better if Bolter kept away!'

The two accomplices gazed at each other intently for some moments; then Mrs Carraway nodded slowly.

So the Dodger's and Fagin's plan had been successful, as far as it went. Mr Grimwig's suspicions had been aroused by Mary's message, and Bumble would thereby be incriminated, should Bolter and Monks get to hear of it, as they most assuredly would. Having dispatched Oliver, the Dodger took a considerable while to summon up sufficient courage to return to Fagin's hide-out; he wandered, nervously and alone, for a good hour, through the city's less-frequented streets, as night approached. It was quite dark when he at last steeled himself to face the worst and entered the dilapidated house near Field Lane.

'Well! Well!' said Fagin's voice in the blackness, as the Dodger arrived in the room. 'At last! The Dodger! Light the candle, will you, my dear?'

'Where's Barney?' asked the Dodger.

'Gone back.'

'You sent 'im back?' exclaimed the Dodger in surprise.

'He takes his chances, as we all do,' declared Fagin. 'Light the candle, my dear.'

The Dodger groped towards the table, found the matches, and lit the candle.

'There now,' said Fagin. 'We can see each other.' He grinned. 'And now,' he continued softly. 'I have a better question. Where have you sent Oliver?'

The Dodger hesitated briefly before deciding to tell the truth. 'To 'is aunt's,' he replied. 'In the country. Where 'e'll be safe.'

Momentarily, Fagin's gnarled fingers clenched, his mouth tightened, and his eyes took on a cold gleam. In an instant, however, he had relaxed.

'Wise as ever, that's our Dodger,' he muttered, chuckling. 'Yes, he'll be much safer there. You delivered the message?'

'It got there all right,' said the Dodger. 'Why? Yer worryin' about Barney?'

Fagin shrugged. 'As you do about little Oliver,' he murmured. 'Human nature, my dear, it's a sickness we all suffer.'

''E's gone to the Cripples, 'as 'e?' said the Dodger.

Fagin nodded.

'And you'd like me to 'ave a look-see.'

Fagin nodded, and smiled slightly.

'If they've nabbed Barney,' said the Dodger, 'an' they get me, too, you could end up with no one to light yer candles for yer.'

'I've been in Newgate Prison, my dear,' retorted Fagin with a shrug. 'You learn to live with the dark.'

The Dodger gazed at him for a few moments before leaving the room and setting off in the direction of the Three Cripples. Left alone again, Fagin let his rage come to the fore. His hands twisted into talons; his face contorted into an expression of blind fury.

'You learn to live with the darkness,' he repeated to himself in a savage whisper. 'And with more than the darkness, my dear. With treachery, my dear, with desertion! But we'll have our day! Oh we'll have our day! And when the time is ripe . . .' His features began to relax again. 'And when the time is ripe,' he murmured, 'Why you can fetch him home yourself, can't you, Dodger? Little Oliver, back with us, at home, where he belongs . . .'

As it happened Barney had most certainly been 'nabbed'. At that moment, he was lying on his back on the table in the private room of the Three Cripples Tavern; Noah Claypole was holding onto his wrists, and the monstrous Kags was towering over him, with a heavy belt coiled about his right fist. Noah Claypole, for his part, was not the kind of villain who relished physical violence, unlike Kags, who assuredly was; and he was now doing his best to avert his gaze from the torture that was about to commence.

''Old 'im tight, can't yer?' growled Kags. 'Monks wouldn't want 'im damaged so 'e can't talk.'

Claypole tightened his grip on Barney, keeping his face turned away.

'Right,' snarled the creature, flexing the belted fist. 'Now we can start . . .'

'I don't dow wot yer after!' protested Barney, with all the courage he could muster in the circumstances.

'To begin wiv,' said Kags, 'where d'yer go, when yer give me the slip?'

'I dever gave dobody the slip!' cried Barney.

Kags raised his fist for the first blow. Noah Claypole shut his eyes. Then, to both Noah's and Barney's considerable relief, there was a knock on the door which caused Kags to lower his hand and swing round, his eyes blazing. Before anyone could say anything, Noah's devoted friend Charlotte had scuttled into the room with a countenance full of breathless panic. The sight before her, however, increased her anxiety, as she stared wide-eyed at the prostrate Barney and the terrifying creature standing over him.

'Charlotte!' exclaimed Claypole, releasing his hold on Barney's wrists and allowing the youth to roll sideways from the table. 'Wot yer doin' 'ere?'

'Get 'er out!' thundered Kags.

'Charlotte,' Claypole continued, ' 'ow many times 'ave I told yer, never to. . . . .'

'It's Mrs Carraway!' squealed Charlotte, 'A message! That friend of Mr Brownlow's, he . . .' She could say no more, for Kags was stepping menacingly towards her, making it abundantly clear that whatever agonies he had intended to inflict on Barney were about to be transferred to her.

'Wait a bit!' cried Claypole.

Kags lowered his fist, but retained a dangerous stance.

Claypole approached Charlotte. 'Grimwig?' he said. 'Wot about 'im?'

' 'E came to the 'ouse again,' said Charlotte, still staring in terror at Kags. 'An' Mrs C says you ain't to come back. Not for now, anyway. Maybe not ever.'

'Wot?' exclaimed Claypole in fury.

'This is wastin' time,' growled Kags.

'Why ain't I?' asked Claypole, ignoring the monster.

' 'E's onto somefink,' Charlotte explained. 'About you an' Oliver, at the 'ouse. Put up to it by someone, 'e was.'

Kags became immediately interested and turned his attention to Barney once more. 'Who?' he demanded, pointing at the youth, who was now crouching beside the table. ' 'Im? Was it 'im?'

'Not 'im, no,' said Charlotte. 'Big an' fat, 'e said. You'll never guess. 'E said the name was *Bumble*.'

A short pause followed this revelation, after which Noah Claypole sent his fist crashing down onto the table-top.

'Didn't I say it?' he cried. 'Didn't I? All the while! Bumble!' His glee at having had his initial suspicions proved correct, almost overrode his fury at having been betrayed; and his agitation as to what might happen as a result of the betrayal. Bumble, after all, was Monks' man; it was Monks who had brought this corpulent traitor to their cause into the whole business in the first place.

Kags, with a sigh, began to unwrap the belt from his fist. Barney rose hesitantly, not daring to indicate his relief, although he was most certainly very relieved.

'It'll be a pleasure,' declared Kags, 'dealing wiv 'Umpty-Dumpty! Wot a fall that'll be!'

'No!' interposed Claypole. 'No, Bumble's mine! I'll find – something 'e'll really appreciate. Somethin' special for Mr Bumble.'

Charlotte gazed in astonishment at her loved one. She had never seen quite such a malignant grin cross his countenance before, or quite such a hate-ridden gleam in his eye.

Mr Bumble had decided not to return to the Three Cripples Tavern until Daniel Possett had led him to Oliver, for he was a gentleman not impartial to glory and adulation, and had received very little of either for some while. If he could be the one, he mused, who brought the boy single-handed before Monks, he would surely enjoy the astonished admiration of that person, and be rewarded handsomely; not merely with money, but with the respectful awe which he felt he unquestionably deserved; and the brutish Kags would never dare to call him 'Humpty-Dumpty' again.

His fleshy features betrayed a gleeful anticipation as he knocked boldly on Daniel Possett's door once more, when darkness had descended. The toy-maker emerged promptly.

'This way, Mr Stalker,' he said, and led Mr Bumble through a maze of dingy thoroughfares and passageways, so complex in its arrangement that Bumble was not at all sure that he would be able to trace his route back to the Three Cripples, once Oliver had been handed over to him. The toy-maker moved very rapidly, too, and Bumble had to exert himself to a greater extent than he had ever done before, in order to keep pace with him.

Occasionally, out of consideration for his bulk, Dan would stop, so as to allow him to catch up.

They reached a narrow, muddy court at last, containing nothing but a small, lean-to-shed, with a door closed by a bar slung across two brackets.

'I got . . . a stitch!' called Bumble, as Dan waited for him. ''Ow – *How* much farther?'

When Bumble reached him, panting hugely and sweating profusely, Dan declared: 'We're there.'

'Wot?'

'We're there,' Dan repeated, pointing to the shed.

''Ere?' asked Bumble.

Dan nodded. 'As I promised,' he said.

'You've got 'im h'incarcerated?'

Dan shrugged, reached for the bar across the door and swung from its supports. 'Safest, for all of us,' he said. Bumble's massive frame was trembling with excitement at the prospect of seeing his quarry at last. Dan pulled open the door, and called to the utter darkness within: 'Oliver? Oliver, it's Dan. Got a surprise for yer, Oliver.'

A strange rustling was the sole response to this announcement.

'Looks like 'e's asleep, Mr Stalker,' said Dan. 'Why don't you give it a try, sir? See 'ow 'e reacts to an old, familiar voice.'

He stepped aside and allowed Bumble to approach the open door. Bumble peered into the gloom and called softly: 'Oliver? Oliver, my dear?'

Again there was no reply but a further rustle.

''Ow about givin' 'im a nudge?' suggested Dan.

Bumble glanced briefly at Dan, and then stepped through the doorway into the shed.

'Oliver? Wot the—?'

It did not take Bumble long to realize that he had been tricked. There was certainly a presence of some kind in the shed; but it was most decidedly not Oliver. He turned frantically back to the door, but it was too late. No sooner had he entered than Daniel Possett had slammed the door shut and swung the bar back onto its brackets.

'That's right, Mr Stalker!' the toy-maker said with a chuckle. 'You give 'im a nudge!'

'Let me out, d'you 'ear?' cried the furious Bumble, beating on the door from within. 'Let me out! It's a pig! A monstrous great pig! Let me out!' His shouts were accompanied by a succession of irritable grunts.

'Right again, Mr Stalker!' Dan called. 'Or is it Fumble? A 'og, the 'eaviest in London, they say! 'E'll be so 'appy yer waked 'im! Enjoy yer night, Mr Bumble!' Whereupon he scuttled off, pursued by Bumble's irate protestations.

The pig, who must indeed have been the largest in London, was not in the least bit pleased at having been so rudely aroused from his contented slumbers; as a result of which the self-important former Beadle and School Porter managed to benefit from very little sleep that night.

The Dodger had turned the corner into Little Saffron Hill on his way to the Three Cripples Tavern when he saw, some distance ahead of him, the unmistakable figure of Daniel Possett scurrying across the street.

'Dan! Dan!' he called, as the toy-maker disappeared into a passageway. He immediately took off in pursuit, but had run no further than a few yards when he tripped and fell heavily to the ground. Dazed and shaken, he rose and turned to examine what had caused such an abrupt interruption to his progress. It was a silver-topped cane, and the owner of the cane was Monks, who had stepped forth from an alley and was glaring at him evilly. Before the Dodger could even attempt to escape, the villain had seized him roughly by the collar and now proceeded to drag him up the street, saying nothing, but allowing a triumphant smile to play across his thin lips. The Dodger struggled manfully, but no amount of effort could free him from his captor's determined grasp.

Noah Claypole had peevishly dismissed Charlotte, and was now trying to settle himself down comfortably for a night in the private room of the Three Cripples.

'Stupid woman!' he muttered, putting his feet up on the bench and covering himself with a thin rug which he had managed to obtain from the landlord. 'Why'd she 'ave to go an' tell Grimwig that story? Can't nobody tell a decent lie round 'ere? Can't even sleep in me own bed!'

'Taint so bad, Bister Bolter,' said Barney, who was sitting in a corner of the room. 'I'll keep yer cobpady.'

Claypole was about to retort that he did not consider Barney's company to be of particular solace, when the door opened and Monks appeared, holding the Artful Dodger by the collar. He pushed the boy forward so that he spun onto the floor, landing on his hands and knees just in front of Barney.

'Dodger!' cried this youth.

'Exactly,' rejoined Monks, grimly. 'Master Dawkins, late of Stalker's Academical Establishment. And now perhaps at last we'll learn the whereabouts of his ex-schoolmate.'

Monks then realized to whom he was talking – none other than the young man who, he thought, should have been undergoing a severe interrogation as to why he had given Kags the slip earlier that day; for he had not returned to the Three Cripples since Kags had arrived to report that fact. Before he could vent his own fury on Barney, however, or even ask where Kags was, Noah Claypole enlightened him as to the nature of recent events and discoveries; not without a certain degree of relish. Bumble, he announced had proved to be the traitor in their midst, not Barney; and he had sent Kags off in search of that disloyal gentleman; instructing the monster, however, to bring him back unharmed so that they would have the pleasure of inflicting a very particular form of punishment upon the villain.

As Noah was hurriedly explaining these things, the Dodger made a rapid dash for the door, but he was quickly prevented from escaping by Monks.

'Tie him up!' Monks snarled. 'We'll question him when Kags gets back!'

Kags had dutifully gone to Daniel Possett's shop, merely to discover that there was no-one there, neither within nor without; a fact which could only arouse his suspicions as to Bumble's treachery still further. Scowling horribly, he had then commenced a thorough and determined search of the surrounding streets, convinced that he would track down the corpulent turncoat sooner or later, even if it took him until morning.

It did take him until morning, as it happened; but another individual had the pleasure of finding Bumble first. This personage was the owner of the irascible pig; the animal in whose company a thoroughly distraught Mr Bumble had had to spend a most restless night. The pigman, as was his custom, had opened the door of the shed shortly after dawn in order to feed his charge, and had seen, to his understandable dismay, a furious gentleman of immense size rising from the straw within and advancing towards him with an expression that could only be described as rabid. Before this dreadful apparition had reached him, the pigman had slammed the door shut again, barred it, and run screeching for help; which was not slow in coming. Within less than a minute, the pigman had returned to the shed in the company of a Bow Street runner.

'In here?' inquired the runner. 'With your pig?'

The pigman nodded. The runner swung the bar up again, pulled open the door and peered into the shed. 'Right then, out you come!' he commanded. 'No nonsense! Let's be having you!'

Mr Bumble emerged, blinking into the light; he was haggard, dishevelled and completely miserable. His coat was in great disarray, and torn in several places. Having spent several hours in close confinement with a pig, he also emitted a most unpleasant and unfortunate odour, which caused the runner to take several paces backward, and the pigman to give him a very wide birth as he approached the door to close it again.

'So, wot was you after? Stealing the pig, was it?' asked the runner.

'I would 'ave you know, sir,' announced Mr Bumble, adopting all the dignity he could muster in his sorry state, 'my name is Bumble and I do not purloin! I 'ave been the victim, sir – not the perpetrator – of a most deleterious prank.'

The runner could not conceal a certain degree of amusement. 'Well,' he said, 'I suppose it would have been difficult for you to drop the door-bar on yourself.'

'Not only difficult – an impossibility!' retorted Bumble. 'I was h'inveigled into these ... premises.'

'Is that so, Mr Bumble?' said the runner. 'Do you wish to lay charges?'

Mr Bumble drew himself up to his full height, which was considerable, and declared authoritatively: 'I most certainly ...' He stopped, as a thought struck him. 'Do not,' he continued. 'That is – I h'am not sure I know the h'individual's name.'

'That so, sir?' said the runner, eyeing him curiously. 'Well, if I was you, Mr Bumble, I'd nip off 'ome an' have a bath an' a change pretty quick. A pig sty ain't the most odorous of accommodations.' Whereupon he saluted and strode off.

Mr Bumble stared disconsolately at the astonished pigman; then, regaining an air of superiority, he turned and walked haughtily from the courtyard.

He had no idea where he was. It had been a long and confusing journey to the shed from Daniel Possett's shop, and he now wandered perplexedly along the street in an attempt to discover some identifiable feature that would help him to establish his whereabouts. He had not walked for more than a hundred yards or so, however, when he realized that he was in Saffron Hill, and that the Three Cripples Tavern was only a short distance ahead of him.

In the private room of the tavern itself, at this moment, the Dodger was seated in a chair with his hands tied behind his back. Kags, who had returned only a quarter of an hour earlier, was standing threateningly over him, his fist belted once more. Barney and Claypole were seated on the bench, and Monks, who was standing by the door, was conducting an interrogation.

'Don't try to trick us, boy!' he hissed. 'What have you done with Twist?'

'Me?' replied the Dodger. 'Wot should I 'ave to do with 'im?'

'I've warned you once. I won't again. Kags!'

Obediently, Kags drew back his fist in preparation for the first blow.

'All right!' exclaimed the Dodger hurriedly. ''E's got away from both of us, ain't 'e? Sure I was 'elpin' 'im! For a share of the money I'd 'elp old Nick 'isself.'

The declaration saved him, momentarily at least, from Kag's brutality. Noah Claypole, who understood greed better than any of the other deadly sins, believed him at once. Monks remained mildly sceptical. Kags merely laughed brutally.

'Makes sense, tho', don't it?' said Noah, glancing at Monks. ''E wants it, I wants it, you wants it. There's enough for all of us.' He rose, turned his back to the Dodger, and winked; thereby making it clear to Monks that he had no intention of allowing the youth to receive the smallest share of the money.

Monks understood this, and now muttered: 'Yes . . .

He can have his share. Once I have Oliver, I'll take care of that.'

'Without Brownlow?' the Dodger inquired with interest.

'That's no concern of yours!' Monks snapped. 'Now. You will take us to Twist?'

'I can't!' replied the Dodger quickly. ''E's gone! Somewhere in the country! Maybe back to old Stalker's! I don't know!'

There was a pause. 'Or maybe elsewhere,' Monks murmured pensively. He turned to the door and opened it. 'Kags,' he said. 'I need you.'

Kags shrugged, disappointed at having once again been denied the pleasure of exacting retribution, and followed Monks from the room, closing the door as he left. Barney hurried forward to untie the Dodger, who, when he was free, began to rise.

'Stay there!' barked Claypole. 'Monks ain't as smart as 'e imagines. Yer knows more 'n you've said. We'll talk again.'

The Dodger slumped back into his seat. Claypole gestured to Barney to join him in a corner of the room.

'Now,' he whispered, once Barney had reached him. 'Yer got it clear, wot yer to do?' Barney nodded. 'Soon as Bumble's back, yer cuts off. I'll deal with the rest. Then we'll . . .'

The Dodger, who had sharp ears, heard every word of this, but further information as to what Claypole and Barney were plotting between themselves, was denied him by the sudden reappearance of Monks in the company of the wretchedly discomposed Bumble.

'Someone you wished to see,' said Monks. 'If scarcely to smell.'

Barney slipped from the room, as Claypole held his nose and cried: 'Cor! Where 'ave *yer* spent the night?'

The response to this question was an inaudible mutter from the malodorous gentleman.

'Where?' asked Claypole, straining forward to hear.

'In a pigsty!' Bumble now bellowed in fury.

'A little visit home, I take it,' remarked Monks, smiling thinly.

'H'oh, most jocular, Mr Monks,' declared Bumble. 'Ha, ha, most jocular. H'if you must know, I was tricked by that mountebank Possett!'

'See?' said Claypole with affected sympathy. 'Don't be unkind, Mr Monks! 'E suffered in the line of dooty!' He grinned at Bumble, who appeared slightly mollified. 'Tell yer wot,' Noah continued. 'Why don't yer 'ave a nice bath an' breakfast at the Spinners Inn? On me. An' yer can drop off a parcel for me, to the barman at the Spinners, Alfie.'

'Wait outside, Bumble, for the time being,' Monks recommended with a sniff.

Mr Bumble nodded disconsolately and left.

'Is this how you reward treachery?' snarled Monks, glaring at Claypole. Claypole merely chuckled, and reached under the table for a large package that was lying there.

'Come an' watch,' he said, still chuckling, as he moved to the door.

'What about Dawkins?' asked Monks.

'We'll attend to 'im later,' said Claypole. 'Where can 'e go?'

The two men left the room, and the Dodger heard a key turn in the door. As it happened, the chair in which he was seated was directly above Fagin's bolthole. Only he, Barney and Fagin were aware of its existence. Ned Fingers was too, of course, but he was on his way to the Ivory Coast, if he had not reached it already. Quickly, the Dodger rose, pushed the chair aside, raised the trapdoor and descended into the hole. Pausing only to blow a kiss in the direction of the locked door, he dropped out of sight into the darkness below, lowering the trapdoor above him as he went.

*

'And that, Mrs Maylie,' declared Mr Grimwig with a face full of shame, 'is as much as I know. I blame myself that it is not more. However, your husband should be here at any moment. You will at least be re-united with *him*.'

Rose Maylie had come to London on her own initiative, impatient for further news; not that her husband had failed to keep her fully informed of his progress, or lack of it, in the search for Oliver. Perhaps, then, she had merely travelled from the country because she missed Harry; a pardonable reason, assuredly, for one so deeply in love as she was. Arriving in London, she had gone at once to Mr Brownlow's house, where she was, to her considerable dismay, denied admittance, and not even allowed to see the housekeeper. She had then walked to Mr Grimwig's home, and the old gentleman, delighted to see her despite his having to recount his own innumerable mistakes, had told her of everything that had occurred and all that he and her husband had managed to discover in the past twenty-four hours, since the visit of the actress Mary and the curious message from Bumble.

'Oliver's note, Mr Grimwig,' Rose now said. 'Can I see it?'

'Why surely, ma'am, surely!' replied Grimwig, rising from his chair and moving to the desk. He opened a drawer and extracted the soot-smudged note, which he handed to her. She studied it intently for a long while.

Grimwig coughed. 'This matter of Mrs Carraway, ma'am,' he said. 'To an extent I can understand her refusing to see you. She herself has been, I am convinced, like Oliver a victim in this . . .'

He stopped short, for at that moment Harry Maylie entered the study. He stared at his wife in a mixture of astonishment and utter joy. Rose, however, was too absorbed in the note to notice his arrival at first, and now said, with a sad shake of her head: 'No, Mr Grimwig, I am afraid that I cannot accept that.'

'Accept what, my dear?' asked Harry, with a smile.

'Harry!' cried Rose in delight. In an instant, the young couple were in each other's arms, and provided a picture of such loving contentment that Mr Grimwig could not refrain from allowing a tear to form in the corner of an eye.

'How pleasant to see you, my love!' declared Harry. 'But what can you not accept?'

'Mrs Carraway's innocence,' replied Rose, 'if this note is genuine.'

'It is!' announced Grimwig, 'or I'll eat my head!'

'Genuine, certainly,' said Harry. 'But its meaning is impenetrable.'

'No, Harry!' exclaimed Rose. 'It's perfectly plain!'

The two gentlemen stared at her in surprise.

'Mr Brownlow is in a nursing home, yes,' Rose continued, 'but brought there by ill-treatment, and held virtually prisoner. And this could not have come about without connivance.'

'By Mrs Carraway?' asked Harry.

'And Dr Hyssop,' replied Rose.

'Hyssop?' exclaimed Grimwig.

'Yes, Mr Grimwig,' said Rose. 'Is such an action on his part inconceivable?'

Grimwig began to splutter confusedly: 'But Hyssop . . . highly respected . . . member of . . .' Suddenly he adopted an air of determination and said: 'Well! There's only one thing to do! Have a second opinion, and without Hyssop's knowledge.'

'That could be dangerous,' said Harry.

'If Hyssop's diagnosis was the truth, certainly,' retorted Grimwig. 'But if not – why, then everything will be resolved! You must leave this to me. I have a certain authority, still.'

The old gentleman crossed purposefully to the door and left the room, pausing briefly to gather up his hat and coat before walking through the front door.

*

Noah Claypole had handed the mysterious package to Bumble, repeating that it was to be delivered to a certain Alfie, the barman at the Spinners Inn, a hostelry at the bottom of Saffron Hill. The corpulent gentleman now walked heavily towards this place, carrying the package which was large and of considerable weight. He stopped, however, when he caught sight of the Bow Street runner who had released him from the pig's shed earlier that morning; this person was approaching him up the hill, in the company of two uniformed policemen. Mr Bumble wondered whether or not to turn back in the direction of The Three Cripples, as innocently as he could. He decided, however, that this would only arouse the runner's suspicions, and proceeded to walk on.

'Ah, Mr Bumble, sir,' declared the runner, as they met. 'Still not 'ad your bath?' He sniffed the air.

'I h'am on my way to the Spinner's Inn,' announced Bumble, with all the dignity he could summon. To his understandable perturbation, the runner now gestured to one of the policemen, who stepped forward and seized the package, quite roughly, from his grasp.

'Your property, sir?' inquired the runner.

'H'in a manner of speaking,' Bumble answered nervously. 'Well – not h'entirely mine. H'actually I h'am delivering it, for a friend, to 'is friend, name of Alfie, the barman at the Spinners.'

'Where the barman's name is Peter,' rejoined the runner, casually, looking down at the policeman, who was now kneeling and unwrapping the package.

To Bumble's immediate misery and dismay, the package which he had been asked to deliver contained a large, branched candlestick; a fine object indeed, made of solid silver, which glittered in the morning sun. At once, the other policeman had seized Mr Bumble by the arm, producing a pair of handcuffs which he immediately attached to the desperate gentleman's wrist.

'Well, sir,' said the runner, 'at least you can have a bath at the police station.'

Bumble tried to protest his innocence, but to no avail. His mouth merely opened and closed silently and his large eyes seemed to want to pop from their sockets as he was escorted from the scene.

Monks and Noah Claypole, who were standing in the doorway of the Three Cripples, witnessed Mr Bumble's sorry downfall with great amusement; as did Barney, who was watching from a place of concealment in a passageway only a little further down the street. This young man now hurried to Fagin's hide-out, where he reported the happening to Fagin and the Dodger, who also found it highly entertaining. No-one, it seemed, could feel sorry for Bumble.

'Arrested on the word of Bister Borris Bolter, Bagistrate's informer!' announced Barney. 'The candlestick was reported purloyed last night.'

'He'll be sentenced to the hulks?' asked Fagin, sadistically.

'Three years at least,' declared Barney. 'Baybe five.'

''E deserved worse,' remarked the Dodger, once he had recovered from a lengthy bout of hysterical laughter. 'But,' he now said seriously, 'where do we go from 'ere?'

'Have you forgotten little Oliver, my dear?' replied Fagin softly. 'We have his name to clear, don't we, my dears; to clear *completely*!'

The Dodger was delighted. 'You really meant it then!' he exclaimed in surprise.

His joy was to be short-lived, however, for now Fagin grinned and said. 'Could you doubt it, Dodger? There's still the money, is there not? And Brownlow's house; and Mr Brownlow dying. And once Oliver's credit is redeemed, and Bolter and Monks are eliminated . . .'

'You bove in!' Barney interposed with glee.

'We all do, Barney,' announced the cunning old gentleman. 'We all move in.'

'Into Brownlow's house?' asked the Dodger.

'Where else, my dear?' replied Fagin.

'With you takin' Bolter's place,' said the Dodger.

'What else, my dear?' replied Fagin, with a disconcertingly sweet smile. 'Whatever else? And we live the life of gentlemen of leisure. For evermore!'

The Artful Dodger did his best not to reveal his helpless, disgust and dismay.

The following morning Oliver Twist arrived at the home of his aunt and uncle in the country, only to find it locked and empty. Immediately perturbed, he ran to the churchyard where, to his comparative relief, he saw Mr Brittles, Harry Maylie's kindly old sexton, tending the graves. Naturally, Mr Brittles was surprised and pleased to see the boy. He immediately informed Oliver, however, that his journey had been wasted, for the clergyman had left for London a week previously, and his wife had followed him there only two days ago.

'You must have passed your aunt on the road, Master Oliver,' said the sexton.

'While I was walking, half the way here,' said Oliver, bleakly.

'Well now, if you were to hurry back . . . ,' suggested Mr Brittles, with a groan.

'I'm too tired,' declared Oliver, shaking his head.

'With half a guinea for coach-fare, though, you might still catch them at Mr Grimwig's, mightn't you?'

The sexton produced a shining coin from the pocket of his waistcoat and gave it to the boy.

'No thanks now,' he said. 'I'm sure your uncle will be happy to let me have it back.'

'Thank you anyway, Mr Brittles!' exclaimed Oliver.

'Best be goin' then,' said Brittles. 'There'll be a stage along presently. It'll bring you to London by midnight.'

'I truly mean it! Thank you, Mr Brittles!' cried Oliver, running for the gate. The sexton waved him on, smiling.

No sooner was the boy out of the churchyard, however, and protected from Mr Brittle's view by a high stone wall, than he ran straight into someone: a brutal, looming, heavy-set creature with a ferocious grin. It was Kags, who had been sent from London by Monks to fetch Oliver back. Before the terrified boy could cry out, the monster had clapped a large hand over his mouth, and seized him by the arm, dragging him away. Oliver struggled to free himself, but such a task was utterly impossible.

CHAPTER TWENTY-SIX

'Smells very tempting, my dear,' declared Fagin happily, sniffing the air as he watched the Artful Dodger stir a pan of clear soup on a trivet by the fire. 'You could have been a first rate chef.'

'A thieves' kitchen's the only one I'll ever see,' said the Dodger. He rose and carried the pan to the table, pouring the soup into two bowls. The old thief-master chuckled.

'D'yer mean wot you was sayin'?' the Dodger now asked. 'About movin' into old Brownlow's 'ouse?'

'Once we have little Oliver safely back in our hands,' said Fagin.

'But won't Brownlow 'isself 'ave somethin' to say about it?'

'He's in a nice, comfortable nursing home, isn't he?' said Fagin. 'Thanks to the good Dr Hyssop; whose fees I shall obviously continue to pay.'

The Dodger was tearing a piece of bread from a loaf when he heard this, and he now halted momentarily. 'The old villain ...,' he thought. He quickly continued to tear at the loaf, however, for he did not wish to reveal his anxiety as to Fagin's intentions; not yet, at any rate. He brought the piece of bread and a bowl of soup to the fireplace, placing the bowl in Fagin's lap.

'Sure you can manage?' he asked.

'Not the bread,' said Fagin. 'I can only handle one thing at a time.' The Dodger took the bread back to the table and sat down. With his unsteady right hand, Fagin raised the bowl of soup with difficulty to his lips, and sipped.

'Mmm . . .' he observed with an approving grin. 'As tasty as dear Nancy ever made.'

'Not bad is it?' said the Dodger, tasting his own soup.

They both sipped silently for a couple of minutes.

'Why'd 'yer want to move into a flash ken like Brownlow's?' inquired the Dodger.

'Style, my dear,' replied Fagin. 'I have plans – to spread my interests further west. And for that I need a bang-up base.'

'Further west?' exclaimed the Dodger. 'You'll 'ave to fight all the gangs in Seven Dials!'

'They won't even know I'm there, my dear,' retorted the old gentleman, softly. 'No violence. I'm too old for that. But inside a year – they'll all be working for me.'

'Wot you got in mind then?'

'A new criminal empire!' said Fagin, his voice rising with excitement. 'Not dipping for handkerchiefs and purses. No petty crime, but large-scale swindles, my dear. The whole splendour of creation is just waiting to be fleeced! Just waiting, Dodger!'

He gazed eagerly at the youth, hoping for an enthusiastic reaction; but the Dodger merely appeared sceptical.

'You don't think I can do it?' Fagin asked, in a disappointed tone.

The Dodger shrugged. 'If anyone can do it, it's you,' he said.

'I shall need you at my right hand, Dodger,' said Fagin.

'You got Barney.'

'Ah, Barney's a downy bird, but he's not the Artful Dodger. Now is he, my dear?'

'Maybe not,' retorted the Dodger, betraying agitation.

Fagin chuckled softly. 'Ah, you're thinking of your promise to little Oliver, are you not, my dear?' he said. 'To go straight. Let it be a lesson to you, Dodger. Never make promises on an empty stomach.'

The Dodger nodded non-committally.

'But where *is* Barney?' inquired Fagin, suddenly anxious. 'He's my eyes and ears. I need 'im!'

'Must've found it 'ard to get away from Bolter,' said the Dodger.

Barney was indeed finding it difficult to escape from the private room of the Three Cripples tavern that night, for every time he rose to leave, Claypole, who had grown very irritable recently, would bark: 'Where yer sneakin' off to then?'

'Stretchin' be legs, Bister Bolter,' Barney would reply.

'Well stretch 'em in 'ere, Barney!' said Claypole. 'Can't stand yer creepin' about.'

Whereupon Barney would lower himself back onto the bench, morose and helpless.

There was a strange mood of indeterminate anticipation in the room, inspired by Monks, who was sitting at the table in a tense and expectant manner, staring into his glass, which Charlotte, who had come to keep her loved one company, would occasionally attempt to refill from a jug of wine. Every time she tried to do so, however, Monks would cover the glass with his hand to prevent her.

'Why d've 'ave to wait 'ere anyway?' asked Claypole petulantly.

'Because I say so,' Monks quietly replied, without looking up.

There were several long minutes of silence, during which Charlotte refilled Noah's glass and kindly offered the jug to Barney, who refused it with a dejected shake of his head.

'An' where's Kags? That's wot I want to know,' said Claypole at last.

'He's on an errand for me,' Monks replied.

'A errand?' exclaimed Claypole. 'Might I remind yer 'e works for *me*? An' I ain't seen 'im for two days!'

Monks stared up at him coldly for a moment, then lowered his head again and murmured: 'He'll be here soon.'

''E'd better be,' said Claypole. 'An' where's the Dodger?'

'I still can't think how he got out of this room,' muttered Monks.

'Under the door; like smoke!' said Claypole.

Barney emitted a short chuckle, which caused both men to glance sharply in his direction. He immediately converted the chuckle into a stupid grin, which he hoped would convince them that his mirth was simply the result of too much drink. The tactic seemed to work. In any case, the possibility of his being discovered was now suddenly averted by the entrance of Kags; who was wrapped in a blanket and seemed even more huge, in a curious way, than they remembered him to be. He was smiling in a terrible and triumphant fashion.

'Well?' demanded Monks, rising swiftly.

'You were right,' said Kags. 'The little bird flew to the country.'

'Wot little bird?' asked Claypole, thoroughly mystified.

For answer, Kags now opened the blanket to expose the cause of his increased bulk. In the crook of his arm, he held Oliver Twist, whose mouth was gagged and whose body was tightly tied round with a thick rope.

'You've got 'im!' cried Claypole, rising with excitement.

'Safe and sound!' declared Monks, exultantly. 'And this time, we'll deal with him once and for all.'

''Ow?' asked Barney, in an anxious tone.

Charlotte ran to Noah and cried: 'You promised you wouldn't 'urt 'im!'

'That,' said Monks, 'depends on Bolter. If now he'll keep his part of our agreement.'

Quite simply, the agreement was as follows: that Oliver should be subjected to being judged by a magistrate on the charge of theft, which Noah Claypole, under the name of Morris Bolter naturally, had lodged against him; he would then be made to undergo whatever punishment the magistrate might deem suitable for such an offence; which would be imprisonment, certainly, and for a considerable time. Oliver would thus find himself discredited, and would be unable to inherit the money that was due to him; and Monks would have had his revenge. The plan was put into action as soon as it could be: the following morning. On reflection, Monks and Claypole had now decided to make Mrs Carraway the layer of the charge, for she was an apparently upright citizen, and would lend the required air of respectability to the proceedings. Noah, in his capacity as Morris Bolter of course, would merely come forward as the chief witness.

Lest the reader should imagine that Oliver, being brought before a sympathetic magistrate – or at least one who was willing to listen – would be able to deny the charge brought against him, and thus avoid being sent to prison, it should perhaps be pointed out that such a possibility had already occurred to Noah Claypole. As a result, he had chosen to let Oliver be tried by a particular magistrate; one who was not renowned for his tolerance or impartiality. Indeed, this gentleman, whose name was Fang, was known far and wide for the very opposite. He was of a waspishly pitiless nature, apparently quite incapable of listening to anything but what he wanted to hear.

Oliver had been tried by this person once before, on an unfounded charge, and had only been rescued from appalling misjustice, on that occasion, by Mr Brownlow. When he was hauled into the courtroom on this particular morning, therefore, and saw the very same magistrate glaring at him from behind the high desk, he concluded that his chances of being dealt with in a just manner were negligible; for there was no Mr Brownlow to save him now. His guardian was a hundred miles away, lying very ill in a nursing home in the depths of the country; indeed, for all poor Oliver knew, Mr Brownlow was already dead.

Mr Fang was a lean, long-backed man with very little hair and an awesomely stern face, which was very flushed from many years spent imbibing brandy.

'Well then!' said this gentleman. 'Enough shilly-shallying! Who's the prosecutor?'

'I am, sir,' said Mrs Carraway, who was standing primly at the side of the courtroom next to Noah Claypole; who, in his role as Morris Bolter, magistrate's informer, had adopted a most official and sanctimonious stance.

'Has she been sworn?' asked Fang.

'Yes, yer worship,' replied Claypole.

'And what's this young vagabond charged with?' inquired Fang, with another sharp glance at Oliver.

'Attempting to steal a set of silver spoons from my house, sir,' said Mrs Carraway.

'Silver indeed?' said Fang. 'Any witnesses?'

'As Fate would 'ave it, yer worship,' said Claypole, stepping forward a pace. 'Myself, sir. I perchanced to be passin' the premises.'

'Good! Good!' said Fang.

Oliver now decided to protest, though he suspected that it would be to no avail. 'Sir, I never—' he began.

'None of your tricks, gallows-bait!' said Fang. Suddenly he seemed to recognize the boy standing before him. 'What's your name?' he barked.

'Oliver Twist, sir.'

'You'd what? Twist me? Never heard such insolence!' said Fang. 'I've had you here before! Stealing books then, as I remember.'

'Please, Mr Fang sir, I . . .'

'Hold your tongue villain!' said Fang. 'Anything known?' he asked, glancing at Noah Claypole.

'H'oh yes, yer worship,' replied Claypole. 'Young as 'e is, a 'abitural thief, sir.'

'Habitual, eh? I've heard enough. Summary conviction. Three years' imprisonment. Clear the court!'

'I never stole anything!' cried Oliver. 'If you'd only listen!'

'Threaten me, would you?!' said Mr Fang. 'Very well then. *Four* years – with hard labour. One word more, and I'll double it! Clear the court!'

Thus it was that British justice, as interpreted by the notorious Mr Fang, sent Oliver Twist to Newgate prison. He was quickly escorted to that place and thrust into a small dark cell. The thick door was slammed heavily behind him, and he stared pitifully around the confined space in which he was destined, without hope of appeal, to spend four inordinately long years. Mr Monks, it is unnecessary to point out, was very pleased.

That same morning, Mr Grimwig had sent for Dr Hyssop. This person duly arrived at Grimwig's house on his guard and very controlled, wondering, naturally, why he had been summoned. Waiting for him in the study were Grimwig, the Reverend Harry Maylie, and a lady and gentleman whom he had never seen before.

'Ah, Doctor!' said Grimwig, smiling in a disconcertingly affable manner. 'Very good of you to come.'

'Your message said that it was a matter of urgency, sir,' remarked the doctor. 'You are not ill, I hope?'

'Not a bit, sir!' replied Grimwig, with a chuckle. 'I have *never* felt better! I believe you've met the Reverend Mr Maylie?'

'I have, sir,' said Hyssop, bowing shortly to the clergyman.

'But not,' continued Grimwig, 'his charming wife, Rose.'

'Mrs Maylie,' said Hyssop, bowing stiffly to the lady, and receiving an unenthusiastic curtsey in return. The doctor now expected to be introduced to the gentleman, who was a distinguished-looking individual with a healthy shock of silver hair, but Mr Grimwig demonstrated no inclination to do so.

'They are aunt and uncle to Oliver Twist, of whom you must have heard,' said Grimwig.

'Indeed, yes,' said Hyssop.

'It was for news of him,' said Harry, 'and of his guardian, Mr Brownlow, that my wife and I came to London.'

'I have no more knowledge of that unfortunate boy than anyone else,' declared the doctor. 'But as regards Mr Brownlow, I am happy to say that his condition shows signs of improvement.'

The gentleman who had not been introduced now stepped forward and said, somewhat sceptically: 'I am relieved to hear it.'

'Ah yes,' said Mr Grimwig. 'Dr Hyssop, may I introduce Dr Losberne?'

'*Doctor* Losberne?' exclaimed Hyssop, suddenly taken aback.

'An old friend of Mr Brownlow's sir,' said Losberne. 'And his physician for many years, until I retired.'

'I see . . .' said Hyssop. He suddenly experienced a desire to extricate himself from what could well prove to be very embarrassing company, and he turned once more to Mr Grimwig, saying: 'You will forgive me, sir. I am delighted to have set your friends' minds at rest as to the state of Mr Brownlow's health, but I am a very busy man.' He moved hastily to the door.

'One moment, Doctor,' said Losberne. 'I had hoped to go with you to your nursing home, to see Mr Brownlow.'

'I regret, sir, that that will not be possible,' said Hyssop.

Dr Losberne smiled. 'Perhaps I should have said "return" to it; since I have already been there and examined him.'

Hyssop was thunderstruck. 'I gave strict instructions that no one was to be admitted!' he cried.

'An order which I countermanded,' explained Grimwig. 'As a Justice of the Peace.'

'I have never heard of anything so unethical!' protested Hyssop.

'Ah,' said Dr Losberne, quietly. 'You presume to speak of ethics, do you, sir? After what I found there?'

Dr Hyssop knew that he had been found out; he could think of nothing to do but escape in terror and shame, but as he turned to the door again, he saw the clergyman standing firmly in his way.

'Mr Brownlow,' Dr Losberne now continued, 'is suffering from nothing more than the toxic effects of being kept for long periods under sedation!'

'I . . . I deny it!' said Hyssop, helplessly.

'You cannot, sir,' said Dr Losberne.

'And we'd find most of the other patients' so-called illnesses to be the same – or I'll eat my head!' cried Grimwig, unable to contain his fury any longer and striking his stick heavily upon the floor.

'That is . . . that is not so!' protested Hyssop; genuinely, as it happened, for it was certainly not the case. 'Not so,' he repeated, broken at last, and feeling for a chair, upon which he sat in a most wretched manner. 'Not so,' he muttered a third time. 'It is . . . it is one of the finest medical institutions in the country.'

He now seemed such a picture of pathetic distress that his accusers, despite their unanimous horror at what he had done, could not fail to feel a certain degree of sympathy for him. Even the irascible Grimwig was moved to silence.

It was Dr Losberne who spoke next: 'I have always heard you spoken of with much respect, Dr Hyssop,' he said, not without gentleness. 'I am at a loss to understand your involvement in the whole sordid affair.'

'Weakness,' murmured Hyssop, pitifully. 'Weakness and greed. All the effort and dedication of my life – for so little return. Then Mrs Carraway suggested a plan whereby we could both . . . make a great deal of money. I . . . I could re-equip my nursing home, and ensure my future, in just a few weeks. Then I discovered the man, Bolter, was behind it.'

'That unspeakable villain!' growled Grimwig.

Hyssop continued: 'I wanted to get out of it; to make amends. But by then, they had me in their power. Since that moment, I have not known one quiet hour . . .'

He leant his head forward, covering his eyes with one hand, and wept, profusely.

Mrs Carraway returned home from the magistrate's office, to find the Reverend Harry Maylie and his wife waiting for her in the sitting room. Charlotte had admitted them, and when the housekeeper had given that young woman a suitably disapproving glare, she adopted a manner that was cool but resolute.

She asked what it was that the couple wanted. The clergyman replied by asking Mrs Carraway in her turn if she might now wish to reveal the whereabouts of his nephew.

'I know nothing,' declared Mrs Carraway, icily.

'Nor do you seem to care, Mrs Carraway,' said Rose.

'And why should I?' demanded the housekeeper.

Harry Maylie reminded her, in case she had perhaps forgotten, that her employer was the boy's guardian, which rendered her lack of concern somewhat suspect.

There was an uncomfortable silence.

'I'm afraid I must ask you to leave,' said Mrs Carraway.

'We have no intention of leaving, Mrs Carraway,' said Rose. 'We are waiting for someone.'

'Indeed!' said the housekeeper, moving to the door and opening it. 'Then kindly wait outside in the street. I thought I had made it clear that relations of that vicious, unrepentant young criminal are not welcome in my home.'

'In *whose* home?' said a voice from the hallway. Mrs Carraway recognized it at once, and froze. It was frail but unmistakable. A moment later its owner, Mr Brownlow, entered the room on his friend Mr Grimwig's arm. The good old gentleman was ashen and weak, but he now freed himself from the support of his friend, drew himself up to his full height and stepped towards his housekeeper, repeating sternly: 'In *whose* home, Mrs Carraway?'

Mrs Carraway saw at once that, for her at least, there would be no forgiveness.

For their part, Noah Claypole, Monks, Barney and the brutish Kags had decided to spend the rest of the morning celebrating the final and irrevocable ruination of Oliver Twist; and what better place could there be for such a jamboree of villains than the Three Cripples Tavern, on Saffron Hill?

'A drop of fine Rhenish wine, Mr Monks?' suggested Claypole.

'Yes, Mr Bolter,' replied Monks, raising his glass for it to be filled. 'For once I *will* drink with you.'

'Oh wery obliged, I'm sure, Mr Monks,' said Claypole, with sarcastic unctuousness. 'Such h'affability! Barney?'

'Yes please, Bister Bolter,' said Barney, grinning happily and nodding his head in a series of little jerks. Claypole filled his glass.

'Kags?'

Kags nodded. Noah Claypole filled *his* glass.

'An' last but not least,' he said, as he poured the wine into his own glass, 'misself. Now. What about a toast?'

'Down the 'atch!' said Kags.

'No, no!' retorted Claypole. 'Somethin' a bit more appropriate.'

''Ere's bud in your eye,' suggested Barney.

'In yours, too!' said Claypole, with mild irritability.

'What about . . . absent friends?' said Monks softly.

'I like it!' declared Claypole. 'In Newgate Prison, yer mean? Oh, wery suitable!'

So they all chorused. 'To absent friends!' and drank, voluminously.

'Well now,' said Claypole, wiping his mouth with the

back of his hand. 'I've kept my part o' the bargain, Mr Monks. It's 'igh time yer kept yours, I'd say. When do I get my three thousand pound?'

Barney listened with particular interest as Monks said innocently: 'Oh? Which three thousand is that?'

There was a ominous pause.

'The money!' said Claypole. 'Wot was left to Oliver! Yer said yer'd arrange to 'ave it transferred. To *me*!'

'But my dear Bolter,' said Monks, a thin smile playing on his pale lips, 'that money was tied up by his guardian in trust funds and investments. There was never a hope of touching it.'

'But yer . . . But yer . . .' Claypole spluttered. 'But yer said yer could fix it!'

'And you believed me?'

Monks smiled piteously and drained his glass.

'Yer knew it!' cried Claypole, in fury: 'Yer knew it all along! Yer've been *usin'* me!'

'For what you are worth, Bolter,' said Monks, rising from the table. 'Which is little enough.' He picked up his cane and moved to the door.

'Kags!' commanded Claypole. 'Get 'im!'

Monks turned and stared at Kags, who did not move.

'Yer 'ear me, Kags?' squealed Claypole. ''E don't get out of 'ere till 'e coughs up! Get 'im!'

Kags shrugged, placed his glass on the table, and approached Monks, who did not seem to be in the slightest bit afraid. Standing before Monks, the creature then turned to Claypole with a grin and said: 'Wot did yer say?'

Claypole was dumbfounded. 'Monks 'as *bought* yer!' he cried.

'I had no need to, Bolter,' explained Monks. 'Kags has always worked for me.' He gave a small, malicious chuckle. 'Poor, poor Bolter,' he said. 'Or is it really Claypole? No matter. Be thankful that one or the other of them is not on your tombstone.'

'So I ends up with *nothin'*?' said Claypole.

It does seem a trifle unfair,' observed Monks, thoughtfully. 'Very well. For your silence and to be done with you, I'll give you fifty pounds.'

'Only fifty?' said Claypole, in an offended tone. Monks turned to the door once more. Claypole rose hurriedly and held out his hand. 'All right! I'll take it!' he announced.

'Not now,' said Monks. 'I'll meet you tonight.'

'I'm not meetin' the likes o' you anywheres tonight,' said Claypole, unable to control a shiver.

'Suit yourself,' retorted Monks with a shrug. 'But Kags and I are sailing for America on the ebb tide. If you want that money, be at the corner of Garnet Street and the Ratcliff Highway at nine o'clock.'

He was gone.

'Thanks for the wine,' said Kags, picking up his glass again and dropping it so that it shattered on the floor. He grinned evilly and followed his master from the room.

Noah Claypole felt utterly alone; but Barney now reminded him of his presence by remarking, hesitantly: 'That idvitation. Wery unwise to accept it, Bister Bolter.'

'Wot?' said Claypole, staring up at him glassy-eyed.

'Lodely place. Dight. Adythid could 'appen.'

'I knows that, blast yer! Get out! Leave me alone!'

Barney quietly did as he had been commanded, shutting the door behind him as he left the room.

In his solitude and desolation, Noah Claypole permitted himself a small, strangled, cry of despair, as he lowered himself slowly onto the bench once more. Further dire tidings were in store, for now the door burst open and his devoted friend Charlotte scuttled in, causing him to jump up with a squawk of terror.

'Charlotte!' he cried. 'Yer wouldn't burst in like that if yer knew'd wot I just been through!'

'Mr Brownlow!' said Charlotte, panting heavily.

'Wot?'

'Mr Brownlow!' the woman repeated. ''E's back! An'

Mrs Carraway and Dr 'Yssop! They've been arrested! Oh Noah, it'll be our turn next! Oh Noah, yer'll 'ave to *do* somethin'! Oh Noah, oh Noah...'

'Stop screechin' an' let me think!' snapped Claypole, instantly pensive. He began to pace the room; his mind had never worked so quickly in his life. He suddenly stopped, and his mouth opened wide at what he considered to be a brilliant inspiration.

'Mr Fang!' he cried. 'I wonder . . .?' And he hurried from the room, leaving Charlotte to gape after him in utter bewilderment and distress.

Barney, for his part, now raced towards Fagin's hide-out near Field Lane. He had not returned there since the previous morning, and Fagin was in the habit of growing very irritable if the young man did not report to him at least twice every day.

'At last!' said Fagin, as Barney entered the room.

'Sorry, Bister Fagid,' said Barney, grinning briefly at the Artful Dodger, who was seated somewhat pensively at the table.

'What's been going on?' demanded his employer.

''Igh jinks an' do bistake, Bister Fagid,' said Barney. 'For a start, Oliver's id jail.'

There was an interested silence.

'Which jail?' said Fagin.

'Dewgate,' said Barney.

''E can't be! 'E's in the country!' exclaimed the Dodger, openly anxious.

'Kags fetched 'ib back,' Barney explained. 'An' Bolter 'auled 'ib straight into the Bagistrate's Court.'

'Which one?' asked Fagin.

'Bister Fadg,' said Barney. ''E give Oliver a laggid' – four years, 'e give 'im.'

'I don't believe it!' cried the Dodger, rising from his chair.

'So Monks got what he wanted . . . ,' muttered Fagin, thoughtfully.

'Ad' dow, it's war, betweed 'ib an' Bolter,' said Barney. 'I dropped Bolter a 'int – 'e'd best get Bunks and Kags first, afore they get 'ib!'

'That's my Barney!' said Fagin, with an approving chuckle.

'Ad' that's dot all,' said Barney, glancing at the Dodger.

'Not all?' echoed Fagin.

Barney approached him and leaned forward to whisper urgently into his ear.

'We'll 'ave to do somethin' to 'elp Oliver,' said the Dodger. Fagin was still listening intently to Barney's whispers so the Dodger repeated, more loudly: 'Did you 'ear me, Fagin? We've got to 'elp Oliver.'

'Yes, yes, my dear,' said Fagin, as Barney finished whispering. 'Of course we must, my dear, of course we must. But first – why have you never mentioned the money left in trust for our little Oliver?'

The Dodger took a step backwards. 'Wot money?' he asked, with all the innocence he could manage.

'The three thousad poud you was' talkid' about to Bunks,' said Barney.

The Dodger knew that it would be useless to pretend to further ignorance.

'Well?' asked Fagin, dangerously.

The Dodger thought quickly and declared with a shrug: 'Why d'yer think I been 'elpin' 'im?'

'Obviously to get your hands on his fortune,' said Fagin.

'That's it, Fagin!' said the Dodger. 'Right first time!' He noticed, however, that Barney was beginning to move round behind him.

'Or was it to protect your little friend?' Fagin suggested, quietly. 'Oh Dodger, I'm sick at heart, my dear. Heartbroken – to find I cannot even trust you.'

He gave a little nod to Barney, who now grasped the

Dodger's arms from behind. A struggle ensued, and the Dodger managed to free himself, pushing Barney sharply away, and running for the door. As he passed Fagin's chair, the old cripple leaped up and seized him, holding his arms tightly with both hands. For all his age, he was still immensely strong; but it was complete astonishment more than anything else that immobilized the Dodger.

'You can . . . You can *walk*!' he gasped. 'You're *not* paralysed!'

'Just another little surprise, my dear,' said Fagin, without loosening his grip for a second. 'Barney! Some rope!'

The Dodger tried to struggle, but Fagin held him firmly.

'Easy, Dodger,' said he, turning the youth round roughly, and thrusting him into the chair by the fireplace. Barney was already standing behind it with a length of thick rope in his hands.

'Wot you goin' to do with me?' asked the Dodger, as Barney proceeded to tie him to the chair.

Fagin smiled. 'That all depends, my dear,' he said. 'I don't wish you any harm, Dodger. But I can't have you interfering, can I? Not now that I've decided to enter the game, myself.'

CHAPTER TWENTY-SEVEN

So now both boys were prisoners; the one at the hands of British justice; the other at the hands of justice's most notorious enemy – the thief-master Fagin, who was not merely alive, but unparalysed, and as dangerous as ever.

It was a very black, very foggy, very cold night. Oliver paced up and down his damp and narrow cell in Newgate Prison, aimlessly and despairingly. He shivered and sat down on the blanketless straw mattress of his bed, feeling utterly alone and wretched. Some distance away, in a still darker part of London, his friend the Artful Dodger was sitting on the chair to which he had been tied by Barney. He, too, was alone, for Fagin and Barney had left the room on a mysterious but unquestionably villainous mission. The Dodger, however, would not allow himself to be overcome by a sense of helplessness, and was strugggling desperately, trying to free himself. Suddenly, by the light of the single candle that guttered on the table, he saw an object that he thought might be of use to him in his attempts to escape; a large wooden beam lay across the back of the fireplace, having tumbled down from somewhere above, and from this beam there protruded a long rusty nail. The Dodger began to jump his chair inch by inch towards it, his lips tight with determination.

At the very same moment, concealed from the view of curious eyes by the night's darkness and the swirling fog, Monks and his monstrous assistant Kags were waiting on a lonely street corner near the docks.

'See anythin'?' said Kags, hoarsely.

Monks shook his head.

'Sure 'e'll come?' inquired Kags.

'He'll come. He can't resist the smell of money,' said Monks.

Kags chuckled quietly and unpleasantly as he raised an evil-looking horse pistol to his eye to check the priming.

'That'll make too much noise. Leave it to me,' said Monks, raising his cane and pulling at the silver top to show his brutal assistant the glinting blade within. Kags grinned, and was about to put the pistol back into his coat pocket, when he suddenly saw something.

''E's 'ere!' he whispered, urgently.

A figure was indeed approaching them through the dense fog, with great caution; but it was not Noah Claypole.

'It's the police!' hissed Monks, recognizing the familiar shape of a tall hat and a dark greatcoat.

Kags was instantly alarmed, and turned quickly, only to discern more tall hats advancing towards him from all sides.

'It's Bolter!' he snarled. ''E's shopped us!' He cocked his pistol threateningly.

'Stand where you are!' called a policeman from the shadows, as the officers now closed in on the villains more rapidly.

'Look out!' cried Monks, stepping away from Kags and raising his hands in the manner of an innocent victim under attack from an assailant. 'Look out! He has a pistol!'

Kags realized at once what Monks was trying to do, and swung at him with his fist; but he was prevented from hitting him by four policemen, who grabbed at his arms. As the monster struggled, the pistol gave vent to a deafening report. There were five officers in all, and since four were required to control Kags and his immense strength, only one was left to seize Monks; this unfortunate gentleman now found himself being thrust viciously aside.

'After him!' he cried, pursuing Monks into the darkness. One of his fellow-officers joined in the chase, while the three remaining policemen continued in their struggle to overpower the desperate Kags.

By now, the Dodger had succeeded in backing into the fireplace in Fagin's hide-out, and was sawing the rope that bound his hands back and forth over the rusty nail. His cuffs were torn and his wrists were bleeding; but no amount of pain could dissuade him from his resolve to escape. At last the rope snapped. With his hands now free, the Dodger quickly untied the knots that secured him to the chair. He jumped up and hurried for the door. Opening it, he ran directly into the hands of a gentleman in a tall hat and red waistcoat, who happened to be about to enter the room at that moment. The Dodger stared up at his captor.

'Got you at last, my lad!' said the Bow Street officer.

The lamps were lit until late into the night in Mr Brownlow's sitting room, for nobody felt like sleeping; least of all Mr Brownlow, who, because of his serious ill-health, was in grave need of rest; as Dr Losberne now pointed out.

'Now, now. Don't fuss!' said Mr Brownlow.

'For weeks your body has been poisoned by criminal doses of chloral and laudanum,' said the doctor. 'You should be in bed!'

'Dr Losberne is right,' rejoined Rose, gently. 'You must rest.'

'I cannot,' said Brownlow. 'Not until there is some news.'

The front doorbell was heard to jangle outside. Everyone looked up in anticipation.

'I'll go,' said Harry Maylie, leaving the room.

'If Oliver is harmed,' observed Grimwig, who was pacing up and down, 'I'll never forgive myself for my . . . stupidity.'

'Hardly that,' said his old friend.

'I'll not be contradicted, d'ye hear!' Mr Grimwig rapped his stick fiercely on the floor. Mr Brownlow could see that he was not angry, however; merely deeply worried and anxious.

Harry Maylie now re-entered the room in the company of a magistrate's officer, who was holding the Artful Dodger by the collar.

'Why've yer brung me *'ere*?' inquired the Dodger.

'No lip now,' said the runner, pushing him into the room and announcing: 'Dawkins, sir.'

'The boy who's been helping Oliver,' said Harry.

The Dodger found himself standing before a pale but kindly old gentleman who now smiled and said: 'Yes, I'm very grateful to you, Dawkins.'

'Are you . . . you must be . . . Mr Brownlow!' exclaimed the Dodger. 'Ow'd you get 'ere?'

'Never mind about that,' replied Mr Brownlow. 'Where's Oliver?'

'In Newgate Prison,' the Dodger answered.

There was a shocked silence.

'We thought you were both in hiding?' exclaimed Rose.

'We was, ma'am,' said the Dodger, turning to the lady. 'From various parties. An' 'is lot,' he added, jerking his head in the direction of the runner.

'But, my dear boy,' said Mr Brownlow. 'For days those officers have been looking for you to *help* you!'

''Elp us?' exclaimed the Dodger in astonishment.

Mr Grimwig now advanced. 'Now tell us,' he demanded gruffly. 'Why is Oliver in prison?'

'Surely not that false accusation of stealing silver from this house?' inquired Harry.

'That's it!' replied the Dodger. 'Bolter an' Mrs Carraway charged 'im in front of a Magistrate.'

Mr Brownlow was astounded. 'But any reputable Magistrate would only have to question Oliver to know the case must be followed up!' he declared.

'Not Mr Fang,' retorted the Dodger morosely. ''E don't listen to nobody 'cept 'is informers. 'E done Oliver for four years?'

'Four years?' gasped Rose.

'Fang!' muttered Grimwig. 'Monstrous!'

'That man again!' observed Mr Brownlow. 'He'll have some explaining to do.'

'Indeed he will!' rejoined Grimwig, decisively. With magisterial authority he then approached the Bow Street officer and said: '*I'll* deal with the prison. *Your* priority is to apprehend Bolter!'

'As good as done, sir,' said the officer and he was gone.

Oliver Twist was no less wakeful, no less cold, and no less wretched when he heard the bolts on the cell-door shoot back and a key turning heavily in the lock. He was so utterly despondent that he could not expect anything but further anguish.

His surprise was considerable, therefore, when he saw the door open and his guardian's old friend Grimwig enter the cell. He remained mildly sceptical, however, as to Mr Grimwig's reason for visiting him at such a strange hour of the night, for the old gentleman wore a very stern and somewhat forbidding countenance.

Another figure now followed Mr Grimwig in, more slowly, and a flood of relief mingled with pity poured through Oliver's heart as he saw who it was. Mr Brownlow was wan and tired, and was leaning heavily on a stick.

'Father,' whispered the boy.

He rose from the bed and ran to his guardian, holding him and burying his face against the kind old man's chest.

'Oh, Father . . . ,' Oliver repeated, softly.

Mr Brownlow put his arms about his ward and murmured, greatly moved: 'My boy . . . my boy . . .'

*

In the private room of the Three Cripples Tavern at approximately the same moment, Noah Claypole and his loyal female companion were busily filling a pair of travelling cases with the most valuable items they could find in the sackfuls of stolen property that Noah had managed to accumulate in his capacity as a thief-master.

'Not that!' said Noah, as he saw Charlotte pick up a large marble clock which she could barely lift.

'But it's pretty, Noah,' protested the woman.

'We can only take as much as we can carry,' declared Noah.

Charlotte sighed mournfully and proceeded to remove from another sack an equally heavy bust of the Duke of Wellington.

Noah Claypole watched her struggle with this ridiculous object for some moments before saying, in a despairing tone: 'Charlotte, my love, yer'd best be off.'

'Where to?' asked Charlotte.

'The shippin' office,' replied Claypole, taking her arm and hurrying her towards the door. 'Book two passages on the packetboat for France – sailin' no later than dawn.' He extracted some coins from his waistcoat pocket.

'France?' exclaimed Charlotte. 'But you said we was safe now!'

'Safe enough,' retorted Noah. 'But it'll do us no 'arm to stay out o' sight for a month or two.' He gave her the money.

'Yes, Noah, dear,' said Charlotte, resignedly.

'Cut along now, my sweet,' said Claypole opening the door. 'An' no window-shoppin'!'

'Yes, Noah, dear,' said Charlotte, as she left the room.

Noah Claypole was beginning to feel very pleased with himself, for everything, it seemed, was working out surprisingly well for him. Monks and Kags, whom he had indeed betrayed, would almost certainly have been arrested by now, and he had also managed to obtain some very helpful papers from the Magistrate Fang, which would protect him in the unlikely event of his being apprehended by the guardians of the law.

He had been so anxious to get rid of Charlotte, however, in order to be left alone with his own happy musings, that he had not noticed the secret trapdoor in the floor opening quietly and someone climbing out. By the time he turned back into the room, the trapdoor had been closed again, and a tall figure in a long shapeless coat and flat, wide-brimmed hat was watching him from the shadows. The figure now stepped into the light, gaunt and implacably menacing.

Noah Claypole knew him at once. He whimpered softly and recoiled. In almost superstitious terror, he turned back, scrabbling for the door-handle. He wrenched open the door; only to find Barney facing him outside.

'Wotcher, Bister Bolter,' said Barney, with a grin that was no longer stupidly friendly, but calculatingly malicious. He pushed Noah towards the centre of the room, followed him in and kicked the door shut.

'Fagin?' said Claypole to the thief-master who was advancing slowly. 'I thought – I thought yer was dead – or near it.' He backed towards a wall.

'Nearer every day,' said Fagin quietly; 'as you are.'

'No! No please!' squealed Noah, raising his hands to protect his face. 'Don't 'urt me! Please! Don't 'urt me! I can't stand pain!'

'I should exterminate you!' Fagin hissed, his face only inches away. 'But,' he then added, 'I have a soft heart.'

Noah gazed at him through the fingers that were still splayed across his face.

'Your life is *mine*!' said Fagin, harshly. 'Do you agree?'

'Yes . . . Yes . . .,' replied Noah, nodding frantically.

'And in exchange for it,' said Fagin, 'all I'll take are these . . . baubles.' He gestured towards the heavily-filled sacks that were scattered on the floor.

'My pickin's?' exclaimed Claypole, in horror. 'All of 'em?'

'All of them!' replied the grim, old gentleman. 'And the papers and letter you stole from me.'

'Wot – wot papers?' asked Claypole, affecting utter ignorance.

'The ones dealing with Oliver Twist!'

'I – I ain't got them.'

'Barney!'

Barney took a threatening step forward.

'No! No!' squeaked Claypole. 'I mean I ain't got 'em *on* me! I've . . . I've 'id 'em!'

'But you are going to give them to me, are you not?' said Fagin.

'Yes! Yes!' announced Claypole.

'Because if you do not . . .'

Fagin was not allowed to complete his threat, however, for now the door opened once more and to Noah Claypole's immense elation, a Bow Street officer entered the room, followed by three policemen. Convinced of his safety, Claypole now pushed past Barney and Fagin and ran to the officer.

'Yer just in time!' he said breathlessly.

'Morris Bolter?' inquired the runner, sternly.

'That's me!' said Claypole. 'I 'ave a wery serious charge to make; against . . .'

'Take him away!' said the runner.

Two of the policemen grasped Noah by the arms.

'No – wait—?' he cried, startled.

'Out with him!' barked the runner.

The two policemen marched Claypole from the room, unmoved by his protests: 'It's a mistake! Yer don't want *me*! Listen! I'm Bolter! I *work* for you! *Wait*!'

'Look at all this,' said the remaining policeman, staring down at the sacks of loot and at the two cases with stolen jewellery.

'Who are you?' inquired the runner of Barney, who was now squatting on the floor, grinning idiotically.

'B-B-Bardey!' replied the young man vacantly, affecting stupidity. 'Pleased to beet yer.'

The runner gazed down at him in disgust.

'And you . . .' said the policeman to Fagin, who was now seated on the bench, a broken, paralysed old man once more, his head nodding shakily. 'I know you. You're Fagin! Get up!'

'Can't walk, your honour,' said the poor, old cripple, with great feebleness.

'Can't walk?'

'Paralysed, your honour. Can't move.'

The policeman surveyed him suspiciously. 'What do we do with all this stuff – an' these two?' he asked the runner.

The officer considered the two villains. They did indeed look thoroughly harmless. 'Oh – lock 'em in here and stand guard, until we get orders,' he said, heading for the door.

The policeman followed him out, locked the door, and obediently stood guard, awaiting orders.

I shall leave the reader to deduce how Barney and Fagin escaped – suffice it to say that they did; and when several more policemen arrived at the Three Cripples Tavern, with instructions to escort the two villains to Newgate Prison, they found the trapdoor open and the room entirely empty, not simply of Fagin and Barney, but of all the stolen property as well.

By the time Noah Claypole was brought before Mr Brownlow in his sitting-room, he had adopted a tone of unctuous civility, tinged with an air of self-importance.

'Why, Mr Brownlow!' he declared with a broad smile. 'Wot a pleasure to see yer! An' you, Master Oliver.'

'Don't try any games, Bolter!' said the officer who had accompanied him there.

'His real name is Noah Claypole,' announced Oliver.

'And under that name he is wanted for theft!' declared Grimwig.

'Claypole I may be, yer honour,' said Noah. 'But the charges was dropped. All settled an' signed – by Mr Fang.' Whereupon, to the assembled company's astonishment and distaste, he produced a folded document from the inside pocket of his coat.

'You cannot deny your involvement in my abduction!' said Mr Brownlow.

'Nor your persecution of my nephew,' said Harry Maylie. 'Even to laying a false accusation against him.'

'A h'unfortunate h'error of judgement, sir,' explained Noah, turning to the clergyman. 'As to my h'involvement with the criminality, that was only a cover – for my perfessional dooties.'

'Yer wot?' said the Artful Dodger, who was standing beside Oliver.

'My perfessional dooties,' Claypole repeated. 'I 'ave 'ere my commission as a Magistrate's Agent – signed by Mr Fang.' Whereupon he produced a second folded document from the inside pocket of his coat. 'An' a free parding,' he continued, extracting a third document, 'for any acts committed in the course of bringin' the potorious felons Monks an' Kags to justice.'

'Also signed by Fang,' snorted Grimwig, 'or I'll eat my head!'

'His payment for informing on his accomplices,' muttered Mr Brownlow.

'All dooly sealed an' certified,' announced Noah, handing the papers to the runner, who began to examine them hurriedly.

'The long an' short of it – not to mention the 'eight an' breadth—' continued Noah, impudently, 'is that yer can't touch me. Can they, h'officer?'

The runner looked up from the papers in disgust and glanced at Grimwig. 'He's telling the truth, sir. Though I'll have 'em checked.'

Claypole tucked his thumbs into his waistcoat and beamed confidently at the gathering.

'Let me get at him!' growled Grimwig, advancing.

'No, Mr Grimwig,' said Harry Maylie, softly, restraining him.

'Don't be so confident, Claypole!' said Mr Brownlow.

'Mr Magistrate Fang already has a number of questions to answer.'

'That's 'is problem, ain't it?' said Noah, with a shrug.

'It may also be yours!' declared Grimwig. 'If his own professional conduct is under inquiry, do you imagine he will risk himself to save you?'

''E told yer,' retorted the Claypole, nodding towards the runner. 'Them dockerments is legal.'

'And I shall dispute their legality in every court in the land!' thundered Grimwig.

'It may not come to that,' said Mr Brownlow quietly laying a hand on his furious old friend's shoulder. 'Much as it disgusts me, Claypole,' he continued. 'I am prepared to strike a bargain with you.'

'A bargain?' echoed Noah, interestedly.

'I shall drop charges against you, if you restore to me the papers relating to Oliver's parentage.'

'*All* the charges?' inquired Noah.

Mr Brownlow hesitated for a moment or two before declaring, reluctantly: 'All of them. Yes.'

There was a pause, during which Noah Claypole appeared to give the matter serious consideration.

'Done!' he said at last. 'They ain't no more use to me.'

There was an immediate reaction of surprise and relief amongst the company. Rose Maylie, who had been standing silently and anxiously all this while in a corner of the room, now hurried forward and asked: 'Where are they?'

Claypole glanced round at them all with a grin before announcing: ''Ere.'

'Here?' exclaimed Grimwig.

'Here?' echoed Mr Brownlow.

Noah Claypole nodded. 'In this wery 'ouse,' he said. 'If yer'll just allow me to show yer the way.'

The papers were hidden in the kitchen; and it was to this place that Claypole led them, chuckling somewhat disconcertingly as he did so. The kitchen was lit by a solitary oil-lamp and by the radiant glow from a blazing hearth.

'In 'ere?' inquired the Dodger.

'In the kitchen, all the time?' said Oliver.

'Safer 'n the Bank of England,' declared Claypole.

'Where? Where are they?' inquired Mr Brownlow.

For answer, Noah Claypole picked up a knife from the kitchen table and crossed to the wainscoting at the side of the fireplace. He slipped the knife under the beading of one wooden panel and levered the panel out. Reaching inside with the tips of his fingers, he withdrew a slim package wrapped in oilcloth. As the assembled group stared at him, he hesitated momentarily before handing the package with a flourish to Mr Brownlow, who quickly stripped off the oilcloth and leafed through the papers that it had contained. There was a breathless silence as he examined them.

'Are they what we hoped for, Mr Brownlow?' asked Harry at last.

'Are they genuine?' inquired Grimwig.

'Yes – Yes,' muttered Mr Brownlow. 'Yes, these confirm Oliver's legal right to a half share in his father's estate – and this letter establishes his parentage.' He looked up at Oliver and smiled. 'The adoption can now go ahead, my boy, without further delay.'

As the happy company began to surround the boy and his kind guardian, offering congratulations and expressing their joy at the wondrous manner in which all had been so suddenly resolved, Noah Claypole remained by the fire with a sour expression, gazing down into the flames; his eyes narrowed calculatingly. Only the Artful Dodger, who remained suspicious of his intentions, watched him fixedly.

'Isn't it wonderful, Oliver?' said Rose.

'Everything we hoped for,' said Harry.

'Just when we'd given *up* hope,' observed Mr Brownlow.

'A miracle, old friend!' declared Mr Grimwig.

'H'if I might make so bold?' Noah Claypole now interposed, taking a step towards the group. There was a sudden silence as they all turned to stare at him. 'H'if I could just 'ave a sight of them,' he continued, ingratiatingly, 'Just to check they're all there?'

Mr Brownlow, who was refolding the papers, eyed him hesitantly. 'Course yer can!' said the Dodger, taking the papers from the old gentleman's hand. He began to push his way through the group, muttering as he went: 'Scuse me . . . scuse me!' He handed the papers to Noah. ''Ere y'are,' he said, cheerfully.

'Oh wery kind – I'm sure,' said Noah with a smile. With the speed of a snake striking its prey, he plunged the papers deeply into the blazing fire, starting back and wringing his scorched hand. Naturally, the action caused utter consternation amongst the assembled company.

'Oh dear Heaven!' cried Harry.

'Save them!' cried Grimwig.

The officer, obedient to Mr Grimwig's command, ran to the fire in an effort to retrieve the papers; but saving them was impossible, for they had flared up at once and were burning fiercely in the centre of the flames.

Claypole chuckled in a harsh, wolfish manner. His eyes blazed viciously as he sneered: 'Yer can forget yer bargain, Mr Brownlow! An' yer can save yer breath, Grimwig! Fang'll uphold my parding!' He stared evilly at Oliver. 'It's worth 'avin' it disputed even,' he cried. 'Yer know why? To 'ave the last laugh on *you*, Work'ouse!'

'How could you do it?' asked Oliver, on the verge of tears. 'How could you do it Noah?'

The runner now turned sharply to the Dodger. 'Why did you give those papers to him?' he demanded suspiciously.

'I didn't,' replied the Dodger calmly. ''Ere they are.' Whereupon he produced them from the inside pocket of his coat and handed them to Mr Brownlow, who leafed through them in complete astonishment.

'But . . . it's true!' the old gentleman declared. 'Here they are!'

Noah Claypole was naturally more amazed than anyone at the extraordinary occurrence. He felt like running from the kitchen, but the shock rendered him incapable of any movement whatsoever.

'But we saw you hand them over!' said the runner to the Dodger. 'What was it he burnt then?'

''Is own papers,' replied the Dodger casually. 'I snitched 'em out your pocket.'

'By thunder – so he did!' gasped the runner, clapping his hand to his side pocket and discovering it to be empty.

Claypole stared in terror at the fire, in which his precious papers of pardon had by now been entirely consumed by the flames, and he slumped into a nearby chair, with an expression of absolute misery and defeat.

'So, Mr Informer,' said Grimwig. 'You burnt your own free pardon. And I'll make certain sure Mr Fang does not issue another! Well done, boy!' he exclaimed, slapping the Dodger violently on the back. The Dodger had room to reflect on the exceptional fact that he had just been congratulated on his pick-pocketing by, of all people, a Magistrate. Oliver saw the humour in this and laughed. The Dodger grinned at his friend.

'Well then,' announced the runner, taking the dejected Claypole by the arm, 'all that remains now is to take him off to prison – where Fagin and his accomplice should already be safely incarcerated.'

'Fagin?' exclaimed Grimwig, glancing at Mr Brownlow.

'Where d'you find 'im?' inquired the Dodger.

'At the Three Cripples,' replied the runner. I had them locked in the snugroom. They'll have been collected by now.'

'Oh no,' said the Dodger, with sudden anxiety. 'Oh no. Not in *there*!'

*

Noah Claypole was duly escorted to Newgate Prison, protesting, naturally, all the way. 'This is all a mistake, I tell yer!' he cried. 'A h'abberation of justice! A gross h'abberation, I tell yer!'

He was still squealing indignantly when the turnkey opened the door of a cell and thrust him inside. 'I'll be out of 'ere by mornin'!' he declared, in an offended tone. 'By the mornin', I tell yer!'

He stopped his outburst, however, when, by the light of the turnkey's lantern, he discerned that the cell already contained another occupant; a huge brutish figure was seated on the bed. This creature glanced up and, seeing Noah, grinned hungrily; his eyes glinted in the manner of a carnivorous beast who has caught sight of a particularly tempting prey.

'No!' screamed Noah Claypole, as he recognized Kags. 'No! Please! Not in 'ere! Anywhere but 'ere!'

But the door shut solidly behind him.

At that moment, as the Artful Dodger had feared, Fagin and his adenoidal assistant Barney were leaving the city in a cart which they had purloined from Covent Garden market. Barney was pulling it, and the merry old gentleman was sitting in the back, comfortably propped up against two heavy suitcases and surrounded by a multitude of very valuable sacks. By the morning, they were nowhere in London, and although a thorough search was made of the metropolis and its neighbouring counties, they could not be found.

And what of Oliver Twist's half-brother, Edward Leeford, better known as Monks? The two policemen who had chased him had reported that, reaching the riverbank, he had plunged into the swirling waters with a last frantic cry of revenge. The night had been exceptionally windy, and the river exceptionally violent; the villain, they concluded, must have been drowned.

'Or swum to the other side,' declared the Artful Dodger sceptically, when he heard the news.

'Well, in either case,' observed Mr Brownlow, 'we are not likely ever to see him again.'

The plans for Oliver's adoption were put into action at once. While they were being implemented, Mr Brownlow took a further, perhaps curious but unquestionably benevolent, decision: he would adopt the Artful Dodger too, if that was what the youth desired. The Dodger was overjoyed at the suggestion, and accepted it eagerly. Mr Brownlow discovered that Mrs Carraway, in his absence, had managed to spend a good deal of his savings, but he concluded that he still possessed enough capital to live on, quite comfortably, and to look after the two boys.

Oliver's uncle and aunt, before returning to their happy home in the country, declared that they thought it an admirable decision. Mr Grimwig, however, if only because he was of a mistrustful nature, remained dubious.

'Two growing boys,' he murmured, raising his eyeglass and surveying Oliver and the Dodger out of the corner of an eye. 'Well, don't say I didn't warn you, old friend. Your troubles are just beginning – or I'll eat my head, sir!'

21448